M000105971

Never take your own revenge, beloved,
but leave room for the wrath of God, for it is written,
"VENGEANCE IS MINE, I WILL REPAY,"
SAYS THE LORD.
R O M A N S   1 2 : 1 9   (N A S B)

VENGEANCE IS MINE

Brian Regrut

author of *Stolen Identity*

INTERVARSITY PRESS
DOWNERS GROVE, ILLINOIS 60515

© 1994 by Brian Regrut

All rights reserved. No part of this book may be reproduced in any form without written permission from InterVarsity
Press, P.O. Box 1400, Downers Grove, Illinois 60515.

InterVarsity Press® is the book-publishing division of InterVarsity Christian Fellowship®, a student movement active
on campus at hundreds of universities, colleges and schools of nursing in the United States of America, and a member
movement of the International Fellowship of Evangelical Students. For information about local and regional
activities, write Public Relations Dept., InterVarsity Christian Fellowship, 6400 Schroeder Rd., P.O. Box 7895,
Madison, WI 53707-7895.

This novel is a work of fiction. Names, characters, places and incidents are either the product of the author's imagination or are used fictitiously. Any resemblance to actual persons, living or dead, events or locales is entirely coincidental.

Cover illustration: John Walker

ISBN 0-8308-1372-1
Printed in the United States of America ∞

Library of Congress Cataloging-in-Publication Data

Regrut, Brian, 1946-
    Vengeance is mine/Brian Regrut.
      p.   cm.
    ISBN 0-8308-1372-1 (alk. paper)
    I. Title.
    PS3568.E47614V46   1994
    813'.54—dc20
                                                      94-28133
                                                      CIP

17	16	15	14	13	12	11	10	9	8	7	6	5	4	3	2	1
07	06	05	04	03	02	01	00	99	98	97	96	95	94			

This book is dedicated to my friends,
Bill and Beth York,
who lead by serving and whose service touches many.

Prologue

"Daddy, oh my daddy," cried three-year-old Jonathan Boget as he clung to his father's left leg. Tears were flowing as freely as the blood from the bullet wound in his father's right thigh.

The little boy could not comprehend all the activity that whirled around Peter Boget's room in Arundel Community Hospital a few miles south of Baltimore. Jonathan had watched lots of television with his sisters and brothers, and had seen blood and mayhem on the screen, but reality was so much more confusing, so much more terrifying. The guns exploding just a few feet from his sensitive ears had started reverberations that still caused his body to quake. And despite his mother's tender hand on his shoulder and her gentle assurances, he continued to tremble.

He searched the faces of his mother, his two older brothers and his older sisters for understanding, but found expressions that were new to him—blank faces that seemed to be asking the same questions he was: What is happening? Who shot my daddy? Why is Mommy shaking? Why is there blood everywhere? Who are the men who fell to the floor, and why were they crying out? Jonathan's younger sister—just a year old—clung tenaciously to her mother's hip, issuing a staccato cry from deep in her chest.

Jonathan felt his mother's hand envelop his as she quietly told her children what frantic hospital personnel had not had time to say: "Let's wait outside." Jonathan didn't want to leave his father's side, now that he had finally seen him after a difficult three-week separation. But he followed, responding to his mother's tug, and walked into the hallway where two large, dark stains on the gray carpet marked the spot where minutes before a sergeant in the Maryland State Police died trying to protect his father. In every direction hospital personnel, policemen and a few of the many visitors to the floor scurried to attend the five people injured in a flurry of gunfire in what had been a quiet hospital corridor.

Jonathan watched from the doorway as his father was lifted from his bed and transferred to a gurney. From his vantage point, he couldn't see the dressings that covered the hole that had been burned into his father's chest, but he could see the bright red stains on the sheet from the gunshot wound in his dad's right leg. And he could see lots of people doing lots of things to his father with little hoses and wires and bags of water that hung from shiny pipes. He watched so intently that he didn't notice the policeman standing just behind him wearing, over his uniform, a yellow gown just like the ones that his mother and siblings were wearing. And he didn't tune in as the policeman spoke sharply to one of the people helping his father. But when that man, who was doing something with one of the tubes running into his father's arm, heard the policeman, he leaped forward.

Jonathan's trembling stopped and so did his heart as the man, looking like a comic-book character, rushed toward him. Only the man's eyes, ears and hands were visible—everything else, except his light-blue cotton uniform pants and his black Reeboks, was covered by a yellow paper gown, mask or hat. The man was coming at him the way his grandfather's huge, gregarious dog did. He jumped to one side to get out of the man's way, but his entire family moved the other way. The man dodged to avoid Jonathan and went airborne to get through the doorway, but the boy didn't move fast enough. The man's foot hit in the small of his back and both went sprawling into the hallway.

Before he knew what hit him, Jonathan was leaning against the man's chest as a powerful arm encircled his waist, locking him in place. The pressure on his body was so great that Jonathan cried out in pain. He felt something hard and cold pressed against his temple, and he saw the gown-covered state trooper pointing a gun directly at him as he and the man rose from the floor.

"Mommy, Mommy! Help me." Jonathan's high-pitched scream filled the hallway. It penetrated the thick, wooden doors behind which bed-bound patients prayed they would not become victims of the terror that was raining around them. A dozen

people watching the stand-off were transfixed.

Jonathan felt the powerful left arm squeeze the air out of his small lungs. He tried to pull away, but there was no escaping the grip of Patrick O'Hearn, who had failed to complete the assassination assignment started by his co-conspirator minutes earlier. Jonathan only knew that his captor was walking backward, away from his father's room.

Jonathan continued to scream, extending his arms toward his mother, who began to follow him up the hallway. He heard her measured voice not pleading but commanding the assassin: "Let my baby go!"

He heard the man clutching him yelling at the policeman walking beside his mother: "Drop your gun, Hanks, and I'll release the boy." But the trooper refused to do so.

With each step Jonathan's ability to cry for help became more difficult as the arm around his waist forced his diaphragm up into his lungs. He gasped for air as his mother advanced. He didn't know that she was studying his eyes and was terrified over the prospect that his captor might pull the trigger on his 9mm Glock and splatter her baby's brains on the walls of the hospital corridor. But she kept coming. At every third or fourth step she issued her command to the gunman with startling boldness. "Let my baby go!"

"Drop your gun, Hanks, and I'll let the lad go." The boy was too terrified to realize that the man was speaking in an accent, just like the "Irish" his mother used when she read poems to the family.

As they passed the nurses' station and elevator lobby, Jonathan continued to plead for help. He felt himself being taken farther and farther from his father's room, not understanding what was happening to him except that he wasn't being allowed to go to his mother. It was hard to breathe, and his ribs and abdomen ached.

Just outside the stairwell door, through which another gunman had exited minutes earlier, the ordeal ended as quickly as it had begun.

O'Hearn relaxed his pressure on Jonathan's chest only long enough to grab him around the waist with both hands and toss him into the air. As he began flying toward the ceiling, the three-year-old refilled his lungs then almost swallowed his tongue as the Glock exploded two feet beneath him. He saw the policeman fall backwards as the bullet ripped the yellow gown in the center of his chest. As he began his drop through eight feet of nothingness, Jonathan watched as his mother dove toward him, arms extended. But he knew she wouldn't reach him. As her face passed in front of O'Hearn's gun, a second explosion erupted from the gun. The bullet *parted his mother's hair as the man called Hanks collapsed to the ground, grabbing his thigh.*

As Jonathan hit the floor, his lungs forced a liter of air through his tiny but enormously effective vocal chords, and for five ear-piercing seconds his scream punctuated the horror of what had begun as a joyous reunion between a lost father and his family. It was a scream like that of a calf seared by a branding iron, and it burned itself permanently into the heart and soul of each member of the Boget family.

*   *   *

Elizabeth Boget bolted from her bed and raced down the hall toward the scream emanating from Jonathan's room. It was the first night since that dreadful incident on Palm Sunday, two weeks earlier, that Jonathan had gone to bed in his own room. Now, after two nights of peaceful sleep, the nightmare had returned.

Sixteen-year-old David was already in Jonathan's lighted room when his mother rushed through the door. The three-year-old was sitting upright in bed. His eyes were open but he was not yet awake and the terror of the nightmare continued. His body shook violently, and both David and Elizabeth knew that he was reliving the exchange of gunfire that reverberated from the stairwell moments after Jonathan had hit the floor.

Finally it was over. Elizabeth knelt beside David, who was sitting on the bed cradling his brother in his arms. Lauren stood at the bedroom door rubbing sleep from her bloodshot eyes. Her thirteen-year-old body was trembling beneath the ankle-length nightgown that her mother had made for her. She couldn't hold back the emotion that was boiling within her. "When will this end, Mom?" her voice quivered. "When will it end?"

Elizabeth Boget raised her hazel eyes toward the ceiling. She wanted to see beyond the confines of the plasterboard and wood of their new home. In her mind she searched the heavens for a God she believed was there, though she couldn't see him. In her pain she called out, but heard no response. In her frustration she begged for a message, but none came. She looked back at her daughter.

"I know this is hard to understand, Lauren," she said as tears rolled down her face. Elizabeth extended her weary arms, inviting her daughter to curl up beside her. Then she turned to David, who was still holding his sleeping brother. "While your father was missing I asked the same question over and over again. But I knew God would carry us through no matter what the circumstances. He's been very good to us, even if right now we can't see what he has in mind for us."

"Then why doesn't he stop Jonathan's nightmares . . . and mine too . . . and what's he doing about Dad's job?" asked the young teenager.

"Lauren, that's next week's worry. Tonight we have to pray that the skin graft will go well tomorrow, and we have to pray for Mr. Downes and Mr. Hendrick. They know your father didn't do anything wrong, and they will fight for him. And the FBI is working day and night to find the people who attacked your father in the hospital. And as for the nightmares," she said almost in a whisper, "it's just going to take time."

1

L iza Morgan was bending over her kitchen sink rinsing her thick black hair when the phone rang. It was her day off and she had hoped to spend it washing her hair, fixing her nails and plunging into her private world of books. Except for reading, there wasn't much else she really enjoyed doing in her small house near the railroad tracks in the tiny resort community of Waveland along Mississippi's Gulf Coast. She had lost half the morning on three telephone conversations, so she decided to let the answering machine handle the call. Even though the voice on the machine was weak and somewhat raspy, and though she hadn't heard it in over twenty years, she recognized it immediately. "Hello, Liza, this is Peter Boget."

Her heart leaped and her head hit the faucet as she jerked her dripping hair away from the sink, swirled a towel around it, stepped across the room, grabbed the handset from the wall phone, took a deep breath and said, "Peter?" Nothing else would come. For half her life she had hoped and prayed for this call. She had practiced her answer a thousand times. Now she was speechless.

"Liza, is that you?"

Cupping the phone with her shaking hand, she took another breath as the towel on her head dropped to her shoulders. She closed her eyes. "Yes, this is Liza."

"This is Peter Boget," he said again. "Do you remember me?"

She wanted to say, "Remember you? I can't remember *not* remembering you." But she didn't. A third deep breath had the butterflies in her stomach flying in formation. "Of course I do. How are you?"

"Great . . . but not good. That's why I'm calling." His voice seemed strained. "How are you?"

"I don't understand. What do you mean, 'great but not good'?"

"I'm having a skin graft today to cover a hole in my chest—"

"What?" Liza interrupted. She was a nurse, and she knew that people didn't have skin grafts unless they had a serious injury or a serious disease.

"—and they're also going to do some more work on my right hand. My thumb and forefinger were burned . . . not as bad as my chest . . . but I still won't be able to use them for another week or two."

"What's wrong?"

"It's a long story."

Liza listened intently as Peter Boget spun an almost unbelievable tale. Driving from his office in Richmond to a company meeting in a suburb of the nation's capital, he had stopped to help a motorist who had a flat tire along the busy interstate. He had intended only to dial for help from his mobile phone and set out flares and continue on his way. He didn't expect to encounter someone who looked like a twin brother. Nor did he expect to trip, knock himself unconscious, and fall on top of the burning flare he was carrying.

"The man I stopped to help turned out to be a drug courier," Peter explained. "He took my car, switched identities and, while doctors tried to keep me alive in a hospital in Baltimore, ended up in Cancún, Mexico, with, of all people, Debbie Steinbaugh."

"Debbie who?"

"Sorry. Debbie Blanton. She lived with the Clarks. Remember, we visited them in Colorado Springs."

Liza's head suddenly filled with images of her home in the foothills of the Rockies west of Denver, of the trees and mountains and rushing streams and the one glorious summer she spent with Peter, the college student, who had returned to Colorado for a second summer. The previous year he had

been the sixth child in the home of the Clarks, Debbie Blanton Steinbaugh's foster parents. But when Liza met him he was staying with the
Bertrands, the leaders for the young-adult class in Liza's church.

Liza remembered Peter's athletic body and broad impish smile. She remembered how he spoke her name, slow and deep, and how he kissed her
as they stood in the middle of a frothy brook high in the pine-and-aspen-
covered hills above the town. But most of all she remembered his eyes, eyes
that spoke more loudly and clearly than the voice of any man she had ever
known. Eyes that said what his mouth never did: "I love you." The memories drew her breath away.

*   *   *

The president of Virginia's largest phone company walked out of his
imposing office atop the Virginia Bell building and across thick carpeting
that absorbed each footfall. He strode past two dark cherry desks at which
secretaries were busily handling the work of the day, and stepped into an
office that was smaller than his but every bit as richly appointed. The
principal difference between the two offices was the artwork. His office was
adorned with magnificent prints of sailboats and lighthouses on Chesapeake Bay painted by local artist John Barber. The walls of this office
featured paintings of blue-and-gray-clad men locked in mortal combat, a
reminder of the tens of thousands of Americans who had fought and died
in the fields and forests of the Old Dominion. The cherry furniture in the
office was traditional, as was all the furniture in the executive suite, and
reflected the conservative nature of a company that, like the Commonwealth it served, was steeped in history.

Mike Downes, the young vice president for external affairs, looked up
from a paper he was reading, laid it down on an open manila folder, and
watched as his boss, Earl Hendrick, slid his large frame into one of the
fabric-covered chairs in front of his desk.

"What is the latest on Peter?" asked Hendrick, whose easy manner and
disdain for using contractions always seemed to slow down communication.

"I talked to him on the phone this morning," Mike said with a smile. "He
sounds a whole lot better than he did a week ago. But he's having his skin
graft today, so he's probably not going to be feeling too good for the next
few days. I'm going by tonight to check on him before I head home." He

paused. "I'm thinking about flying back to Colorado for the weekend."

Hendrick squinted his eyes and gave Downes an I-cannot-believe-I-am-hearing-you-right look. "I thought that, after all your travels the last three weeks, you would not . . ." Earl caught the gleam in Mike's eye. "It is that woman," he said, and a grin crawled across his broad face as he slowly shook his head.

"Debbie, yes," said Downes, grinning back. "I can't seem to get her out of my mind."

Hendrick acknowledged the comment with a nod. "Look, Mike," he said. "Emily and I are going to take a long weekend and sail to Crisfield. She is picking me up here at noon so we can be on the water by three or so. We probably will stay until Monday, and when we get back we will drive directly to D.C. I have the Boget files, and that . . ." he frowned, "that vial of skin, and will bone up on them for the executive committee meeting on Tuesday."

The smile disappeared from Mike's face. "I know there's not much there, but we have to stop Mazzetti. He's bent on making sure Peter never comes back to work here. But considering all that family's been through, it would be a crime to tell Elizabeth that, in addition to everything else, Peter's out of a job."

"Well," the president said slowly, "I know they must be worried, and I am certainly going to do what I can to see that Peter returns to the office. He is a good man; I have always believed that. His people love to work for him and he gets results. But he is kind of crazy and has done a few," the president extended his hand and rocked it back and forth, "shall we say, questionable things. Still, I would expect that from someone who is always looking for new and better ways to get the work out."

Downes laughed. "*Different* ways, anyway. I think it's safe to say no one is going to engrave the company logo on his gravestone."

"No, I would not think so, but then I hope nobody puts one on mine either. I would prefer to have a sailboat . . . ," said Hendrick, sweeping his hand through the air as if tracing words on a marble monument above flower-bedecked sod in some quiet cemetery. " 'Here lies a man whom God blessed with a loving wife, a wonderful family, a rewarding career and favorable winds.' "

"Hope they're favorable for you this weekend."

"The weather bureau says they are going to be perfect!"

The president stood and slowly made his way to the door. "By the way, when are you coming back from Colorado?"

"Sunday night, I guess. I just plan to fly out for dinner."

Earl Hendrick tugged at his belt and pushed in his shirttail as he responded to the vice president, twenty-one years his junior. "You know, if it was anyone but you, I would never believe that a man would fly halfway across the country just for dinner." He backed through the door. "Have fun."

*   *   *

From the phone beside his hospital bed, Peter Boget continued to tell Liza about the previous weeks. "Debbie was vacationing with a friend when she saw this Barry Whitehead guy who looks like me," he explained. "Anyway, he tried to rape her. When her friend, Jan, came to her defense, there was a fight and she was killed."

Liza gasped. "Debbie?"

"No. Jan died. Debbie ended up in jail for murder."

Liza was only half listening to the story. She didn't want to hear about anyone but Peter. He included too many details, and she was losing track of the story.

"The doctors thought I was going to die while all this was going on, but a friend of mine, my boss, Mike Downes, found Debbie and then tracked down Whitehead. Then he found me."

"I can't believe it. I just can't believe it." Liza wanted to say more, much more, but she continued to listen.

"I told you that Barry Whitehead was a drug runner. Well, it seems he skipped out with a million dollars' worth of cocaine, and the owners weren't happy. Since he left me by his car, with his wallet, the hospital assumed I was Whitehead. So did the people looking for the cocaine. They tried to kill me three times."

The whole story was too bizarre. Liza tried to imagine Peter lying in his hospital bed, but couldn't.

"Anyway, that's why I'm calling." She heard him pause and take a deep breath. "Liza, this past week the whole matter of life and death has continually been on my mind. After going through what I and my family have gone through, I can't help but look back at all the decisions I've made through the years and all the mistakes." His voice trailed off.

Then, as he continued, Liza could hear the melancholy in his voice: "I've thought about the missed opportunities and the time frittered away on things that don't really count in the long run. And, for some reason, I've thought a lot about relationships, especially the fact that I so often let circumstances, not my heart, govern my actions. I think that's what happened with us back in Colorado. I was headed back to college, and I couldn't figure out how to fit you into my life back then. So while my heart was telling me one thing, my circumstances dictated another. And through the years, despite the fact that I found and married a pretty special woman, and raised a great family, I've never been able to get you out of my heart.

"I guess it all came together this morning. I picked up the devotional book the church passes out every few months, and the reading for today was entitled 'What would you do if you knew that this was your last day on earth?' "

Liza couldn't believe what she was hearing. Earlier in the morning she had sipped her first cup of coffee after the children left for school and read the very same page in *Our Daily Bread*. She started to believe that the connection to Peter she had felt all these years was real after all. She didn't notice the towel dropping from her shoulders or the tears dripping from her cheeks. Her heart was pounding as he continued.

"Well, after all I've been through, and all I have yet to go through—and I'm not just talking about a skin graft, or having to go through life with a thumb and forefinger that aren't what they once were or even having to find another job, if it comes to that," he said sadly. "Anyway, for the past few hours I've been thinking long and hard about the answer to the question in that devotional book.

"Here's what I think I'd like to do on my last day on earth. After I filled twenty-three hours and fifty-nine minutes with taking care of business, saying goodbye to my wife and children . . . and after making sure my life was right with God . . . I think I'd take a minute to say something I never got around to telling you." He stopped, as if realizing that he shouldn't be thinking these thoughts, much less expressing them. "Please don't get me wrong. I'm not trying to start anything here. I guess what I really want to

do is bring closure ... or something like that ... to our wonderful summer."
Then he paused.

Liza wasn't paying attention to Peter's words of caution. She was waiting
for what she wanted him to say. The silence was electrifying. Then Peter
Boget spoke the words Liza Morgan had always imagined were on the tip
of the tongue of the only man she had ever really loved. He spoke them
quietly, almost in a whisper.

"I love you, Liza Bellamy." The words kindled a flame that swept through
Liza's body like a forest fire driven by late summer winds. "I always have
... and I always will."

                              *   *   *

Living two lives was easy for Mary Kennedy. Her closest friends weren't
all that close, and her employees at her small Norfolk, Virginia, architec-
tural firm knew only that she had a keen awareness of what clients wanted
and a shrewd ability to make money by giving it to them. Not one of her
associates would have guessed that this shapely, stylish, red-haired Irish
woman was also a major distributor of cocaine. She had so refined her
acquisition and distribution chain that only seven people could link her to
the illegal activity. There had been nine, but two had recently met untimely
deaths. Closing in on her were the FBI, the Securities Exchange Commission, and one angry customer, Mark Randolph, to whom she was speaking
on the phone. For the first time in years, she felt vulnerable.

Randolph was sitting in the kitchen of a house along Old Colony Road
in Hartsdale, an affluent suburban community twenty miles north of midtown Manhattan. It was the home of George and Jeanette Miles, a childless
couple who left home early each morning to commute to their respective
jobs—he an accountant, she a lawyer. George Miles was of one of a half-
dozen friends with whom Randolph had maintained a relationship since
his college days at Brown University. These friends shared more than a
common alma mater; they all had turned their backs on their rich families
and had become leaders in antiwar activism during the late sixties and early
seventies. When their cause died a natural death following the withdrawal
of troops from Vietnam, they began migrating back into mainstream society
using their families' names and influence to secure good positions. Though
outwardly they looked like the other yuppies in the neighborhoods they

populated, all had become involved in activities that allowed them to continue to exercise their antiestablishment leanings, and all had come to the aid of one another during times of oppression from governmental authorities. Though none had taken on an activity that rivaled that of Mark Randolph's cocaine dealing, all understood the need to respond, without questioning the reason, to requests for shelter. Mark Randolph was enjoying that shelter and a strong cup of coffee in the empty house as he listened to Mary Kennedy.

"I've located eighteen kilos," she said.

"Not enough. I need twenty-nine." Randolph spoke quietly, stating his need the way he conducted portfolio management for his clients at Michaels and Trent. "I'm not worried about the customers that Glenn handled as much as I am with those whose accounts I manage. As soon as one blows the whistle—and who knows, they may already have—the SEC is going to be doing a lot more than just snooping around a computer."

"Sorry, Randolph, I've got my own troubles. I don't see any more goods for two weeks, and that's if I can come up with the cash. Right now I can't touch a penny without some investigator asking me questions," Kennedy said. "If you want the eighteen, I can have them delivered to you or your customers this weekend. No names, no money. The rest will follow whenever I can get it." Kennedy didn't sound nervous, but she was. "I know you're unhappy about the lost shipment, and I'm sorry about Segal." She spoke with little remorse over the killing of Randolph's partner, Glenn Segal. He died along with two Maryland State Troopers in a bomb blast associated with the attempted retrieval of what Segal thought was the forty-eight kilos of cocaine that Whitehead never delivered to New York.

"Believe me when I tell you that Segal did himself in," she continued. "He was about to spill his guts and bring us all down with that big mouth of his."

Although he had only met her once before, in a dark bar, Mark Randolph could imagine Mary sitting in her handsome office overlooking the Lafayette River. His now-deceased partner had described the sprawling residence-turned-office in glowing terms. He also had remarked that the woman was a knockout. But Randolph wasn't thinking about her appearance now.

"My buyers are scared," he said. "They all want the goods or reimbursement. Now. I had an insurance policy on Glenn, but I can't walk in and ask for the money or I'll end up in jail. As for the eighteen kilos," he said, calculating how best to distribute what she was going to send, "when can you make the delivery, and how?"

"Drop shipments would be best," she said. "Post the addresses, amounts and times in my e-mail. The goods will be there."

"And the other eleven?"

"I'll have to get back to you."

"Two weeks," he said, "or I shut off your cash flow from Charlotte and Baltimore."

"You can't do that."

"You're forgetting that I set up both operations and trained both of your clients. I can and I will get into their systems and make a mess of your transfers if you don't cooperate."

Mary Kennedy didn't like other people telling her what she could and couldn't do. She had been assured from both of her customers that no one could perform the hidden transactions used to transfer money from co-caine buyers to Kennedy unless they were at a computer terminal in the offices of the investment firms where the customers worked. She also knew that, as soon as Randolph had completed his work, all the passwords had been changed.

"Randolph, you can't touch the operations in Baltimore or Charlotte and you know it. So don't give me a hard time. I'm already going way out of my way to help you keep your customers satisfied, so shut—"

"Check with Max at four o'clock today," Randolph interrupted, referring to her contact in Baltimore. "Ask him if five hundred shares of DuPont enters and leaves your account today. Then think about what I said." Randolph was bluffing, but he was betting that she wouldn't call to check. "Make sure you deliver the eighteen tomorrow," he said forcefully. "And get me the other eleven by May 1. I'll have a list of drop locations to you by three. Make sure there are no screwups."

Kennedy was angry, but she held her tongue. She needed Randolph as much as he needed her. But he was a liability. He knew too much. "There won't be any screwups," she said. "Just make sure you don't start talking to authorities."

Randolph laughed. "There's not a cop around who can find me. Anyway, I don't talk about anything to anybody."

*   *   *

Mike Downes picked up the phone on his desk and dialed his daughter's number. As he waited, he looked through the window to the imposing Federal Reserve Bank building. It towered above the James River that was churning through the city with the accumulated runoff of late spring rains that had drenched the mountains far to the west.

"Anna?"

"Yes, Dad."

"I'm going to be a little late for dinner tonight. I'm stopping by the hospital to see Peter."

"Oh, I'm so sorry, I forgot to tell you. Martin and I have just been invited to go up to Wintergreen for the weekend. We had hoped to eat early and get on the road."

Downes stroked his chin. "Well, I'll just head home, then."

"No, Dad, come on over," she said. "We may be packing when you get here, but I'll hold your dinner. I've got beef stew in the slow cooker and was going to stop by Ukrops for a salad and some dinner rolls."

"Sounds good to me."

"And I'll pick up some bagels so you'll have something in the morning if you want to stay over."

"Thanks, I think I will."

After talking to his daughter, he pulled a telephone credit card from his wallet, punched in an 800 number, then an authorization code then a phone number.

"Rocky Mountain Savings, this is Mrs. Steinbaugh."

"Hi, Debbie, this is Mike."

"What a pleasant surprise." Her voice was melodic.

"I know this sounds crazy, but how about dinner tomorrow night?"

Debbie felt her throat go dry. "You're in Richmond, aren't you?"

"Yes, but I'd like to see you, and . . ." Mike's heart was racing. "I can get an early-morning flight out of Richmond. I could be at the airport in Denver before noon. I can rent a car and pick you up before three. That is, if you're interested."

The blonde-haired woman at the other end began to stutter. "Well, I—

I guess so. I mean, I mean . . ." Though they had talked each evening since he had taken her home to Colorado Springs the previous Saturday, Debbie was still having trouble believing that Mike Downes was for real.

At last she recovered from her momentary loss of speech. "I've got a better idea. I'll meet you at the airport."

2

F or three weeks since his accident, Peter Boget had undergone the daily ritual of having a nurse remove his wound dressing and pull away rotting skin from the area of his burn. The procedure was slow and painful, but tweezersful by tweezersful the destroyed skin had been removed. Granulation tissue had formed over the badly charred sternum, and a good vascularized bed was ready to accept the graft. When the day finally arrived, Elizabeth Boget was at her husband's side as he was wheeled to the operating room.

At the door to the room, Elizabeth stopped the gurney, leaned over and kissed her husband. Then she whispered in his ear, "I think the whole world is praying for you, and I am too. But I really want to tell you that no matter what happens, I'll always love you."

Peter smiled and pulled her ear to his mouth. "Nothing's going to happen. But even if it does, I want you to know that I love you too."

Though the surgical risk was minimal, Dr. James Gill, who headed the team of surgeons and students performing the graft, was aware that Peter's lung capacity had been diminished from both smoke and flame inhalation. Just before the anesthesiologist began his task, Gill delivered the reminder he issued before every procedure he performed. It could have sounded trite, like the directions on seat-belt use rattled off by flight attendants bored with hearing their own voices on the intercom, but it wasn't.

"Remember," he began solemnly, "there is no such thing as routine surgery. Every time you walk in here, life and death are in your hands. Never forget it. On this table, this man is not just a patient. He's somebody's son, somebody's husband. He's somebody's friend and somebody's father. Those people are the ones who will be grading you long after you leave this school."

After receiving a nod from the anesthesiologist, Gill scanned the faces of the eager men and women in the operating theater. "Let's go."

The team members worked fast, removing the dressing from the chest wound and exposing the patient's left thigh from which the donor skin would be taken. Jason Wordel, an intern at the medical college, began the slow, delicate process of removing a three-inch wide, nine-inch long strip of skin from the smoothly shaved leg with a device that resembled a wire cheese slicer with a roller to ensure a slice of even thickness. Unlike a cheese slicer, the device's blade oscillated to facilitate the cut. When Wordel finished, another student picked up the limp, paper-thin slice of pink skin, pressed it into a tool that sliced hundreds of small slits in the skin, and handed it to Dr. Gill. Even as the skin was beginning to lose its color, Dr. Gill pulled it apart at the slits, giving it the look of a crocheted doily. By pressing each individual strip into the bloody surface, rather than trying to get full continuous contact from a sheet of skin, the doctors greatly increased the chance of the graft performing well.

Once satisfied that the new skin was properly in place, a student began stapling the edges of the donor skin to the unburned flesh surrounding the wound. Another student, under the close supervision of Dr. Gill and with the aid of a trauma nurse, carefully placed sterile dressings over the entire chest while others dressed the donor site, which now looked like a terrible, symmetrical, bloody abrasion.

*   *   *

Mary Kennedy loved New Orleans almost as much as she loved her native Ireland. But she wasn't in town to peruse the shops along Royal Street or to carouse on Bourbon Street. The thin, stylishly dressed architect with her closely cropped red hair and sensuous smile stepped into a taxi and rode the dozen blocks from her French Quarter hotel to the offices of Holland Engineering in a high-rise two blocks west of Canal Street.

A young receptionist greeted her as she stepped from the elevator lobby through a double set of glass doors. "Would you please have a seat?" she said, motioning to two austere contemporary chrome and leatherette chairs and matching sofa that flanked a glass and chrome table.

"I hope Mr. Holland is in a good mood today."

Diplomatically the receptionist replied, "I'm sure he will be delighted to see you."

Moments later she was sitting on a leather couch across a carved mahogany coffee table in Jack Holland's elegant office.

"Good to see you again, Mary. I trust all is well." He knew it wasn't, but he was a Southern gentleman who went to great pains to make his guests feel at ease.

"Nothing is well, Jack. That's why I'm here. I can't pay you for the next shipment."

"You came all the way here to tell me that?"

"No, I've come to tell you that I have an order in for twenty-three kilos, but I need thirty-two. And I've got to take delivery by May first."

"But you have no money, is that right?"

"I'll pay you as soon as I can free up some cash. But now I can't lay my hands on anything without having the feds jump all over me."

"I like you, Mary, but we operate on a cash and carry basis. No exceptions."

Her response was smooth and cold. "Fine. If you don't want to play ball, I cancel the order."

"You what?" he said in an intense whisper.

"Cancel my order," she said matter-of-factly. "Either you play ball with me or I go elsewhere."

"Don't threaten me."

"Then don't tell me you can't help out while I'm in a jam."

"Oh, really," he said in a condescending tone. "But I suppose you still want me to handle the engineering on the Fountain Square building."

"That I can pay for. It's the other that I can't handle at the moment," said Kennedy. "My primary distribution network has been wiped out, my driver's gone, my number-one man is back in Ireland recovering from gunshot wounds, and my number-two man was killed in a shootout. The cops have thirty of the forty-eight kilos you shipped last month, and an ex-cop has the other eighteen. And on top of all that, the feds have been in and out of my office like it's a doughnut shop. I've got to take care of existing customers and new ones I'm cultivating. But I've got to control the flow of cash to avoid suspicion."

"Look, I'm sorry you're having trouble," Holland responded graciously. "But I'm afraid that your next order is already on the move, and when it arrives in two weeks, I'll need four hundred thousand. I don't cover that kind of money, not for you, not for anyone."

Mary Kennedy was an expert at dealing with adversity and with manipulating men. A shrewd businesswoman as well as a skilled architect and designer, she had achieved an unusual level of success before she turned thirty. But as successful as she was, she sought another avenue to fund her secret passion—support for the Provisional Irish Republican Army. Hers was not a passion born of a deep understanding of and compassion for the disenfranchised Irish Catholics of Northern Ireland. Rather it was very personal. The only man she ever loved was killed when a Protestant paramilitary group fired shots into a pub in Londonderry, where he had stopped for dinner one evening while on a business trip. Her interest was avenging that loss by funding as much mayhem as she could afford.

Working with two New York securities brokers, she found that she could afford a lot. They came up with the perfect scheme to sell cocaine to businessmen who were willing to pay a premium price to obtain the drug through professional channels without having to deal with cash or street hoodlums. The program worked so well, she moved into other cities with large financial communities where there was a high probability of locating prospective customers with the knowledge of computers and securities required to make the scheme work. But these new operations only worked as long as Mark Randolph brought his computer expertise to the operation. That's why Kennedy needed Randolph and was prepared to do whatever was necessary to make sure that he was taken care of. But there were no alternative drug suppliers she could work with. She needed Holland's cocaine.

"Jack," she began quietly, "I can't lay my hands on that kind of money without the feds swarming all over me. I've got to be squeaky clean until this blows over and hope my securities transactions records hold up."

Holland sat impassively.

"For almost three years we've been making this work. I've hit one snag. I need you to work with me."

"Sounds like a lot more than one snag."

"A courier who knows too much is on the loose, but I'm taking care of him. My problem is Mark Randolph, my customer in New York. Among other things, he's a computer wizard, and he can make things happen . . . good *and* bad. He's the only one who has the complete picture. He knows me. He knows the plan."

"And?"

"And he told me that he's going to get revenge for the death of his partner, unless I can help him make good with his customers. If I can take care of them, he'll work with us."

"Us?" Holland asked indignantly. "I like you, Mary, but this is business. I don't extend credit, I don't employ hit men, I don't do a lot of things that people think goes on in this business. I have merely set up the cover for bringing the stuff into the country. I play by one set of rules for everyone. Considering you're so dependent on one man—and maybe not a very happy man—making things work for you, I want no part of it."

Holland was prepared for a lot of eventualities, but not Kennedy's charm. She let her mouth hang open slightly and then slipped the tip of her tongue across her upper lip. "Perhaps a down payment would help." Then she stood up and leaned over the coffee table, allowing her black dress to blouse open in Jack Holland's face. "Let's discuss this over dinner." She laid on the accent seductively. "Come by the Monteleone at seven. We can go out . . . or just order from room service."

Holland leaned back in his chair and smiled, "Okay, Mary, you've got me. But I've got a better idea. Forget the Monteleone. You can come over to my place in the Garden District. With the AIA convention here in town, I've invited some of my top clients for dinner."

Holland continued to smile but Mary couldn't tell if she had him or he had her. He pulled out a business card, turned it over and scribbled an address on the back. Then he handed it to her. "It's pronounced Ca-ron-de-let," he said, accenting the second syllable. "It's only twenty minutes by cab, or you can—"

"Take the trolley," she finished his sentence. "I know. I've been out to St. Charles more than once. What time?"

"Cocktails at six, dinner at seven."

*   *   *

Mike Downes was agitated. Two FBI agents were sitting in his office and asking questions he wasn't ready to answer.

"Okay, let me put it to you this way," he said. "I know the man you're talking about. He's in jail in Mexico for accidentally killing a woman. And I've made a commitment to get him out. If you can show me how you will help me in that endeavor, I'll cooperate. But if all you want is information, and don't care about the person providing it, then I won't." Downes paused for emphasis and then, touching his right forefinger to his temple, he said, "What's up in his head is his only ticket to freedom. I don't plan on pulling that ticket until he is on the plane."

"You've been sitting on this for two weeks?" Tyrone Giddings, the lead agent, demanded.

Quietly, Downes replied: "I've been waiting to find out which way the investigation was going, to determine just how important his testimony might be. I've kept my ear pretty close to the ground and I still haven't heard anyone asking about him."

Giddings, sitting in the same chair that Earl Hendrick had sat in five hours earlier, leaned across the desk. "Mr. Downes, we're trying to get the people responsible for killing four law enforcement officials, for shooting you and Peter Boget, for traumatizing his entire family," Giddings's voice was rising, "for dealing cocaine, for terrorizing a hospital, and who knows what else." The FBI agent, who once had played linebacker for Howard University, rose slightly out of his seat and glared at Downes. In a powerful, raspy voice, he said, "And you want to dictate to us the terms of your cooperation?"

With a flippancy in his voice that made the two FBI agents want to reach across the desk and punch him, Mike said, "You haven't shown me why you need Whitehead."

"He can identify the people he was working for."

"So can I. And anyway, you already know who she is, so what's in it for Barry?" Downes was feeling testy. It was late and he was trying to get out early. "If you plan to seek extradition on a specific charge, or so that Barry can testify against Kennedy, then I'll be glad to help, but a fishing expedition . . . no way."

"I'm sure we'll be able to find him," Giddings shot back. "I just figured you could save the taxpayers some money."

Downes laughed. "Since when have you guys worried about taxpayers' money?" he said cynically. Then he stood up to signal that the conversation was over.

"Sit down!" The command by Rex Middleton, the second FBI agent, took Downes by surprise. Though younger and smaller than Giddings, Middleton left no mistake that he, too, meant business. "We've tried to have a civil conversation with you, Mr. Downes, but you don't seem to understand. You are in serious trouble. And I suggest you get a lawyer quick, because the next time we come here, you're going to be facing arrest for aiding in commission of a felony, for being an after-the-fact accomplice, for interstate flight to avoid prosecution, for obstructing a criminal investigation and whatever else I can find to hang on you!"

Middleton continued: "Now tell us where we can find Mr. Whitehead and we'll talk to the prosecutor and let her decide whether or not Whitehead's information is sufficiently valuable for her to initiate extradition. If you choose not to tell us, you're going to find yourself behind bars. It's as simple as that."

Downes was noticeably subdued, but wasn't ready to roll over. "I don't know the law, but I don't believe you can charge me with anything, unless you had a warrant out for Whitehead's arrest before I helped him. You didn't know he existed until after I got to him. And I didn't interfere with an FBI investigation, because you weren't conducting one on him, were you?"

"I think you better shut up before you say something you wish you hadn't," Giddings interrupted. "When you start telling me that you've actually thought about whether or not you were committing a crime—and you're a pretty bright guy, judging from this office—I start hearing a man in serious trouble with the law. Now, for the last time, I'm asking for information on Barry Whitehead."

"Until I get a lawyer, there isn't much to say. But I'm not looking for trouble, either; I've had enough this last month. So I'm going to tell you that he's in jail in Cancún on a manslaughter charge. His lawyer is Jorge

Soto." Downes opened his top desk drawer, pulled out a slip of paper and wrote down a phone number. "Here's how you can contact him." Downes put his hand to his forehead. "Look fellows, I'm sorry. It's been a long week, and I'm trying to get over to the hospital to check on Peter Boget. Please do whatever you can to help Barry, that's all I want."

Giddings shook his head. "Excuse me for saying so, but you've got a lot to learn about people. Don't get personally involved with losers, they'll only bring you down."

"Thanks," Mike said with hard-to-miss insincerity. "I've been given that good advice once before."

*   *   *

Liza Morgan couldn't contain the elation that continued to surge through her body. As she pulled open the screen door and stepped into her small but tidy kitchen, she gave her husband a smile he hadn't seen since before they were married. Randy Morgan didn't smile back. The electrician waited until his wife set the bags of groceries she was carrying onto the counter. Then he reached forward, grabbed her chin and pulled her face toward his. "Where have you been all day?" he demanded. "And who's Peter Boget?"

Liza gulped. The name that had been like honey on her lips for hours now came back like a fist in her stomach. In her ecstasy she had forgotten to reset the answering machine. She had abandoned her thoughts of reading and had hiked down to the community pier to look out past the shrimp boats, freighters and oil tankers that glided across the horizon, to look out across the nothingness of the Gulf of Mexico. In the stillness of midday, she had become lost in her memories of the man she wished she had married. Now she had to face the other man in her life, her husband of twenty years.

Jerking her head out of his grip, Liza glared at him. He was tall and strong and pleasantly handsome, but behind the attractive exterior he was another man altogether. "I told you I hate it when you do that to me. When are you ever going to treat me like a lady?"

"When you start treating me with the respect I deserve! Now, where have you been, and who's this Peter guy?"

"You know who he is. Why are you asking?"

"I think you talked to him today." His tone was surly.

Liza snapped back, "If you must know, he called to tell me that Debbie Steinbaugh, one of my friends from back home, was imprisoned in Mexico for murdering her friend." Her voice was rising as she spat out the words the way a Gatling gun spits out bullets. "And that the man who really did it was a drug dealer who looked like him, and he stole cocaine and the owner tried to kill him three times, and he's going in for a skin graft and . . ." She paused and regained her composure. "I'm sorry, Randy, but it's really nothing to concern yourself with." Liza turned and stepped through the doorway, holding the screen door so it wouldn't slam shut behind her.

He didn't understand all he heard, but he had seen a gleam in his wife's eyes he had never seen before. As he watched Liza skip down the stairs, a jealousy-fueled rage filled Randy Morgan.

* * *

By the time Mike Downes arrived at MCV Hospital, Peter Boget was asleep. He was heavily sedated and his face looked unusually drawn. His wife, Elizabeth, looking equally sallow, sat quietly by the bed.

"The graft today took a lot out of him, I'm afraid," she said.

"Looks like it took a lot out of you too," Downes responded.

Elizabeth Boget smiled faintly. "These days everything seems to be taking a lot out of me. What's his job look like, anyway?"

"It's in Earl's hands now," Mike said. "He's taking a few days off to relax before tackling the executive committee next week. He's got enough evidence to cast suspicion on Mazzetti, and I'm pretty sure he'll use it. Your evidence would be good," he reminded Elizabeth, "if Frank would consent to a blood test. But let's face it, he's not on trial, Peter is. And what Mazzetti has makes Peter look bad." Glancing at the man asleep on the bed with tubes attached to his body, Downes said, "If he had only told me what he was doing or hinted that he was gathering information that would be helpful to the company, I could testify on his behalf. But I'm out of the loop."

"And my statement . . . *our* statement?"

Downes shook his head. "It's not flying."

Elizabeth stood up abruptly, as if injected with a stimulant. She stretched to her full five foot nine and brushed back her thick brown hair with her fingers. "I'm so sick and tired of being the victim," she said. "I'd like to go to that executive committee meeting myself and let those men—those men who are more interested in profits than people—hear just what kind of man that Frank Mazzetti is. And if they still take his word over Peter's, I'd go over to Mazzetti and rip his face open just like I did on the floor of the PR office last week when he was walking away with Peter's computer files. Then I'd take his flesh to the medical examiner's office and prove that he tried to destroy my husband."

"Whoa!" Mike held up his hands in front of himself. "This doesn't sound like the Christian woman I'm used to seeing in here."

"I'm sorry, Mike, but I'm weary of this whole mess." She paused and turned to the window. Her shoulders sagged along with her voice. "What am I going to do with five kids and a husband who's going to need who knows how much more medical treatment? I haven't worked since David was born, and even if I went down to the hospital personnel office right now, what's the chance they would hire a physical therapist who hasn't seen the inside of a rehab center in sixteen years?"

Downes's voice was soothing, "Earl Hendrick, above all else, is a man of integrity. Everyone in Mid-Atlantic Bell knows that. A few days on the bay and he'll be back refreshed and ready to take up Peter's defense. I think you can count on that."

Elizabeth dropped her head. "I hope so," she muttered. "I hope so."

*   *   *

The call Mary Kennedy made to Roland Hanks was routed through a mechanical switchboard at an orphanage in Ireland. It was how she made sure that her telephone number was lost en route to Maryland and to the home of the young police officer who had helped to thwart the killing of Peter Boget. Roland Hanks was spared a life-threatening gunshot wound to his chest because his Kevlar vest had stopped Patrick O'Hearn's bullet. The wound in his thigh, that dropped him to the ground alongside Elizabeth Boget in the hospital corridor, was healing quickly.

"Roland," she said in a voice that sounded like a purring cat. "How was Cancún?"

Roland Hanks hated his first name. Kennedy knew that and found that by using it on her newest helper she could get him agitated, which seemed to make the former state trooper more compliant.

"I wasn't there long enough to find out," he said.

"But you did find Whitehead, and he's been taken care of, correct?"

"Will be."

"What do you mean, *will* be?"

"You don't just walk into a jail and kill someone," he said indignantly. "But don't worry. I've got it taken care of."

Kennedy didn't trust a man who had stolen eighteen kilos of her cocaine and tried to double-cross her twice. But she liked his freewheeling style, and while her most trusted aide was recuperating three thousand miles away in Belfast, Hanks was going to have to do for some of Kennedy's odd jobs. He was still smarting from his embarrassing dishonorable discharge from the state police for trying to be a hero at the expense of the lives of fellow officers, and she knew that her offer of employment would be the best the twenty-three-year-old would get in quite a while. She tried him out on a small errand to Mexico. Now she was going to give him a bigger test.

"Congratulations, Roland, you've finally passed your first exam. I guess from now on I can call you Hanks, if that's what you prefer."

"It is." Hanks had a smart reply on the tip of his tongue but swallowed it. "Thank you."

"Your next assignment is to make some deliveries of my goods—the ones you have in your possession."

"I figured that's what it would all come down to." The resignation in his voice was readily detectable. He had in his possession cocaine valued at about four hundred thousand dollars—double that on the street. Yet he didn't dare sell an ounce of it unless he wanted to be looking over his shoulder for the rest of his life.

"There's a Kinko's in Landover. Go there at eleven tonight and wait for a fax. It will tell you everything you need to know." Mary Kennedy remained warm and friendly, even though it was clear that she was the boss and Hanks was the subordinate. "Five thousand will be delivered to you when you return on Tuesday."

After he hung up the phone, the former policeman cursed the air. He picked up a half-filled beer can and threw it over the counter in his small but comfortable apartment. It hit the refrigerator door and spilled onto the floor. He cursed again.

The boy who had planned of becoming a supercop was now a man reduced to running errands for an unseen criminal. He lived for action and dreamed of fame, expecting to become financially comfortable along the way. Now, despite Kennedy's assurances of action and money, Hanks realized that he was just like the scores of men and women he had arrested through the years—people who compromised their principles for a quick buck or a cheap thrill. He hated the thought, but he hated worse the police department that had stripped him of his uniform and the power and prestige that it engendered.

He knew that once he said yes to her a week earlier, Mary Kennedy would control his destiny. He didn't expect she'd control his day-to-day life as well. He checked his watch, picked up the phone and canceled his date for the evening. He had four hours until the fax arrived. Hanks slumped into an easy chair, picked up a remote control unit from the table beside him and flipped on the TV.

*   *   *

The taxi in which Mary Kennedy was riding crossed Canal Street and picked through traffic for several blocks before rounding the monument of Robert E. Lee. It slipped under the long approach ramp to the Crescent City Connection, the twin-span bridge that connects downtown New Orleans to the communities south of the river. The taxi headed southwest on St. Charles Avenue, the broad, tree-lined boulevard with parallel roadways between which trolleys clatter along two sets of tracks carrying commuters and tourists from the French Quarter through the city's historic Garden District. St. Charles arcs southwest and then around to the northwest, following the bend in the river that gives the Crescent City its name. There, huge oak and pecan trees shade the large old homes and shops that line the avenue that ends just beyond bucolic Audubon Park.

The driver turned right just west of the Garden District, drove one block to Carondelet and stopped in front of an imposing home framed by trees on a pretty corner lot. Kennedy paid the fare, along with a generous tip, and stepped onto the sidewalk. She surveyed the home, trying to assess its age and worth, then opened the iron gate and glided up the twelve steps to the front porch. Just as she reached for the knocker, the door swung open and she was greeted by a middle-aged, dark-skinned woman wearing a black uniform with white collar and cuffs.

"Good evening, ma'am," she said politely. "Mr. Holland and his guests are in the garden. May I show you the way?"

"Thank you," she said, stepping inside.

The moment Mary Kennedy entered the hall, she knew she liked Jack Holland's tastes. From the Oriental rugs on the floor to the antique table and mirror along the left wall, to the plaster relief work on the ceiling fourteen feet above, from which a simple but elegant chandelier was suspended. She glanced to her left into the library and to the right into the living room. Both exuded wealth yet both looked remarkably friendly. She was surprised, since his office was more contemporary.

The maid led her to a door that opened onto a porch overlooking a lush garden along the side of the house. Six men and two women, all holding drinks, were talking to one another beneath the banana and plum trees. Several flower beds were nestled into groupings of azaleas, all accessed by winding brick walkways. In the center of the garden, a bronze fountain gurgled and spilled water into a small pool of large golden fish that swam among the water lilies.

"Hello, Mary," Holland called from the base of an enormous pecan tree that provided a green canopy for the entire garden. He beckoned her to come down the wooden steps and walked to meet her.

"This is gorgeous, Jack," she gushed.

"I thought you'd like it. I've wanted to have business meetings here before, but Martha was so dead set against it that I finally had to divorce her so I could do it!" He snickered. "What would you like to drink?" he asked, motioning her to the bar under the porch. "Wait, don't tell me. A Bloody Mary." He laughed raucously at his feeble attempt at a joke.

She smiled. "Just some bourbon and water, please. Let's save the bloodletting for another day."

After a round of quick introductions, Mary eased into conversation with two male architects who were immediately captivated with her accent and her charm. Glancing at her frequently as he made the rounds of his clients, Holland observed a woman who could light up a party. He hoped she wasn't lighting up one of the guests, because he was looking forward to whatever extracurricular activities she had in mind for him.

*   *   *

Torn between getting home to the children and staying to talk with her heavily sedated husband, Elizabeth chose the former. "I've got to go now," she whispered as she bent down to kiss Peter. "I'll be back with the kids tomorrow."

Bill McGuire and his wife, Joyce, were also in the room. Together they had provided the most help and the most consistent support for the Boget family throughout their month-long ordeal. Joyce, in particular, had spent many hours with Elizabeth lending an ear as well as a hand, continually guiding her back toward God when she sensed that Elizabeth was reaching the end of her rope. Bill stepped to the side of the bed across from Elizabeth, while Joyce put her arm around the beleaguered mother and wife. "Let's pray before we go," he said.

When he was through, Peter looked up from his pillow. "Thanks, Bill," he said weakly. He looked toward his wife. "Get a good night's sleep, Elizabeth, and don't worry about coming tomorrow. Tell the kids I'll be rooting for them and to score some goals for me."

*   *   *

Jack Holland was nearing fifty, but seemed older. He might have looked distinguished, but instead, with small eyes on a full face and a large belly protruding through his opened suit jacket, he looked rather ordinary. It was not his appearance that attracted Mary Kennedy, and they both knew it. But a few drinks and a heavy dinner clouded Holland's thinking, and Kennedy had little trouble getting her cocaine supplier to talk about his second business.

"What you do sounds so daring. Don't you think someone suspects?" Kennedy asked smoothly.

Holland laughed. "Around here everyone suspects, but no one cares. We bring the goods in on a banana boat. It used to come into New Orleans, but Gulfport, over in Mississippi, took away the business. Not that it matters. I've got a shrimp boat out of Bayou Caddy that gets the drop out along the shipping channel and brings it in." Holland downed another glass of whiskey and kept talking. "Lots of guys tried to bring the drugs right up the Mississippi, but they were always getting picked up; some would take shrimp boats all the way to the coast of Cuba, but they kept getting intercepted by the Coast Guard. I don't know anyone who uses a working shrimp boat. In the winter, it's tougher, because there's fewer fisherman, and . . ." He started to say that without the shrimp nets, the pickup is more difficult, but he didn't want to give away all his secrets. "Well, you understand. This time of year it's better."

Kennedy coaxed him on with kisses to his cheeks and neck. "So what boat's bringing my cocaine?"

"The *Maiden Pr*—" He stopped and smiled, then shook his head to signal that was all she would get out of him. "You don't need to know that."

"And then you pack the cocaine in ice with the shrimp and fly it to Norfolk?" she persisted.

He tried to laugh, but all he could muster was a drunken guffaw. "Don't you think it's funny that people drive from Pittsburgh and Cleveland to Virginia Beach to eat the same shrimp and oysters they could eat if they visited restaurants in their own towns?"

"Yes, and to think, the same cocaine that comes ashore with the live shrimp on the—" She waited for a response and, without thinking, he gave it.

"*Miss St. Loo.*"

"—right, on the *Miss St. Loo*—leaves packed in ice with the same shrimp to Norfolk," she said. Then she leaned over and kissed his lips. "You're such a genius, Jack," she whispered.

Before Holland fell into an alcohol-induced sleep, Mary Kennedy was able to learn how many people handled Holland's merchandise, what kind of security he had in place, and the procedures for transferring shipments.

3

Saturday, April 14

At 6:00 a.m., with Debbie Steinbaugh the only thing on his mind, Mike Downes was headed east on Interstate 64 toward the airport.

The night before, he had stopped briefly at his house to pack for his Colorado trip, and then arrived at Anna and Martin's place after they had left for the mountains. The Windsors lived in a beautifully restored townhouse near Virginia Commonwealth University in the city's Fan district, and Friday nights there were special for Mike. He liked the company of his daughter and son-in-law as much as he enjoyed spending the night in something other than his home—a structure that now housed only him, his dog, Goldie, and memories. This weekend, though Anna and Martin were gone, he also took pleasure in the fact that their house was fifteen minutes closer than his to the airport.

Though usually very diligent, he hadn't told anyone but Hendrick where he was going. He decided not to activate call-forwarding, since he wasn't going home after dinner, and he didn't bother to check his answering machine or his voicemail at the office. He didn't want to be distracted from his primary objective—getting out of town to see Debbie.

For the first time since his wife died of cancer, Mike was fully occupied with thoughts of a woman.

*   *   *

With the burn census down, the Burn Intensive Care Unit at the Medical College of Virginia Hospital had opened its doors to patients experiencing a wide variety of traumatic injuries. Filling the otherwise quiet morning were the sounds of monitors tracking the vital signs of a woman who had been caught in the crossfire of rival drug dealers in the city's Blackwell neighborhood.

Despite the pain medication, Peter Boget was awake and listening to those sounds after a fitful night of sleep. The pain from the skin donor site exceeded that of the graft on his chest, but he smiled when he realized that the two new pains made him temporarily forget about the bullet wound in his right thigh.

He pulled his laptop computer from the stand beside his bed and turned it on. Connected to both a power supply and to a telephone outlet Boget accessed CompuServe to look for any electronic mail he may have received overnight. There was none. He dialed up several bulletin boards over which he had exchanged information with a wide range of computer users, including a few hackers who frequently explained the how-to's of their nefarious deeds.

The process was more difficult than it had been before the accident because the bandages on his right thumb and forefinger all but negated his ability to use his right hand for typing.

The digital clock in the corner of his computer screen read 7:02:36 when he found what he was looking for, a query to "Hack Attack" from "Mark-the-Shark." It simply said, "CIS address?"

Bulletin boards are not the place to discuss intimate secrets, though under the veil of anonymity a lot of information changes hands. Peter knew that if he posted his CompuServe address, anyone on the bulletin board could learn who he was. When he was investigating people who provided detailed information on how to steal or disrupt telephone service, the release of his identity would surely thwart his work. But Peter Boget wanted to talk to Mark-the-Shark. He posted the number and logged off. As he set his Powerbook on the small table at his side he wondered who, besides the man he was intending to reach, would be looking up his name and profile on CompuServe. He squeezed a button to release a small dose of painkiller into his intravenous solution and laid his head on his pillow.

*   *   *

Fifteen miles southwest of the hospital, in a large home nestled among mixed hardwood and pine trees in the lakefront community of Brandermill, Elizabeth Boget was waking up her son Daniel. His soccer game was at 8:30, and she planned to take him while Lauren baby-sat Jonathan and Kristin. David was already downstairs in the kitchen making himself some scrambled eggs. A bagel glowed inside the toaster oven. He was dressed and ready to be picked up by the McGuires for the long drive to Williamsburg for a league game at ten.

"Mom, do you really think Dad will be home by next Saturday?" David asked.

"That's what the doctors are saying." She tried to sound cheerful despite all that was weighing on her mind.

"I sure miss him . . . especially when he isn't at my games."

"I do too."

David looked out the window through the screened-in porch to the yard beyond. He looked at the bright green blades of grass shimmering where a lazy sun knifed through the trees and danced off the morning dew. It reminded him of the soccer field where his father had spent so many hours running with the youngsters he coached. "Do you think he'll be able to play ball again?"

"If I know your father, he'll be out running around before the new skin on his chest stops oozing."

David laughed. "I know. It's just so hard to see him in a hospital bed, and to hear him breathing like that."

Elizabeth pulled a cereal box from a shelf and began filling a bowl for herself. She was tired, having spent most of the night drifting in and out of consciousness waiting for Jonathan, whom she had brought back to her bed, to have his nightmare. The other half of the night she relived the terrible incident in the hospital.

"Do you remember his eyes, David?"

"Whose eyes?"

"The man holding Jonathan," said his mother.

It took a moment for David to get his mind in sync with his mother's. "The man with the gun?"

Elizabeth nodded. "I can't get those eyes out of my mind."

David looked quizzically at her.

"It's nothing, David, I'm sorry. It's just so hard for me to believe that he could do what he did to your father and Jonathan and to that poor policeman and get away scot-free. It doesn't make sense."

"Like you said, Mom, the FBI will get him sooner or later."

Elizabeth shook her head, then sat down at the kitchen table. "It's going to be hard to rest until I know that those eyes have been closed . . . forever."

*   *   *

The same sun that was shining in the Bogets' backyard was brightening the sky over the Gulf of Mexico, filtering through the trees around the home of Liza and Randy Morgan and their three children. But Liza didn't see it. She was sitting at the nurse's station in the emergency room of the Hancock Medical Center.

The one-story, gray-brick building with the distinctive blue pyramids marking the building's entrances was the pride of Bay St. Louis, the coastal community that adjoined Waveland and wrapped around the western side of a beautiful bay. The night had been uneventful, so Liza had time to begin a letter to the man who was on her mind continually.

Dear Peter,

You will never know what I am feeling right now. It's as if sparklers and fireworks are exploding in my head and carousels are riding around in my stomach. Though I am sitting calmly here at the desk in the hospital where I work, a whole world of wonder is swirling within me. If I were to stand at this moment, my feet would leave the floor and I would dance until I drop.

You will never know how often I have thought about you and how I willed you into my life. You will never know how many times I sat writing you letters I never sent. You will never know how often I ran from the physical and verbal attacks of my husband, looking for you along the road or down at the beach.

From the moment we met, I believed that someday we would be together. When you left to go back to school, I wished, hoped, prayed you would come back for me. Then I learned that you were to be married to Elizabeth, and I cried, oh how I cried. I've kept track of you the same way you've kept track of me, I suppose—through the Bertrands. And as I heard about your growing family and your wonderful life with Elizabeth I have to admit I spent more than a few moments being very jealous. I wanted to be your wife. I wanted to be the mother of your children.

But I have learned to go on with life. Randy's not the best husband, nor the best father, but we've never gone hungry and I did marry him for better or worse (and there has been a lot of worse), for richer or poorer (and there's been a fair amount of poorer), and I plan to be faithful for as long as the two of us live, but (excuse me if I have too many buts here, but you probably understand) I never imagined you would actually reenter my life, and oh, Peter, I can't tell you what it means to me to know for sure what I always believed.

And Peter, let me tell you what in my tongue-tied condition on the phone I didn't spit out: I, too, love you, Peter. I always have and I always will.

Liza continued to write, spilling her heart on the pink pages that she filled quickly with her open, sweeping handwriting.

"Are you okay, Liza?"

She looked up from the letter into the face of Norma Jenson, one of the emergency-room doctors in whom Liza had often confided about her marriage and her difficulties. A smile blossomed on Liza's face and a sparkle illuminated her eyes. "I'm more than okay," she beamed through the tears that streaked her face. "Today I'm the happiest woman in the world."

*　　*　　*

Mary Kennedy was dressed before Jack Holland awoke. She was combing her hair in front of a spacious dressing table just outside the door to the bathroom when Holland, in a sleepy voice, asked, "Did you spend the night?"

"You forgot already?"

"I must have had too much to drink." Holland rolled over. "I'll be up in a minute."

"Don't bother," said Kennedy as she checked her makeup. She dropped her comb into her purse and walked toward the door that opened onto the hallway. "I plan to do some shopping down in the French Quarter, but I wouldn't mind a ride into the country. How far away is Bayou Catty?"

"Caddy, with a *d*," said Holland reflexively. But he was suddenly very awake. "Why do you want to know?"

"Oh, nothing. You just mentioned that's where our goods come in and I thought it would be fun to see it."

"I told you that?" Holland said as he stepped out of the bed. He wrapped a silk robe around his large belly. "Oh, right, I remember. I can't get over there today, but if you're going to be in town this evening, I could take you over to the casino. It's right on the bayou."

At the mention of gambling, Kennedy's ears perked up. "Casino? in Mississippi?"

"Yeah. Riverboat gambling is bigger over there than here. To be honest, it worries me. It's changing some of the family beach communities like Gulfport. I don't have to tell you gambling attracts people with problems, and people with problems attract cops, and the last thing I want is cops sniffing around in my neighborhood." Holland walked toward the bathroom. "But if you'd like to make a night of it, I can pick you up at five."

Kennedy looked at Holland. Absolutely nothing attracted her to him physically or emotionally. But she hadn't finished her weekend's work. "That's great. Remember, I'm at the Monteleone."

"How could I forget?"

*　　*　　*

Despite the pain, Peter Boget focused on his work. All morning, he reviewed the notes he had compiled during the previous weeks. After lunch he laid them out on the two bed tables he had requested. Though his range of motion was limited, his long arms allowed him to take his pile of 3 × 5 cards and spread them out across the two tables, with leftovers covering every surface as far as he could reach. He had learned the card technique for studying a problem at a company-sponsored management-development program. Now he was rearranging the array before him. His wife was standing at the head of the bed.

"Look, Elizabeth, I think I've got it," he said as he walked her through his scenario. "When I take all the information I've been able to glean from the FBI agents who've been visiting me in here, and when I take what you and Mike have told me about what went on in Baltimore, and when I remember what I heard when people thought I was sleeping in that hospital bed in Maryland, I think I've figured out what's going on. I don't think the police have put it all together yet."

He pointed to one of the cards on the table just above his waist. On it was written:

Mark-the-Shark

M&T = Michaels and Trent

Dealer?

"So?" Elizabeth asked.

"He's the missing link," Peter beamed. "Right now the FBI believes that Mary Kennedy was after me because she thought I was Barry Whitehead and that I had made off with her cocaine. But there's no link. They need Barry, but I don't think they know where he is. I know Mike hasn't said anything to anybody."

"Are you telling me that even the FBI doesn't know where Barry White-head is?"

"I don't think so. Mike's been very tight-lipped about the whole thing."

"Maybe. But he did tell me last night that the FBI called on him just before he came to the hospital."

"And?"

"He didn't elaborate."

"Well, even if they catch up with him, Barry isn't going to be much of a witness."

Elizabeth smiled. "Why are you trying to be investigator, prosecutor, judge and who knows what else? You're supposed to be resting and recuperating so you can get back on your feet."

Peter didn't smile back. "Look at me. I've been in a hospital bed for a month."

"So?"

"I'm about to lose my job."

"Peter, I—"

"And I've come to see how short life really is. I want to make sure I don't waste a minute of my time. So if I can help the police land the creeps who tried to kill me, that's good, but it's not why I'm doing this. This is about Frank Mazzetti."

"What?" Elizabeth said in disbelief.

"I haven't figured it all out, but there's a link here. I know there is a link here somewhere. I've just got to put it together. And that's why I'm trying to talk with Mark Randolph."

"Who?" She looked deep into his face. "You can't be serious about Mazzetti doing drugs, can you?"

"No, nothing like that, but, but . . . I just don't know." Peter looked at the cards spread out around him. He picked one up. "I think Mark Randolph is Mark-the-Shark. On one of the computer bulletin boards he described a way to change telephone numbers so that someone else ended up with a long distance bill. That's when I first noticed him and saved his information. I tried it myself and it worked. That's one of the things Mazzetti found in my computer. Anyway, if we can get to Mark Randolph—and right now I bet the FBI has no clue where he is—we can get Kennedy, and maybe we can get Mazzetti too."

Those words got Elizabeth's attention, but she didn't understand what stealing telephone services had to do with Mary Kennedy.

Peter continued, "One of the other things this Mark-the-Shark bragged about was how he accessed a certain type of computer to have reports generated without the computer retaining information that was used for the reports. It seemed complicated at the time, so I just saved it and forgot about it. But this past week, on those backup disks you brought me from home, I found it, and I think the M&T that Mark-the-Shark referred to is Michaels and Trent, the investment firm that the FBI was talking about. If I'm right, then Mark-the-Shark's scheme is how the men paid Mary Kennedy for the cocaine."

"Do you ever turn your mind off?"

"Some people may want to turn it off for me," he said, referring to the attempts on his life, "but no, I can't stop thinking about possibilities."

Leaning forward to kiss her husband on the forehead, Elizabeth whispered, "That's why I married you: you're always coming up with so many ideas. You always keep life so interesting."

"And I thought you married me for my body!"

"Good thing I didn't," she parried, "since what you've got left isn't much to talk about!"

Peter started to laugh, but when he did, pain knifed through his body. He grimaced. "Touché."

*   *   *

Mike Downes walked up the warm, tunnel-like ramp from the plane to the terminal, his heart racing as he thought of Debbie. He could scarcely remember the first time he saw her at the jail in Cancún. She was gaunt, foul-smelling and in shock. It had only been a month ago, but it seemed like years.

As he stepped through the door, Debbie Steinbaugh was the only person Mike Downes saw. Her shimmering golden hair and her radiant smile were like a lighthouse beacon penetrating the darkness. As he approached her, he dropped his carry-on bag and extended a bouquet of flowers. But Debbie wasn't noticing flowers or suitcases. She saw only the face of the man who had brought her hope in her darkest hour and deliverance from her wretched nightmare.

*   *   *

As Elizabeth turned to leave, Peter stopped her. "I'm sorry, Elizabeth, I forgot to tell you that I spoke with Liza Morgan on Friday."

"You what?"

"You know I've been making calls to some of our old friends, and I thought Randy and Liza might like to know about Debbie and what I've . . . what we've been through."

Elizabeth knew of Liza and Randy from conversations with the family Peter lived with in Denver. But she hadn't met the Morgans until Liza and Randy made a short stop at the Boget home when their youngest was a toddler. The Morgans had been on their way to Washington for a rare vacation. Elizabeth had been totally surprised by the visit, for which she had but an hour's notice, but she had insisted they stop, despite the fact that Peter was in New York on business.

From time to time Elizabeth and Peter had talked of Liza and their summer in Colorado, but other girlfriends came up in conversation too. When he mentioned Colorado, he more often talked about the Clarks and Debbie. So Elizabeth never believed that Peter and Liza had more than a passing interest in one another, though she remembered that her husband seemed more than a little disappointed when he learned that Liza had been to the house and he had missed her.

"You just called her out of the blue?" she asked.

Peter nodded. "She's become a nurse since you saw her. And she's still married to Randy, but she didn't say much about him."

"And her children—how old must they be by now?" Elizabeth began some calculations in her head.

"I forgot to ask."

"How are they doing?"

"I don't know that either."

"Typical." She slowly shook her head. "What kind of an information-gathering expert doesn't find out the vital details? What did you talk about?"

"Mostly what happened, you know, and the skin graft."

Elizabeth huffed. "Men don't know how to talk about anything important!"

*   *   *

Roland Hanks was playing mailman. He was good with maps and directions, and he had no trouble making his New Jersey merchandise drops at parking lots along U.S. 22 in Scotch Plains and Union before heading west to the Short Hills Mall.

Each encounter was the same. A man wearing a red shirt stood next to a car in the designated area of a parking lot at the predetermined time. Hanks, carrying two shopping bags, walked up to the man and asked, "Having car trouble?"

"No," the man would reply, "I'm just waiting for my wife."

"Is she still shopping?"

"I don't know," the man would say. "She's probably talking to friends about our trip to Aruba."

At the mention of Aruba, Hanks would give one of the shopping bags to the man and walk on across the parking lot, bag in hand, to his car. The second bag held some clothes he had bought on his way north to give him something to carry after making the handoff. The exchanges went flawlessly.

Hanks got slowed up for a while in traffic on Northfield Road before making a drop in West Orange, then picked up the Garden State Parkway for a delivery at the huge Garden State Plaza in Paramus. It was his last stop before crossing the George Washington Bridge into Manhattan for one curbside exchange. Then he headed north into New York's Westchester County and on to Long Island for his final deliveries.

                                    *   *   *

By the time Debbie and Mike hit Interstate 25, the north-south route that connected the Colorado cities on the high plateau east of the Rockies, they were changing their plans. Instead of turning south to Colorado Springs, they continued west.

"If you've never been up in these mountains, that's where we need to go!" Debbie couldn't contain her excitement. "We can head to Vail, swing south through Leadville to Buena Vista, and then come back through the Florissant Fossil Beds and down into the Springs."

"And how long will this take?" Downes asked patiently.

"When does your plane leave?"

"Tomorrow at six. Why do you ask?"

"We might just make it," she said, tossing her blonde hair backward.

Mike looked at the woman behind the wheel of the Mustang and caught the impish grin that crossed Debbie's face. "And what about dinner?" he asked.

She turned and looked at the handsome man sitting beside her. Her grin widened into a full smile as she asked, "Who's hungry?"

Traffic was light as they sped across the city and started the climb into the foothills. "This is beautiful," Mike said. "Are you trying to tempt me or something?"

"Just want you to see why the prospect of spending a lifetime in a Mexican prison nearly killed me. And I figured that anyone who'd fly two thousand miles to see me for a weekend ought to see what I love about this place I call home." Before Mike could respond, Debbie added, "I thought about calling the Clarks and telling them you were coming, but I decided I'd keep you all to myself."

As the Mustang raced past slow-moving trucks, Mike leaned back and contemplated the beauty around him—the woman at the wheel whom he had only known for a month and the majestic mountains that rose before him. "I haven't been this happy in years," Mike said. "A couple more hours and I'm not going to want to go back to Virginia."

"You sound like Peter. After that summer he spent with our family, we were all sure he'd move back here after college, but it just didn't happen."

"Maybe," Downes said thoughtfully, "he didn't realize how beautiful you'd become."

"Maybe he noticed that I was only a little brat at the time!"

*   *   *

Despite her exhaustion, Liza Morgan couldn't sleep. She never liked having to sleep during the day when she worked the overnight tour at the hospital, but with time she had gotten used to it. Her children were usually quiet around the house when she slept, and this day was no exception. Junior was off at college, Amy was visiting one of her high-school friends, and Eric, her youngest at fourteen, was hanging out on the town's fishing pier.

But it wasn't noise that kept Liza awake, it was elation. She wanted to call Peter but knew that she had better not. Randy was sitting at the kitchen table with his tax forms, checkbook, and stacks of documents spread before him, but she knew that her husband's attention span was short. With the house empty he was likely to crawl into bed with her. Anyway, she didn't know what she would say to Peter, or how she would say it. She rolled on her side, pulled the light blanket up to her neck and prayed that sleep would overtake her.

*   *   *

It was dark and Roland Hanks was weary when he pulled into the Roosevelt Field Shopping Center in Garden City on Long Island. He circled the mall until he spotted a man leaning against the hood of a BMW in front of the J. C. Penney's. The man was younger than the others Hanks had seen during the day, under twenty-five he guessed. The man's red shirt looked almost black under the mercury vapor lamps, but Hanks could see that the man, like himself, spent a lot of time in a weight room. Hanks found a parking spot two rows away and backed in. With shopping bags in hand, he walked to the mall entrance and then turned and headed in the direction of the BMW.

"Having car trouble?" he asked.

"No, I'm just waiting for my wife."

"Is she still shopping?"

"I don't know," the man said. "She's probably talking to friends about our trip to Aruba."

Hanks turned and walked between the BMW and the car beside it, dropped one of the bags he was carrying, and walked on.

"Did you drop something?" the man called after him.

Hanks's heart suddenly pounded in his ears. It was a setup. "Sorry, I didn't notice," he said, and turned back to retrieve the bag. When he reached for it, two men with guns drawn leaped from the car directly across from the BMW. The man on the car pulled a firearm from under his red shirt. "Stand still," he said quietly to Hanks. "You're under arrest."

4

Sunday, April 15

Hey, Mom!" yelled a breathless David Boget, bursting through the front door, "we're on the front page of the Metro section." He dropped most of the Sunday paper on a chair in the kitchen and placed the Metro section on the table. His two younger brothers scrambled for a look at the family photo as Lauren elbowed in. Elizabeth reached for her reading glasses and stepped to the table. She peered over Jonathan's shoulder.

"Listen to this," David said. Then he deepened his voice and tried to sound dramatic as he read the headline above the photo of Elizabeth and her children sitting on their front porch.

"Family caught in bizarre case of stolen identity discovers holes in corporate safety net."

David quickly read aloud the first few paragraphs of the story that had been written at Peter's instigation. A previous story had focused on the search for and discovery of the phone company's PR manager and the assassination attempts in the hospital. This one focused on the unpleasant surprise Elizabeth got when Peter was missing and his paycheck, along with his benefits, stopped.

Near the end of the article, several paragraphs focused on Elizabeth's feelings now that the worst seemed to be over. David tried to imitate his mother's voice as he read her quotes.

"As a full-time mother it was difficult to face the prospect of losing all that we had built up over the years," said Mrs. Boget. "We work as partners. He brings home the money, I stay home and take care of the house, and together we raise our family."

Asked if she planned to change anything once her husband returned home she responded boldly: "The first thing I'm going to do is get some of our money out of the company savings plan and into an account where I can access it if something like this ever happens again. Then I'm going to do whatever needs to be done to see that the people who tried to kill my husband and kidnap my son are locked up for good."

Elizabeth winced as she read the last sentence. As soon as the reporter had left her home she knew that line would end up in print. She wished she hadn't said it, even though it reflected a thought that she tried continually to erase from her mind.

*   *   *

While the Boget children were fawning over their family's photo in the *Richmond Times-Dispatch*, Frank Mazzetti was reading it intently over breakfast in the Greenhouse Restaurant at the Hyatt Richmond. When he finished, he tore out the article, folded it and slipped it into his pocket.

*   *   *

For the first Sunday in over a month, Elizabeth Boget sat in church not bothered by fear, doubt or anxiety. She had her first good night's rest in over a week. All of her children slept through the night, and now the three oldest sat with her during worship. The members of Lakeside Community Church had provided financial, emotional and spiritual support for the family throughout their ordeal, and as Elizabeth scanned the church's sanctuary, she was struck with how many sitting there had become closer and dearer friends in just a few short weeks. But when the sermon began, Elizabeth's feelings of thanksgiving and praise gave way to thoughts of the future.

" 'Do not be anxious for your life, as to what you shall eat, or what you shall drink; nor for your body, as to what you shall put on.' "

The pastor was quoting Jesus, but Elizabeth wasn't hearing. She already knew God would take care of her needs. She and her family had seen evidence of that for years, and never more so than recently. But now that her needs were once again being cared for, Elizabeth found a few wants clouding her thoughts. "The man with the eyes, Lord," she prayed. "Is it too much to ask that he will never again bother my family? And Mazzetti . . . take care of him, Lord. Please see that he gets what's coming to him." No sooner had the prayer filled her mind than another, deeper prayer took its place. "Forgive me, Father. Please control this desire for revenge."

*   *   *

Jack Holland was a gracious host but not much of a cook. "How about breakfast at Brennans?" he asked Mary Kennedy, who was sitting in her long silk bathrobe at the round table in the corner of her hotel room. She was looking through the sheer curtain that softened the view of the flower-filled courtyard below. She turned back toward the bed where Holland, under the quilted bedspread, was propped up on one elbow. "You better hµrry. I've made reservations for noon."

"I'm all ready except for putting on my dress," she said as she lifted a cup of coffee to her lips. "I've already taken a walk to the levee and back, showered, and put on my makeup. You've missed out on a beautiful morning."

"I was savoring a beautiful night," he said as he rolled from the bed and headed to the bathroom.

"Are you still pleased with our business proposition?" Mary asked.

"Absolutely."

"Good, then we can discuss the details at breakfast."

Thirty minutes later, Kennedy and Holland walked through the doors of one of the grandest dining establishments in the heart of the French Quarter. It was crowded as it always is for breakfast on the weekends, but a friendly maitre d' quickly whisked them away to an elegant table for two in one of the nine dining rooms. The table, draped in pink linen, sat across the aisle from tables that looked out onto a courtyard where additional tables were nestled among the trees and flowers.

"Is that who I think it is?" Kennedy whispered across the floral arrangement, using her eyes and a nod of her head to point to a large man with a big smile who was laughing infectiously with three other people at a nearby round table.

"Rush Limbaugh? Yes," Holland whispered back, though he knew that even in his normal voice he wouldn't be heard over the laughter. "And that's the manager there with her husband. I don't know the other man." Holland thought for a minute, then said, "Rush is a good man. It's just too bad the people in Washington don't listen to him. Taxes are killing me."

"I can believe it. I pay taxes on all my transactions, because I don't ever plan to go to jail. Too many people in this business end up going down on tax evasion charges," Kennedy said seriously. "But that's one rap they'll never be able to hang on me."

A waitress walked to the table, set glasses of champagne before the couple and asked, "Are you prepared to order?"

When she departed, Holland and Kennedy resumed the discussion they had begun in the hotel room.

"You drive a hard bargain, Jack," mourned Kennedy. "I turn over to you a company worth one point one million and get in return only twenty-five percent of a company worth two million?"

"No, twenty percent, and that's only if I make delivery of the goods as planned and you are not able to pay cash within thirty days."

"You didn't say anything about thirty days."

"Look, Mary, I can't string you out forever."

"I need at least sixty days. Ninety would be better."

"It's thirty or nothing. I'm sorry."

"Then I get twenty-five percent."

Kennedy had looked over Holland's books and judged that the real value of Holland Engineering was half a million more than he stated, but she didn't know for sure. In any event, she figured that she stood to lose a quarter of a million on the deal unless she could make the cash payment in thirty days. On the other hand, as a principal owner of Holland Engineering, she might be able to sink her teeth into his other line of business.

Holland knew that whatever the outcome, he couldn't lose. He knew he had to give up some of the ownership in his company to prevent law enforcement officials from looking too closely at the transaction, but he knew from personal investigation and some inside information that the real worth of Kennedy's firm was closer to one and a quarter million. He liked the idea of gaining control of Kennedy and Associates so that he could keep track of Mary. "That's fair enough," he said reaching for his champagne glass. "Have we got a deal?"

Mary Kennedy lifted her glass. The ring of crystal striking crystal was swallowed in the laughter from a nearby table.

*   *   *

"He's where?" Tyrone Giddings couldn't believe what he was hearing on the phone. "What's he doing in Colorado?" the FBI agent demanded.

"I don't know. No one's been able to find him yet. I just thought you'd like to know that he bought the tickets at the airport yesterday morning."

Giddings didn't get out of church until 1:30, and by the time he and his family had finished dinner, he was ready to settle down to watch basketball, not head to the office. "You're telling me that Downes got on a plane yesterday morning and it took you twenty-four hours to find that out? Come on, Rex, you can do better than that."

Agent Middleton ignored his partner's ranting. "I just got in here, and I can tell you that a lot of leg work has been done ever since we learned that Whitehead isn't in Cancún. Nobody, and I mean nobody, knew that Downes was going to Colorado. We even tracked down his daughter at Wintergreen and she said he was supposed to come over for dinner on Friday night and he said he'd be late, that's all." Middleton flipped through some notes on his desk. "Elizabeth Boget may have been the last person he talked to, but he said nothing to her. His secretary was genuinely flabbergasted when I called her back and asked her if he had said anything about Colorado."

"So?"

"Listen to this. We talked with the Consular Agent in Cancún—the woman Downes worked with to get Debbie Steinbaugh out of jail—and she said that she saw Whitehead in the jail last week but that he has disappeared."

"And the police?"

"They say they have no record of him."

"How about Steinbaugh? Did you reach her?"

"No."

Giddings was hoping that he could enjoy the rest of the basketball game, but he began to suspect that wouldn't be the case. "Have you talked with the prosecutor?"

"Williams did," said Middleton, "and I can tell you she's not happy. She's upset with us that it took so long to find Whitehead. Now that it looks like Downes has led us up a blind alley and then skipped town, she's going for an arrest warrant if he's not back tonight."

"Do you need me for anything?"

"I don't think so."

"Good. Today's supposed to be my day off," Giddings said with a sigh. "Don't call me until you locate Whitehead or Downes."

*   *   *

Delivering a kiss to his cheek, Mary Kennedy said goodbye to Jack Holland. She had gotten everything she had come for, but the price exceeded what she was willing to pay for it. She didn't know what she was going to do, but even as she stepped from the car, she was plotting her next move. She needed the drugs, but she wasn't about to give up control of her company.

By the time she was on her plane, two possibilities came to mind: reduce the value of her company by transferring its assets to a holding company and then leasing them back, or just help herself to the drug shipment. Both had serious drawbacks. But just imagining how Holland would react when he discovered he had been outsmarted by a woman made her smile.

*   *   *

Though it seemed to Mike Downes that the Rockies would go on forever, Debbie's Mustang wouldn't. Just east of Vail it threw its timing chain, and the mechanic on duty at Pinnacle Auto Repair had to send to Denver for a replacement. The new chain didn't arrive until Sunday morning. But that didn't seem to bother the couple as they enjoyed a leisurely breakfast and walked the streets of the resort community. Ducking in and out of shops, Mike and Debbie spent more time looking at each other than the merchandise on display or the snow-covered mountains that ringed the tourist mecca. Cancún and Richmond seemed far away in miles, time and climate.

Mike liked the cold. It gave him an excuse to hold Debbie close.

"I probably should call and make another plane reservation," Mike said while investigating several cable-knit sweaters. "Even if the car is ready now, there's no way we'll make it back to the airport in time for my flight."

Debbie didn't want to think about him leaving. "Did it ever occur to you that maybe you aren't supposed to go back?"

"It occurred to me from the moment I stepped off the plane."

Debbie smiled. "Me too," she said, as she slipped her hand into his.

Mike glanced around the small but busy shop and dropped his voice to a whisper. "I think they call this love."

"I think you're right," she whispered back.

*   *   *

Peter Boget tried to ignore the pain in his chest and leg, but it wasn't going away. He didn't feel much like doing anything but sleeping, but sleep wouldn't come. Elizabeth sat quietly by his bed holding his hand. She had told her friends at church that Peter wasn't up for visitors, so the room was peaceful. Eventually she broke the silence.

"I never imagined what the words of our wedding vows really meant until this," she said. "Here we are facing richer or poorer, sickness and health. Our whole world has been turned upside down—and even though it's coming back around, you're still here in this bed and I'm still worrying about how we're going to pay our bills." She wiped away a tear. "I'm so confused, Peter. Why is all this happening to us?"

She wasn't looking for an answer, and Peter offered none. His medication was making him groggy. And soon he was asleep. Elizabeth caught herself dozing off and finally she stood up. Her movement awakened him. "Elaine is staying with the kids, but I'd like to get home in time to put them to bed," she said before leaning over to kiss him. "I'll be back after lunch tomorrow."

*   *   *

"There's nothing tonight," Mike told Debbie. "Too many skiers heading back to the East Coast."

"Unfortunately, I've got to get home for work in the morning," she said. "I can drop you at a motel near the airport, then I'll drive on back to the Springs."

Mike thought about her suggestion and reluctantly said, "That's fine." He reached for her hand and headed for the door. "But right now I really don't want to think about car repairs or airplanes or work. I don't want to think about anything but you."

* * *

Sunday evening was unusually subdued at the Boget household. The strain of the preceding month was clearly evident in the mood in the house. The television was off, and David sat at the kitchen table working on his homework. He eschewed the desk in his room because he liked to listen to music on the family stereo while he "studied." Lauren was squirreled away in her room talking with a friend on the phone. Daniel and Jonathan were playing with their Sega in the rec room. That left Elizabeth in relative peace to bathe Kristin and put her to bed.

She was pulling the baby out of the warm water when the doorbell rang. David answered the door and then called to his mother, who didn't want to talk to anyone until she had Kristin in bed for the night.

"It's Agent Middleton," he yelled up the stairs.

When Elizabeth finally arrived in the living room, the FBI agent stood up and greeted her. "I'm sorry to come out here tonight, but your line has been busy for hours."

"Must be the kids. I'm sorry about that."

"I just wanted to ask you a few questions about Mike Downes and Debbie Steinbaugh."

Elizabeth looked at the man quizzically. "Why are you asking me?"

Holding up his hands to assure her that she wasn't going to be asked anything she didn't want to answer, Middleton gently said, "Mike has left town. In fact, he's gone to Colorado, and both he and Ms. Steinbaugh are, shall we say, unavailable."

"What do you mean, 'unavailable'?"

"We can't find them."

"But I told you yesterday he didn't say anything about what he had planned for the weekend."

"I know, but you know Ms. Steinbaugh, don't you?"

Elizabeth shook her head. "Not really, except for all the stuff down in Cancún. Peter knows her better than I do. He knows Mike better too. What are you getting at?"

"My job is to track him down, that's all," said Middleton. "I'm just running out of leads."

"Well, if Mike went to Colorado to see Debbie, she probably took him for a trip up into the mountains. He's mentioned that he had never been to that part of the country and, after getting a taste of it when he went to Colorado Springs to find Peter, thought he'd like to go back. Doesn't seem like any big deal to me."

"It is a big deal," the FBI agent said. "A very unhappy prosecutor in Norfolk is about to make life difficult for Mike. If he doesn't show up tonight, she's going to throw the book at him."

Elizabeth's countenance changed. She turned her head and called to David to go up and get his sister, who was crying in the crib. Then she motioned Middleton into the living room, switched on a lamp and sat down in a wing chair. Middleton sat facing her on the sofa.

"This is serious, isn't it?"

"Very. A potentially key witness that Mike Downes has been hiding from us has disappeared. And now Downes has too."

Elizabeth leaned forward, her head in her hands, her elbows on her knees. "And you think he's run away?"

"Maybe."

"No way," Elizabeth said softly. "Not Mike. He doesn't run from trouble."

5

Monday, April 16

Mike Downes didn't like the idea of letting Debbie drive to Colorado
Springs so late at night, but she insisted she would be okay when
she dropped him off at the airport at midnight. He had booked
space on a 4:35 a.m. flight to Washington's Dulles Airport
with a connection to Richmond.

He called his answering machine, and his voicemail at work. Both contained messages from the FBI, and both had messages from his daughter.
All asked him to call the FBI immediately. He looked at his watch and
decided that, as tired as he was, he didn't want to get into a discussion with
the police. He called his secretary's number and left a voicemail message:
"Hi, Sharon, this is Mike. I've run into some problems and won't be in the
office until mid-afternoon. I'm coming in from Denver and will call when
I change planes at noon. Would you please call Agent Giddings and find
out what he wants? Tell him I'll call between twelve and twelve-thirty."

He chose an empty seat in the gate area for his flight, tucked his carry-
on bag beneath his legs, set the alarm on his watch for 4:15, and, as best
he could, stretched out to sleep.

*　　*　　*

Nothing helped Earl Hendrick get his job out of his mind more completely than taking the helm of his thirty-three-foot yacht and skimming across the choppy waters of a breezy Chesapeake Bay. But this day nothing could clear his mind of the events of the preceding two weeks and the report he had to make to Mid-Atlantic Bell's executive committee on Tuesday.

He was tacking across a fourteen-knot southwesterly wind on his return from Crisfield on Maryland's eastern shore to Deltaville at the mouth of the Rappahannock. He had knifed through Kedges Strait at the north end of Smith Island and was heading toward Smith Point. He hoped to cross the twenty miles of open water at the confluence of the upper bay and the Potomac River and get to the shelter of Virginia's western shore before dark. He was so preoccupied with his personnel problem he didn't realize the boat was dragging a crabpot snagged off Solomon Island.

Hendrick turned to his wife, who sat on the cockpit's starboard bench gazing into the wake created by the boat. "I am not going to let Frank Mazzetti get away with that," he told her.

Emily Hendrick had heard the story of Frank Mazzetti, Mid-Atlantic Bell's vice president for administration, but this time it sounded different. "I know, honey. Frank's playing by his own rules."

"No, that is not it." Hendrick paused. "What a fool I have been."

Emily turned to look into the full, well-tanned face of the man to whom she had been married for as long as she could remember.

"For two weeks I've been wracking my brain to come up with an explanation why Frank is hell-bent on destroying Peter Boget," Earl said as he looked out over his boat's covered cabin into the choppy bay. "I have been so focused on Frank's desire to spite Mike and me because we defended Peter last year when he wanted to fire him that I have overlooked the possibility that Frank is trying to force me to retire early. I think he is trying to create a crisis by implying that I have lost my objectivity and am allowing an employee who has violated company rules in the past to continue as an outlaw here in Virginia. He sees this as his opportunity not only to force me aside, but to step into my job, clean up the dirty laundry he's created and then use his golden-boy image to carry him to the presidency of Mid-Atlantic Bell."

"They wouldn't send him to Virginia," she said with mock incredulity.

"Appoint Mazzetti? Yes, I think they would." His response was serious. "I may not like his methods but his results are phenomenal. Except for his occasional abruptness, he can charm the scales off a snake."

Emily smiled at her husband as he spun the wheeel abruptly to starboard. "Sounds to me like he *is* a snake."

Ignoring the comment, he continued in his slow, deliberate manner. "That is the problem. He has everyone convinced that Peter's accusations about finding him altering files in Peter's computer and having a fistfight with Peter's wife in the middle of the night are ludicrous. He already has everyone in D.C. convinced that the man should have been fired long ago." Hendrick took a deep gulp of the cool salt air. "He has brought in testimony from doctors that say that the medication they use with burn patients causes them to imagine that all the breathing and feeding tubes they have inserted in their mouths and up their noses are worms or snakes, and because they are not really unconscious, they hear what is being said about them and get confused and say and do strange things."

Emily waited for more.

"The burn doctors even say that the medication sometimes gives the patients such a feeling of well-being that they just get up and walk out of the hospital—the way Peter did—and then they usually end up back there in a few hours when the excruciating pain returns. That is why it is going to be so hard on Tuesday to try and defend Peter when Mazzetti has so much against him. What the security boys found in Peter's computer—and Peter's admitted it was there, though for very different reasons—sure could lead someone to believe that Peter was plotting to take revenge on the phone company. Mazzetti's shown me a scheme that he says Peter could have used to prompt our switching equipment to misread a telephone number and cause a long distance call to be billed to someone else's number. Peter also apparently had some information on how to find secret passwords in electronic mail systems."

"How do you defend a man who does that?"

"You don't. Unless . . ."

Hendrick was quiet for a long time. Emily sat just as quiet listening to the swoosh of water racing by the hull and the hum of air pressing against the stiffened sails.

"I had real trouble with Peter's story. I mean, how could I believe that a man in intense pain from burns on his chest and hand and a gunshot wound in his leg would sneak out of a hospital bed at eleven o'clock on a Saturday night and hobble a dozen blocks to his office just to remove a file from his computer? It was too preposterous." He paused and brought his hand to his chin. "But it fits . . ."

Emily watched while her husband arranged the puzzle pieces in his mind.

"Peter's wife meets him in the parking garage and brings his key so that he can get into the building. And when he gets to his office, Mazzetti, of all people, is at Peter's computer altering files to make Peter look bad. Because Peter's access to the building was with his own electronic key, it was recorded by the security computer. No matter what Peter did, it could be used against him."

"But if Peter went to alter files, wouldn't you think he would have taken out the ones that could have gotten him in trouble?"

"What Mazzetti found in the computer was not what he was looking for. He expected to find personal letters to Debbie Steinbaugh, copies of ones he found in Peter's personal laptop when Peter first disappeared. If he had found them, Peter would be in clear violation of company rules against using a company computer for personal business. If that happened, even I would have fired him on the spot. But Peter is no fool. I think he learned his lesson last year. I cannot believe he would have anything of a personal nature on his office computer. That is why I have to believe that what Frank found was business related—and I believe he found it on Saturday night like Peter says and not on Monday morning like Frank says."

"So all you have to do is prove that Frank was in the building on that Saturday night?"

"Well . . . ," he stretched out the word, "there is almost no evidence that anyone but Peter accessed the building. Let's face it, the head of company security can make just about anything work to his advantage. I have no idea how he got in or got to the tenth floor without his key showing up on the logs, but I'm sure he could have fixed the records. That's why the only evidence I do have is so important."

"Evidence? You didn't tell me about any evidence."

"After Elizabeth brought Peter home—after the incident—she scraped what she says is Mazzetti's skin from under her fingernails and put it in a test tube she took from the chemistry set of one of her kids. She said she ripped the skin from his face when they were fighting on the floor of the public relations office. I think I told you this before."

Emily said nothing and let her husband continue. "She took the test tube back to the hospital when she brought Peter back and some lab technician analyzed it and prepared a report. I have the report and the test tube in my attaché case."

"You do?" Emily's eyes brightened.

"The only problem is Frank is going to have to voluntarily allow someone to test his skin and blood to see if it matches."

"That sounds like a big problem," his wife whistled.

"A huge problem, so I am going to have to finesse it. Mike had an idea, and I am warming up to it. At Tuesday's meeting, after I tell Peter's side of the story to the executive committee, I will pull out the report and the test tube. The shock value alone could upset Mazzetti enough to allow his true colors to shine through or to shame him into disproving the allegation."

"What if the skin doesn't match?" Emily asked.

"I do not even want to think about that possibility," admitted Hendrick.

*   *   *

Ignoring the pain and the itching on his chest and leg, and the odor of luncheon meat going bad—a common byproduct of skin grafts—Peter Boget continued to check his CompuServe mailbox for a message from Mark-the-Shark. Just after three his persistence was rewarded. The message was short: "What do you want?" His response was not much longer:

Does Mary Kennedy ring a bell?
How about Michaels and Trent?
I'll check in every half hour.

*   *   *

Emily Hendrick tugged at the Baltimore Orioles baseball cap she had pulled down over her windblown auburn hair. Then she climbed down into the cabin and brought her husband's sleek, watertight, black aluminum attaché case to the deck. Earl smiled as she opened it and pulled out the test tube with the cork wedged into the top. She swirled the fluid in the tube and watched the tiny pieces of skin spin in the preservative solution that the lab technician had added. "Earl," she said, while a smile filled her sun-weathered face, "when Mazzetti sees this he's gonna flip out . . . mark my words."

Preoccupied with the Boget issue, the Hendricks were not hearing the warnings on the weather radio in the cabin below. They didn't know that a line of dangerous thunderstorms that had moved through central Virginia earlier in the afternoon was intensifying and bearing down on Chesapeake Bay. They didn't know that a tornado watch had been issued for eastern Virginia and southern Maryland. They also didn't know that the buoy and line attached to the crab-filled, steel-mesh basket they were dragging through the bay was entangled in their boat's propeller.

*　　*　　*

FBI agents Giddings and Middleton were waiting in Downes's office when the telephone executive walked through the door. The greeting was terse. Charles Piper from the company's security organization sat down next to Giddings, across the desk from the vice president. Piper spoke first.

"I'm sorry I have to be here, but you understand that we have to be involved whenever a law enforcement group is conducting an investigation. Mr. Mazzetti has been notified."

At the mention of Frank Mazzetti's name, Mike's blood pressure rose and his heart rate accelerated.

"Mr. Downes, I have a warrant for your arrest," Giddings said.

Mike appeared impassive, but fear and anger were working within him. After enjoying the most exciting, romantic weekend in years, he wasn't prepared for what he was hearing.

"I thought you were after Whitehead. He's the bad guy, not me. I told you what you wanted on Friday, didn't I?" The three listeners sat quietly. "Look, I caught the bad guy and persuaded him to voluntarily go to jail. You don't arrest citizens for that, do you? What's the charge against me?"

Giddings pointed at his partner and said, "On Friday, Agent Middleton told you that what you did was obstruct a criminal investigation and aid in the commission of a felony. That's what this warrant is for, but there could be more."

"Wait a minute. I didn't commit a crime. You guys didn't know Whitehead existed. Sure, I knew he took Peter's car and wallet, but how was I to know that he was mixed up in some huge FBI investigation of a drug kingpin?

At worst, I figured that if what he told me was true, the police in Maryland might want him for transporting drugs. I had—"

"At *worst?*" The big man exploded from his chair and clutched the edge of Downes's desk. "You figured that at the worst he would be wanted for transporting drugs? Maybe you don't think drugs are any big deal," Giddings bellowed, "but don't try to tell that to the mothers who are watching their kids die in every city in America. Don't try to tell that to the cops who are putting their lives on the line to keep this poison out of our neighborhoods. And don't try to tell that to your friend Peter Boget, who almost died because of those drugs. How dare you presume that you know what's best for a man delivering a million dollars' worth of death!"

Giddings dropped back into the chair, and his partner jumped into the conversation. "The problem is that you lied to us on Friday, and we haven't been able to find you all weekend."

"I've been in Colorado, and I didn't lie."

"You told us Whitehead was in Cancún. He isn't. You said some guy named Soto would help us. He hasn't. You said you'd call at noon today. You didn't."

"What are you talking about?"

Giddings was angry, but he kept his voice controlled. "Barry Whitehead is not in the Cancún jail and officials say he never has been."

"What do—"

"We couldn't find Soto either. I don't know what you think you're doing, but I hope you have a good lawyer because you're going to need one."

Downes was subdued as the gravity of his situation started to sink in. "I'm telling you, the last time I saw Barry Whitehead he was in the Cancún jail. That was ten days ago. The guards saw him, Soto saw him, the judge saw . . . That's it! The judge—did you contact Judge Cabrillo? Call him, he'll know."

Giddings wasn't swayed. "Mr. Downes, I'm afraid you are going to have to come with us." He motioned to Middleton, who had pulled handcuffs from his pocket. "I'm sorry," he added.

*   *   *

As the wind shifted to the northwest and began blowing down the Potomac, Earl Hendrick knew trouble was coming. With binoculars he could make out the Smith Point lighthouse, but the sky behind it was nearly black, obliterating the setting sun. Working quickly, he asked Emily to take the helm while he started the diesel engine. He wanted to be under power while he reefed the mainsail and ran up his storm jib on the forestay to serve as a weathervane.

Though he tried repeatedly, the engine wouldn't start.

Distress calls from other boaters already engulfed by the storm filled the radio. Then one voice cut through all the rest. It was the voice of a desperate woman. "Help me, I don't want to die. Help me, somebody help me, we're all going to die," she wailed before her voice was silenced by the storm.

"This is going to be worse than I thought," Earl said, emerging from the cabin. "Something is wrong with the engine," he told Emily as he slipped on his life jacket. "The only thing I can figure is that something is caught in the propeller. Turn into the wind while I check it out."

The boat slowed and Hendrick climbed down the stainless-steel ladder on the boat's stern. He checked to make sure that the line he had secured to a gunwale behind the cockpit was securely tied through the loops on his life jacket. The winds had climbed to twenty knots and the boat was pitching as waves splashed against the hull and sprayed the cockpit.

His hunch was right. Peering into the water, he could see heavy fishing line wrapped around the propeller. Three times he grabbed for the line only to lose it when it was ripped from his wet hands. The numbing cold of the forty-eight-degree water began to burn at his fingertips as he tried to reach the line.

When the stern rose out of the water, he saw something that made him sick. At one end of the line was a buoy that was now wedged between the propeller and the hull. Hanging from the stanchion, he kicked at it, but could not dislodge it. For five minutes he struggled with the buoy and the line, all to no avail. Cold and wet, he climbed back into the cockpit.

"It is no use," he told Emily with a hint of trepidation in his voice. "We're going to have to ride this one out. Get me a sweater and my mackintosh, please, and get ready for trouble."

Emily didn't need any further instructions. She and Earl had spent many hours on the bay and had been caught in more than a few storms. Within minutes of disappearing down the companion way she had tied down everything that could move, put on her own sweater and rain gear, strapped on her life jacket, and emerged from the cabin with clothing for Earl. The noise of wind and water required her to raise her voice as she told her husband of the many distress calls that were continuing to come in on the radio. She took the helm while her husband quickly dressed.

Earl Hendrick was a large man but relatively agile for his size and age. He was strong but he was also smart. He knew that he was no match for the elements. He secured a lifeline before climbing out of the cockpit and up onto the deck that ran along both sides of the boat.

"Be careful!" Emily shouted above the roar of the huge mainsail flapping in the wind.

*   *   *

Rain was already falling heavily onto the offices of Kennedy and Associates from one of the many storms sweeping across eastern Virginia. The torrents were filling storm drains and pouring into the Lafayette River. But Mary Kennedy was more interested in her conversation with Roland Hanks than the weather.

"It's a good thing that was my last drop," said an agitated Hanks as he talked about his encounter with the police at the Long Island shopping center. "And it was a good thing I'm a fast thinker, or they would have nailed me."

"Hanks, considering the circumstances," Kennedy tried to soothe her new problem solver, "I think we're fortunate that we only had one problem."

" 'We'? This isn't a 'we' thing. You didn't stick your neck out. You didn't get arrested!" retorted Hanks.

"And you didn't either, did you?"

"Of course I did—sort of. But I asked them if they always pull guns on someone who drops a bag in a shopping center, and when they got done searching me and my car and turned over two garbage cans looking for the stuff, they let me go."

"And the merchandise?"

Hanks retold the story with pride. "I smelled trouble. The man in the red shirt looked too much like a cop, so I stashed the stuff behind a tire on the back of a Blazer. Then I guess I got lucky. I went back two hours later and the Blazer was still there."

"You've got it with you?" asked a surprised Kennedy.

"Are you kidding? You think I want to get picked up with a key of cocaine? No way. I went back to the mall, bought a food processor, stuffed the bag in the box, got it gift wrapped, and told them it was a surprise for my girlfriend and that I was going to send her to the store to pick it up before Monday night. So, just send whoever is looking for the stuff to Penney's, and tell them to ask for the package for Michelle Jefferies."

6

C harles Piper stepped out of the vice president's office first and asked Sharon Tisdale, Mike's secretary, not to discuss what she saw or heard with anyone. Patricia Massey, the president's secretary, was given the same message. The two women then watched in stunned silence as two FBI agents escorted a handcuffed Mike Downes to the elevators.

Turning back to his secretary, Downes smiled. "Don't worry, this will all be resolved." To Giddings he said, "Let me try to get Soto on the phone, I'm sure we can work this all out right here. Maybe Kennedy got to Whitehead."

Giddings shook his head and scowled. "You just don't get it. We want Whitehead, not excuses and delays. Now let's go!"

* * *

The response from Mark Randolph showed up in Peter Boget's electronic mailbox minutes after the original memo was posted. It simply said, "Yes. Yes. I'll stay on."

Boget posted back, "The FBI is looking for you. Mary Kennedy tried to kill me. I need your help to get her and whoever tried to kidnap my son. I'll post more later. Lay low."

Then Peter signed off and was gathering up the cards he had spread out when Elizabeth walked through the door. The Boget children remained in the hall outside the burn unit.

Peter was elated as he told his wife, "I found Mark."

*　　*　　*

The sky blackened quickly and, before Hendrick had the mainsail cranked down the fifty-foot mast, marble-size hail beat up on the wildly tossing boat. Emily tied the wheel and then pulled the lines to stabilize the boom and keep it from sweeping her husband into the bay. Her thick hair and the sweater under her mackintosh softened the incessant blows from the hail. But Earl was struggling to bring the main under control, and the hail first ripped his hat off and then split open his balding scalp in half a dozen places. The jib tore from the forestay and wrapped itself around the mast as hail punched holes in the flapping fabric.

Grabbing the mainsail and pulling it over his bleeding head, Hendrick wrapped his arms and legs around the mast and held on tightly as twelve-foot waves washed across the boat.

A waterspout emerged port side and whirled with deadly speed as it approached. From her place at the helm, Emily, who had returned to the wheel and tied herself to it, watched in horror as the tornadolike funnel bore down on them. Though her husband was less than twenty feet away, there was no way to warn him.

Within seconds, the spout tore the bow pulpit from the wooden fore deck, and then flipped the 2,000-pound boat on its side, plunging Emily beneath the surface of the icy water. Yanking the slipknot, she freed herself from the wheel and surfaced near the boom that she grabbed to avoid crashing back into the deck. She saw her husband pulling himself toward her, hand over hand, along the floating boom. He strained against the waves and the driving rain that had mercifully replaced the hail.

Both knew that if they could reach each other, they would be all right. But each swell that washed over them drained a portion of their strength. When Earl finally reached Emily, she could see the gaping wounds in his head continually washed clean by the frothy sea and the torrents that fell from the sky. She could see in her husband's swollen eyes that he was near the point of exhaustion and that shock from the frigid water would soon set in.

He saw the terror in her face and above the roar of the storm he yelled, "Hang on, we'll make it!" Neither one believed it, yet the two clung to each other's life jackets with one hand and the boom with the other.

Amid the din of destruction, the unmistakable sound of the mast snapping reverberated in their ears and they, along with the mast and boom, were set adrift. Even with their sweaters and slickers, they knew from their training that sub-fifty-degree water would suck away their body heat, and then their lives, within two hours.

The release of the mast and boom and its water-filled sail had the positive effect of allowing the boat to right itself. Earl let go of the boom and grabbed the stanchion just forward of the cockpit with his right hand. With his left he tugged on Emily's life jacket as she released the boom and paddled to the pitching boat. Earl tried to boost his wife onto the deck, but each time she got on, waves washed her back into the water.

"Go to the stern," Earl yelled in to his wife's ear. "Maybe the ladder is there."

"I can't," Emily shouted back. "There's nothing to hold on to."

When the boat dropped into one of the deep troughs, Earl pulled himself out of the water and saw that two sections of stanchions, the half-inch thick railings that ringed the boat, were missing. His body was freezing, his mouth was filled with salty water, and his head felt like it had been beaten with a baseball bat. But somehow he summoned the strength to pull himself high enough on the deck to smash one of the cabin windows with his fist and secure a handhold around the window frame. Despite the numbness in his hands, he knew that a shard of glass had punctured his palm, but he hung on. Laying prone on the wave-washed deck, he extended his other hand to his wife. She grabbed his arm and began to climb up his body, gripping his life jacket and finally securing herself around his waist.

"At the top of the next swell," Earl yelled, "crawl to the cockpit and tie yourself to the wheel. I'll come on the next one."

It took another ten minutes, but they finally reached the relative safety of the cockpit. Though the boat was swamped, they were mostly out of the water and that meant they now had a chance of survival if help reached them quickly—and if Earl didn't lose too much blood. They crawled to the post that once supported the wheel and encircled it with their legs and arms. Emily removed her rain hat, pulled it down over Earl's head and snapped it under his chin. She leaned toward his ear and yelled, "We're going to make it, honey!"

*   *   *

Seven blocks north of the imposing Virginia Bell building a much smaller and much older edifice reminds tourists to historic Richmond what life was like in the years before America's independence. The former home of John Marshall, the nation's first chief justice of the Supreme Court, graces the street that bears his name. A block away from the white, clapboard Colonial structure, and in stark contrast to its classic Georgian architecture, is the glass and marble Federal Building that rises twelve stories above the street. There, in the sixth-floor offices of the U.S. Marshal Service, Mike Downes was fingerprinted, photographed and given an opportunity to retain an attorney.

It was also in the marshal's office that Tyrone Giddings placed a call to the Mexican lawyer who had helped obtain the release of Debbie Steinbaugh and who assisted in the plea bargain for Barry Whitehead.

"Mr. Soto? This is Tyrone Giddings calling from Richmond, Virginia. I'm an agent with the Federal Bureau of Investigation. Mike Downes has given me your name and says that you may know where we can find Barry Whitehead."

"How do you do, Mr. Giddings. How is my friend Mike?" The lawyer was friendly and chatty.

"He's fine," said Giddings with a hint of irritation in his voice. "But it's not Downes I'm concerned with. I'm looking for Whitehead."

"I'm sorry, I don't believe I'll be able to help you. Why don't you ask Mike to call? I'd be glad to talk with him."

"He's right here," the agent said, handing the phone to Downes.

"Jorge! What's going on?"

"I just wanted to be sure that I was really talking to the FBI. I tried to call you since Friday, but got no answer. A man was here in Cancún asking a lot of questions. He was looking for Whitehead. By the time I got the tip, he was gone. I don't know who he was or what he wanted but something didn't seem right so I called my uncle, Judge Cabrillo, and he agreed to move Whitehead and give him a new name. I didn't leave a message on your answering machine because I wasn't sure who might be listening."

An excited Mike Downes stopped his friend. "Thank you, Jorge, thank you so much. Now, would you be so kind and retell this to Agent Giddings?"

"I will," he said cautiously. "Is something wrong?"

"Talk to Giddings. I'll call you later." Downes handed the phone back to the man who had arrested him.

*   *   *

Without his glasses, Earl Hendrick couldn't make out his wife's features in the stormy darkness. But he didn't need glasses to see the monster that emerged from the gloom on the port side of his boat as he clutched the wheel post waiting for the fury to end. It towered above the frightened couple like a black beast from the deep, and then the 11,000-ton Polish freighter *Gdania,* bringing machine tools from Europe, bisected the tiny yacht with the ease of a butcher cleaving a rib roast. Earl and Emily Hendrick, still clinging to the wheel post and to each other, were washed beneath the roiling waters.

When they emerged they were on the ship's port side, less than ten feet from the ship's hull, thirty feet from the bow. Earl saw his wife before she saw him and thrashed through the water to her. She was coughing saltwater out of her lungs when he grabbed her life jacket and spun her around. "Swim, Emily, swim!" Earl shouted above the din of the driving rain and the churning sea. Though he knew that any expenditure of energy would reduce their survival time, Earl was more concerned that they might be dashed against the ship's hull or, worse, be sucked into the ship's propeller.

They clawed frantically away from the freighter and soon found themselves bobbing in its wake, colliding with twisted and broken reminders of what was once their home on the bay.

As quickly as it had come upon them, the storm subsided. The sun reappeared, but Earl Hendrick didn't see it. He had slipped into unconsciousness while clinging to the floating sheet of foam-filled fiberglass that once made up the hull of their boat. Emily had pulled herself onto the same slab of wreckage and dragged her husband aboard. Now she held Earl in her arms. His breathing was labored and intermittent, his pulse weak and slow. His skin felt like ice.

Emily's tears mingled with the water that dripped from her hair. "Don't leave me Earl. Oh, God, don't take him now," she sobbed. "Oh my love, hang on. The sun is out, Earl, can you see it?" Her voice trembled uncontrollably, "Don't die! I love you . . . I love you."

She pulled his limp body to her breast and gently rocked him in her arms as her eyes surveyed what was left of their yacht. The bow was bobbing in the becalmed waters two hundred feet away. Other pieces—some identifiable, others not—littered the water around her.

Despite the reemergence of the sun, a cool breeze made her throbbing head feel as if it were packed with ice. Shivers raced up and down her back as she drifted in and out of consciousness. Through glassy eyes, she looked down at her husband's face. An hour before it had been full and red. Now it was bruised and swollen and blue. Blood oozed from wounds on his forehead and trickled from beneath his hat. "Is this all there is?" Emily Hendrick whispered as tears fell on the face of the man to whom she had devoted her life and her love. "Is this all there is?" She laid her head on his and joined her husband in sleep.

Forty feet away, Hendrick's attaché case bobbed just below the surface of the frothy bay.

*   *   *

Something was wrong. As she walked to her car in the parking lot of the Garden of the Gods branch office of Rocky Mountain Savings Bank, Debbie Steinbaugh felt a strange detachment from the world around her. She was oblivious to the gray skies and the light drizzle that covered her car with tiny beads of water.

All day she had waited and prayed for a call from Mike, but it never came. A hundred reasons entered her mind. She dismissed all but one. Over and over again she asked herself if she had come on too strong during the weekend. Had she pressured him into doing something he didn't want to do? In her mind there could be no other explanation.

She opened the door of her Mustang, slid behind the wheel, pulled the seat belt across her lap and fastened it into place. Then she closed her eyes and rested her forehead on her hands that gripped the top of the steering wheel. She started to cry, but as the first tears dripped onto her hand she pulled herself upright, pushed her yellow hair from her face and said aloud, "This is crazy. He's fine. I'm fine. He probably got tied up at the office."

She started the engine, turned on her windshield wipers, and headed for her apartment.

At home she walked straight to the bedroom where the answering machine on the table next to her bed flashed. She listened as the machine rewound through three messages. Then the voices began.

"Hi, Debbie, this is Trish. I've been trying to get you all weekend. Are you okay? I didn't see you in church and wondered if you're planning to play on the softball team. Give me a call when you get in."

Beep.

"Oh, hello, Miss Steinbaugh, this is Mrs. Washington from the Disabled Veterans. Our truck is going to be in your neighborhood on Wednesday, and we would appreciate anything you can put out for them. You should have gotten a blue bag on your door this weekend. Thank you."

Beep.

"Debbie, this is Mike," the voice sounded unusually somber. "It's eight-thirty. I must have missed you at the bank, and I see you're not home. I had a good but exhausting flight to Richmond. I hope you're doing weil. I sort of wish I had stayed, because when I got back to the office I had a welcoming committee. There's no easy way to tell you this, but I was arrested."

The word *arrested* took her breath away. She sat down on the edge of the bed, placed a clenched fist to her breast and continued listening.

"I'm waiting for my lawyer but don't know how long this might take, or even if I'll have to go to jail tonight, so I wanted to call. It's all over my involvement with Barry. I told you about it Saturday. Anyway, I wanted you to know. I'll call as soon as I can." Then the voice got quieter. "I don't know what all this is going to mean. I'm sorry, Debbie."

The news was just one more shattering experience in a life that had known more than the average amount of pain, much of it self-inflicted. As she sat transfixed on the bed, her thoughts drifted back.

It was twenty-three years ago, in April, when her house burned, killing her mother and father. She was taken in by the Clarks, her parents' best friends, but she never quite fit in with their four children. Although Peter Boget was a strong positive influence for her the summer he also lived with the Clarks, within five years she was well-acquainted with several boys her own age and let her grades go the way of her morals. She dropped out of school at sixteen and was pregnant within the year. She married the baby's father and had another child, but she couldn't cope with children. She discovered that alcohol could ease her through the day. It also led to her divorce at twenty-four and the loss of her two girls in an uncontested custody agreement.

She hit bottom and tried to end her life, but instead she ended up at an alcohol rehab center in Arizona where she met Jan Stevens, who helped turn her life around. After seven years of living on the edge, she returned to the Clarks, returned to church, and began seeking something to quench her spiritual thirst.

That's about the time Peter walked back into her life, when he made a surprise visit to the Clarks while attending a business convention in Denver. The day had been one of the high points of her life, because after attending church together, Peter took Debbie up to the falls where he had taken her as a kid, and sitting alongside the sparkling water that cascaded through the forest, he offered quiet encouragement as she poured out her heart.

As Debbie continued to sit on the bed with her damp raincoat still wrapped around her, the memories became more current. She replayed in her mind the whole episode in Cancún where she was vacationing with Jan Stevens. She remembered catching a glimpse of Barry Whitehead and, thinking he was Peter, she tracked him down. She discovered that Barry wasn't who she thought, but she also learned that he was passing himself off as Peter Boget. Without thinking through her actions, she confronted him—a confrontation that had deadly ramifications.

It was Jan's timely return to the hotel room that thwarted Barry's brutal rape attempt. Sadly, she remembered how Barry tossed Jan into the night-stand where her temple was punctured and her life was lost. And then the jail. Had it only been five weeks since she landed in the bare-walled, bed-less, roach-infested prison? It seemed like an eternity since that nightmare began. And then it was over. Mike Downes had brought her out.

As she replayed his message on the machine, she realized that in giving her a new lease on life, Mike Downes may have sacrificed his own freedom. She looked at the clock radio. It was 6:40. She had missed his call by less than five minutes. Her head spun and her stomach churned. With her raincoat still pulled around her and tied at the waist, she lay down on the bed and curled herself into a fetal position.

*   *   *

For people who never turn off U.S. 90, Bay St. Louis, Mississippi, looks like just another gulf-coast community of strip shopping centers, fast-food outlets, gas stations and a casino. But once off the main drag, no one would mistake the picturesque village for those other communities. Steeped in history, the community encompasses Old Town, block after block of antique shops, gift galleries and stores displaying a wide variety of arts and crafts—many housed in old residences in the resort village. From the jetty at the foot of Washington Avenue, the beautiful white-sand beach runs west for seven miles through Waveland and on to Buccaneer State Park.

It was from the beach that an ambulance delivered a fourteen-year-old girl to the emergency room of Hancock Medical Center. She had been riding on the back of a motorcycle when the driver turned too fast onto the jetty that stretches into the gulf and threw the girl onto the large slabs of broken concrete that define the beach's edge. The girl had been wearing a helmet, which probably saved her life, but her cuts, bruises and broken arm left her in great pain. Large patches of skin had been rubbed raw.

Dressed in their teal uniforms of cotton slacks, v-neck shirts and thin, white jackets adorned with tiny flowers, Liza Morgan and Nancy Stark, the two registered nurses on duty, went about their work quickly. While Morgan was washing the wounds to better judge their severity, she leaned over to Stark who was standing beside her and whispered, "I'm glad we got something serious to work with. I'm tired of taking temperatures and looking down the throats of kids who should be in a doctor's office, not a hospital emergency room."

"I know what you mean. Let's just hope she's not as bad as she looks."

"Her pressure's ninety over forty-eight, so she's not too bad off," said Liza nonchalantly.

The two worked quickly, while the physician, Norma Jensen, who had shared most of her twelve-hour shifts of the preceding two weeks with Liza, gave the girl a complete check. Although she was already crying, the teen-ager managed to issue louder screams to indicate the places on her body that hurt most when touched.

Once the girl was stabilized, Liza walked to the chair at the nurses' station and began to fill in information on the patient's chart, but she had trouble concentrating on the words before her. Dr. Jensen noticed the dreamy look in Liza's eyes and said, "If I didn't know better, I'd think you had a man stashed on the side."

Liza laughed. "Wouldn't that cause a sensation?"

Jensen turned a bit somber as she leaned over the four-foot-high counter that separated them. "But I wouldn't blame you after putting up with Randy all these years. You deserve something better."

Liza couldn't get the lovesick grin off her face. "Maybe you're right." Then, with resignation, she added, "But I've made my bed, and I'm going to lie in it."

"You know I don't think much of divorce, Liza, but if anyone should think about it, you should. Excuse me for saying so, but every time Randy barges in here and does some of the things he does, we're all embarrassed for you. And I remember some of those 'falls' you said you had that gave you those bruises on your face. Do you think for a moment I didn't know what he had done to you?

"You have a very expressive face," the doctor went on. "I can tell when you're in trouble and when you're hurting. But I've never seen you like this."

"It shows that much?" said Liza almost apologetically.

"Let me put it this way. If you don't get that look off your face, your husband's going to begin thinking you went over to Casino Magic and snagged some highroller, and the next thing we know you'll be coming into the emergency room all right, but through that door," she said, motioning to the double glass doors of the ambulance entrance.

Liza looked sheepish. "Are you saying I look that different?"

The doctor spoke as if she was delivering some confidential information, but she couldn't suppress the grin on her face. "Do Cajuns eat catfish?"

7

Tuesday, April 17

D an Hart, Mid-Atlantic Bell's fiery CEO, always seemed to be on his
way to the next meeting. After rising rapidly through the ranks, he
had consolidated control of the geographically and culturally diverse
telephone companies and other nonregulated subsidiaries of the
telecommunications giant. He also personally negotiated the acquisition of
cable TV companies he was integrating into a communications empire.

Unlike many old-school company officers who had little understanding
of the importance of public relations and corporate image building, Hart
was a master of both. He insisted that problems be exposed quickly and
handled expeditiously. In his twenty-five-year career he had only once
deviated from his get-it-out-in-the-open-and-get-it-out-of-the-way philoso-
phy. It was when he learned that a fellow manager was supplying cocaine
to Hart's affluent neighbors in one of northern New Jersey's suburban
communities. He demanded and received the man's resignation. Then he
collected and destroyed all copies of the security report. Or at least he
thought so. One copy had ended up between the lower left-hand drawer
and the thin, plywood bottom of a walnut desk inherited by Frank Mazzetti.

"Has anyone heard from Earl this morning?" Dan Hart voiced irritation
more than worry. It was ten o'clock and every member of Mid-Atlantic Bell's
executive committee was in the boardroom except Earl Hendrick. He slid

out a shelf suspended under the mahogany top of the long boardroom table, picked up the phone that was on it and called his secretary.

"See if you can track down Earl. Let me know where he is and why he's not here."

In rapid succession, Hart dispensed with a dozen items on the committee's agenda. Then he looked down the table to Frank Mazzetti. "Earl's not here, but I want to hear what you've got on Peter Boget."

Mazzetti expected a fight. Instead, he got a chance to tell it his way.

"This is rather clear-cut. Earl Hendrick asked that the Peter Boget matter be put on today's agenda. He was deeply concerned that Mr. Boget's family has already suffered a great deal as a result of his disappearance, his injuries and the attempts made on his life in the hospital. He is therefore requesting that Mr. Boget not be subjected to disciplinary action for his second violation of the company's guidelines on personal responsibility." Although no formal investigation had been conducted, and although Earl Hendrick never acknowledged Peter's alleged wrongdoing, Frank Mazzetti had implanted Peter's guilt in the minds of everyone in the room.

"Our security personnel discovered that not only was Mr. Boget continuing to use his computer for personal use, he was gathering information on ways to subvert the integrity of the telephone network." Mazzetti's air of confidence left the allegation unchallenged. He picked up and dropped a pile of papers on the table. "I've brought the documentation." Murmurs traveled around the table. "I was going to let Earl discuss this, but in his absence I thought you should know what's going on."

Mazzetti then launched into his own version of the Peter Boget story. He reviewed the man's first run-in with the security organization a year earlier, when one of its investigators discovered that Boget had allowed an employee in an acute, short-term financial bind to extend beyond thirty days the repayment of a small corporate cash advance. The guilty-until-proven-innocent investigation that ensued allowed unfounded allegations to damage the reputation of Boget, an employee who had consistently earned outstanding ratings for his performance.

Peter was one of many employees caught in Frank Mazzetti's company-wide crackdown on violators of the company's policies. Though many of the violations were serious breaches of Mid-Atlantic Bell's ethical guidelines, many were not; yet Mazzetti called for dismissal of employees for the slightest offense. He thereby achieved some of the company's downsizing objectives at far less cost than other force-reduction measures. Earl Hendrick and Mike Downes had rallied to the defense of their public relations director, saving his job at the expense of his paycheck.

Frank Mazzetti didn't like losing any of his cases, but he found a silver lining in Boget's troubles. He figured that if he could ever find Boget violating another rule, he could drum the man out of the company and destroy the reputation of Downes and Hendrick in the process. He waited and he watched. When Peter disappeared, Mazzetti decided to use the incident to accomplish his objectives. Under the guise of trying to find clues to Peter's disappearance, he had his men investigate every part of Peter's office, including every item in his computer. The only suspicious thing they found was an encrypted computer file. It was that file that Mazzetti decided to use against Peter, regardless of what was in it.

As Mazzetti told the executive committee about what his security investigators found in Peter's computer, he omitted any reference to stopping by Peter's hospital room and tricking the injured man into giving up the password to his encrypted file, or manipulating the file to cast suspicions on Peter.

"I'm not sure why there has been so much interest in protecting this man, considering his previous history with the company," Mazzetti said, concluding his version of the Boget story. "I recommended that Mr. Boget be terminated. However, at a time when we need to focus on regulatory reform and garnering support for our cable TV ventures, any more negative publicity won't be in our best interest . . . and this man's story, including his wild imaginings about encountering me in the public relations office, is certainly capable of generating negative publicity." Mazzetti scanned the faces along either side of the table and gently nodded his head to garner support for his plan. "In light of what happened in Richmond yesterday, we can't afford any more bad press."

Murmurs again traveled around the table as executives wanted to know what happened in Richmond. While Mazzetti had already informed Dan Hart, the CEO had asked that he say nothing until the executive committee gathered. Mazzetti continued matter-of-factly, "Yesterday afternoon, Mike Downes was arrested by the FBI for his involvement with a man who transported drugs between Norfolk and New York."

The bombshell had precisely the effect he sought. The room erupted in crosstalk, and by the time the CEO called for order, nine men and two women were questioning Downes's judgment and wondering aloud if Earl's absence had anything to do with it.

Anne Cortland, the company's chief financial officer, was the only one who came to the defense of the men. She looked across the table at Mazzetti and then turned toward Hart. "Is there more to this than meets the ear?" she asked. "I've known Peter Boget for years. I've worked with him in Maryland and Virginia and I can tell you he's a solid company man." She made eye contact with as many of the others at the table as she could. "And is there anyone at this table who questions the abilities and integrity of Mike Downes? I'm not sure I'd jump to conclusions."

In a strong but controlled and almost loving voice Frank Mazzetti began to drive the nails into the coffins of his rivals. "That's why this is such a sad day for the company. The men involved in these activities are not people anyone would readily point to and say, 'I'm not surprised.' No, these are people who do everything right, who are looked up to, who are admired. That's why to ignore the severity of their actions—particularly those of Peter Boget—would signal every one of our 9,000 employees that if you've been around here long enough, or if you've got the right connections, you can, with impunity, violate company rules, rules established to protect this company's assets, its revenues, its profits, its employees and its good name."

Dan Hart liked what Mazzetti was saying and Frank knew it. Before anyone at the table could respond, Mazzetti continued: "Mike Downes was released last night on his own recognizance. But the company will likely receive a fair amount of bad publicity when the news gets out. This would be the absolute worst time to dismiss the company's PR director, so I was going to recommend to Earl this morning that we arrange to keep Peter Boget on long-term disability for three months, then demote him and offer him a transfer to an undesirable location in lieu of termination."

Dan Hart asked for comments. None were forthcoming.

"Okay, Frank," Hart said, "I'll talk to Earl when he gets here. Now as for the Mike Downes incident, we don't have all the information we need to make an informed judgment, but I will get that to you as soon as it becomes available. Now, the next item of business . . ."

* * *

Embarrassment, confusion and exhaustion combined to keep Mike from placing the call to Debbie that he knew he had to make. He planned to call her at home at seven, but by then it was nine in Richmond, and he was in a meeting with the other vice presidents. By the time he got back to his desk, he knew she would be at the bank. He picked up the phone and called.

"Rocky Mountain Savings, this is Sue. How may I help you?"

"May I speak with Debbie Steinbaugh?"

"Just one moment, please."

The moment stretched into a minute before the familiar voice came on the line.

"This is Debbie, may I help you?" Her voice was official, not hinting of what was going on inside her.

Mike spoke discreetly. "Hello, Debbie."

"Mike, where are you?" she blurted out. "Are you in jail?"

"I'm in my office, and I only have a minute. The charges are serious, but my lawyer says he believes we may be able to work out a plea bargain. I just wanted you to know that I'm still here, I'm all right, and you are very much on my mind. I just don't know what the next few days hold. I might not be able to get back to you for a while."

"I understand," she lied. "I'll be here for you."

"I know you will, and when this gets resolved . . . well, let's just wait till then."

"Mike," she said, "I'm sorry if I came on too strong this weekend."

"I didn't notice." He tried to project a smile through the phone line. After a moment's hesitation, he continued. "Debbie, I want to pick up where we left off, but right now I'm overwhelmed."

Debbie was trembling. "They can't do this to you!" Her loud whisper drew stares from her coworkers. "Don't they know what you did to help me? Don't they know that Barry is in jail? Why are they arresting you? Don't they know the difference between the good guys and the bad guys? They can't do this, I won't let them . . ."

*   *   *

Despite the terrible itch on his leg that had set in where the skin had been removed for the graft, Peter Boget had rested reasonably well and was checking his electronic mail on CompuServe. The first item didn't interest him, but the second jumped out like an illuminated billboard along a dark interstate.

To: Peter Boget

From: M. T. Stewart

Peter, this isn't from M. T., it's from me, Liza. I borrowed my friend's account to post this. I can't believe we've been this close for this long. Don't know if anyone else looks in on your mail. Let me know with a reply here.

With all that was going on in his mind, Peter was totally unprepared for the message. It was one thing to place a one-time, ill-conceived telephone call. It was something else to reopen a relationship that belonged in his past. He had thought a lot about his conversation with Liza Morgan, worried that she might have misunderstood his intentions. He wanted to follow up with another contact but knew that calling wasn't appropriate and figured that a letter might be awkward. It hadn't occurred to him that she might be accessible via e-mail. He took a deep breath and typed a response.

Liza:

I'm here at the hospital. No one accesses but me. Do you think this contact is wise?

Peter

* * *

Dan Hart's secretary stepped into the meeting room and laid a note in front of him as he addressed the executive committee.

He stopped in midsentence. The room was eerily silent for thirty seconds while Hart read and reread the note. His face, which had been looking paler than usual, lost its remaining color. "It's about Earl," he finally said, not looking up from the table. "He's in a hospital in Kilmarnock. A boating accident and a heart attack. He's not expected to live."

Boyd Nielson, Mid-Atlantic's vice president for corporate communications, headed to the door. Hart, knowing that the man would need to coordinate the release of the information to the public, nodded his assent and then looked at Mazzetti. "Frank, will you please head down to Richmond and look after things for the next few days? I think we'll be all right here without you."

"Yes, sir," was the subdued reply from a man who was having trouble concealing his elation. "I'll take care of Virginia." He excused himself and the meeting continued.

*   *   *

Shortly before noon, FBI agents Giddings and Middleton stood by Peter Boget's hospital bed. The rush of adrenaline Peter was feeling seemed to reduce the postoperative pain and the itch on his leg and chest.

"I believe I now have put together all the pieces of your puzzle—except how Mary Kennedy gets her cocaine and what she does with her money," he told the agents. "But I believe I can show you how she moved cocaine to New York, how she was paid for it by Glenn Segal and Mark Randolph, how they manipulated the books at Michaels and Trent to effect the trade, why she killed Segal, and . . ." Boget stopped. He looked at the lead agent. "You said Mike couldn't come, but you didn't tell me why. I think he should hear this."

"I'm sorry," Giddings apologized. "I didn't want to upset you. But I guess you should know that Mike Downes has been arrested for his involvement in helping a fugitive leave the country."

"No way!"

"It's a pretty serious offense. He's been released, but we didn't think it was appropriate for him to be here."

"Appropriate? What could be more appropriate? This is why he got into this in the first place." Peter's initial excitement was tempered by the information. "You guys put Mike Downes in jail? I can't believe it. He placed his whole career on the line to run around Mexico trying to find me. He even got shot, but that didn't stop him from doing the impossible—getting a woman, falsely charged with murder, out of a Mexican prison." His voice rose with irritation, making the raspiness more noticeable. "And he did it by convincing a criminal to give himself up. For that he gets arrested?"

"I'm sorry," Giddings said. "Look, he may be a hero to you, but we can't have people going around taking the law into their own hands."

"Does the same go for criminal investigations? Because if it does, I'm going to shut up right now."

"Look," Middleton said. "We're here because you said you wanted to show us how we can put away Mary Kennedy. That's what we all want. If you can help us, we'll certainly work with you to help Mr. Downes. Now, why don't you tell us what you know?"

*   *   *

Earl Hendrick clung tenaciously to life in the emergency room of the small but well-equipped hospital in Kilmarnock, the largest town on Virginia's northern neck. John Caldwell, the Coast Guard's lieutenant junior grade, was standing in the nearby waiting area. It was he who had accompanied Earl Hendrick on the helicopter flight from the cutter to the hospital. Now he was telling—for the sixth time—the story of the rescue, this time to Hendrick's niece and husband, the first family members to arrive at the hospital.

"We passed the freighter northeast of Smith Point and stopped to pick up six people whose boat had been swamped by the storm. We proceeded south to respond to another distress call when we ran into the debris on the water and spotted your aunt and uncle. We sent divers into the water to put rescue lines around them. Both were very cold and unconscious. Mr. Hendrick's pulse was barely detectable, and he was in shock when we pulled him onboard. His body temperature was down to eighty and he was bleeding from his head and hands. Mrs. Hendrick was in much better shape. She suffered some lacerations and hypothermia, but she regained consciousness on our boat and told us about the collision with the ship. She seems to be doing well."

"Will Uncle Earl live?" Janet Watkins asked bluntly.

"I think the doctor can tell you more about his condition," Caldwell said. "The main thing is that I wanted someone in his family to know how proud they can be of Mrs. Hendrick."

"Aunt Emily?"

"Mrs. Hendrick had pulled your uncle onto the piece of hull and locked herself around him in such a way that he couldn't have fallen back into the water. It's amazing that they made it through the storm in the first place. It's incredible they survived that encounter with the freighter."

*   *   *

Peter Boget's analysis of the events of the preceding month impressed the two men at his bedside. He had fit pieces together in a way that no one else had.

"How do you know that the receipts Mary Kennedy has in her possession are frauds?" asked Agent Middleton.

"Mark Randolph told me."

His visitors' eyes opened wide when Peter suggested he was in contact with the object of a nationwide manhunt.

"You've spoken to Randolph?" the men asked in unison.

Boget knew he had to be careful that he didn't compromise his source. "I discovered his work on a bulletin board—an electronic bulletin board. His methodology was explained, though the code was never posted. Look. I want to see Mary Kennedy locked up, but more than that, I want to see the man who tried to kill me taken out of circulation."

"But you don't know who he is."

"No, I don't. But when you find him, you'll probably have the man who set the charge that killed Glenn Segal and those officers in Maryland. Kennedy knows who he is, Randolph probably knows, and I wouldn't be surprised if Whitehead knows. And I'll tell you this: my wife will be able to identify him if you can bring him in. She'll never forget those eyes."

*   *   *

Joanna Harris, a reporter for the *Richmond Times-Dispatch,* sat in a comfortable chair across a coffee table from Mike Downes. She wanted more than just a statement from the vice president; she wanted the whole story. And she deserved it. She had reported on Peter Boget's disappearance and had been sensitive in covering the family's plight and their reunion. Mike knew that if anyone would present the story fairly, it would be this woman. And having learned a lot about public relations from Peter, he knew that an article in the daily newspaper would reach the desk of Dan Hart and the others on the executive committee who would be influential in the decision to replace Earl Hendrick. In addition, he felt he had to counteract the misinformation that he imagined Mazzetti was spreading in Washington.

Sitting on the sofa alongside Downes was Janice Bland, the company's news media relations manager, who was also acting director of public relations in Peter's absence. Her tape recorder sat on the table in front of her, running alongside the one Joanna Harris had brought.

"Yesterday," Harris began, "you were arrested for harboring a fugitive—the man who left your employee Peter Boget to die on the beltway." Harris laid the foundation for the question, but did not editorialize in the process. "Can you tell me what you did, and where the man is now?"

Frank Mazzetti startled the three people in Downes's office when he cleared his throat as he stood in the doorway. "Excuse me. May I speak with you a moment?" he said, signaling to Downes. Both women stopped their tape recorders as the men exited the room.

Downes said nothing as he walked behind Mazzetti to the president's office. Once inside, Mazzetti closed the door.

"What are you doing here?" Downes demanded.

"I've been sent by Dan to oversee this company until we can get things straightened out," said Mazzetti with just a hint of arrogance in his voice. "Our first order of business is to refrain from talking to the news media about your arrest. The second thing is that I suggest you take a few days' vacation until the dust settles. The third thing is to send Miss Bland in here so I can give her instructions as to how we should be handling the information on Earl. Got that?"

Mike Downes did not get to where he was by rolling over at the first hint of trouble. He also knew that insubordination would get him fired and, whether he liked Frank Mazzetti or not, the man had the rank and apparently the authority to issue the orders. "I don't know what you expect to achieve with all this, but here in Virginia we don't take kindly to strangers coming in and riding roughshod over our operations and our people."

"I'm not riding roughshod. You know the rules. My job is to see that they are not violated. Lately, you people here in Virginia seem to have forgotten that."

"Frank, relax." Downes was seething, but tried to maintain control. "I'm not going anywhere. I haven't been convicted, and with Earl out of the picture for a while, I've got my hands full. We've got a regulatory reform filing set for the end of the month, and I'm not going to let that slip just because we have a few problems down here. Second, I'm not going to refrain from talking with reporters about what I do on my time with my life. As far as Earl's situation is concerned, we have that well in hand. Now, I'll be happy to bring Janice in here to brief you. She and Boyd Nielson spoke for over an hour this morning and have developed a strategy. I already spoke to the other vice presidents this morning to let them know what's going on."

Despite the fury that was causing Mazzetti's neck to turn red, Downes continued. "Now, if Dan Hart has sent you down here to take care of the Virginia company, fine. I suggest you sit back and let the company run itself. It's been doing very well for a very long time, and we don't need someone like you coming down to throw a monkey wrench into the works."

"I think you've said quite enough." Mazzetti removed his suit jacket and draped it over one of the seven chairs in Earl Hendrick's spacious office that, like Mike's, overlooked the James River. "You may resent the fact that I've been asked to look after things down here. But to let you know that I'm not some evil monster from the north, I asked the executive committee this morning not to fire Peter Boget. If Earl okays it, we're going to ask Peter to remain out on long-term disability for ninety days, and then quietly demote him."

Mike shook his head in disbelief. "I'll tell him."

"Please do." A smirk tightened the corner of Mazzetti's lips. "He needs to know how lucky he is."

At the door, Mike stopped and looked back at Mazzetti. "You're looking good, Frank," he said sarcastically. "Those gouges in your face from Peter's wife are hardly noticeable." Downes expected a strong reaction from Mazzetti. Instead, he saw only the smirk, so he threw another barb. "Did I tell you she scraped some of your skin and blood from underneath her fingernails, saved it in a test tube and had it analyzed? I gave Earl the test tube and the report. He was going to show it to the committee this morning."

Mazzetti's countenance didn't change, but Mike's words gnawed at his insides.

"The good news for you is that the test tube is probably at the bottom of the Chesapeake," he said, as Mazzetti's glare turned cold. "The bad news is, I have a copy of the report."

8

Wednesday, April 18

The itching was driving Peter Boget crazy, and he was weak from lack of sleep. But neither of those concerns came close to those he had about saving his job. He knew he was in a precarious position with the company. He also knew that he and Elizabeth had poured every cent they had into their new home. Even then, their mortgage payment was twice that of their previous home. He had banked on a substantial performance bonus to pay off some immediate debts, but he lost that because of the actions that led to Security's first investigation last year. And his salary had been cut. He could not get at the shares of stock the company was holding in his name, and he could only access what little remained in the company savings plan if he was willing to absorb a stiff tax penalty. With firms throughout the Richmond area cutting public relations positions, local employment prospects were dim.

The concern over the prospect of losing his job propelled him to find Mark-the-Shark. He believed that if he could somehow prove that the data he was collecting from computer bulletin boards was not for personal gain, but to aid the company in catching criminals, he would be seen in a different light. The most obvious target of his pursuit was Mark-the-Shark.

He dialed CompuServe on his Macintosh PowerBook and went to his electronic mailbox. The first post was from Mark.

Interesting theory you have. I've been reading newspapers too. Check for connection to Sinn Fein.

The last thing Peter dreamed of was a connection with Sinn Fein, the political and fundraising arm of the Provisional Irish Republican Army. He picked up the phone and dialed the FBI office.

"Agent Giddings, please."

"I'm sorry, he's not in the office yet. May I take a message?"

"Is Middleton there?"

"No."

"Does anyone else know about Mary Kennedy?"

"Just one minute, I'll find out. Your name, please?"

"Peter Boget."

Moments later, a high-pitched voice came on the line. "Bartok." The salutation was curt.

"Good morning, this is Peter Boget."

The agent said nothing, waiting for more.

"Has anyone considered the possibility that Mary Kennedy is providing money to the IRA?" Boget began.

Bartok listened intently.

*   *   *

The public relations office in Virginia was abuzz as rumors crisscrossing the company caused the phones to stay continually busy. Mid-Atlantic Bell's PR department was helping to deal with the national news media that had picked up the Associated Press article about Downes's indictment and were retelling the original Peter Boget story. Reporters were also trying to link the accident of Earl Hendrick with the other activities going on in Richmond.

Frank Mazzetti, Spencer Ferguson, the company's vice president for legal matters, and Mike Downes walked into the company library a few minutes before nine to address the assembled staff. Mazzetti's demeanor surprised those who had never met him. Though vilified for his hard-nosed approach to the company's security issues, the man seemed warm and friendly and spoke with compassion.

"I want to commend you—all of you—for the work you are doing during these difficult times. I was asked by Dan Hart to come down and help where

I'm needed, but it's clear to me that this Virginia team doesn't need much help from me." His compliments seemed genuine. "I know that a lot of rumors have been circulating about Mike and Peter, and I want your help in squashing them. As Mike told you yesterday, Peter will be out for several months and in the interim Janice Bland will continue to manage this office. Mike's unfortunate situation, which you've been reading about, is obviously a misunderstanding that will soon be cleared up. Like you, we in Washington admire his capabilities and his commitment to his employees. Nothing that is going on now will cause us to think otherwise. I'll be available to help with general administrative issues, but will not be involved with the day-to-day operations of the company. And Spencer here," he turned to the gray-haired lawyer who was ten years his senior, "well, why don't you just explain."

Spencer Ferguson, who was a usually jovial, somewhat overweight, and balding lawyer whose entire wardrobe consisted of dark blue pin-striped suits and multicolored bow ties, adjusted his wire rim glasses. "I want you to understand that, from a legal standpoint, Virginia Bell is not involved in the activities surrounding Peter Boget's disappearance, his discovery, and the various incidents that have been precipitated by that affair," he said, weighing his words. "The serious charges lodged against Mike Downes here concern us as individuals, of course, but are not directly related to the activities of this company. Therefore," he said as he straightened his bow tie, "we must not comment on them internally or externally in any official capacity. In fact, no one associated with the public relations office nor any of our spokesmen in the field should comment to the media privately, since even private comments could be construed as company policy."

The employees sitting around the large table tried not to look bored as the lawyer explained what they all knew.

"Obviously of great concern," Ferguson went on, "is the condition of our president. We must be prepared for his passing, even as we plan for his return. I presume his biography is up to date."

"It is," interjected Janice Bland.

"And we have current photographs?"

"Last year."

"Earl is loved by employees throughout this company. We need to be sure that they are the first, not the last, to receive information about his con-

dition. I'd like to recommend that for the next few days someone be available around the clock to update *Newsline.*"

"The schedule has already been posted." Bland was quick with her response. She glanced at Downes and caught his smile of approval.

"Finally, beyond the words I've already approved in the event of Mr.
Hendrick's death," Ferguson said, "please don't say anything else to the
news media until I've had a chance to review it." Janice nodded.

"And, please, to protect their privacy, no discussions of either Peter's or
Mike's situations beyond what I've told you," added Mazzetti.

After Mazzetti dismissed the group, Lucy Williams, editor of the company
newspaper, followed Janice Bland to her office and sat down across from
her. "What do you think the disability leave for Peter means?" she asked
in a hushed voice. "I thought Peter said he could be back as soon as next
week."

"He did," Janice whispered. "I think Mazzetti stiffed him. With Earl out
of the way and Mike handicapped by the arrest, I think this is going to be
a cakewalk for Frank."

Lucy frowned. "He has all the right words and all the right gestures . . ."
Her voice trailed off, and she shook her head slowly. "I hope sooner or
later he gets his comeuppance."

"Don't we all."

*   *   *

The second CompuServe letter scrolled up Peter's computer screen.

Peter, oh Peter, where have you been all my life? I wrote you a letter the
other morning, but didn't think I'd better send it. But now that I know
you're here, I've typed it up. I hope you understand.

The words scrolling up his screen sucked Peter Boget back into Liza Morgan's life. Lost in his memories, he didn't notice the man standing at the
foot of the bed.

"You look like you're a thousand miles away," Mike Downes said.

Peter was startled. "I guess I am."

"What are you working on?" Mike asked. "Have you zapped Mary
Kennedy yet?" He wanted to keep the conversation light, but he couldn't
hide the concern that wrinkled his brow.

Peter dimmed the screen and looked at his boss. "What's wrong?"

"Why do you think something is wrong?"

"It's written all over your face, Mike. Is it Earl?"

Mike decided that the best way to handle the situation was to get the bad news out fast. "No, Earl's still hanging on. It's you I'm worried about. The executive committee agreed with Mazzetti. They aren't going to fire you, but you're on disability for three months and then you'll be offered a demotion and transfer."

Peter didn't want to know where. "Why am I not surprised? I guess it could have been much worse. At least I'm not fired, and if I'm out on disability, maybe I'll have time to look for another job."

Downes admired how Peter always seemed to know how to make the best of a bad situation.

"Don't tell Elizabeth. This is going to be hard on her and the kids," Peter said. "Elizabeth's got a lot on her shoulders right now. So, what's the scoop on you?"

"Mazzetti would like me to take a leave of absence until the trial. But there's no way I'm going to let him start dictating company policy."

"Is he here?"

"Moved right into Earl's office."

"Unbelievable." Boget looked at Downes thoughtfully. "Whatever you do, don't tell *that* to Elizabeth, or she might just pay the man a visit we'll all be sorry for!"

*   *   *

When the news of her husband's job situation reached Elizabeth Boget, she responded quietly. "I'm glad you called to tell me, Peter. I guess we're just going to have to turn this over to the Lord and go on with life."

"I know, Elizabeth. Considering what we've been through, I really am not all that surprised." Peter too spoke quietly. "Yet somehow I can't help but feel that Mazzetti shouldn't be allowed to get away with this."

Peter couldn't see his wife nodding assent nor could he read on her face the hostility that was rising within her. When it finally reached her tongue she had to vent it.

"It always comes back to Mazzetti, doesn't it? He's an evil man, and I'm beginning to think he's more evil than Mary Kennedy and her henchmen." She stopped to take a deep breath. "With Kennedy, you know she's bad, but

Mazzetti is a whole different creature. He looks too good, fools too many people who fall for his charisma. He's a snake, and he needs to be caged." Her voice was rising. "Peter, I know you love the phone company, and you've never worked for nicer people than Mike and Mr. Hendrick, but how can you go back to work for Frank Mazzetti? Why would you want to?"

"I don't, but there is the matter of food and the mortgage. And David's college is just around the corner. No, I don't want to go to work for Frank Mazzetti, but I may not have to. First, he's not been crowned king down here. At least, not yet. I still haven't had a fair hearing, and I could make enough noise to force that to happen." Peter shifted the phone from his right ear to the left and picked up the stack of cards he was working with from the small table on his right. "Let's look at the bright side. Right now I've got three months off with seventy percent of my pay. I'll use that time to try to straighten out this mess and look for another job."

"I thought you've been saying there isn't much around."

"There isn't—least not here. But do you remember John Markich?" he asked, recalling a former coworker who had left years earlier for a job with Bell South.

"Sure."

"Couple of months ago he was looking for someone to take over PR for one of their new subsidiaries. And I know a guy down at Texaco in New Orleans—do you remember me talking about him when I came back from the last PRSA convention? He always seems to know where the good job openings are."

*   *   *

The jail on the western edge of Cancún, though deplorable by United States standards, had been vastly superior to the tiny, filthy, overcrowded jail in central Yucatán, halfway between Cancún and the state capital in Mérida, where Barry Whitehead now resided. Whitehead, who was listed on the jail's records as Barry Norton, shared a cell with an American accused of stealing artifacts from a Mayan temple west of the town. Joining the two Americans were three locals in for various minor offenses.

Constantly swatting flies and crushing the large roaches that roamed the floors and crawled the walls, Whitehead waited for the guards who would transport him to Mérida. His five-day stay in the lockup fifty miles west of

Cancún was designed to allow him to take on a new identity before proceeding to the prison where he would serve out his five-year sentence for killing Jan Stevens.

The move took Whitehead by surprise. In a brief weekend encounter, his lawyer, Jorge Soto, told him only that the move was a security measure and that he was to tell no one about what transpired. The man who shared so many physical attributes with Peter Boget again looked like Boget's twin brother. Under the close supervision of a guard, a local barber who served the inmates cut short the hair that had reached Barry's ears, leaving the sandy-colored locks on the floor. What remained was his naturally dark brown hair. Barry had already shaved the beard he had grown to disguise himself following the incident with Jan and Debbie. It had begun to irritate him in the Mexican heat.

When the time came to complete his journey to Cancún, a guard arrived at his cell door. "Señor Norton, come with me."

Whitehead turned as he walked through the thick wooden door set in the concrete wall. "Good luck, Jim," he said to the other American. He turned to the Mexicans and, drawing on the little Spanish he had picked up during his three-week imprisonment, he said, *"Cuídate."*

"Adiós. Buena suerte," they responded in near unison.

Though the sun was hot and the humidity high, Whitehead found the air outdoors to be such a refreshing change that he almost forgot he was still a prisoner. Only the discomfort of leaning on the hands cuffed behind his back diminished his exhilaration.

He felt free as the car in which he rode raced through the jungle that opened onto small plots of land cleared for farming. The smell of gasoline occasionally mixed with the sweet air blowing in the front windows and swirled across the back seat.

The driver eased off the macadam along a lonely stretch of road fifty minutes outside Mérida. Both the driver and the guard sitting in the back got out of the car and walked into the tall, thick vegetation that lined the thoroughfare. Barry figured that the men, who had already downed two bottles of soft drinks, were going to relieve themselves, but thought it strange they would leave him alone. Though the road was devoid of traffic and the jungle on either side of it looked forbidding, Barry contemplated escape. But he knew that a handcuffed man in the middle of a jungle in a foreign land where he couldn't speak the language wasn't likely to get very far. Still, he didn't think there would be any harm in stepping outside to stretch.

He leaned against the door and tried to lift the handle with his knee. It wouldn't budge. Hearing the sound of another vehicle, Whitehead looked out the back window and saw a dust-covered pickup slowing as it approached. He scanned the jungle for his driver and guard but saw no one. Whitehead slid across the seat to the driver-side door, but out of the corner of his eye he realized the truck wasn't stopping. Then he saw a man in the truck holding what looked like a dark ball.

Concern overtook Whitehead and he slid back across the seat. As Barry moved, the man threw the dark object through the front window of the car, and the truck raced off.

Cautiously, Whitehead peered over the seat back. On the floorboard in front of the passenger seat was a five-gallon gas can with no cap on the two-inch opening. It must have been there during the entire trip; some of the gas had sloshed out and was dripping down the sides. On the front seat was the dark object that had just arrived through the window.

It was a hand grenade, and the handle was open.

Barry lunged for the door that opened onto the road. He pulled up the lock button with his teeth, slid his knee under the handle, and drove his shoulder into the door. The door flew open and he rolled to the pavement. As he did, the car exploded into a fiery hell.

*   *   *

Roland Hanks was giddy as he relayed the news to Mary Kennedy. "I guess that takes care of everything," he smugly intoned.

"I'm afraid not. All we've done is eliminate one voice. There are others—like the people at the hospital. You know who they are, you were there. I need a list of everyone who has been asked to identify subjects. You've still got contacts; use them."

*   *   *

The news of Whitehead's misfortune was relayed to Mike Downes by Jorge Soto the same time it reached Mary Kennedy.

"I'm sorry, my friend, I'm terribly sorry," said the Mexican lawyer. "Somehow someone knew of his transfer and set this up."

"And the guards? They weren't questioned as to why they survived?" Downes asked.

"Let me explain," said Soto. "The people transporting Barry were not policemen. The original guards were hijacked. One was found tied and gagged outside Valladolid. The other is missing."

"You mean to tell me that someone blew up a car with Barry in it and that's that?"

"I wouldn't put it quite so bluntly, but yes, the car was the one he was riding in, and what's left of his charred body was lying on the road. I'm afraid officials around here aren't going to get too worked up over the death of a murderer and drug dealer—even if he is an American."

"And you're sure it was Barry."

"That's what I'm told. The handcuffs were still in place and he was wearing his wedding ring." Soto filled in the details as he knew them and added, "I'm guessing the man who was down here looking for Whitehead last week reached some people. I'm sorry, my friend. I know how much you did for this guy."

"No, Jorge, I didn't do anything," said a devastated Mike Downes. "That's the problem. I promised to protect him from Mary Kennedy and bring him back to the States. Two weeks later and he's dead. How can that happen?"

"Listen, my friend, this isn't your fault. You did what you could . . . and we did what we thought was best."

*   *   *

By the time word of Whitehead's death reached Peter Boget, he was preparing to go to sleep. He wanted to escape the smell emanating from the dressing on his chest. He also wanted to be relieved of the unrelenting itch that had him running his hand up and down the bandage on his thigh almost continually.

"Funny thing," Peter said mournfully to Mike Downes. "As much as I wanted the man to get what was coming to him for all he did to Debbie, I was feeling kind of sorry for him. He seemed rather pathetic."

Mike sat down on the end of Boget's bed in the yellow room that, under the fluorescent lights, seemed washed out and sterile. He noticed that several of the bouquets of flowers around the room that brought so much life when the sun shone in now looked dull and lifeless. Their weak fragrance didn't begin to mask the hospital odor. Downes was fidgeting, looking for a comfortable position.

"He was rather pathetic," Mike said thoughtfully. "And I guess I really started to like him by the time I left Cancún. It's hard to imagine he's gone."

"I know this hasn't turned out the way you would have liked. It's certainly not what I had hoped for. Somehow we've all lost something through this." The two men sat quietly for a few seconds then Peter continued, while Mike stared vacantly at the wall. "I'm sorry I stopped to help Barry. It was a stupid thing to do."

"Stupid? I don't think so. Not enough of us have the courage to help a stranger in need. I saw a bumper sticker the other day that made me think of you. It said, 'Commit Random Acts of Kindness.' That's good. And look at the positive side of all this," he said as his face brightened. "I found Debbie, didn't I? And beating you on the tennis court is going to be much easier." Both men laughed. "Seriously, though, a lot of good *has* come out of this. I've had a chance to reassess what I'm doing with my life. I've had a chance to repay you, at least in a small way, for all the kindness you and Elizabeth showed me and my family when Susie was dying. And I really can't say enough about Debbie."

"She's special, isn't she?" said Peter.

Mike didn't answer directly. "It's scary to see how youthful indiscretion can wreck a life. I wonder if she can ever be whole again."

"What do you think?"

"Well, I've never had the faith that you and Elizabeth seem to have, but I've seen a lot of prayers answered over the past month, and I guess I'm beginning to realize that most of what goes on around us is beyond our control. So, in a roundabout way, I'd say that . . . yes, I believe she can be made whole, but it's going to take time."

"How do you think she's going to take the news about Whitehead? She owes him her freedom."

The question remained unanswered as the conversation moved in other directions. Finally, Mike stood up and placed his hands on the end of the bed. "I'm heading down to Kilmarnock in the morning. The report is that Earl's stable. I don't know exactly what that means, except that he's still alive, and that's good news."

* * *

Barry Whitehead's nine-mile trek through the jungle ended at a small construction site in one of the villages along the road from Valladolid to Mérida. He had rolled free of the burning car, landing in a ditch filled with water from which he crawled into the thick vegetation. There he had twisted his handcuffed wrists under his legs and gained the advantage of having his hands in front of himself as he raced into the jungle.

He had no way of knowing that he wasn't being pursued nor that as he ran, his death was being staged by the two men who walked into the jungle just before the grenade was tossed into the police car. Finding Whitehead gone, they pulled the charred remains of the original driver from the trunk and dropped him by the car door. Then they took Whitehead's ring, which they had stolen from the envelope containing his new identification and personal effects, and slipped it over a blackened finger. Finally, when their getaway truck arrived, they drove over the blackened body, drenched it with gasoline, and lit a second fire before driving off. The men who staged the incident did it for fun and two hundred dollars apiece. That Whitehead might show up later did not concern them. They assumed the man was badly injured and would be quickly swallowed by the jungle.

But Barry's injuries were minor. A few bruises and scrapes and singed hair and eyebrows were all he carried away from the blast. Now, as he approached a church, he cautiously looked for signs of law enforcement officials. Instead he saw a fair-skinned man in his midtwenties wearing a T-shirt emblazoned with what looked like a stylized sun with a church building silhouetted against it. In an arc above the sun were the words *Hands Across the Gulf*. Beneath it in smaller letters read *Elm Street Presbyterian—Church Builders*.

Whitehead stood in the shadows of a large tree and called to the man in a loud whisper, "Hey, you."

The man turned in the direction of the voice.

"Come here, please."

The man walked in the direction of Whitehead, but stopped when he saw the handcuffs. He was about eight feet away when he cautiously asked, "What do you want?"

"Some people are trying to kill me. I need help."

9

_____

P eter Boget awoke refreshed after his first good night's rest in a week. To the amusement of the nurse who had stopped in at seven to see how he was doing, Peter was typing on his computer.

"Up early this morning, aren't you, Mr. Boget?"

"Thought I'd get a jump on the day."

"I think you spend too much time on that computer."

"You're probably right," he said, then looked down at the screen and continued typing. He was fast becoming a one-handed typist as he found it hard to keep his bandaged right forefinger and thumb off the keyboard when he tried to use the three fingers that still worked. He was composing his first response to Liza since receiving her message.

Where do I begin? Maybe with an apology. I realize now that I shouldn't have called you. I shouldn't have walked back into your life. Yet I can't begin to describe the emotions I have been experiencing since we talked last week. Fortunately, I've been quite preoccupied with trying to save my job. But I can't get you out of my mind. I'm almost afraid to tell you this, because you might mistake what I'm saying. This is for information, nothing more, but I want to tell you that every now and then through the years I've thought of you.

I especially think back on that wonderful summer. Dare I call it idyllic?

What a great time we had discovering our shared interest in writing, music and the great outdoors.

Though I have never wished that I didn't marry Elizabeth, and though I plan to spend the rest of my life with her and with my family, there have been a couple of times I wondered what life would have been like if we had become husband and wife. I guess that summer was too short and our times together too few to allow our relationship to flourish.

When I received that graduation song you wrote for me, I went into a real spin because by then I was engaged, and I knew that Elizabeth and I were well on our way to starting our new life—a life that has been great. But somehow that song and the personal note you included have always stayed with me. I've probably played the tune on the piano a thousand times (please don't ever tell anyone that) and sung those lyrics in secret places. The music sheet is still tucked away in a cardboard box with a bunch of old baseball cards and stuff I picked up at ballparks through the years. Every now and then I'll pull it out and remember how I felt the day I received it. I'll never forget walking to the student union on campus and sitting at a big old upright piano and playing it over and over for more than an hour. Yes, every time I think of that day, the memories of you come flooding back into my mind. It's ironic that now that I'd like to play it again, I can't because of my burned fingers.

While I'm reminiscing, I've got to tell you that the one memory that stands out most, besides our trip to Crystal Lake, was driving in that old Volkswagen to the top of Pikes Peak while you sang "Climb Every Mountain." Do you remember the sun shining on the snow and that old car coughing and choking as it crawled up that gravel road?

I've sometimes wondered what it would have been like to have that kind of music in the house. Do you still sing? Do you still play the piano and guitar? I've kept up my playing through the years and write a song every now and then, and the older kids have taken some piano lessons, but it's never really caught on here and I miss that. Elizabeth loves poetry and has read it a lot to the kids, but as far as music goes, it's mostly the stuff the kids like to listen to on the radio. I bought an electronic keyboard a few years back and that has sparked an interest in Daniel. I get it out and play some songs, but the kids prefer I don't sing. I don't have much of a voice.

I'm sorry to hear that life with Randy has been so difficult. Maybe someday we'll be able to sit around a campfire and tell our stories to one another. It would be fun to compare notes, but I'm afraid that seeing you would be bad for both of us. I'm sure we're not the people we were twenty-two years ago, and a meeting might be awfully disappointing. Worse than that is the possibility that we are the same people we were then. If so, who knows what might happen if we ever got together.

I hope you understand that in calling I wasn't trying to open up old wounds or establish a new relationship. Without violating my marriage covenant or intruding on yours, I just wanted to close a door that's been open too long.

Peter

He proofread the letter, ran the spell checker, and then dialed up CompuServe.

*   *   *

While a cold rain fell on the city, and thick clouds blocked the sun, Elizabeth Boget stood in her brightly lit suburban kitchen, packing the last of the lunches for her children. David and Lauren had already headed to the bus stop along the parkway that wound through the community. Daniel was eating a leisurely breakfast, knowing that he had half an hour before his bus squealed to a stop at the top of his cul-de-sac. Jonathan was still asleep. Kristin was wide awake and restless in her highchair when the phone rang.

"Hello," Elizabeth answered, tucking the handset under her ear so she could continue working on Daniel's lunch.

"Mrs. Boget?" The man's voice was muffled and crackled with the sound of a cellular phone.

"Yes?"

"Was David on bus two-thirty-nine this morning?"

Elizabeth's heart stopped. "Why? What's happened?"

"Nothing, nothing at all. I was just wondering. And I suppose Lauren's two-sixteen is just now rolling into the bus loop at Swift Creek Middle School."

Elizabeth's panic turned to confusion. "Who is this?"

"And Daniel, what a messy morning to be putting him on a bus to the

THURSDAY, APRIL 19 ⬜ *105*

elementary school. In this kind of weather there's no telling what might happen."

The anger mingled with fear. The man was too smooth, too professional. "What do you want?" she demanded, startling the two children eating breakfast. "Who is this?"

"Calm down, you have nothing to worry about. I'm just calling to talk to you about an unfortunate incident that took place in Maryland several weeks ago. Do you remember?"

"Is this some kind of joke?" There was no immediate response so she continued. "Look, I don't know what this is all about, but I don't think you're very funny."

"Mrs. Boget, I've been asked to call and let you know that if you and your family forget what you saw and who you encountered at the hospital, no harm will come to your children. But be advised that, if you should testify, your children may not get off the bus one day."

Even though the connection was noisy, Elizabeth thought she recognized the voice.

"Tell no one but your husband that you received this call."

The line went dead.

Elizabeth hung up the phone, then grabbed it off the hook again and laid it on the counter. She pulled a phone directory out of the cabinet above the desk in the kitchen and thumbed through the first few pages. She knew there was a way to trace calls if she put in the right code—Peter had talked about it—but she couldn't remember the procedure. She only knew that she had to get the code in before she made or received another call. She finally located the information and dialed *57.

She hung up and made another call.

"Oh, hi, Elizabeth," Peter said. "I'm surprised to hear your voice so early." She took a deep breath and said, "Somebody is after us."

*   *   *

By midmorning Heather Priddy, a federal prosecutor in Norfolk, Virginia, was in court awaiting the findings of the grand jury. The Justice Department had selected the venue because of its proximity to Mary Kennedy, her records and her employees. Priddy had presented a largely circumstantial case based on the stock trading patterns of Randolph and Segal on behalf of dozens of individuals, including two men arrested for cocaine possession and trafficking. She had also introduced the testimony of Barry Whitehead that Judge Cabrillo of Cancún had secured on Tuesday.

The key to Priddy's case was the identification of the assassin gunned down at the Arundel Community Hospital. She showed that the man who tried to kill Peter Boget, thinking he was Barry Whitehead, was almost certainly Richard Donovan, an employee of Mary Kennedy. Donovan allegedly returned to his native Ireland the weekend of the shooting, but he had not been in contact with friends or family members since. Priddy also had shown that Mary Kennedy had offered to send Richard Donovan to retrieve Whitehead's car, which was loaded with cocaine, from the police impoundment in Maryland.

The grand jury handed down the indictments that Heather Priddy sought.

At 11:20 a.m., six agents of the Federal Bureau of Investigation arrived at the offices of Kennedy and Associates to serve a warrant for the arrest of Mary Kennedy. Two had blocked the building's driveway with their car. Two others, carrying umbrellas to ward off the rain, walked to the rear of the building while two walked up to the front porch of the sprawling house that served as the home of Kennedy and Associates.

The agents opened the ornate wooden door, fitted with a large oval of beveled glass, and stepped inside. They crossed the Oriental rug in the spacious entrance hall, ignoring the renderings of brick and stone homes that hung on the walls.

At the desk of Lila Westfield, the firm's receptionist, Agent Sid Jones announced their presence. "We'd like to see Miss Kennedy, please," said Jones to the petite woman peering over her half-frame glasses. "We're with the Federal Bureau of Investigation."

"I know," said Westfield politely. "You've been here before. Let me ring her office."

Before she picked up the phone, the unmistakable sound of Kennedy's heels caused the men to turn toward the sweeping stairway fifteen feet away.

The tall woman descending the stairs looked like a model for *Working Woman* magazine. Dressed in a turquoise fitted suit with matching shoes and earrings, Kennedy glided across the floor to the agents. She extended her hand to greet Jones and his partner. "What brings you here today?"

"We have a warrant for your arrest," Jones said.

*   *   *

For Janice Bland and the staff of the public relations office, the lull in news media and employee inquiries was welcomed. Bland was finalizing a plan to tell the company's newest deregulation story to its various constituencies. She was in daily contact with Peter Boget to discuss strategies for ensuring that the company be properly positioned in the emerging communications battle with opponents of the company's entry into the cable TV arena. Bland knew that Peter wasn't coming back soon, and she had taken it upon herself to become fully acquainted with the committee work Peter was involved in at Mid-Atlantic Bell. She also had instituted a strong rumor-control center with extended hours, to head off the many rumors circulating through the company.

She and Lucy Johnson met for lunch at Aunt Betty's Kitchen just off the lobby of the phone company building. Because of the rain the eatery was unusually crowded and noisy, providing the needed cover for their private discussion.

Janice spoke between bites of her Greek salad. "What am I doing wrong? It seems like I've been on Mazzetti's bad side since he arrived, and that's been, what, forty-eight hours? He's called me a dozen times making suggestions on how to run this shop, and even when I tell him that things are under control he doesn't seem to believe me. I know that Earl called Peter a lot, and Mike was often out of the loop, but this is different."

Lucy cupped her pita bread filled with sliced chicken breast, shredded lettuce and narrow wedges of tomatoes. The oil and vinegar dressing was making the bread soggy. "What's he want now?"

"That's what's bothering me. I don't know." Bland looked perplexed. "He seems to want information on how Peter ran the office, but every time I tell him about certain projects and meeting schedules he cuts me off like that's not what he really wants. Twice he asked me—"

"Well, if it isn't the Peter Boget fan club!" Megan Churchill interrupted. The office busybody, holding a tray of food, slid into a chair at the small table. "Mind if I join you?" Before the two women could object, Megan started in with her latest gossip. "I heard that Peter got the shaft at the executive committee meeting in D.C. He's history, and so is Downes. You know he shacked up with that woman that everyone thought Peter was with in Mexico. Not that I'm surprised, he's a real hunk, and if I could find a way—"

"Megan, shut up." The scowl on Janice Bland's face communicated more than the words did. "I wish you'd learn to keep your opinions and rumors to yourself. Peter only suspected you were the one causing trouble down here, but I know. And as long as I'm in charge, I'm not going to allow you to continue."

"But—"

"But nothing. Consider this a warning. I'm going to enter this conversation in your personnel record and I'm going to make sure it ends up on your quarterly review." Bland continued firing as Megan extricated herself from her chair. Lucy looked on in delight. "Your rumor-mongering is absolutely unprofessional and counterproductive to all we're about in the public relations office."

An embarrassed Megan slinked away. Lucy was laughing when Janice turned her attention back to her salad. "You really let her have it," she said.

"You're darn right I did. Too bad she's so good at what she does. Otherwise I'd have her out of here in a month!"

"It's also too bad that her rumors have an uncanny way of being true," said Lucy.

Janice slid a plastic forkful of lettuce and feta cheese into her mouth and nodded in agreement.

"You were talking about Mazzetti's questions," prompted Lucy.

Bland finished chewing. "Right. He keeps asking if Peter talked to me about what happened in the hospital in Maryland. When I tell him no, he doesn't seem to believe me. And he keeps trying to get me to talk about the fight Elizabeth and Peter were supposed to have had with him, but he never comes right out and asks me about it."

"He just wants to see how much you know."

"Or how much I believe."

Lucy leaned forward. "And how much do you believe?"

"Well, I'd say there is more to the story than we know. "

"I don't like to get into speculation," said Lucy, "but I think Peter was on to something that Mazzetti was doing."

"Like what?"

"Like violating some company rule or having an affair or something."

"You think so?"

"Look, there's a lot more going on here than a hotshot vice president trying to throw his weight around. Mazzetti has cast a spell over the whole executive team up in Washington. I've been doing some checking with my counterparts in the companies where Mazzetti has worked. You know what? He's always been good at what he does, but he didn't take off until just a couple of years ago. He used to be an ordinary, hard-nosed manager with a decent amount of compassion progressing through the ranks at the usual rate of speed. Then, boom, he raced through two levels in three years, climbing over everyone to get into the job he now has—the job that has given him control over all company security. That's lots of power. So why would he want to exchange that for the top job in Virginia? So he gets the word *president* in his name?"

"He's got to be president of an operating company if he ever wants to become Mid-Atlantic's chairman," Janice responded. "I think that's all there is to it."

"Maybe," Lucy said around a mouthful of sandwich. "But I bet there's more here than meets the eye."

                              *   *   *

"Mike, I'm so glad you've come," Emily Hendrick told Downes as the two sat outside Earl Hendrick's hospital room. "We've had heart specialists brought in from Richmond." She shook her head slowly. "The word is that right now only God can make a difference." The woman who had her own close encounter with death just four days earlier looked remarkably strong and well, but she spoke with a great heaviness of heart.

"Just before the storm hit we were talking about you and Peter and the whole Mazzetti mess."

Downes responded cautiously. "Earl won't be too happy when he hears that Frank's sitting at his desk right now and that I was arrested for helping Peter."

"I heard."

"Frank's game plan is to force Peter out in three months, after all the hoopla subsides."

Emily shook her head slowly. "We've got to pray that Earl makes it. He's got Mazzetti's number and he's ready to expose the man for what he is."

* * *

The hallmark of a good manager is the ability to resemble an accomplished juggler, keeping many balls in the air at one time. From that standpoint, Peter Boget was a master. But even the best jugglers have limits, and Peter was stretching his. He called the FBI and explained the threat his wife had received and the warning that came with it. In reply, the FBI agent told him that they had arrested Mary Kennedy. In addition to his concern for the safety of his family, he was still plagued with thoughts of Liza and worries about his financial future and the prospect of a demotion. As if that weren't enough, the continuing itch on his chest and leg was driving him to distraction.

At 3:10 p.m., FBI agents Giddings and Middleton entered his room. "Mr. Boget, the last time we were here you said you were in contact with Mark Randolph," Giddings said.

"I said I learned of his work and believe he is one of the people who regularly share their computer insights on some bulletin boards I've logged onto."

"Can you contact Mark Randolph?"

Boget hesitated. "Why?"

"Mary Kennedy has been arrested, and her request for bail was denied because the prosecutor demonstrated that there is a high probability she may try to flee the country if released. Unfortunately, with the death of Barry Whitehead, the prosecutor's not going to have much of a case against Kennedy when she goes for arraignment." Agent Giddings leaned forward. "Unless we can get Mark Randolph to testify."

"What makes you think I can get him?"

"I believe you've contacted him. If you have, you have an obligation to help us. If we get Randolph, we get Kennedy. And if we get Kennedy, your family can get on with life."

"And what about the man who took my boy hostage in the hospital? When you get Kennedy, will you get him?" Boget was testy. "I don't care if Mary Kennedy is a drug kingpin, it's the other guy I want to see locked up. I don't know who he is or where he is, but I'm going to find out. When I do, I expect you to do what's necessary to put him away. Permanently."

"Let's start with Kennedy," Giddings said. "Let me know when you make contact with Randolph,"

*   *   *

At the Plumrose Inn, beyond the boisterous group of men and women at the bar, beyond the young man who was practicing his dart throwing, four men and two women huddled around a heavy wooden table in a dark corner of the narrow, low-ceilinged Irish pub.

Patrick O'Hearn gulped a breath of the beer-scented, smoke-filled air and spoke in a measured rhythm. "Barry O'Donnell and Patrick Vincent and Peter Clancy and Sean O'Farrell have not died in vain. We needn't be reminded, but we must never forget. There is work to do and I have come for your help."

Ten eyes were riveted on the man who, four weeks earlier, had eluded New York police in a footrace through midtown Manhattan and who was still recovering from two bullets he received at point blank range from a Maryland state trooper. "Our battle is not just being fought here in County Tyrone or in Belfast or Londonderry. It is a worldwide battle and the blast that brought down the financial district in London was just the opening round of the final push to oust the bloody British. They keep talking about peace, but they're killing our brothers and sisters and our mothers and fathers in the pubs and streets of Belfast every week. Unless we get out from under the Brits, we'll never be truly free."

The faces of the young men and women seemed older and harder in the dim light. They looked eager to avenge the deaths of their friends who had died at the hands of the British Army in an ambush in the parking lot of St. Patrick's Church on a cold February evening.

"We have a friend in America who is in trouble," O'Hearn continued. "I've been told that you are trained and ready for the work that needs to be done."

A collective "Aye" resonated from their lips.

10

T he cold front that had brought the previous day's rain moved off-
shore, sucking cool, dry air from the Midwest into central Virginia.
Set among the trees in the planned community southwest of Richmond, the Boget residence was skirted with a dazzling display of
nature's beauty as water droplets scattered the rays of the bright morning
sun across thousands of white and lavender azalea blossoms. The plants
were large and full of color, a rare sight at so new a house, but their size
and beauty were no mystery to the neighbors. Peter and Elizabeth had
begun working the red clay around the house's foundation before they
moved in.

Elizabeth and her children were waiting indoors for Bill McGuire, who
had agreed to drop by to pick up the children and take them to school. As
his Dodge Caravan pulled into the driveway, David, Lauren and Daniel
hugged their mother in quick succession.

"Everything will be fine, Mom," David assured her. "No one's going to
bother us. Just don't worry about anything."

Lauren was not so at ease, but she echoed her brother's sentiments.
"We'll be fine. I'll see you later."

Elizabeth bent over to kiss Daniel, who tried to dodge her lips. "I don't
need any kisses. Nobody's going to bother me," he said, smugly sweeping

the air with a karate chop. "If they do, they're going to regret it."

* * *

Mark Randolph's response to Peter's request for help was curious.

Check the Atlantic Quest BB and look for a message from SIMM DR. Boget quickly logged off CompuServe and onto the bulletin board Randolph had mentioned. He located the message from someone identifying himself as SIMM DR, one of the many colorful names that bulletin board aficionados give themselves. The message wasn't what he expected. It was part of a collective story being written by those logging onto the bulletin board.

"I am not going to come in and testify to my association with her. That would be crazy. To damage her I'd have to implicate myself," said the money man. "That would expose me not only to the criminal justice system, but to her goons as well. Maybe she got the fat man, but she isn't getting me."

His friend looked at him carefully. "From what I hear, you and the fat man were big-time dealers of death."

The money man interrupted. "Wrong. The people I deal with are recreational users who've grown up with the stuff and don't want to get caught up in the riffraff who buy and sell on the street. That's too demeaning and too dangerous."

"And you don't consider murder dangerous?"

"It wasn't supposed to happen that way," the money man said defensively. "If it hadn't been for the breakdown, none of this would be an issue."

His friend said, "That stupid flat tire nearly cost me my life. None of this would have happened if you weren't selling drugs."

"Sorry. Things happen."

SIMM DR's portion of the story ended and another author picked it up. Boget scanned backward through the story, but the other contributions by SIMM DR were innocuous.

* * *

Patrick O'Hearn's plan needed work, but more importantly it needed secrecy. The comings and goings of Catholic young people, especially men, were monitored to the point of annoyance by the Royal Ulster Constabulary, the police force referred to locally as the RUC. Because of that, O'Hearn took extra precautions to minimize his contact with his recruits. Each was given a separate itinerary, allowing forty-eight hours to reach the rendezvous point in Belfast. The team O'Hearn was assembling was unique in that none of the members had ever been arrested. Their profiles were not in the government's terrorist files; their fingerprints were only on the inside of their gloves.

Their brigade of the Provisional IRA had made two daring and successful attacks on army munitions storage facilities, seizing a cache of arms before blowing up what they didn't want. They had no remorse for their fellow countrymen who had died by their hand.

Now the focus had changed. Mary Kennedy's drug money had funded their training and mission. The skills they had acquired would now be pressed into use; the tactics would be the same, only the objective would be different.

O'Hearn had placed a series of calls to Virginia. His persistence paid off: drawings of the correctional facility in which Mary Kennedy was being detained were faxed to him during the night.

*   *   *

Though he should have been resting, Peter Boget was dialing his bedside phone.

"Mr. Hanks, this is Peter Boget. I've been trying to catch up with you for almost two weeks."

"Oh?"

"My wife and I really haven't had a chance to thank you for standing with us in the hospital. And I'm sorry to hear that you've lost your job with the Maryland State Police." Peter's voice resonated compassion. "I guess you've got more reason than we do to be angry with the man who shot you after tossing our Jonathan in the air. Is your leg better?"

"Yes," Hanks said with a note of caution. Then he was silent.

"Let me tell you why I'm really calling. I suppose you got the same call we did about not testifying against Mary Kennedy. Well, we're not about to risk our family a second time. Anyway, I'm more interested in finding the man with the gun."

"Oh?"

"It's something my wife mentioned. She said that the man called you by name." Peter was fishing, but he thought he might be onto something. He listened very carefully for not just the words of the answer, but Hanks's expression as well.

"I don't think so. He probably just read my name off my badge."

"Well, it was a long shot. If you think of anything, give me a call."

After Boget hung up the phone he turned to his computer and clicked on the project-management program into which he had typed the information from all of his 3 × 5 cards. He scrolled to the box that contained the name of Roland Hanks and added a few notes.

* * *

While Peter Boget was busy with his computer, Liza Morgan was busy with hers.

Dear Peter,

I should be sleeping, because I just got off work. I work twelve-hour shifts from 7 to 7, usually three or four days in a row, then a few days off. It's been a long week and I need to get some sleep. But I'm not sure I can sleep. You are on my mind day and night. I know the feelings I have are wrong, but never before have I felt more like tossing caution to the wind and leaving here to meet you out along the road, to climb into the seat next to you and drive with you back to the mountains to escape to a secret sanctuary.

I can't tell you how many times I have thought those thoughts—of you driving up and taking me away from here forever. It's hard to explain. Even though you're 1,000 miles away, I feel as if you've already come for me. Does this seem stran ʒe? You're like a breath of mountain air, wonderfully refreshing. If I never see you again, if for the rest of my life all I have of you are memories of this week—memories of what you said, and what I've felt—I will still know a joy that I have never previously experienced except that summer with you. For the first time in my life I feel as though someone really cares about me. I feel so free with you, Peter. I feel I can tell you everything.

For two hours, Liza's hands danced across the keyboard as her computer screen filled with words—words that told her story of a troubled marriage tempered by the privilege of raising three bright, talented children. She talked about her openness and how, particularly in her early, immature years, it got her into trouble with her husband, friends and coworkers.

Peter, I guess I've told you more than you ever wanted to hear. I've been composing this letter in my mind all week, but I've waited for my day off to write it all down because I knew that once I got started I wouldn't be able to stop. I know that by now I've probably driven you off, and if you don't acknowledge this I'll understand. Meanwhile, I want to thank you for making me the happiest woman in the world.

*   *   *

"Elizabeth, does 'Hanks' ring a bell?"

"Sure, he was the policeman who was shot by the man who had taken Jonathan."

"And you said that the gunman called him Hanks."

"Yes, he did."

"But he was wearing a gown over his uniform and his name tag would have been covered."

"So?"

"So how did he know that trooper's name was Hanks?"

The veil began to lift from Elizabeth's eyes. "They knew each other?"

"Maybe." Peter tapped a finger on his forehead. "Think about it. Nobody knows exactly why Hanks was at that hospital that day—or at least no one's reported on it. Maybe he was somehow part of the plan, some kind of insurance—I don't know. Maybe something went wrong."

"And?"

"And I know this is a long shot, but you told me that the man who called you yesterday seemed familiar. Could the call have come from Hanks?"

Elizabeth pondered the question. "I don't know. It was muffled. I'd probably have to hear his voice again."

"Wanna try?" said Peter, lifting the phone from the receiver.

"Let me think about what I need to say."

*   *   *

Earl Hendrick didn't need to think about his first words since entering the hospital on Monday evening. As he awakened from his coma he uttered a barely distinguishable, "Emily." It wasn't much, but for the woman sitting by his side it was the most exciting thing she could imagine.

Standing across from Emily Hendrick, a physician smiled. "I think the worst may be over."

Emily gently squeezed her husband's hand. "I'm right here, honey." Turning to the doctor, she added, "Many prayers have been answered."

"A lot more will have to be before he leaves this hospital, but this is an encouraging sign. Both of you are incredible people. I'll bet your story ends up in *Reader's Digest* or in a book somewhere."

"Right now all I'm thinking about is getting him well enough to take home." Emily gazed lovingly at her husband, whose face had regained a bit of its former color. "I think it's time to leave the phone company and get on with retirement."

"I don't suppose that retirement is going to include any more sailing."

Emily looked into the face of the doctor, who was younger than her children. "Now what makes you think that?" she asked as a wry smile crossed her face. "I'd like to think that, statistically, we'd never hit a storm like that again."

"I guess you're right, statistically speaking." He laughed. "But, statistically, you shouldn't be here today, and," looking into Earl's full face beneath the bandages on his scalp, the doctor added, "and, statistically, he shouldn't be alive."

* * *

"Have you taken care of business?" Elizabeth Boget asked Roland Hanks. She didn't use her normal speaking voice. Rather, she spoke in the cultured Irish accent she often used when reading to her children the poetry and stories of her father's native Ireland.

"Who is this?"

"I just want to know if you've made all the calls."

"I don't know who you are. But if you are trying to imitate someone, you're not doing a very good job."

Peter didn't have to ask Elizabeth if the man on the phone was the one who threatened her earlier in the week. Her face recorded the revulsion she felt as she talked.

"I'm sorry, I must have the wrong number," she said, and then hung up the phone.

"I must not sound like Mary Kennedy," Elizabeth said to her husband, "or they have some code or something. But that was him, all right."

"So do I tell the FBI?"

"You've got something else on your mind, Peter?"

"I don't know, I've got to think." Peter swung his legs over the side of his bed and stepped down. He held his chest erect as he limped across the room, ignoring the continuing itch and irritation of the bandaged wound on his thigh. "If the FBI questions Hanks, what's he going to say? He's working for Kennedy? Not a chance."

"Maybe he's some sort of double agent," Elizabeth offered.

"I can't imagine a double agent threatening innocent people. There's more to all of this than meets the eye." Boget started to bend down to pick up a scrapbook that sat with a stack of newspapers along the wall of the room. When he flinched, his wife scooted around the bed and reached down to pick up the book for him. "Still hurts?"

"Not much," Peter said as he laid the scrapbook on the bed and began to leaf through it. "Here is that story on Hanks the hero." He skimmed it quickly, remembering the details from previous readings, then he looked up. "Hanks could be the wild card in all of this. What if he was bought after the incident? Here we have a hero who loses his job days after he gets ink in every major newspaper in the country. If these quotes are accurate, he's got a big ego, and he loves action. He goes to the hospital to net a big-time drug dealer and ends up with nobody." Boget stopped. "There are a lot of holes here."

"Like the gunman knowing Hanks."

"Yeah, that's part of it. I'm going to have to sleep on that one," Peter said.

*   *   *

Mike Downes was always a welcomed guest, and on this night, Peter had more than the usual to talk about with him. He hoped that no one else would drop in for the next thirty minutes.

"So that's what I have," Peter concluded after presenting his findings of the day. "What do you make of it?"

Despite the fact that Boget employed the same analytical tools for problem-solving, the two men often came at problems from differing perspectives. Downes tackled problems hoping to solve them in the most expeditious way. Boget liked to look at the bigger picture and determine the environment in which the problem occurred. He would often say that fixing a problem is not enough. You've got to change the environment that allowed the problem to occur in the first place.

Downes, sitting in a chair between the bed and the window, said, "I think it's interesting. Have you told the FBI? I think they would want to investigate and possibly build a stronger case against Kennedy."

"I haven't told anybody, and I'm not sure I have enough to go to the feds. Listen, if Hanks was working for Kennedy before he came to the hospital, what was he supposed to be doing? He wouldn't make the trip just to visit me. But if he came to kill me, why would the others be there? And of all people, why would a bigtime drug dealer get messed up with all that nonsense? And that scene with Elizabeth and Jonathan," he said thoughtfully, "was that staged? I don't think so, but remember the two bullets that the other guy fired? One hit Hanks in the chest, but he was wearing a bulletproof vest. Was the second shot also supposed to hit him in a way that would just injure but not kill him?" Boget's mind swirled. "I think Hanks may be on Kennedy's payroll, but I bet we're missing something. Like he's some kind of peripheral player—maybe a drug user, like Whitehead was, or someone who got too close to Kennedy's operation or something."

"So you don't want the FBI involved? That could be risky."

"What, not telling the police that I have some theories?"

"Just be careful. Everyone working on that case is awful edgy. I heard today that the prosecutor is worried that she may not have enough to keep Kennedy in jail, that Kennedy's hired some hotshot lawyer."

"Why am I not surprised?" Peter interjected.

"He's from Washington, a former Justice Department lawyer who quit over the drug-kingpin legislation that he believes seriously undermines the Constitution. The lawyer working with me says that Kennedy will be out long before a trial starts."

"That's not a happy thought."

"Not when she employs killers to watch over her business."

Peter looked at his friend and thought back to the mayhem that Kennedy's men created at the hospital in Maryland. Softly he said, "That's why I'm going to get her." Boget stopped and lightened his demeanor. "He's got to have a name."

"Who?"

"Irish Eyes. That's what I'm calling the guy who grabbed Jonathan. As soon as I get out of here, I'm going to find Irish Eyes, and the first person I'm going to talk to is Roland Hanks."

Downes stood up and looked out the window as he began speaking. "Peter, I know your family has been through hell, and you're not particularly fond of Mary Kennedy and this Irish Eyes fellow. But you've got a young family, and you're in no shape to undertake a personal vendetta against anyone." Downes turned and walked the few steps to the foot of the bed where he grasped the bed rail and continued. "When I went after Whitehead, I wasn't chasing some criminal, I was looking for you. I didn't do anything to harm anybody. What I did was try to find you because no one else would or could. And I helped Debbie because she needed me." Downes pressed his argument. "You're talking about revenge, and that's not right. You want to see Kennedy and Irish Eyes in the electric chair? That's what we have police and the FBI and the Justice Department for. You're my friend, Peter. Please think about what you're saying. I don't think you really want to take matters into your own hands."

Mike sat down and pulled Peter's Bible out from under a copy of *Our Daily Bread*. "You're the Bible scholar. Doesn't it say in here somewhere that you're to love your enemies? You know, 'Vengeance is mine, saith the Lord' and all that."

Mike set the Bible in his lap and looked into Peter's subdued face. "Look, as soon as Earl gets back to work, we'll go after Mazzetti, we'll get your job reinstated, and then you can get on with life. In the meantime, go home and spend time with your kids and Elizabeth. I think they'd like to get you back for a while."

Before Downes left, the evening parade of visitors from church began. When it ended at 9:15, Peter began to log onto CompuServe. Then he stopped. He needed time to think. He needed time to pray—something he had been neglecting lately. He didn't want to hear Mike's message but he couldn't block it out. He didn't want to hear God's Word because he wasn't interested in doing the right thing. Not when it pertained to Mary Kennedy. He thought about her dead, with Irish Eyes beside her.

11

I don't know what's going on, but this Boget character is asking too many questions." Roland Hanks nervously glanced out the window to his left, scanning the Burger King parking lot in Landover, Maryland, just off the Capital Beltway. He kept a styrofoam cup of coffee at his lips.

"Like what?" said the man across the white plastic table.

Hanks told the story of the call he had received the previous day. "The guy is hot to get Mary, and I think he put someone up to call me and pretend she was Kennedy."

"What did you say?"

"I know a setup when I see one," said Hanks indignantly. "I didn't say anything. But it's clear that they suspect I called in the threat."

"So, why are you here?"

"I need to know who shot me."

"Why do you need to know that?"

"I'd like to know who my teammates are."

"This isn't baseball. Maybe all the guys at the police station knew each other, but you're safer if you don't know the details. You're getting paid—that's all you need to know. Oh, you might also like to know that Mary was released last night."

*   *   *

Elizabeth was with her husband when the call came.

"That was Mike," he said afterward. "She's out. I can't believe it!" Peter dropped his chin onto his chest. "With Randolph and Whitehead out of the picture, and without strong evidence to bolster the government's case, there's not gonna be a case."

After a long silence, Elizabeth said, "Look at the bright side. If they have no case, she'll have no reason to threaten us."

"Unless we tell the newspapers something we shouldn't," Peter said with a smile, remembering his wife's comment in the newspaper that he thought might have triggered the threatening call.

"I didn't want to tell you this, but Jonathan had the dream again last night. You just don't know how terrifying his screams are . . . and how disruptive they are to the whole house."

"I'll be home soon, Elizabeth. We'll be able to help him together."

Peter heard talking in the hall. Then Dr. Gill walked in with two interns and Nurse Spencer trailing behind.

"Are you ready to send me home?" Peter asked hopefully.

"That's what we're here to find out."

"Mrs. Boget, if you'll wait down the hall . . ." He didn't have to finish the sentence. Elizabeth was on her feet and ready to leave. She would be changing enough dressings once Peter returned home; she didn't have any desire to watch or smell as the dressings were removed. And she certainly wasn't eager to watch them pull two dozen staples from her husband's chest.

Like most of the physicians on the staff, Dr. Gill was both an excellent physician and a good teacher. As much as possible, he let his students do the hands-on work. Once Elizabeth was out of the room, the students worked quickly but gently to uncover the skin graft and the donor site.

"It looks good, very good," said Gill, observing the reddish-pink chest. "Let's get the staples out."

Though the removal process wasn't supposed to hurt, Peter winced each time as the remover hooked one of the staples and withdrew it from his tender chest.

"The waffle pattern will pretty much go away," Gill told him. "But that skin's going to be sensitive for a long time."

"You told me."

"Just a reminder," he said, as much for the benefit of his students as for his patient. "Keep the sun off it. It's going to be more sensitive than baby skin."

While one intern removed staples, the other trimmed dead skin from the edges of the graft. In less than fifteen minutes the procedure was complete and Elizabeth was invited in to review the dressing technique. When class was finished, Peter looked up at the teacher. "Does this mean I can go home?"

Dr. Gill's yes was much more than a short answer to a simple question. It marked the end of an ordeal. Hearing the answer, Elizabeth began to cry. She knew that her life finally was going to be put back together. She walked to the head of the bed and leaned to kiss her husband, who also had tears in his eyes.

"I'm ready to take you home," she whispered.

"I'm ready to go."

*   *   *

As she often did on Saturday mornings when she was off work, Liza Morgan drove to Ruth's Bakery in neighboring Bay St. Louis for a cinnamon roll, coffee and engaging conversation with the dozens of people who made the gathering place the liveliest morning spot in the historic community. From its weathered blue and white paint to its well-worn wood-and-glass door, the structure, which doubled as an antique store, looked more like a Salvation Army outlet store than a place for political and social discussions. Outside, a small, hand-painted sign said it best: "Where the Elite Meet to Eat, Greet & Rest Their Feet."

After an enjoyable forty-five minutes of conversation, Liza headed to Delchamps to do some grocery shopping. She returned home to a kitchen cluttered with breakfast fixings and a torn-apart carburetor. Liza wanted to see if Peter had posted a response on CompuServe, but she knew she couldn't even think about looking while Randy was around the house.

It was late morning when her husband informed her that he had to go to an auto-parts store and then to Wal-Mart for some other supplies. As soon as Randy's truck pulled onto the street, she turned on the computer and modem, waited impatiently for her applications to come up on the screen, and then instructed the computer to dial.

At log-on, when she did not see the "You have mail waiting" message, she knew he hadn't responded. Questions swirled in her mind. Had he read it? If not, why not? If he did, why hadn't he written a reply? Had she said too much and driven him off? She knew she couldn't do anything about the situation, so she dashed off a note:

I guess you must be on your way home by now. How I wish I could be the one nursing you back to health. Just to touch you once again . . .

She hoped that neither her son nor her daughter, who were both watching television ten feet away, would come over to see what she was doing. She added another line.

Sorry, I won't get off on that again. Just wanted you to know that I'm here waiting to hear from you but always wishing we were a thousand miles closer.

She logged off just as her husband walked into the house, taking her by surprise. She hoped Randy wouldn't notice the glow of wonder that was on her face from thinking about Peter. But he did.

"What are you doing?" he demanded.

Twelve-year-old Eric and his seventeen-year-old sister, Amy, knew another fight was coming, so they quickly dispersed to their rooms.

"Nothing. Why?"

Randy walked to the computer and looked at the screen. She had closed the communications program just in time. "Why's the modem on?" he asked. His voice was growing louder. "Who's sending you messages?"

"Nobody." She uttered a half-truth, knowing that anything more might result in verbal if not physical abuse. "The modem's been on since you logged onto Prodigy last night. I noticed it this morning and was just about to turn it off." This time she was lying, but Randy couldn't remember if he had turned it off or not.

"Get in the truck. I'm taking you to Wal-Mart with me and then we're going to McDonald's."

"Randy, it's my day off and I have work to do around here. And Eric has his game. Why don't we wait and go to McDonald's after church tomorrow?"

He was in a sour mood. "I don't know what's going on here, but I don't like the look on your face, and I'm not going to leave you alone to get into trouble with some other man."

"For gosh sakes, I'm not a little kid," she said indignantly. "I'm forty-four, and I've been faithful to you for as long as I've known you. I don't have a boyfriend and I resent your accusations. Why is it every time I look happy you think I'm running around on you? I'd think you'd know me by now."

"Get in the truck."

Liza Morgan had often fought with her husband, but through the years she had learned to acquiesce when the outcome didn't significantly alter her lifestyle.

When their children were all in school, she had begged Randy to allow her to go back to college and get a nursing degree, but he was adamant that she stay home and try to have more children. When she stood up to him, she won a huge moral victory for herself. But it came at the expense of a year-long reign of terror because of her husband's fear that she might meet someone at school and leave him. Randy Morgan jealousy guarded his wife, not for her safety or her well-being, but for himself. Liza understood that and tried to serve him in a way that would show him that she had given—and was continuing to give—her all for him. But as much as Liza gave, it was never enough.

"Let me go to the bathroom first," she said with a sigh.

Morgan looked at his watch. "Can't you wait and go at Wal-Mart?"

Liza, not wanting to dignify the comment with a response, turned and walked away down the hall.

*　　*　　*

Even with Bill McGuire's help, leaving the hospital wasn't easy for Peter. The piles of papers that he had accumulated, his computer and accessories, his clothing and his plants were all stacked onto two carts. Several members of the burn-center staff said their farewells as Peter was pushed in a wheelchair to the entrance where Bill's van was waiting. Peter carefully climbed into the second seat. Elizabeth slid in next to him.

"Home?" Bill asked, swinging the van past a parked car and out onto the narrow street that separated two of the hospital's large buildings in downtown Richmond.

"Actually, I'd like to stop by the office and get my mail," Peter said, trying to suppress a grin.

Elizabeth, realizing he was joking, smacked him on his thigh. Peter let out a mournful cry. Bill stopped the van and in his rearview mirror saw an anguished look sweep across Peter's face. A gullible Elizabeth searched for ways to apologize. "Oh, Peter, I'm sorry! I didn't mean to—"

Peter's eyes twinkled as his face transformed itself into the picture of a prankster. "Wrong leg!" he said, laughing.

"I think Peter Boget is back," his wife intoned. "Don't know if I can stand it, but he's back."

*   *   *

In three separate cars the men and women had made their way to Belfast's Aldergrove Airport and were now minutes away from becoming airborne. They looked as much like tourists on holiday as anyone else on the plane.

Billy McMillen was a chunky five-nine. His fair skin accentuated the freckles on his face and hands, and his arms and chest bulged beneath a tight-fitting shirt. He looked like a boxer, except his nose was still thin and prominent. Like everyone else in the group, he could handle himself with or without a weapon, but only he and O'Hearn had the skill to assemble and detonate a range of explosives.

Across the aisle and two rows back, Liam O'Donnell and Eileen Adams looked like newlyweds, which they hoped soon to become. Both were relatively small, with dark hair. They did not look like martial-arts experts, which they were, or appeared capable of killing anyone, which they had.

Behind them sat Patrick O'Hearn and Kathleen McKenna, who looked much older than her twenty-six years. She was quick and strong and an expert in small arms. More important for this mission, she bore a striking resemblance to Mary Kennedy.

Missing from the group was Paddy McKee, a thin, wiry investment counselor who lived in London. Following the meeting at McGurns, he had departed for America and now was enjoying brunch in a Manhattan hotel. At just over six feet, he was the tallest of the group. His short hair was as dark as his eyes. Wire-rim glasses gave him the look of a man who spent most of his time in a library or behind a computer console. Only a handful of people knew that, though he was very British in all his dealings, his private loyalty was to the Irish Republican Army. Growing up in Belfast he had heard stories told by his parents of how police mistakenly arrested his grandfather and tried to force him to testify against people he didn't even know. His grandfather had died from blows to his head during the interrogation.

As a youngster, Paddy decided that if ever there was an opportunity to avenge that killing, he would do it.

*   *   *

Bill McGuire's van sped west on the downtown expressway, exited onto the Powhite Parkway and crossed the James River. Bill chatted with Peter and Elizabeth as they breezed along through the trees and residential areas that flanked the toll road. He exited at Courthouse Road, sooner than he should have by Peter's calculation. "Going to the soccer field," said McGuire casually, as he lifted his car phone, tapped a few buttons, and hung up. "Don't mind, do you?"

"Do I have a choice?"

"Daniel's game is about half over, but I know he'd love to see you show up on the sidelines," said Elizabeth, who had arranged for the detour to the Coalfield Soccer Complex. "David and Jason's game is probably over," she said, mentioning the name of Bill McGuire's son and David's best friend. "They'll all be at Daniel's Field."

Elizabeth was wrong. David wasn't at Daniel's Field. He was standing at the referee's shelter next to the parking lot waiting for his dad. Jonathan was riding on his shoulders "keeping lookout." Lauren was by his side. All looked anxiously toward the road. Behind them, taped to the shelter's roof, was a bright blue-and-white sign that read, "Welcome Back, Dad!" Next to it, another read, "Coach Boget, Hurray!"

As the van traversed the last two miles across Lucks Lane, Elizabeth pulled a blue shirt from under the seat. "I think you better change," she said. As quickly as he could, given his painful chest, Peter, with Elizabeth's help, removed the shirt he wore out of the hospital and donned the blue one emblazoned with an "MYSL Staff" logo.

"I'm afraid I'm not ready for coaching," he said as McGuire drove onto the large, gravel parking lot.

"No," said Bill, turning around, "but the kids are ready for you."

*   *   *

Roland Hanks stewed for several hours after his breakfast meeting at

Burger King. Then he climbed into his red Corvette, heading for Norfolk and the office of Kennedy and Associates.

He didn't expect to find anyone in on Saturday, but felt compelled to see for himself the place where Mary Kennedy conducted her business. The door was locked so he walked down the steps from the porch and encircled the building. A white Mercedes-Benz was parked in the backyard that had been converted into a small parking lot overlooking the river. It looked like the kind of car Kennedy would drive.

He scanned the building for signs of life and noticed lights on the second floor. He checked the back door but it was locked, so he rounded the building slowly, looking for an opening. Finding none, he returned to the front porch, pressed the lighted button alongside the door and waited. He pressed it again and heard the chime ring from the other side of the door. He leaned close to the glass and peered into the reception area.

He heard the sound of a car starting. Before he could get to the sidewalk, the Mercedes raced down the driveway and spun into the street. Hanks could tell that the driver was a red-haired woman, but she never turned toward him and he didn't get a look at her face.

Hanks sprinted to his car and pulled out in pursuit. Within six blocks he had caught up with her. At the stoplight at Colley Avenue and Thirty-eighth Street he pulled alongside and beeped his horn. She didn't turn to look at him, but she didn't need to. When he saw her, Hanks knew she was the woman he had seen stepping onto the elevator at Arundel Community Hospital fifteen minutes before the shooting began.

He pressed his horn again. Kennedy remained impassive, but when the light turned green she maneuvered her car with surprising deftness. She floored the accelerator and the car leaped into the intersection. Hanks in his Corvette did the same.

Almost immediately, Kennedy slammed on the brakes and, while Hanks accelerated through the intersection, she swung her car to the right, barely avoiding a pickup truck waiting for the light on the cross street.

Through his rearview mirror, Hanks saw the Mercedes disappear down Thirty-eighth. He slapped the steering wheel and swore. He thought about trying to catch her, but traffic at the next intersection blocked his progress. He sat stewing for the second time that day. Mary Kennedy was always one step in front of him, and that made him furious.

Defeated and dejected, he drove aimlessly around Norfolk for forty-five minutes before heading north to the interstate and the long drive home. At Mercury Boulevard in Hampton he stopped for a burger and called his answering machine. The recording made him even angrier. He pressed a number to rewind the tape and listen to the message again.

"Roland, Roland, Roland. When will you ever learn? I guess I'm going to have to drop you from the payroll unless you grow up. You and I are not to meet, do you understand? We both have too much to lose."

Hanks slammed down the phone and then picked it up again. He dialed the State Police Barracks in Landover, Maryland, and asked to speak to one of his former coworkers.

"Casteen." The trooper was abrupt as always.

"John, this is Hanks. I need a favor."

"Well, if it isn't Super Cop. You planning to do some more grandstanding?"

"Cut it, John. I need a favor, nothing big. If it amounts to anything, I'll let you know."

Dropping his voice, Casteen said, "Hanks, you know that if I do anything to help you, I could end up on the street too. You are persona non-grata around here."

"I know, but listen, I think I've got a bead on Mary Kennedy. But I need to know her home address."

"Check the telephone directory."

"If she was in the telephone directory, I wouldn't be making this call."

"What makes you think I'd give that information to you?"

"I think you know."

"If you want a favor, that's one thing. If you want to blackmail me, that's something else."

"Whoa!" Hanks interrupted. "That's not what this call is all about. I'm joking, that's all. If you've got the address, that's fine. If not, it's no big deal."

"Hold the line."

*   *   *

Sitting across from his wife at McDonald's, Randy Morgan spoke as he chewed a Big Mac. "I want to talk to you, Liza, about what's going on in your mind. The other day I saw a look on your face that I have never seen before. You look like you're in love, and I don't think it's with me. Would you mind telling me what's going on?"

"Nothing's going on. I've been happy about the good weather, and work's been going well . . ."

"Come on, the *weather*? Who's the other guy?"

Morgan raised his voice and Liza was afraid he would make a scene.

"There's no other guy," said Liza emphatically. "I have not been seeing anyone, I don't have a boyfriend on the side, no one's sending me flowers or cards, no one is even flirting with me . . . except you."

"I'll be watching. In a little town like this, if you do start to fool around everyone will know about it." He smiled. "One thing's for sure. You'd be out of the church choir in a heartbeat."

"You never did like me joining the choir, did you?"

Randy's response was predictable. "Your job is a wife first, a mother second. When you aren't around to give the kids a bath and put them to bed because you're at choir practice, then no, I don't like you singing in the choir."

"Randy," Liza said with a sigh. "Our children haven't needed me to give them baths for over ten years, and it's not like you haven't been around. You could have pitched in and helped now and then." Before she finished the last sentence she wished she could retrieve it.

"Now it's me," he exclaimed. "You're always trying to blame me for your shortcomings. It's my job to work to keep food on the table and a roof over our heads and clothes on our backs. All I ask of you is to take care of the house."

"And have sex seven nights a week," she whispered, hoping the smile on her face would defuse the tension. But he mistook her comment for a putdown.

"That's your obligation!"

Liza shook her head. "I give up," she said. Then she slid out of the booth, grabbed her tray and walked to the trash bin.

Randy jumped up, grabbed her by the arm and squeezed tightly. "Get back here. I'm not through."

"But I am," she said as she spun out of his grip and headed for the car.

Randy followed her to their pickup truck. "Don't you ever walk away from me when I'm talking to you, do you understand?"

Liza said nothing. More than anything she wanted to awake from what she wished was a bad dream and find herself with Peter.

"You're not listening to me," Randy growled. "I want you to understand something. I love you, Liza, and I expect you to love me in return."

Liza looked at her husband and began to cry. "I'm not sure you know anything about love. You don't know how to be gentle, you don't know how to be tender, you don't know how to be like . . ." She stopped.

"Be like who?" Randy demanded.

"No one."

He reached over and grabbed her chin and pulled her toward her. "Be like who? John? Dale? Max?" He ran down a list of names of men they both knew, mostly men at the church.

"Yes, like all of them!"

He pressed her for more answers as anger rose in both of them. She pushed his hand off her chin.

"Leave me alone and take me home," she said.

Then Randy said the name Liza had hoped he had forgotten. "Peter. Peter Boget. That's who it is, isn't it? This all started when he called you, didn't it? And that's what you were doing today, wasn't it? You were sending a message to Peter Boget on Prodigy, weren't you?"

"No," she said emphatically, glad that he had added the name of the information service the family used and not her friend's CompuServe. But her face was more truthful than her mouth.

"Don't tell me no. It is Peter, isn't it? Isn't it?" His voice grew louder. He reached up and pulled her face to his. "Don't lie to me, Liza. Just tell me."

"What if it was Peter? Why would you care? He's in a hospital bed a thousand miles away from here."

Just hearing her mention another man's name further infuriated an already angry man.

"He's married and has five children and isn't fooling around with anybody."

"If I ever see you with Peter Boget, you're going to be the sorriest woman that ever walked this earth."

*   *   *

Finding Mary's house near Lafayette Park was easy for Hanks once he got the address. It was just a few blocks from where she had outmaneuvered him at Colley and Thirty-eighth in an older residential area near the water.

He parked several blocks away from the home and walked down the street. When he saw the Mercedes in the driveway, he mounted the front stairs and rang the doorbell. When the door opened, Mary Kennedy reached out, grabbed him by the collar and pulled him into the foyer. She slammed the door behind him and pushed him into the living room just off the entry hall. Though shorter and sixty pounds lighter than Hanks, Kennedy had no trouble maneuvering the surprised man into a chair. She sat down on the sofa opposite, crossed her legs, which were concealed in a pair of jeans, and folded her arms over a blue sweatshirt emblazoned with *UVA* in orange letters.

"What are you doing here?" she asked. Her voice was calm, but her face radiated contempt. She started to say something else, but didn't.

Now that he was in her presence, Hanks was unable to speak. She waited.

"I had to see you face to face," he said at last.

"Now you have." She stood up. "It's time to go."

"Wait, I want to know a few things."

"There is nothing for you to know right now. Stay by the phone and wait for my call."

"What about your man?"

"What man?"

"The one you sent this morning."

Kennedy masterfully hid the fact that she had no idea what Hanks was talking about. "Did he give you instructions you don't understand?"

"No, I've done everything he's asked."

"And?"

"I don't like threatening women and children."

"Did you tell him that?"

"Look, I signed on for the money and the action," Hanks said. "I just want to know the team I'm playing on."

"Roland, this is not a game, do you understand? This is business. The last person who asked too many questions—and came to see me despite the fact that I told him not to—won't be asking any more questions and won't be visiting again. Don't let the same thing happen to you."

She walked to the front door and held it open. Hanks stepped onto the front porch and turned around, but Kennedy was already closing the door behind him.

He wanted to hit something or somebody, but he didn't know who or what to strike out against. Instead, he walked to his car, pulled a gun from the glove compartment, and pushed it into his belt. He took his jacket from the passenger seat and put it on to conceal the weapon. Then he walked back in the direction of Kennedy's house.

*   *   *

In the cab of the Morgans' pickup, the air was warm but the atmosphere was frosty. Randy and Liza remained silent throughout the ten-minute trip home from McDonald's. Only after stepping through the kitchen door did Liza speak.

"Oh, Eric," she said apologetically to her youngest who was standing in his baseball uniform with his cleats dangling from two fingers. "I'm sorry. When's your game?"

"Two-thirty."

Liza looked at the clock on the microwave. The blue glowing numbers showed 2:07. "Let's go."

As she turned to go back out the door, Randy stepped through it and said, "You're going to be late for your game, son. You better get a move on."

"Are you coming?" the surprised boy asked expectantly.

"Your mother will take you. I'll be along in a few minutes."

Eric dropped his head and followed his mother out the door. For as long as he could remember, his father would tell the children the same thing whenever their activities would come up: "Your mother will take you. I'll be along in a few minutes." Sometimes he wouldn't show up until the ninth inning, or the last quarter of the football game, or after the curtain dropped on a school play. Sometimes he wouldn't show up at all.

Randy liked his children and was proud of their accomplishments. Randall Jr., known to all his friends as Junior, was a third-year starting pitcher for LSU and a good student majoring in marketing. Amy, who had leading roles in school plays for six years, was also the editor of the high-school yearbook and a strong off-the-bench player for the girls' basketball team. Eric was following in his brother's footsteps with an added interest in music. Both he and his sister played the piano, and he played the trumpet as well.

But the children never seemed to be important enough to warrant Randy's attention. He was always attempting to fix things, taking them apart and never getting around to putting them back together. Or he was piddling with electronic gadgets he'd build or order from offbeat catalogs. The fact that his attitude toward his children contributed to their distance from him eluded him. He figured his kids were being brought up by a woman who was teaching them to disrespect him, so he regularly chided her and spoke sternly to them, ordering them to sit on his lap or give him a hug when he went out in the morning.

Now Eric, still young enough to want his father's support and encouragement, called back through the door, "Dad, I'm the starting pitcher today, if I get there in time. Won't you please hurry and watch me play?"

His father issued a grunt and added, "I'll see what I can do." Then he headed for the laundry room where he stored some of his tools.

*   *   *

When Hanks reached Mary Kennedy's front door a second time he not only rang the doorbell, but pounded on the door as well. When Mary opened it, he pushed her and the door backward.

"I just want you to know that I'm not some wimp you can push around." He pulled from his belt his Smith & Wesson 9mm semi-automatic and held it flat against his chest to let Kennedy gauge the full impact of the silver barrel. A smirk emerged on his face. But his fun was short-lived.

From over his left shoulder an arm reached forward, encircled his neck and bent back, locking his head in place. The cold steel barrel of a gun was pressed into the soft flesh directly under his mouth. Then Mary spoke.

"You are trying my patience, Mr. Hanks. Another screwup like this and you'll be found floating face down in the Elizabeth River." She reached forward and took the gun from his hand and stuffed it back into his belt. In a condescending tone, she added, "Don't get me wrong, I like your spunk. Just keep it focused."

Hanks never saw who held him, but he realized that whoever it was had probably overheard the conversation when he was in the house a few minutes earlier. When the man threw him onto the porch, Hanks didn't turn around. He stood up, walked to his car, and headed back to Maryland.

12

Sunday, April 22

Peace had come to the Boget household Saturday night. Lauren slept through the night, Jonathan was not awakened with nightmares, and, for the first time in more than five weeks, Peter slept soundly in his own bed.

"It's so good to be home," Peter whispered to his wife as morning light brightened their bedroom.

"It's good to have you back."

Peter yawned, threw back the thin cover and sheet, and eased himself out of bed. "Gosh, I'd love to take a shower."

"Three weeks," Elizabeth reminded him, as she slid out of bed and raised the window shades. "Do you want me to run some bath water?"

"No, I just want you to stand there so I can look at you awhile. I've missed seeing you. I mean . . . here, like this."

"You've missed a lot. And if we don't get the kids going, we're going to miss Sunday school."

"Wait," Peter said as Elizabeth was opening the bedroom door. "I'd like to wake the kids." He stepped gingerly across the floor and then, realizing that his leg felt pretty good, strode into the hall.

Knocking on doors, Peter sang out his "Good morning!" It ordinarily had the effect of irritating children who didn't believe anyone should be so joyful so early in the morning. But today David, Daniel and Lauren all greeted their father's voice with a pleasant "Good morning" of their own. Jonathan bolted out of his bedroom and hugged his dad.

Before long the house was filled with commotion as everyone readied for church. Breakfast was interrupted twice by calls, but by nine the family was ready to roll out the door. David was fastening Kristen into her car seat and Lauren was climbing into the back of the family station wagon when the phone rang for a third time. Elizabeth grabbed it and answered with a hurried "Hello."

"I'm calling for Peter Boget."

"Just a minute." Elizabeth covered the mouthpiece and yelled to Peter, who was walking through the door to the garage with Jonathan in tow. "It's for you, Peter."

"Can you get Jonathan in his car seat?" Boget asked his wife. "I'll be there in a minute."

Elizabeth handed Peter the phone and listened to his words as she slowly walked toward the garage.

"Hello?" Peter listened intently for nearly a minute. He concluded the call with a reluctant yes and walked out the door.

"Who was that?" Elizabeth asked as Peter climbed into the passenger seat.

"I don't know."

When Elizabeth turned to look into her husband's face, what she saw frightened her. He had lost his color and his buoyancy, and fear wrinkled his brow. "What's wrong?"

"Nothing."

"It's written all over your face."

"Not now," he said icily. "Let's get going to church." He looked at his watch. "We're going to be late."

*   *   *

Finishing his morning run through his fashionable West End neighborhood, Mike Downes pulled the Sunday paper from the box alongside the driveway. With his golden retriever beside him, he walked to the front porch. He was soaked with sweat but he had over an hour to get ready for church. In the meantime he decided to peruse the news and business sections before taking his shower.

On page two of the Virginia section a headline caught his eye.

FBI Apprehends Suspect in Money Laundering Case

He read the article with keen interest.

FBI agents arrested Mark Randolph, a suspect in a money laundering and cocaine dealing operation. The New York stockbroker was picked up at a Virginia Beach hotel late Saturday and an array of computer equipment was seized.

Randolph is believed to be a link in an alleged scheme allowing cocaine users to pay for drugs through stock transfers to alleged drug kingpin Mary Kennedy, a prominent Norfolk architect.

Kennedy was arrested earlier this week but was released after authorities learned that a key witness against her had died in an auto accident in Mexico. Justice Department sources said Kennedy was linked to the attempted murder of Virginia Bell's public relations director, Peter Boget, who was mistakenly identified as a drug courier.

A spokesman for the Justice Department refused to discuss any of the charges against Randolph or Kennedy, indicating only that the Kennedy investigation was ongoing.

Downes raced to the phone and dialed Peter, but there was no answer.

* * *

After four hours' sleep, Mark Randolph was again being interrogated by FBI agents and federal prosecutor Heather Priddy. But despite his weariness, Randolph maintained a clear head and repeatedly invoked the fifth amendment as he had done repeatedly the night before.

"Let's start again," said Priddy in the spacious, brightly lit interrogation room in the federal courthouse. "You're telling me that you weren't concerned that two dozen of your clients were consistently losing money in the stockmarket."

"It's their money."

"And did you happen to notice that Mary Kennedy was amassing a fortune with a series of incredibly lucky trades?"

"Some people just catch the flow of the market."

"And how do they catch that flow?"

"You watch what's happening and make decisions."

Priddy, who had been sitting across the table from Randolph, stood and walked to a window. "You controlled Mary Kennedy's portfolio."

"I believe Glenn Segal had a significant portion of it."

"And you executed trades outside the company's system."

"That's not possible."

"Then how do you explain the fact that Kennedy has receipts for trades that don't show up in any of your company's records? How do you explain the fact that her four-hundred-thousand-dollar investment has quadrupled at a time when the market has only grown twenty percent? You were manipulating her account so she'd get the money without the company suspecting."

Randolph said nothing.

"You were doing that to pay for cocaine that you then distributed to the clients who were," Priddy held up two fingers on both hands and stroked the air, "quote losing unquote their money on the market. They weren't losing it at all. They were making payments. They were buying cocaine and you were their dealer."

"I have never—wait a minute—I don't want to get caught telling you a lie." Randolph paused. "But it's been almost twenty years since I've touched any illegal substances."

"But you have touched computers, haven't you, Mr. Randolph? In fact, you've become quite a computer expert." She looked for an indication of satisfaction or pride on his face but saw none. "So good that you were able to get inside the Michaels and Trent computers and fool around with the trading program. Now you're down here to get something straight with Mary Kennedy, aren't you? You came here to make sure you got your story straight, didn't you?"

"No, I didn't. I came down here on vacation because the rates at the hotels along the beach are cheap," said Randolph. "Look, I told you I'd talk to you about why I dropped out of sight after Segal was killed—it was because I was afraid. Word is that my friend and coworker is blown up because he's mixed up with drugs."

"When did you find out?"

"I don't remember."

"Are you telling me that someone brings you the news about the death of a close friend, a friend with whom you have a joint investment fund of nearly one million dollars, and you don't remember when you heard it or who told you?"

"I told you I got an anonymous tip."

"By phone? Did someone come to the door? Did you get it over your computer lines? Did someone send something to Mark-the-Shark?" Priddy was fishing, but she needed something.

"I don't know what you're talking about."

"Mark-the-Shark doesn't know what I'm talking about?" Priddy fired back. "The people on the bulletin board said you were the best. I bet you never thought you'd get caught."

"I don't know any Mark-the-Shark," said Randolph emphatically.

"Just one more question, Mr. Randolph." Priddy was trying to get more out of the man before a lawyer intervened and blocked the spontaneity she wanted. "Do you know Matthew Silverman?"

"I believe he's one of my clients."

Priddy returned to the table and sat down opposite Randolph. Two FBI agents remained seated at either end of the dark wood table with the scratched, laminate top.

"Matthew Silverman lost fifty thousand dollars on stock trades in just three months, and you churned his account so much that you collected over twenty-five thousand in commissions."

Priddy's voice was rising, but Randolph remained calm. He had been arrested numerous times during his days as an activist in the peace movement and had learned to remain in control no matter how much pressure the police brought to bear on him. Compared with some of the run-ins with the law that he'd had over two decades earlier, Priddy didn't phase him.

"He was arrested in New York when one of your boys tried to make a delivery."

Randolph said nothing.

"Mr. Silverman said that you ruined him and that he would do anything to see you hanged."

"Have you ever met Matthew Silverman?"

"No," Priddy admitted.

"The man's brains have been scrambled. I'm not surprised he's mixed up in drugs, he seemed to be on them perpetually. You do know that I filed a letter with the company pointing out that Mr. Silverman's trading requests were so bizarre that I would not take responsibility for the losses he was incurring because of raw stupidity. If you've done your homework you also found notations in his file that I routinely advised him against making trades that I knew would cost him money." Randolph leaned back in his chair, folded his arms and announced, "Case closed."

Priddy had been given the file on Silverman that contained the notations Randolph mentioned, but the investigator from the Securities Exchange Commission had found similar letters and notations in the files of each of the clients that was "losing" money. Every person who was contacted, except Silverman, acknowledged receiving letters from Randolph or Segal disclaiming responsibility for losses incurred through reckless trading. The investment counselors had covered their tracks extremely well. Priddy pressed on, looking for a break.

"Why do you go by 'Mark-the-Shark' on the RSC bulletin board?"

"I don't know what you're talking about."

"Do you know Hack Attack? Peter Boget? He says he knows you and is willing to testify that you bragged about getting into the Michaels and Trent computer. Do you want to tell me about it?"

"Actually, I want some sleep. And the next time I talk to you, it will be after I've spoken with a lawyer."

Priddy was out of ammunition.

*   *   *

Mary Kennedy wasn't taking any chances, not with Randolph in custody. She reached Patrick O'Hearn in a Long Island motel a few miles from JFK Airport.

"Randolph's been picked up. We go with phase two today."

"Ma'am," replied the Irishman, who was nearly back to normal after receiving a chest full of lead at the hospital shootout in Maryland. "I can't be ready until tomorrow."

"Today. It's got to be today."

After she hung up, she reviewed some of her papers, then called British Airways and changed her reservations for a seat on the evening flight from New York to London's Heathrow. She then called back and reserved the seat next to hers in the name of Paddy McKee. Then she went into a closet off her bedroom, pushed aside hanging clothes, and opened the safe built into the wall. She removed the duplicate passport she had purchased from a man who specialized in forged documents for IRA operatives.

*   *   *

At 10:50 a.m. FBI agents Giddings and Middleton arrived at the crowded parking lot of Lakeside Community Church. Middleton, who was behind the wheel, drove the white sedan directly to the handicapped parking space next to the walkway that led to the church's front door.

A light breeze was blowing across the 1,800 acre crescent-shaped lake that was dotted with sailboats crisscrossing the rippled blue water. The moist air filtered through the dogwood and large oak and pine trees and drifted across the parking lot, cooling the churchgoers chatting outside the worship complex.

Though dressed in suits and ties, the two law enforcement officers attracted attention. Giddings's dark skin was in stark contrast to that of most of the men, women and children getting ready to enter the sanctuary. But it was more than his skin color that attracted attention to Giddings. His hulking frame strained to be released from the confines of his suit. Middleton was smaller, but not by much.

Peter Boget was talking with a group of friends in the lobby when Giddings and Middleton entered the modern building. Both Peter and Elizabeth looked up immediately.

"Mr. Boget, we're sorry to interrupt you just before church, but we need to talk with you right away," said Giddings, scanning the lobby for some privacy.

Peter recoiled. Elizabeth looked perplexed. "What's going on?" she asked with trepidation.

"Perhaps an empty classroom," Giddings suggested.

Boget, with his wife by his side, led the two agents into a vacant Sunday-school classroom, closed the door and sat down.

Giddings spoke first. "We've picked up Mark Randolph."

"I know."

Elizabeth glared at her husband for not disclosing that information to her.

With Boget offering nothing more, Giddings continued. "We'd like you to talk with the prosecutor in Norfolk. She's been interrogating Randolph and needs more specifics on the computer transactions you talked to us about on Wednesday."

"Can't this wait until tomorrow?"

"I'm afraid not. Would you be willing to talk with her on the phone right now?"

"Do I have a choice?"

"Yes," Middleton broke in, "you do, but this may be the breakthrough we're looking for. We don't want to blow it."

"I'm sorry, I can't."

Giddings ignored Peter's response. "Is there a phone in the church we can use? If not we can go out to the car."

"I just told you I can't."

"Why not?"

Peter looked at Elizabeth, then Middleton and finally Giddings. "I'd rather not say."

"Who reached you?" asked Middleton.

"I don't know, but he said it would be in the best interest of my family if I didn't cooperate in the investigation of Mark Randolph."

Elizabeth knew the morning's conversation was bad, but had no idea how bad it was. She reached out with one hand and placed it lightly on Peter's thigh. She put the other hand on her forehead.

"If we offer to take care of the family, will you help us? I know how much putting Mary Kennedy out of business means to you," Giddings said. "This could be the break we need to do just that."

Boget asked for some time to think it over. Elizabeth and the two FBI agents left the room. Once in the hallway, Elizabeth asked one friend to find her children and bring them to the classroom and another to find the McGuires.

A few minutes after eleven, the Boget family, along with Bill and Joyce McGuire, huddled in the middle of the bright classroom to pray and discuss options. When they finished, Bill McGuire opened the door and invited the two FBI agents back into the room. The pastor, who on any other Sunday would be in front of the congregation, was, instead, with them.

Peter spoke first. "How will you protect my family?"

"I've just talked with the prosecutor and with the marshal's office. We can take them to a safe house today or post guards at your home."

Color drained from Peter's face as tension tightened the muscles in his back and neck. His eyes looked deeply into the face of his wife, and then one by one into those of each of his children. Then he asked all but

Elizabeth and Giddings to leave the room. When the room was empty he said, "I'll try to help you, under one condition. Nobody but those here in this room know what I'm doing, and I'm not asked to testify. All I can do is show you what I found. I can't—I *won't*—put my family at any greater risk than they are in now."

"I understand."

From the pastor's study, Boget spoke by telephone with Heather Priddy.

"Mr. Boget, I'll understand if you say no, but I'd like you to consider saying yes to my next request."

He didn't respond.

"Will you bring that evidence down here—today—along with whatever it takes to access those bulletin boards? I think I would understand this all better if I could see it. I also have a computer expert flying in this afternoon who's worked on this case in New York. I'd like you to explain your findings to her as well."

Peter cupped the phone and looked at his wife. "She wants to see what I have."

Her eyes said no, but her mouth issued a reluctant "Is it necessary?"

"I think so," he said glumly.

Elizabeth sighed. "Why are we in so deep?"

"I don't know, but I think this will go a long way toward getting us out."

"I know," she said, nodding her head slowly. "I know."

Boget removed his hand from the mouthpiece. "May I bring a friend?"

"Sure, if you would like."

"Okay."

"Good. Let me talk with Agent Giddings."

Thirty minutes later, Peter Boget said goodbye to his family outside their home and climbed into the front seat of the agents' car, beside Middleton. Two U.S. marshals stood with the family in the driveway.

Giddings looked out from the back seat at Elizabeth. "We'll have him home this evening," he said.

*   *   *

Sunday was always Liza Morgan's favorite day—even when she had to work, though days off were infinitely better. She was brought up in church and always felt a special closeness to God on the first day of the week, worshiping in his sanctuary.

Her morning started as most nonworking Sunday mornings did, with a quiet time before anyone else awoke. She then rode her bike to the beach to sit and listen to God's creation in the ripple of the water on the sandy shore, the squeal of the gulls diving for fish and the whisper of the wind as it danced through the sprawling live oaks that lined Beach Boulevard. She mostly gazed across the placid blue-gray water dotted with fishing boats and an occasional pleasure craft. But sometimes she'd turn back toward the road and admire the majestic trees that had stood for so many years as the first line of defense against the tropical storms that plied the gulf. She loved to watch the gentle swaying of the lacy sashes of Spanish moss that cascaded from the oaks' sinewy branches.

Upon returning from her brief sojourn to solitude, she awakened Eric and Amy, turned on the coffeemaker, and slid bagel halves into the toaster oven. She entered the tiny bathroom off the master bedroom, showered quickly and dressed. Back in the kitchen she started the toaster oven and waited for the bagels while she poured her coffee. Her children were already dressed and eating cereal at the kitchen table.

No one mentioned Randy. He would rarely drive with the family to Sunday school at the First Baptist Church in Bay St. Louis. More often he would arrive for the morning worship service, entering the sanctuary after the service had begun. Liza assumed that was his way of avoiding discussion with people at the church. Whatever the reason, his late arrivals were a source of embarrassment for the family.

This morning he was true to form. In the middle of the choir anthem, ignoring the ushers' request to wait until the music was completed, Randy Morgan walked through the doors of the former military chapel, sauntered down the green-carpeted center aisle, and sat down in the second row from the front.

Liza wanted to become invisible. In midverse she closed her eyes and asked God to forgive her for the thoughts she was having; if they came true, her husband would be dead.

As she prayed, she realized that Randy was not the only man on her mind. Looking out over the congregation, drenched in the golden glow of sunlight filtering through the church's yellow windows, she imagined that Peter was sitting among the members, that he had come to hear her sing once again and to take her forever away from Randy: to take her back to where they had fallen in love. As she sang, the words flowed out of her mouth, but the worship wasn't there. She heard not one word of the sermon. By the time church was over, she was emotionally drained.

"You sang good today, honey," Randy said when he caught up with her outside the sanctuary. She was walking under a covered breezeway toward the choir room in another building.

She answered curtly. "Too bad you didn't get here in time to hear the whole thing."

Randy followed close behind her. "Why don't you give me credit for just getting to church? That's what you want, isn't it?"

Liza stopped and stepped out onto the grass to let people pass. "You don't come to worship God. You come to hear just enough of the sermon to find something new to use against me. You come to make sure I don't talk with another man. You come to embarrass your children. As much as I'd love to have you here worshiping by my side, I wish you'd just stay home rather than continuing the charade of being a good Christian father. This was a wonderful day until you disrupted the whole service by coming in twenty minutes late." She turned and walked into the choir room. Before she took off her robe, she stepped back out. Randy was still standing on the lawn.

"Let me tell you something," she said. "If you really loved me, you'd change your ways. You'd make Sunday morning a good family time, not a time of Mom plus the kids versus Dad. You'd give me more latitude to talk with the people here at church and develop deeper friendships."

"You've already got lots of friends."

"But *we* don't have friends," she stressed as she continued to talk to her husband in hushed tones. "You never want anyone to come to visit us. When we do have company, you act like our guests have leprosy."

Randy peered into Liza's face. "This isn't about church or about friends or about people coming over, is it? You don't really want me to change; you want me to get out of your life so you can find someone else. No, you've already found someone else, haven't you? And everything I do reminds you that I don't measure up to this standard of yours. Isn't that right?" Anger was filling his voice. "I've figured this all out. You're in love with another man and you're looking at all my faults to justify your thoughts and actions. Well, let me tell you, you ought to be listening to your preacher. He says that adultery isn't just getting into bed with someone else, it's lusting after them in your heart. From what I've seen on your face this week, I know you're lusting after someone and it isn't me." He was surly, but still in control. "Right here and right now I want you to promise me you'll be faithful to me for the rest of your life, that you'll never, ever think about another man, and that you'll stop complaining about my shortcomings and start appreciating all that I do to keep a roof over this family and food on the table."

Liza didn't know how to respond. She was confused. She knew all the biblical passages on adultery but wondered if God really meant her to have to go through life with a man who inflicted so much pain on her and her children. She also knew Randy wouldn't touch her in public, but that the current argument would be continued out of view of the churchgoers—and a slap or a punch might punctuate the discussion. She turned away and headed for the choir room.

Liza's failure to answer her husband spoke as much to Randy as if she had said Peter's name. He went uncommonly silent. Then redness rose along his neck and his eyes widened as his mind fit together the pieces of a puzzle he had been trying to assemble for days. The phone call wasn't long distance; it was local, he believed. The call came on Liza's day off—the man had to have known. It wasn't to tell the story of something that happened in Virginia, Randy thought, it was an invitation for a rendezvous. The look on Liza's face had been the look of someone who had just been with her lover. Her refusal of him in bed. Her defiance. It all added up to one thing: Liza was having an affair with Peter Boget.

His instinct was to find and destroy the man, but the only target nearby was his wife.

Randy Morgan went ballistic. He stepped forward and spun Liza around by her arm. Heads turned to observe the conflict.

"Peter Boget!" he shouted. "That's it. You've been screwing around with Peter Boget." Liza felt like shriveling up and dying. She tried to say no, but he held her so tightly she couldn't make her mouth form the word. By the time he finished saying the name a second time his entire face was red and his eyes were wide with anger. With a jerk, he released her and headed for his truck.

Liza stood on the lawn, her choir robe still covering her bright green dress. Her eyes filled with tears as she hung her head and walked toward the choir room. She tripped on the threshold of the door and tumbled to her knees. Bursting into tears, she pulled herself up into a chair, whispering, "I've never been with Peter Boget. I've never been unfaithful to Randy."

Liza's words were true, but not truthful. In her heart she was emotionally estranged from her husband—and had been for most of their married life. She stayed in the relationship out of fear, and because she believed in keeping the commitment she had made to Randy on their wedding day. But now someone else had returned to her life, someone she had lost and found again.

As she thought back to the moment when she had stood in her kitchen with her wet hair, listening to that wonderfully raspy voice on the phone, she heard over and over in her mind the words Peter had spoken. In that moment, she began to see the world from a new perspective. Her very existence had taken on new meaning. In the nine days since his call, she had begun to see how easy it was to let go of deeply held beliefs, to start imagining a world unencumbered by a husband who treated her like a second-class citizen . . . to start believing that some day, in some way, she could begin a new life with Peter Boget.

*   *   *

Mary Kennedy packed quickly, loaded her car, and drove to a warehouse along the Elizabeth River. The industrial area was deserted, and no one observed her driving her Mercedes into the warehouse. She pulled out in a white van and headed to a shopping center on Military Highway. There she planned to wait in a Chinese restaurant until her flight time drew closer.

*   *   *

Agent Middleton exited from Richmond's downtown expressway and pulled up alongside the city parking garage at Ninth Street. Mike Downes was standing by the curb and climbed into the back seat next to Giddings. Before the greetings were completed, Middleton was back on the expressway for the run to Norfolk.

Giddings felt uncomfortable sitting beside the man he had arrested earlier in the week, but he decided to make the most of it. "So, Mr. Downes, how are you doing?" he asked.

"I would be better if I didn't have to worry about how much it's going to cost me to defend myself in court." Downes then directed his comments toward the front seat. "How are you, Peter?"

"If you want to know, I'm sore. Real sore. When was the last time you had twenty-seven staples taken out of your chest? Let me tell you, it's not pleasant."

"Why did you want me along—besides for the moral support?"

"I want you to see what I tell these people, so you can tell the boys in Washington that I'm not some criminal bent on stealing telephone service, like Mazzetti tries to make out."

"Hopefully, Mazzetti's days are numbered. Earl is doing much better," Downes said. "I talked with him on the phone last night. He's still weak, but fighting to get back. The next few days will tell a lot."

13

Sunday, April 22

I n a Holiday Inn east of JFK Airport, Patrick O'Hearn faced his team from one of the two chairs in his room. Paddy McKee, who shared the room with him, sat in the other. Liam O'Donnell and Eileen Adams sat on one of the beds with Kathleen McKenna. Billy McMillan was perched on the low dresser next to the TV.

"Phase two goes today," Patrick O'Hearn informed his surprised team members. "We were spared our primary mission of springing Mary from jail. But a key witness has been picked up, and to be safe we need to get Mary out of the country tonight. She'll be trading places with Kathleen, who will pose as Mary on the British Air flight to Heathrow at 7:30. Mary will fly as Kathleen on an American Airlines flight at 8:10. Since the U.S. government has pulled her passport, we don't think anyone will be looking too closely for Mary at the airport. If they do, Kathleen's diversion should take care of the problem long enough for Mary to still get out. Let me show you what we'll be doing to ensure the switch goes smoothly." After detailing the plan, O'Hearn sent Kathleen McKenna to get food for the group.

A half mile from the hotel, McKenna pulled her van into a gas station, walked to a pay phone and placed a call. For nearly three minutes she waited, furtively watching. Finally, the man who had first answered the phone came on again. "Lieutenant Ryan will be with you in one minute."

McKenna was sweating. A car that resembled McKee's rental car was coming from the direction of the hotel, moving slower than the other cars. She knew she would never be able to explain what she was doing at a phone. She couldn't wait for Ryan. She spoke quickly into the phone. "Tell him I'm trading places with Mary Kennedy. She'll be leaving New York on an American Airlines flight to London at 8:10." Before she hung up she realized her call had been swallowed by the electronic "hold" of the telephone system in a British army barracks in Northern Ireland.

The car McKenna was eyeing pulled into the gas station. But bright sky reflecting off the windshield prevented her from seeing who was sitting behind the wheel. As unobtrusively as possible, she slipped away from the walk-up phone and climbed into the passenger-side door of the van. Just as she did, the driver of the car opened the door and stepped to the concrete next to the gas pump. It was no one she knew.

McKenna slid behind the wheel and drove out of the gas station.

*   *   *

Agent Middleton had a heavy foot, and less than two hours after he had left the Boget household he was exiting from Interstate 64 onto Norview Avenue heading to Norfolk's airport. "This should only take five minutes," he said.

The agents were asked to pick up new evidence that had been flown from Baltimore and to bring it to the Federal Building on their way in.

Driving west on Norview, Middleton had to stop for the traffic signal at Military Highway. When the light turned green he proceeded through the intersection, barely noticing the white van waiting to turn from Military Highway onto Norview. But the driver of the van noticed Middleton's car— she had an eye for cop cars, even unmarked ones—and she certainly noticed the passenger sitting in the front seat.

By the time Mary Kennedy was able to make her turn, the car was too far ahead for her to see. But when she reached the terminal she saw it again, noticing a large black man emerge from the back seat and enter the terminal. She drove past the car slowly but could only see the driver and the man in the seat directly behind him. What she saw convinced her she was looking at a car containing two of the men she had last seen in the Maryland hospital—Barry Whitehead and the man who had been standing next to him. She circled into the parking lot and waited until the car departed. Then she walked into the terminal and called Hanks.

"I thought you told me that you took care of Whitehead." Her tone was harsh.

"I did," he boasted indignantly. "Why do you—"

"Then explain why the cops have him."

"The cops don't have him—he's dead!"

"I just saw him."

"Maybe you saw someone who looks like him. Maybe you just saw Boget."

She considered the possibility. "You figure out who it is and do it fast. I need to know why he's here in Norfolk. I'll call you back in fifteen minutes."

* * *

When Kathleen McKenna carried in lunch, O'Hearn was hanging up the phone.

"Everything's set. But I've been advised that the ticket agents study passport photos very closely, so while you'll be flying as Mary, she'll personally check in at the counter. You'll do the same for her at American Airlines." O'Hearn spoke with the knowledge and authority of a seasoned veteran. McKenna listened intently and nodded her understanding. O'Hearn pulled a plastic ziplock freezer bag from a suitcase and handed it to her.

"Here's five hundred American dollars," he said. "If you're picked up you tell the officials that this money was given to you by Mary Kennedy to take her place on this flight. Mary's fingerprints are on the bills. You may need that proof, so don't handle the bills until you get home."

* * *

"I'm calling for Peter Boget," Hanks said, trying to disguise his voice in case Elizabeth or Peter were listening in. "Is he there?"

"My father is resting right now," David Boget said. "May I take a message?"

"No," Hanks said, surprised. "I'll call back later."

When the teenager hung up the phone, one of the two marshals standing beside him smiled. "Good job, son. That was probably nothing, but we can't be too careful."

*   *   *

Heather Priddy, who had a distracting habit of pushing against the bridge of her glasses, and Dawn Early, the computer whiz from New York, watched studiously as Peter Boget displayed and explained his electronic files. They confirmed several of Early's findings at the offices of Michaels and Trent.

"So that's why you think Mark Randolph is Mark-the-Shark?" said Priddy.

"Is there any doubt?" Peter said, trying to mask his weariness.

Downes piped in. "I thought Mazzetti destroyed all those files."

"He did, sort of. Before he trashed these files in my computer at work he encrypted them. I got Marge to recover them from the hard disk and I decrypted them."

Peter was beaming with self-satisfaction, and this kind of exuberance was one of the things Downes disliked about his friend. Though it was often couched in humor, it was one of two traits that most often would get Peter into trouble with coworkers. His exuberance looked to some like arrogance, and his lack of humility could be irritating. The other trait that rankled Downes was Peter's frequent testing of boundaries. That was what nearly got Peter fired in the first place. It also was what had put Peter's continued employment with Virginia Bell in question. And now it was on display too.

"I got lucky on the decryption," Peter said, smiling. "Frank—can you believe it—used the same password he uses on his company electronic mail."

Mike stared incredulously at his friend. "You know Frank Mazzetti's password?"

"How do you think I found out what he was up to?"

Downes retained his seriousness. "Have you been reading Frank Mazzetti's e-mail?"

"Yes," Peter said without remorse.

"But that's in violation of company policy."

"It's against company policy now, but it wasn't ten days ago," Boget said. "Don't you read the updates that are made to the executive instructions?"

"Of course not, no one has time to read all that stuff."

"I do! A year and a half ago, buried in twenty-five pages of updates was the addition of one sentence to the subsection on electronic mail. After the sentence that forbids one employee from accessing another's e-mail without written consent—like I give Marge when I'm away—this was added, 'unless such access is required to investigate illegal activity or the misuse of company property,' or something like that. I figured that Mazzetti got the wording changed so that he could have the cover of executive instructions for all his snooping." With a shrug of his shoulder and a smirk on his face, Peter added, "I figured that if Mazzetti was up to no good—and I had it on very good authority from within his own organization that that was the case—then Instruction 46.13.5b gave me the license to investigate him. That's what he found out when he broke into my computer the night before Easter. He discovered that I had some of his e-mail. That's what I didn't want anyone to learn because the raw data, out of context, made Mazzetti look real bad. But I didn't have anything verified. That's why I went to my office to get that out of the computer."

"Why didn't you tell me before?" Mike asked.

"I did, sort of, when I tipped you off to the dirt he had fabricated on Earl Hendrick. But I couldn't tell you everything since the new executive instruction was back dated to the first of March—placing me in violation, retroactively, and ensuring my firing."

The two men had become so engrossed in the discussion of company security matters they became oblivious to the others in the room.

The prosecutor interrupted. "Mr. Boget, I'm going to let you and Dawn Early here discuss your work in more depth a little later. But before I do, I want to know if you would like to meet Mr. Randolph."

The request caught Peter off guard. "Are you kidding? I've got a family to worry about. I'm not even supposed to be here, remember?"

"I thought maybe you could say something that would help, because he's not talking to us at all. Miss Early will be studying the computer we brought from his hotel room, and that'll probably yield some useful information, but . . ."

As he listened to the prosecutor, Mike Downes studied his friend. Then he turned and looked up at Priddy. "How about if I go in? I've been involved since day one."

The tired prosecutor stood up. "Come with me, Mr. Downes."

Giddings and Middleton stayed seated at the gray, steel table on which Peter's Macintosh PowerBook opened a huge window on Mark Randolph's world.

"Oh, Mike, did I tell you?" Boget called out. "He was a big antiwar activist when you were in Vietnam."

Downes looked back from the doorway in surprise. "Great, now you tell me."

Across the hall, Downes and Priddy entered the interrogation room. It was easy to guess which of the four men seated at the table was Randolph.

Priddy kept the introductions short. Then she spoke to Randolph, who was now flanked by a lawyer. "You've been talking with Mr. Boget. I thought you'd like to meet a friend of his."

Downes extended his hand. "I'm sorry we have to meet like this." Randolph tried to smile but it wouldn't come. Mike continued. "I don't know what these people want to do to you, but I have no quarrel with you. In fact, I have enough of my own troubles; I don't need to be involved in yours. But, to be honest, I am involved: I was arrested earlier this week for helping Barry Whitehead leave the country."

Randolph raised his eyebrows.

"I know that you have access to Mary Kennedy and that she's behind an awful lot of what's happened to my friend, Peter Boget, and his family. That man is scarred for the rest of his life because of you and your drug delivery that never made it."

"Wait a minute," interrupted Randolph's lawyer, who had arrived only an hour before the man from Richmond. He looked at Priddy. "I thought you said he might have something to say to my client that might be helpful. He has no right making these accusations." Downes pulled off his tie, unbuttoned his shirt and pulled it down over his shoulder to expose a bright pink scar. "The hole in Peter's leg and this one under my arm will forever remind us that Mary Kennedy will stop at nothing to silence those who know something that could hurt her. I don't know what you've said or what you're going to say, but as long as she's out there you'll never be able to walk down the street without hearing footsteps. You'll never be able to go to bed without worrying that you won't be waking up in the morning."

The lawyer interrupted again, but Randolph waved him off. "She is a client of mine. I'd like to hear what he has to say about her."

Downes buttoned his shirt. "Barry Whitehead is dead. Your friend, what's-his-name, is dead. Four Maryland state troopers are dead. A family has been subjected to an act of terror that no family should be subjected to and, even now, they are being threatened by this woman."

Randolph shifted his glance from Downes to the table and back again.

Downes took a handkerchief from his pocket, wiped his face and then continued. "I know you marched in antiwar rallies while I slogged through the jungles of Vietnam."

Randolph and his lawyer frowned at Mike's comment, as if he had no right knowing that about Randolph.

Downes continued. "But that was long ago, and from my perspective I see our country far worse off today than it was back then. At least then we had some sense that what we were doing was good for America and the people who lived here. But not anymore. Now it seems like most of us are in it just for ourselves. We've got the guys hustling to make a buck and the punks trying to take it away. Even if Mary Kennedy's ideals are noble, which I seriously doubt, her methods are those of a punk. She doesn't respect life. She doesn't care about people. She's a piranha, and you and me should be doing whatever it takes to put her out of commission before she sinks her teeth into her next victim." Downes paused long enough to collect his thoughts and concluded, "I pray that the Boget family or I or even you aren't hurt in the process."

Randolph looked into Downes's face and started to say something. Then he stopped. Downes turned toward Priddy beside him and said, "I think it's time to go. Is there anything else?"

"No, Mr. Downes. Thank you for coming."

*   *   *

At 5:15 Mary Kennedy and Paddy McKee walked into the British Airways terminal. It was busy and few people took notice of the couple walking to the baggage-check line. McKee was dressed in dark slacks, a white knit shirt and a tweed jacket. Over her simple black dress Kennedy wore a gray raincoat. A floppy hat made out of the same gray material as her coat concealed most of her red hair. After a thirty-minute wait, an attendant checked her bags, reviewed her passport and issued her boarding pass. McKee was checked next and both walked together through the long tunnel-like corridor that connected the ticketing and baggage-check area to the gates.

Halfway up the tunnel, Eileen Adams discreetly fell into step alongside

Kennedy, caught her glance, and walked ahead toward the women's rest-room. Kennedy followed her in and waited until the next-to-last stall was vacant. With Eileen idling just outside, Kathleen McKenna and Mary Kennedy exchanged outer garments just as they had done an hour earlier at the American Airlines terminal where they ran the same drill. After they emerged from the stalls, they stared at each other's reflection in the mirror above the sinks and laughed. Though similar in appearance, the two pro-jected two different images. McKenna had little of Kennedy's sophistication, and the latter lacked the toughness etched into McKenna's face. That dif-ference might go unnoticed to the casual observer, but not to someone accustomed to checking passports. That's why Kennedy had taken such precautions to have a face match the photo.

McKenna walked out of the restroom first. McKee was waiting for her. Kathleen had to make another telephone call, but knew she couldn't pull it off. She and McKee walked to the gate and sat down for the fifteen-minute wait until boarding.

Kennedy and Adams slipped out of the restroom and disappeared into the mass of travelers coming through the tunnel. They crossed the lobby, exited the building, and spied a taxi driver unloading a passenger. They climbed into the empty cab. The driver stuck his head in the door and, sounding like a standup comic imitating Archie Bunker, said, "Hey yous gals, you can't do dis. You gotta go downstairs to get a hack. You'll get me in trouble doing dis."

Kennedy flashed a hundred.

"You know how much that medallion costs?" the indignant man said, pointing to the metal tag that gave him the right to operate a taxi in the city.

"Shut up and drive," snapped Kennedy, pressing the bill into his hand.

*   *   *

By the time Peter Boget arrived home he was exhausted, mentally and physically. He spent a few minutes talking with the children and Elizabeth, who were assembled at the dinner table. Without bothering to eat, Peter moved to a recliner in the family room and Elizabeth joined him, sitting nearby on the arm of the sofa.

"You got several calls," Elizabeth said. "Everybody wants to see how

SUNDAY, APRIL 22 ☐ *157*

you're doing. We just told people you were sleeping."

"And the marshals?"

"One will stay the night, another will come in the morning. They don't expect anything, but they want to be prepared."

"Good. Tomorrow will be a better day, I'm sure." Peter tried to assuage her fears. "But right now, I'm exhausted." Peter closed his eyes and fell into a deep sleep.

*　　*　　*

Once past the boarding gate, McKenna breathed a little easier. She had expected to go on with the team and find out what else they might be up to, but was not unhappy about going home. She understood her role in the switch with Kennedy and was relieved that her affiliation with the British Army continued to go undetected.

McKenna enjoyed Paddy McKee's friendly banter while the plane filled with passengers. She also liked the view from her window seat where she could watch the daylight slip away as container after container of luggage was loaded into the 747's cavernous hold.

"Would you like a mint?" McKee asked as he pulled a tin of Altoids from his jacket pocket.

"Thanks," she said.

McKee stood up, removed his jacket, and began placing it in the overhead bin. Suddenly he grimaced and grabbed his back.

"You okay?" McKenna asked.

"It's my back," he said in a pained whisper. "This happens now and then," he explained, moaning as a stewardess arrived on the scene.

"Are you all right?" the stewardess asked.

"No," McKee said, "I don't think I can sit down."

"But you'll have to, we're ready to leave."

"Ma'am," he said, "there's no way I can sit on a plane for six hours in pain like this."

"Do you want to get off?"

"No, I've got to get to London."

A steward and a ground attendant approached McKee.

"I'm afraid you'll have to be seated or come with us off the plane," the ground attendant said. "We're already late."

McKee wanted to make sure that McKenna did nothing and said nothing that might suggest they were traveling together. "I'm glad to have made your acquaintance," he said, gritting his teeth. "Perhaps we'll meet again, Ms. . . . ?"

"Kennedy. Mary Kennedy," she said.

Hunched over with one hand on his hip and another holding his jacket, McKee gingerly shuffled off the plane.

A perplexed McKenna turned back to the window. The last traces of dusk dropped behind the New York skyline as the 747 lifted off the runway. It climbed steeply over Sheepshead Bay and banked left over the Atlantic, heading toward England. McKenna briefly enjoyed the silhouette of the city but soon was looking out onto the blackness of the ocean. An uneasiness tightened her chest. She turned off her overhead light and stared out into the night. The flashing light on the wing's tip had a hypnotic effect on her, and she was soon dozing off.

*   *   *

Elizabeth shook her husband awake. "Do you want to take a call?"

He nodded sleepily. She handed him the cordless phone. The marshal was on the extension in the upstairs rec room.

"You just don't get it, do you?"

"Who is this?" said Peter, suddenly very awake.

"You were told to stay away from Mark Randolph."

Before Boget could respond, the line went dead.

Marshal Ed Costen flew down the steps and into the kitchen. Peter had already dialed in the code to trace the call. The Caller ID display on the desk in the kitchen indicated that the call had come from a phone that was not equipped with number identification equipment.

Costen looked at Peter, then at Elizabeth. "I'm not taking any chances. With four entrances, and all these windows, this house is indefensible. I'd like to move you."

*   *   *

In a quiet cove along the shoreline of Virginia's Northumberland County, a few miles north and east of Kilmarnock, Norm Worthington was checking his anchor and securing his yacht for a night on the Chesapeake Bay. His wife, Carol, was in the cabin below making a fresh pot of coffee and warming some doughnuts in the microwave. In the dark water a rectangular object reflected the beam from his flashlight.

"Hey, Carol," he called to his wife. "Look at this."

She climbed the three aluminum steps and moved to her husband's side at the stern of their forty-foot sailboat. She followed the beam of light to where it pierced the surface of the murky water, illuminating what looked like a small suitcase. "What d'ya bet it's drugs?" she said.

"That's what I'm thinking," said the thirty-five-year-old dentist in a hushed voice. "Or money. Do you think we should get it?"

"Of course," Carol said in a whisper, knowing how sound carries across still waters. "Doesn't look like there's anyone around."

Norm peered into the darkness along the shore then handed the flashlight to his wife. "Let me get something to pull it in."

Within forty-five seconds they had the metal attaché on board. Like two kids who found a lost wallet, they scurried below deck. Carol pulled the curtains over the cabin windows while Norm wiped the container dry. Together they flipped open both latches.

"It's not locked," said Norm, stating the obvious. He carefully lifted the lid. Much to their disappointment the case contained neither drugs nor money.

"Just papers," Carol wagged her head and laughed.

"And this," said Norm as he lifted a liquid-filled test tube to the light.

*   *   *

The British Airways 747 gently banked to the left on a heading that would take it across the western tip of Long Island, up along the Atlantic coast toward Newfoundland and then on to Ireland and England beyond.

In the baggage compartment immediately below seat 38K, six pounds of plastic explosive were attached to a pressure-sensitive detonation device. As the plane climbed through 18,000 feet the pressure switch closed and twelve volts of electricity surged through the blasting cap encased in the explosive. The force of the blast tore a fourteen-foot hole in the side of the airplane just above the left wing. It ripped apart hydraulic and electrical lines and shredded the floor beneath Kathleen McKenna.

For the dozing woman, the end came quickly.

*   *   *

In their suite at the Hyatt in Richmond's West End, the Boget family sat transfixed as CNN reporter Holly Jacobson described the incident. The correspondent stood on the beach with dozens of flashing red and blue lights creating an eerie backdrop. Beyond the lights was the huge airplane lying on its belly in the sand, its tail towering above the gently breaking waves. It was bathed in the blue-white glow of halogen spotlights. Except for the gaping hole just above the wing, the aircraft looked to be intact, if out of place, on the Long Island beach two miles short of the Suffolk County Airport.

"We still don't have word on what caused the explosion," said Jacobson, "but we do know that six officers of the British Army who had just finished teaching a seminar on handling urban terrorists were on the plane. Two of them are among the missing, and one is dead. We understand that 244 passengers and crew are now accounted for. Four are confirmed dead and six are missing."

The camera pulled back to show a man wrapped in a blanket standing next to the reporter. "I have with me Reggie Keckering, who was near the back of the plane when the explosion occurred." She turned to the man who, though shaken, was not injured. "Can you describe what happened?"

The man spoke quickly in a British accent. "One minute I was sitting quietly reading a book, the next minute a roar filled the plane and it shuddered violently. I was thrown into the seat in front of me and then backward as the plane pitched forward. That's when the smoke hit us, and I figured we were goners.

"I was in the middle of the center group of seats and couldn't see much. There was a wall separating our section from the one where the explosion happened, but everyone was screaming and everything started flying around. I pulled my seatbelt as tight as I could, bent over and started praying.

"The crew members told us the pilot was going to try to get us to an airport and for us to remain calm." The man chuckled. "It's hard to stay calm when your life is flashing before your eyes. Then for what seemed like forever, we were dropping out of the sky. There was lots of screaming and some smoke, but not much. I was sitting near the back of the plane, and what we got was the smoke and cold air. Then a voice on the speaker told us to prepare for impact, and the next thing I knew, we were bouncing along the ocean. I thought that we were going to have to jump out into water."

The man talked excitedly. "We bounced along and then heard a terrible grinding sound, and then we were sliding down emergency landing chutes into the surf. We just walked up onto the beach. It was a miracle. It really was. I was never so scared in all my life. I never thought we'd make it."

The Bogets watched for nearly an hour as other survivors recounted the harrowing ordeal. The best stories of heroism came from those closest to the blast site, where passengers and crew members risked their lives to pull passengers from seats that eventually fell from the plane and to extinguish flames that reached luggage and passenger belongings in overhead bins.

Finally, Peter turned off the television and led the family in prayer before he and Elizabeth tucked the children into their beds. David and Lauren understood the threats the family had received; the younger children did not. For Daniel and Jonathan the unexpected trip to a motel was more like vacation than protection. The two had little trouble getting to sleep once Elizabeth drew up their covers and extinguished the lights.

14

Monday, April 23

Peter fell asleep from sheer exhaustion while Elizabeth stirred restlessly. In their two-bedroom suite, David and Daniel shared one room, Kristin slept in a crib in her parents' room, and Lauren bedded down on the pull-out couch in the living room that connected the two bedrooms. Jonathan was asleep on the king-sized bed between his mother and father. It was past two in the morning when Elizabeth, unable to sleep, got up and left the room.

"Is that you, Mom?" Lauren said.

"Yes, dear," she whispered back, sitting down on the edge of her daughter's bed. "Why aren't you sleeping?" A nightlight allowed Elizabeth to see the traces of fear etched into her daughter's face.

"What's happening to us, Mom? What have we done to deserve this?" Lauren's whisper got louder as anger took control of her tongue. "Why did Dad have to go to Norfolk today? Why does he always think he has to be the one to fix things? Or to stop and help people who really don't want to be helped?"

Elizabeth quietly answered. "I know you're upset, Lauren, but don't take it out on your father. You know what a wonderful man he is. He spends more time with you children than many fathers. And he helps others because he believes—*we* believe—that's what God has called us to do. It doesn't always turn out the way we like, but look at how he's helped others understand God through his life and his work."

"Yeah," Lauren said sarcastically, "and look at how he embarrasses us when he does it."

"He doesn't embarrass us, Lauren."

"You don't think it's embarrassing when my friends read in the newspaper that my father stopped in the middle of the beltway to help someone change a flat tire? Is that stupid, or what? Or volunteering to come to my American history class to talk about the impact of Christianity on the settlement of America. I could've crawled into a hole."

"How many other parents visited your class?"

"None!" said Lauren indignantly. "Just because the teacher asks, doesn't mean you're supposed to come. I mean, it's just too embarrassing."

"I understand how you feel . . ."

"No, you don't," Lauren pouted.

"Look at it from another perspective."

"What perspective?"

"Mine," Elizabeth said, placing her hand on Lauren's. "When I met your father in college, I thought he was the craziest guy in the world. He talked too much, had a new idea every minute, was very impulsive. But at the same time he was gentle. He showed a respect for people I didn't think existed. No, he didn't have the 'Yes, sirs' and the 'Yes, ma'am's' we hear around here, but he had something else. He had a way of giving of himself. And all through our marriage, that's the kind of person he's been."

Lauren looked as if she didn't want a lecture, but Elizabeth persisted. "It's hard to read his feelings, sometimes, but watch what he does. He gives of himself for you kids and for the people at church and at work and at school and to strangers."

In the soft glow of the dark room Elizabeth paused to listen to the stillness and to see in her mind the man with whom she had spent so many happy moments. The quiet lasted for a minute or more, then the tired mother spoke again. "I think, Lauren, in a few years you'll learn to appreciate your father much more than you do today." Elizabeth nodded to reinforce her message but Lauren was staring at the shadows on the wall. "Your father went to Norfolk today because he truly believes that the sooner Mary Kennedy is put in jail, the sooner we'll all be able to rest. That's really all we want, isn't it?"

"I guess so. I just wish things were different. I can hardly sleep what with Jonathan's screaming. And look at Dad's chest. It doesn't smell as bad as it did last week, but *look* at it. Is he going to go to the pool looking like that?"

Elizabeth laughed quietly. "I don't think you have to worry about your father taking off his shirt at the pool or on the beach or anywhere else. The new skin will be sensitive, and he won't be able to let any sun on it for a year."

"Well, that's a relief."

The mother and daughter conversation continued intermittently for nearly thirty minutes as the middle-schooler opened up to her mother about a number of things that were on her mind. Elizabeth knew that, as much as anything, the hormonal changes going on in Lauren's body contributed to her mood swings and affected her perspective on her father, her siblings and life itself.

Toward the close of the conversation, Elizabeth quoted a poem that she had learned at her father's feet, and she told it in the same Irish brogue that her father had told it to her. She knew that Lauren was particularly fond of hearing her mother "speak Irish."

All in the April evening,
April airs were abroad;
The sheep with their little lambs
Passed me by on the road.

The sheep with their little lambs
Passed me by on the road.
All in the April evening,
I thought on the Lamb of God . . .

Before Elizabeth finished the Katherine Tynan poem, Lauren was asleep. Elizabeth looked down at her daughter and patted her relaxed hand. "Have a good sleep, Lauren." Then she bent over, kissed her on the forehead and returned to the bedroom.

*   *   *

Mike Downes was up early and out for a run through his neighborhood. His eight-year-old golden retriever ran by his side. The morning was cool and damp, but the forecast was for sunshine and temperatures in the low eighties. Downes loved spring, and his stride reflected a buoyancy that belied his troubled mind.

Given his tenuous legal position, he knew that his standing within the company was shaky, especially with Mazzetti being so close to the company's seat of power. Also of concern was just how much he should do to fight for Peter's job. He knew that it would be difficult, if not impossible, to defend a man who accessed the electronic mail of a company officer—even if the action did not violate the letter of the company rules.

Sweating and breathing hard, Downes stopped at his mailbox to grab the morning paper then jogged up the driveway to the front porch. He cleared the three steps with a single stride and opened the front door. Goldie followed him through the door and kept on walking to the back door. Mike opened it and let him out to his food and water dish on the screened porch. Then he flipped open the newspaper so he could see the entire front page. He turned on the small TV sitting on the kitchen counter.

From the refrigerator he took a container of orange juice and poured a glass. It was five to seven and the local news was being introduced. When the anchor began speaking, Downes was not surprised that the airplane crash was the lead item. He was surprised with the woman's first sentence.

"A Norfolk architect was among the eight now confirmed dead in the crash of British Airways flight 1629 on the beach on New York's Long Island. Mary Kennedy, owner of Kennedy and Associates, who was an alleged drug kingpin, was killed when an explosion ripped a hole in the side of the 747 18,000 feet above the Atlantic. She and four other passengers were thrown from the plane at the time of the blast."

Without taking his eyes off the set, Downes reached for his telephone. He hit Peter's number on the quick dial and waited. No answer. Frowning, he hung up and redialed. After ten rings, he gave up. More perplexed than concerned, he headed for the shower.

*   *   *

When she tumbled into bed, Elizabeth figured she would finally get some sleep. The children would all be sleeping in since they wouldn't be going to school. Peter would be sleeping in because he was exhausted. And, with any luck, now that she had on a dry diaper, Kristin might sleep until 8:30. But Elizabeth figured wrong. Shortly before 7:30, she was awakened by the thrashing of the little boy sleeping between her and her husband.

Peter was awake too. It was the first time he had seen Jonathan acting so strange. His arms flailed and he kicked his feet. His mouth made a gurgling sound, but he said nothing. Enough light was seeping in around the dark drapes to allow Peter and Elizabeth to observe wildly active eyes beneath their closed lids.

Elizabeth shook her son to try to awaken him. He opened his eyes, but they darted wildly. Suddenly, the boy jerked himself upright and let out a bloodcurdling scream that stopped only long enough for him to gasp for air.

Todd Scott, the U.S. marshal stationed outside the hotel suite, burst through the door with his gun drawn, startling a bleary-eyed Lauren who had been awakened by the scream. Scott flipped on a light, quickly scanned the room, then stepped to the bedroom door from behind which the screams were emanating. He opened the door carefully and stepped into the bedroom.

Elizabeth was cradling Jonathan, while Peter was throwing back the bed covers so he could reach Kristin's crib and calm her as well.

"Excuse me," the marshal said. "I had to be sure that nothing . . ."

"I know. Thanks," Peter responded. "It's these nightmares . . . We'll be all right."

Returning his gun to his shoulder holster, Scott reminded the Bogets that he was outside if they needed anything. Then, he turned to go. As he reached the door to the hall, he noticed it was being pushed open slowly. On edge from the screams, and knowing that protecting the family was his number-one responsibility, the marshal didn't wait to identify the intruder. He drove his shoulder into the door, slamming it shut while yanking out his gun.

Lauren, already unnerved by the screams from the adjoining room, glared at the man with a gun just a few feet from her bed. Visions of the events in the Maryland Hospital filled her head: the guns, the blood, the screams, the concussion of bullets, the smell of death. She couldn't believe it was happening all over again. Trembling, she pulled the covers over her head and curled up into a ball.

"Scott, what's going on in there?" yelled a man in the hall.

"Is that you, Giddings?"

"Yes, it's Giddings. What's happening?"

Marshal Scott peered through the peephole and then opened the door. "Nightmare," he said matter-of-factly. "What are you doing here?"

"Is Boget awake?"

Scott pointed his thumb toward the screaming that continued in the bedroom. "Could you sleep through that?"

Giddings pushed past the marshal and strode to the bedroom door, completely ignoring the young woman peering through the covers on the sofa sleeper. He knocked loud enough so that he could be heard above the sound of two crying children. "Peter, it's Giddings. I'd like to speak with you."

"Not now, please."

"It's very important."

There was a pause. "Just a minute."

"I'll wait in the hall."

It was ten minutes before Peter helped get Jonathan back to sleep and Elizabeth quieted Kristin. Peter brushed his teeth, combed his hair, pulled on a pair of slacks and gingerly donned a shirt. When he finally opened the door to the hall, Giddings was chatting with Scott. The FBI agent was wearing a grin that lit up his dark face and told Peter that something good was up.

"What are you doing here so early in the morning?" Peter asked. "And where is your sidekick?"

"It's not that early. May I come in?"

"My daughter's sleeping in there . . . or trying to."

"We can talk here." Giddings lowered his voice. "Mary Kennedy's dead," he said in a whisper.

Boget's eyes opened wide. He backed into the suite and beckoned the law-enforcement official to do the same. "When? How? Are you sure?"

"Quite sure."

"Just a minute," Boget started toward the bedroom door. He motioned to Giddings to sit down at the table. "Elizabeth, Agent Giddings is here. You've got to hear this." Then he quickly walked to the sliding glass door and pushed back the room-darkening drape, letting the morning light filter in through the thin translucent curtain. He returned to the table. With Kristin in her arms, Elizabeth joined them in the living room. She could tell from their faces that something important was happening, but neither looked as if it was serious.

"Mary Kennedy is dead," said Peter. Then he looked to Giddings for details.

"A plane from New York to London went down in the Atlantic last night, and—"

"We saw. She was on it?" Elizabeth said.

"Yes. It's all very strange," he said. Then he looked at Peter. "Apparently your theory about her being connected to the IRA is wrong, because she didn't know the flight she was on was going to be bombed."

"By the IRA?" Peter asked.

"Maybe. You see, it was carrying six officers of the British Army—experts in counter-terrorism—who have extensive experience in Londonderry and Belfast fighting the IRA. There were supposed to be eight, but two canceled their reservations yesterday afternoon, freeing up the only window seat on the plane. That's the one she got."

"That's too unbelievable," said Peter. Elizabeth nodded.

"I'd say so too, if it wasn't for the witnesses. Two flight attendants, one member of the ground crew and one of the surviving army officers all saw her on the plane. Like one of them said, you notice an attractive redhead like that."

"What was she doing there?"

"Going to England, I guess," said Giddings glibly. "She had booked a flight for tonight, but switched it. Her ticket was changed at the gate. It's going to take us a few days to review the case, but in light of what's happened, I wouldn't think anyone's going to be bothering you anymore."

None of the three were able to register compassion for the dead woman, though Elizabeth came the closest. "I never thought it would come down to anything like this. I expected drawn-out court battles, or to read that she had been shot to death by someone, or that she was financially destroyed." Elizabeth was thoughtful. "I can't think of a worse way to go. Can you imagine being thrown out of an airplane and falling a couple of miles before hitting the water?" She cringed. "I think I'd die before I ever saw the water."

"She probably did," said Giddings softly. "She was on fire at the time."

A pained look crossed Elizabeth's face.

Peter closed his eyes and bowed his head. "I know this sounds awful, but I feel a bit cheated. I've never had the opportunity to meet her face to face—to see the eyes of evil, to tell her what pain she's brought to our family."

"Peter, not now." Elizabeth cradled Kristin in her left arm and with her right hand reached across the table and touched her husband's forearm. Then she looked up at Giddings. "Can we take our children home?"

"The marshals will be discussing all this later this morning with our office, but I suspect the worst is over."

"What about Irish Eyes?" Elizabeth asked. "Was he with her?"

The FBI agent studied the woman. Her face spoke the vengeance more clearly than her tongue did. "I don't know. The man who was seated next to her got off the plane before it took off. He's probably thinking he's the luckiest man alive right now."

"Who was it?" Peter asked.

"Haven't heard yet."

Giddings stood and walked to the door. "I'll be in touch later this morning." He stepped into the hall and closed the door behind him.

Peter and Elizabeth sat looking at each other. Kristin was restless, and, though the baby was nearly weaned, Elizabeth allowed her to suckle her breast. Lauren had resumed her sleep and both bedrooms were quiet.

Peter broke the silence. "There's so many loose ends, I don't know where to start." He looked up at the lamp that hung over the table. "If Mary Kennedy was in New York heading for England, why was someone calling me last night? If she's dead, where does that leave Mark Randolph or Roland Hanks? If she's not connected to the IRA . . . No, she has to be. Maybe they were trying to kill her." He looked at his wife. "Am I crazy, or does this make sense somehow?"

"Peter. Turn your mind off for once. It's not your business. It's over. Let's just try to get our family back to normal. If you want to think about something, think about how you're going to save your job." She stopped and clutched her child. "I'm sorry. I'm tired, and all of this just hasn't sunk in yet. Let me get Kristin down and then I'm going to try and get some sleep.

You should too. The boys will be up soon and then there'll be no resting."

*   *   *

It was close to eight o'clock when Mike Downes arrived at his office. He was surprised to see Frank Mazzetti already at Earl Hendrick's desk. Downes stepped into the president's office and, trying to be as cordial as possible, asked, "What are you doing here? I thought you were going to be up in D.C."

"I'm just cleaning up some odds and ends that I didn't get to on Friday. Dan wants a rundown on the regulatory reform tariff filing," he said, referring to a request made by the CEO. "I thought I'd better go over this so I can speak intelligently about it."

"Let me know how I can help," Downes offered.

"Mike, I heard about Mary Kennedy getting killed. How's that going to affect your case?"

Mazzetti seemed to express genuine concern, but Downes didn't believe the man was capable of caring about anything or anyone except himself. He thought for a few moments and then replied, "Who knows? My lawyer says they don't have a case unless Barry Whitehead comes back from the dead and tells them either I coerced him into going to Mexico, or that he enlisted my aid to avoid prosecution. But even then they have to prove that I knew an FBI investigation was going on and that I intentionally tried to circumvent the law."

"You did, didn't you?"

"Did what?"

"Know you were breaking the law."

"No, I didn't think about it." Mike was wary of Mazzetti's questioning. "And like we told the prosecutor, at the time we left the country there was no outstanding warrant on Whitehead; I'm reasonably certain that will prevent the case from getting to trial."

"Wings clipped?" Mazzetti asked.

Downes pushed his suit jacket back, slipped his left hand into his slacks pocket and leaned against the door jam. "I'm supposed to limit my travel to the area served by the Fourth Federal District. And they asked me to surrender my passport. But the funny thing is, I don't have one." He paused while his mind processed a thought. "Don't you think it's strange that

Kennedy had hers? I would have thought with all they had on her, they would have taken it from her."

"Maybe they did. Maybe she left without one."

Downes smiled. "Maybe." He pulled his hand from his pocket and walked the few steps to his office.

"Good morning, Sharon," he said to his secretary, who was watering the philodendron that cascaded over the front of her cherry desk.

"That's the same Mary Kennedy, isn't it?" asked the woman.

"Yes."

"What a tragedy," she said, shaking her head while she turned to check the moisture level of one of four plants that sat on a horizontal file cabinet behind her computer. "What a terrible way to go. Do you think that will change what's going to happen to you?"

Mike shrugged as he passed her. "I don't know. I really don't have any idea how these things work."

He hung his jacket in the closet that adjoined his private restroom. Then he sat down at his desk and skimmed his e-mail messages. There were three, but none of any consequence. His voicemail was equally devoid of messages of importance. He called the Boget house but only got the family's recording. He hung up the phone and dialed Debbie Steinbaugh.

"Hello," came the tired voice on the other end of the line.

"I didn't wake you up, did I?"

It only took one sentence for Debbie to be wide awake. "My alarm just went off."

"Did you hear about the crash?"

"Which one?"

"The plane in New York."

"I guess I missed that."

"Mary Kennedy was on it. She was killed."

"You're putting me on!"

"No, it's true."

"What does that mean for you . . . for us?" She bit her lip. She hadn't wanted to do or say anything that suggested she was trying to force a decision.

"I don't know," Mike said with a hint of discouragement. "I think I have a long way to go before I'll be able to answer that question. As soon as I get some additional information, I'll let you know."

"Wait," Debbie shouted into the phone.

"Yes?"

After a long hesitation, she said, "I love you, Mike."

Mike was reluctant to respond. Debbie was the first real companion he had since he lost Susie, but he was afraid of what the relationship might lead to. He always considered the choices the two would have to make if their previously unspoken love was to progress to its logical conclusion. More than just 2,000 miles separated them. They were separated by different backgrounds, different educational levels, different views of life and different sets of obligations. Always the pragmatist, Downes didn't want to ask Debbie to leave Colorado Springs because he knew she wanted, above all else, to be close to her daughters. And he hesitated to consider moving to Colorado because of all he would have to leave behind. He would have to give up the opportunity to become a leader of one of America's largest corporations; he would have to leave his native Virginia, his family and friends. Yet the mountains and the beauty of Colorado were like a magnet to him, and he could easily imagine walking onto a new stage with a new partner, with the Rockies forming the backdrop to a new life.

Mike looked up from his desk to make sure that no one was lurking outside the door to his office. The keys on Sharon's computer keyboard were clicking rapidly so he suspected that she had on headphones listening to dictation. He swiveled in his seat so he could look out the window and cupped the mouthpiece to further mask his voice from anyone who might wander into his office.

"I love you too," he responded.

15

Monday, April 23

Martin Vonich knew he was in trouble, but he didn't know how much. The baggage handler for British Airways was being grilled by ATF and FBI interrogators in a small room in the bowels of the huge terminal building at JFK Airport.

"I'm telling ya that's all I know," the New Yorker said for the tenth time. "He showed me this box. He opened it up. There was a tape recorder inside, and it didn't look like no bomb. So he told me that some men on the plane sitting in seats 35 J and K had stolen some secrets from his company and figured that they'd probably be talking about them on the way to London." He shrugged. "Let's face it, things like that happen. So he tells me he's put a mike and a transmitter in the overhead compartment, but he needs to hide the receiver, I think he called it, and a tape recorder in the baggage area near the seat."

"And you just took an electronic device—a bomb—and placed it in the plane?" asked Special Agent Derrick Johnson.

"Look, I'm telling ya, it weren't no bomb!"

"Do you know what a bomb looks like?"

"Yeah, I think so. I've been to lots of movies."

The agent placed a small shoe-box-size container on the table. The bottom of the box was about one-and-a-half inches thick. Lying in the center was an audio cassette recorder. The agent removed the cover and pushed it toward the baggage handler. "Did it look like this?"

Vonich looked surprised. "Yea," he said. "It was a tape recorder, like that, but there weren't no bomb in there."

"So it sorta looked mostly empty, like this?"

"That's right."

"Lift up the box," the agent ordered. "Right now you're holding enough plastic explosive to blow the hands off your body, the head off your neck and every one of these walls right out of this building."

Shock crossed Martin Vonich's face. Gingerly he lowered the box to the table and shoved it back to his interrogator.

"Aren't there rules about what goes into this plane?" the agent asked.

"Yeah."

"Yet some stranger comes up to you and asks you to put a bomb on—"

"I'm telling you, I didn't think it was no bomb. You think I'm crazy? You think I want to kill people? Or lose my job?"

"How much did he pay you?"

"Nothin'."

"I said, how much did he pay you?"

"And I'm telling you, nothin'."

"Everybody at this airport is on the take. Before I lose my patience, I want to know what you got out of it."

Vonich held up his hands. "All right, already. Five thousand bucks."

"So some guy comes up to you and says, 'Here's five thousand, buddy, please stick this on the plane for me'?"

"No, he only offered me a hun'erd but I told him there ain't no way I'm putting my job on the line for chump change." Vonich was sweating. "He asked what I wanted, and five thousand sounded like a good number."

"And you didn't think anything was funny when he pulled five thousand out of his wallet?"

"You know how much it costs to live in New York? My wife's got doctor bills I won't be able to pay if I work till I'm a hundred, and that's after insurance. A guy comes along and offers me five thousand bucks, I didn't think nothin'. I just took the money."

"I sure hope it buys you some guilt relief, because you're the last person who had the power to save those innocent lives," Derrick Johnson said.

"Let's go over this description again."

"Wait a minute. I didn't do it just for the money. He told me Romano gave the okay. If Antony says it's okay, it's okay."

The agent looked into Vonich's face. "You didn't say anything about Romano." The man's eyes shifted downward, and Johnson knew the man was lying, but he didn't know about what. The interrogation continued relentlessly for thirty minutes. And after each round of questions, Agent Johnson came back to the punch line, "What did the man look like?" and got the same, predictable response.

"I can't remember."

Johnson slammed his fist against the table. "You can't remember, because you don't want to remember, because it wasn't a stranger who told you to put that box into the plane, it was someone you knew, wasn't it? It was Tony Romano, and he didn't give you a penny to put it in there, did he?" Johnson was bellowing and his hot breath fell fully on Vonich's face. "He told you that you had better put that box exactly where he told you or you'd lose your job, didn't he? Because nothing moves in and out of these planes unless he says so, isn't that right? And you and I know that there's no way you'd stick something on a plane just because some stranger asked you to."

Vonich started to cry.

"You'd better cry. You let some pint-sized jerk tell you when to stand up and when to sit down." Johnson sneered at Vonich. "And if he tells you to put a bomb on a plane . . . well, you do that too. And for what? So you can get up tomorrow and come down here and say, 'Good morning, Mr. Romano, I'm so glad I can work here at the airport. Mr. Romano, may I kiss your feet this morning?' "

"You don't understand," Vonich interrupted. "I've got a family to feed, and my wife's sick all the time. And he promised me a five thousand dollar bonus. I swear I'd never do anything to hurt anybody, you've got to believe me." He folded his hand as if to pray and begged, "Please, it was an accident . . . I wasn't thinking . . . I never did nothing like this before. Just don't send me to—"

At that point FBI agent Dennis Boyd stepped into the room and signaled Johnson to join him in the hallway.

"Tony Romano is dead," Boyd said.

Johnson stared at him in disbelief. "Where?"

"Janitor found him in a housekeeping closet. His throat was slit."

Johnson tried rubbing the stiffness out of his neck, but it was no use. "Do me a favor, Boyd. Get Vonich out of here. We're back to square one."

*   *   *

While Vonich was being questioned in New York, Paddy McKee was under intense interrogation in London. By the time everyone was satisfied that McKee was little more than the luckiest man who ever lived, lunch time had come and gone.

Unlike the others who had flown to New York with O'Hearn, McKee was financially well off and took frequent trips to New York to attend the theater and to shop. His history of weekend trips from his loft in London to the Big Apple were well documented, as was his history of back problems. Of course, O'Hearn knew that when he recruited the man to fly as Mary Kennedy's bodyguard on a return trip to the UK.

With suspicion averted, McKee left Gatwick Airport, where his plane had arrived an hour after the scheduled arrival of flight 1639 at Heathrow. He rode the train north into London smiling, pleased that he could do his part for the cause.

*   *   *

Roland Hanks wasn't smiling. If Mary Kennedy was dead, he was out of work. His plans for a life of action, adventure and wealth were out the window. Considering the fact that his nest egg of eighteen kilos of cocaine was gone, he was more than irritated. It was only ten in the morning but he was on his third beer. When the phone rang, he lunged for it.

"Mr. Hanks?" The voice sounded familiar. "This is Peter Boget. I called you last week. Friday, I think."

"Sure, I remember."

"We just heard that Mary Kennedy was killed."

"Yup, I saw it on the news." Hanks spoke as if someone was waiting for him to go somewhere.

"Did I catch you at a bad time?"

Hanks grunted what sounded like a no, so Peter continued. "I wondered if you think this means we're not going to have to worry about her gunmen and her threats anymore."

Hanks thought the call was mighty curious and responded carefully. "Look, Mr. Boget, I've heard about Kennedy. But I really don't know what any of this means. I wouldn't think she would be threatening anyone, would you?"

"No, but I was sort of wondering if you think there's much chance of the police picking up the man who shot us."

"Sooner or later they'll get him."

"Will you let me know if you hear anything? My wife and I want to see him again . . . before they send him to the electric chair."

Hanks erupted into laughter. "The chances of ever seeing that man again are slim and none. If you don't pick up a trail within forty-eight hours, you're in trouble, and from what I hear, the man has vanished without a trace. Even if they arrest every man in the country with an Irish brogue, you might not get him. Someone tough and cunning like that has probably melted into the woodwork in Ireland or England or who knows where. If anyone finds him, it will be a stroke of luck. Anyway, I hope that's the last we hear of Mary Kennedy." He started to hang up the phone but stopped himself. "Mr. Boget, are you there?"

"Yes."

"I'm sorry, I should have asked how you're doing."

"Much better, thank you."

"And you're out of the hospital?"

"Yes."

"I guess you must be glad to be out traveling again."

Peter's antenna went up. "Traveling? No, I'm home and that's where I'll be for quite a while, I'm sure."

"I'm glad you're feeling better."

After he hung up the phone, Hanks walked across the living room of his apartment. He still had a slight limp from the bullet wound he had sustained during his encounter with Patrick O'Hearn. When he reached the far wall, he drove his fist into the plasterboard, opening a ragged hole in the wall three times the size of his hand. He watched as plaster dust floated to the carpet below.

*   *   *

"Who was that?" Elizabeth Boget asked as she emerged from the bedroom. The TV was on in the suite's other bedroom and all the kids except for Kristin were huddled around it. The crying baby was perched on Elizabeth's shoulder.

"Hanks."

Elizabeth's drawn face lost what little color it had. "Hanks? Did he call here?"

"I called him. I wanted to gauge his reaction to Mary's death."

"And?"

"I couldn't tell much," Peter said thoughtfully, "but I don't think we're going to be getting any threatening phone calls, at least not from him."

"Who else would call us?"

"I'm working on that," he said, lifting a cup to his lips. "Oh, come and get some coffee. I had room service send it up. I don't know who's paying for this, but we don't get out to digs like this very often, so I thought I'd splurge."

Elizabeth grinned. "You know who's paying for this: taxpayers. And we shouldn't be doing any kind of living it up until we get our finances on an even keel and we know if you have a job."

"Don't remind me."

*   *   *

In the public relations office of Mid-Atlantic Bell, a rumor was spreading rapidly that the director, Peter Boget, had been fired. Megan Churchill was making sure that the rumor reached every employee. Lucy Robinson, editor of the company newspaper, was trying just as hard to squash it. When the two met in the women's restroom, their animosity erupted.

"Oh, here you are," Robinson said, seeing Megan at the sink freshening her lipstick. "Did your flapping tongue wash off all your lipstick?"

"You're just worried that your mentor has taken a dive and you won't have anyone to champion your cause. Not that it matters, because your people don't seem to need mentors; you get promoted just for showing up."

Lucy was infuriated. "Another crack like that—"

Megan laughed and said, "I didn't mean that as anything racist; I just call it like I see it. And the way I see it is that blacks get promoted and whites don't, and Peter Boget is history and Frank Mazzetti is here to stay."

"In case you haven't noticed, no one is getting promoted around here," Lucy shot back. "Peter hasn't been fired, he's home trying to put his life back together. And I'll still put my money on Mike Downes over Mazzetti."

Churchill brushed past Robinson on her way out. "Let me tell you, sweetheart, you aren't going to get anywhere kissing up to Boget or Downes. If you want to get ahead, mark my words. Mazzetti is the new top dog."

* * *

While Patrick O'Hearn's team were making themselves scarce, Mary Kennedy was making over her appearance. In a town where few knew her, the "dead" architect added a wig of reddish-blonde hair that was fuller and longer than her natural hair and complemented her fair skin. Freckles showed through her light makeup. Her new wardrobe of loose-fitting, casual clothes contrasted with the fitted dresses and suits she usually wore.

Every change was essential. The hair, makeup and clothes all helped her to look younger, and even on close inspection she could easily pass for the woman pictured in Kathleen McKenna's passport, which she now carried. From all appearances, she was a young Irishwoman on vacation in New Orleans. But she hadn't come to the Big Easy to party. She had work to do and little time to do it.

Kennedy stepped from her room at a low-budget motel in Metairie, west of the city. She looked down from the narrow outdoor walkway to the cars parked below. The one she had rented looked exactly like three others in the lot.

She turned and strode briskly to the concrete stairs that took her to ground level, oblivious now to the world around her. She had only one focus, one target: Jack Holland.

* * *

Eight hundred miles to the south, in a coastal village of northern Colombia, a tube that looked like a scaled-down version of the space shuttle's main rocket engine was being packed with 144 kilos of cocaine. Each kilo was placed into a clear plastic bag, and then set into a thin plastic container the size of a coffee-table book. The container was sealed, numbered and slid into the steel tube. Three men verified the weight of each container while a fourth carefully logged the information into a laptop computer. Two other men brandishing fully automatic assault weapons stood guard just inside the door of the windowless building.

Within three hours, the packing and recording process was complete, the tube was sealed, and the strong electromagnet powered by a bank of batteries inside the tube was tested. Satisfied with their work, the three packers and the recorder used a winch attached to ceiling rafters to lift the 600-pound tube and place it on the back of a pickup truck to await overnight transport to a small fishing boat. Then they departed, locking the building's only door and leaving the two guards behind.

Jack Holland's shipment was about to begin its dangerous trip to Mississippi and destinations throughout America.

*   *   *

Mary Kennedy wasted no time traversing the twelve miles to downtown New Orleans. She parked in a garage and walked to the high-rise building that housed the offices of Holland Engineering. Holland would not be happy to see her, since he would undoubtedly believe by now that she was dead, her company was his, and he wouldn't have to send a teaspoonful of cocaine to Norfolk. She waited impatiently for the elevator.

Within minutes she was walking through the glass doors and was greeted by a receptionist. She was glad it wasn't the regular one, though she did want to try out her disguise.

"May I help you?"

"I'm here to see Mr. Holland," she accented her words to make sure the receptionist was aware that she was from Ireland.

"May I tell him your name?"

"McKenna. Kathleen McKenna."

The woman picked up the phone and called Jack Holland. After she hung up the phone, she demurred. "I'm sorry, Mr. Holland is unable to speak with you at this time. Could you leave a card?"

"Please tell him I'm Mary Kennedy's sister."

She dialed again and relayed the message. "He'll be right with you."

Before the words were out of her mouth, Jack Holland rounded a corner and walked into the lobby. He wasn't wearing a suit jacket, and Kennedy noted that he looked thinner without one. He extended his hand.

"Ms. McKenna?" When he looked into her face, he was startled. "My, you look like your sister." He almost choked on the words.

"Yes," she said. In an accent stronger than she had used previously with Holland, she continued. "Many people have said we do. And, to tell the truth, when we went to school the teachers could never tell us apart. Except Mary was older."

"I'm so sorry to hear . . ."

"Yes. I was on my way here when it happened."

"Excuse me," said Holland, realizing they were standing in the lobby. "Please come to my office."

"Thank you," she said, and followed him to the room with which she already was quite familiar.

He motioned for her to sit down on one of a group of chairs clustered around a coffee table. "What brings you to New Orleans?"

"When my sister landed in jail, she asked me to come over and look after business for her during her absence. Things have not been going well for her recently. I'm not an architect. That part of the business is being handled by Jay Silverstein. I work at an orphanage, but Mary kept me apprised of certain other transactions and wanted me to work with you to be sure all is going okay. Let me see," she said, pulling a date book from her purse. "Our shipment is due in Norfolk on Wednesday, May 2, and it has been prepaid. Is that correct?"

"Yes, ma'am, everything is in order." Changing subjects, he said, "It's terrible what happened to Mary."

"Actually, it hasn't sunk in. I'm sure it will before the day's out. I had planned to stay for a few days. She told me about the casino at Bayou Caddy and the shrimp boats, and I wanted to take that in, and it was a thrill to think I'd have some time in New Orleans; I've always heard so much about it. But I've got to head back to Norfolk. I talked to my brother this morning, but we don't know what to do about a service at this time. With all the talk about her being a drug dealer, I don't think too many people will want to show up."

Holland nodded in agreement and said, "I guess not." Then he changed the subject again. "Excuse me if I looked like I'd seen a ghost when I saw you this morning. She was quite a woman . . . in more ways than one." Holland raised his eyebrows.

"Oh?"

"She was very good at everything she did . . . very persuasive, if you know what I mean."

Kennedy smiled broadly. "I'm sure she was. Now, I must take my leave." She stood to go, and Jack Holland escorted her all the way to the elevator. Neither the receptionist nor Holland noticed the startled look on her face when her eyes met those of a visitor waiting in the lobby. Though the encounter could be measured in fractions of a second, both knew that their secrets had been uncovered.

Immediately after the elevator door closed on Mary Kennedy, the out-of-work draftsman who had been waiting for a job interview stood up, brushed past Jack Holland, and covered the twenty feet to the stairwell door. Twelve floors later, he caught sight of the woman as she exited the building. He stayed well back as she walked the two blocks to a parking garage.

The draftsman followed Mary into the garage, staked out an observation site behind a concrete pillar near the exit, and waited. Four minutes later his wait was rewarded. He watched as the woman paid for her parking and drove out of the garage. He had a clear view of the woman's full face. In that moment he was absolutely sure that, despite what the networks were broadcasting each hour, a prominent Norfolk architect was not among those killed in the bombing of British Airways flight 1629.

*　　*　　*

"This was the neatest day, Dad," said Daniel Boget as the family's station wagon stopped in their driveway. "This is better than the movies—I mean, with the marshals and the FBI and the real guns and—"

"Daniel," his mother interrupted. "I agree, this has been exciting. But remember, those real guns killed people and put a hole in your father's leg."

"Sorry," the boy replied sheepishly.

The marshals' car pulled in behind the Bogets' wagon. Both Peter and Elizabeth were comforted to know that for several days the family would continue to receive protection from the government.

Once inside, life quickly returned to normal—as normal as a house can be with five children, a federal marshal and a husband home on disability. Elizabeth checked her calendar to see who was driving the soccer-practice car pool, and then called to say she wouldn't be going to the Women's Circle meeting at the McGuires' house. Joyce answered the phone.

"Are you okay?" Her friend sounded deeply concerned. "Bill went by to pick up the kids, and when no one was there we got very worried."

"Oh, Joyce, I'm sorry. We never called, did we?"

"No. What happened?"

"It just got so crazy here last night. The marshals were concerned about the threats we had gotten and decided to move us to a hotel where we could be protected better. We were over at the Hyatt."

"Not too bad." Relief was evident in Joyce's voice. "We heard about Mary Kennedy. I can't believe it."

"I know. But I'm glad it's finally over. Maybe now Peter can rest his mind and think about getting back to work . . . or a new job or whatever." Elizabeth's weariness colored her speech. "He's practically been obsessed with solving this whole mystery, but with Mary dead, I may be able to get him to relax and concentrate on reentering a world he's been out of for over a month."

"Do you really think your husband is going to change?" Joyce's smile was carried in her voice. "I've known him for—how many years?—and I don't think he knows what *relax* means. Quite frankly, I don't know how you keep up with him. Or should I say 'put up with him'?"

Elizabeth laughed. "I don't try, but I've always told him if he could can and sell that energy, we'd be rich."

Peter, who was sitting at the kitchen table listening to his wife's comments, smiled along with her, then walked over and kissed her on the forehead. "I'm going upstairs to rest," he whispered.

Elizabeth placed her hand on the mouthpiece. "We'll leave you alone. I'll take Kristin with me to soccer practice. Joyce said she'd drive, but I've missed so much that I said I'd do it." As Peter turned to go, she removed her hand and said, "I'm sorry, where were we?"

In the bedroom, Peter plugged his computer into the second telephone outlet, the one that accessed the children's line he had installed to keep the main number free. It hadn't worked that well. Now two lines were tied up most of the time. No one was on now when Peter dialed up CompuServe and quickly downloaded his mail. The all-consuming events of the weekend had drawn him close to his wife and family. But they also filled him with desire to escape from his circumstances. The letter from Liza offered that escape, at least for his mind. As he read her words he was quickly drawn into her world. He wanted to cross the miles and years and right the wrongs she had experienced, to undo the pain she endured. But most of all he wanted to look into Liza's eyes and tell her that from this day on life would be better.

He knew that it would be wrong to see her, but that didn't stop Peter from retrieving a road atlas from a dresser drawer full of maps and travel information.

He calculated that Waveland was about equidistant between New Orleans and Biloxi, just as he had thought. He went back to the bed and typed a response to Liza.

Right now I feel like I'm two people—the Peter Boget of the past twenty-two years, the one joyously married to Elizabeth, the one who's a happy father of five children, and the other Peter Boget, the one who's still connected to you, the one who's never forgotten your melodic voice, your wonderfully friendly face and the good times we shared.

But that's the past, and though a part of me would like to see you again, the other part tells me no, that the very thought is all wrong. I thought I was confused a few days ago when you first made contact on CompuServe; now I know I am. Everything I've ever heard, everything I ever observed and experienced, says that we should stop this right now. Even though I'd like to know a bit more of your story, and I'd like to tell you a little more about what my life's been like. Even though in some small way I'd like to be a part of your life. I can't. Right now, I'm facing the prospect of no work, my salary's been reduced while I'm on disability, and there is still so much to do to finish our new house. Yesterday I went to Norfolk, my first trip in over a month, and thoroughly enjoyed being out again, seeing the trees and flowers, and inhaling springtime.

I'd love to share some of this with you, but . . . there's always a "but," isn't there? I must get back to my world. Please know I remain.

Affectionately yours,

Peter

*   *   *

Mary Kennedy exited from Interstate 10 and turned into the motel's parking lot. The car that had been trailing her stopped alongside the adjoining restaurant.

Kennedy nonchalantly got out and walked through a breezeway between two of the units, emerging on the other side. She ran to the end of the building and looked to see if the car was still parked at the restaurant. It was, but it was empty. She raced up the steps and knocked on the second door she came to. Billy McMillan opened it cautiously and Kennedy pushed her way inside.

"I'm being followed," she said, gulping for air as she spoke. "Holland put a tail on me and I couldn't lose him. The car's a blue Ford. Here's the license number."

McMillan was out of the room before Mary finished her sentence. The car was driving away just as he reached the parking lot. When he returned to the room, O'Hearn was there. He and Mary were discussing the man in the lobby of the office of Holland Engineering.

"If that's him, then we've got problems. We're losing track of the players here and I don't like it." Mary's mind was racing as she tried to sort through the information. "Get Hanks on the phone and let's see if we can get him down here. Before this is all over, we're going to need an extra hand. And someone who doesn't have an Irish accent."

16

A s it approached the main shipping channel that served Gulfport, the *Miss St. Loo* looked like the hundreds of other shrimp boats that plied the shallow waters of the Gulf of Mexico. A powerful four-cylinder diesel engine droned beneath the cabin, propelling the forty-foot, steel-hulled boat. The cramped, clothes-strewn cabin smelled of stale smoke, sweaty bodies and day-old fish. It was the home for four fishermen who stayed on the water for up to a week at a time.

From the back of the cabin to the boat's stern, a flat deck sheltered the nearly full hold that contained almost 2,000 pounds of shrimp layered between chips of ice. It was the work area for the men who snagged shrimp in the large nets suspended from either side of the boat. The work area was covered by a large tarpaulin to protect the fishermen from the relentless intrusion of the sun that was two hours from rising above the eastern horizon.

The catch of the previous four days was good, but a far more profitable catch was minutes away.

Crossing in front of the *Miss St. Loo* was one of the huge container ships that bring bananas to Gulfport from the countries that ring the Caribbean. The man at the wheel of the shrimp boat didn't have to read *Tropical Delight* on the bow of the ship to know that it was the one carrying a torpedolike container filled with cocaine.

The sleek container had begun its journey in Barranquilla, the Colombian port city on the Magdalena River. There it was attached by electromagnets to the ship's hull six feet below the water line at the point that the squared hull tapers to funnel water to the ship's twin screws. Although the batteries, windings and cocaine combined with the container's steel casing to weigh over 600 pounds, air pockets were strategically sized and located to keep the cylinder horizontal and two to five feet below the ocean's surface once the power to the magnets was cut. A tiny homing transmitter that signaled the cylinder was still attached to the ship would soon help the crew pinpoint it as it drifted in the ship's wake.

One of the four fishermen punched a code into a digital transmitter, which then emitted a signal from an antenna towed behind the *Miss St. Loo*. Another watched the radar screen to ensure no other boats were in the area. "Clear."

"Released."

"It's free."

With its shrimp nets dragging through the calm water, the *Miss St. Loo* passed through the wake of the *Tropical Delight* and snagged the cylinder. Once beyond the sight of the banana ship the crew scanned the moonlit horizon for signs of the Coast Guard and other shrimp boats. Feeling safe, the fishermen retrieved the sealed tube before pulling the shrimp-filled net out of the water. While two men handled the chore of separating fish from the shrimp, two others inspected the canister, dropped it over the side of the boat, and activated the electromagnets to attach it to the hull below the water line. Their work complete, three of the four fishermen headed to their bunks while one stayed at the wheel and guided the boat westward.

*   *   *

Morning came early for Mike Downes. After his two-mile run, he showered, shaved, dressed and then packed a garment bag for a long weekend at a friend's home in Annapolis. He had a ten o'clock meeting in Baltimore and was going to take the afternoon off to relax on the water. An intense week of work on regulatory reform, coupled with many hours working with his lawyers on his legal defense, had left him exhausted. But it was exhaustion tempered by the elation he felt with each of his daily telephone conversations with Debbie.

Woven through his week were periods of contemplation of the plight of Barry Whitehead. Mike was thinking about Barry as he climbed into his car and backed out of the garage. It was 6:15. This would be his first trip back to Baltimore since that chaotic, deadly Palm Sunday.

As the asphalt roadway of Interstate 95 fell away behind him, Downes recalled many of the events that had occurred during the preceding five weeks. By the time he was crossing the Woodrow Wilson Bridge, which carried beltway traffic over the Potomac from Virginia to Maryland, he realized that he should have taken this drive sooner. It brought back memories that would help in his defense.

Downes spoke into his handheld recorder as he wove through rush-hour traffic that clogged the four northbound lanes. He looked for the spot where Peter fell on the flare, but was past it before he realized it. When he saw the sign for Landover, he remembered the policeman, Hanks, and wondered what had happened to the man whose quotes got picked up and disseminated nationwide by the Associated Press. Into his machine he said, "Trooper Hanks. Why was he in the hospital? What was his role? Where is he now?" He added a few other thoughts then picked up his car phone and dialed directory assistance.

*   *   *

The long week was finally drawing to a close for Elizabeth Boget. She and Peter sat across the table on their screened porch drinking coffee and enjoying the warm breeze. The first real summerlike day had arrived.

The grass in the backyard was thick and green and needed to be mowed. The variety of wildflowers that edged it were in bloom. The trees that formed a backdrop for the pastoral setting were in full leaf, radiating freshness in the midmorning sunshine.

At the edge of the yard, three swings hung suspended from a stout beam fastened to two oaks. On the middle swing, Jonathan was excitedly mastering his newly acquired skill of pumping his legs in rhythm with the motion of the swing to make it fly. Kristin was practicing her walking as she circumnavigated the table at which Peter and Elizabeth were sitting. Here idle chatter mingled with the songs of the birds that flitted from tree to tree and the occasional squeal of a power saw from the site of a home under construction in another part of the neighborhood.

"It's so good to have you home and to know that life is finally almost back to normal," said Elizabeth. "God has been so good to us."

"Elizabeth." Peter looked a bit distant, and the way he spoke her name told her he hadn't been listening to her. "Have you ever wondered why things were the way they were?"

"Of course. Why?"

"Something's been happening to me these past two weeks, and I'm not sure I understand it."

"That's something of an understatement!" laughed Elizabeth, leaning over to stroke Kristin's head as the little one passed her on one of her trips around the table.

Peter was far more serious than she realized. "It's more than that, but I don't know where to begin."

"Begin what?"

"Begin . . . begin telling you about what's been going on in my life since just before the skin graft. Do you remember I told you about calling Liza?"

"Did you finally remember what she said about her family?" Elizabeth was watching Jonathan on the swing, who was calling to his mother to watch him.

"Not exactly."

"What, then?" she asked, waving to Jonathan.

"There's more."

The "more" got Elizabeth's attention. "Don't tell me—you told her all about being in the hospital and feeling bad and she said, 'Oh, Peter, I wish I was there to make you feel better.' "

"Not exactly."

"I give up, then." Elizabeth was smiling. Kristin made another round of the table, stopped, and reached up to grab her mother's elbow.

Peter saw that this just wasn't the time. "Talking to her reminded me about that summer, and the memories have been a distraction lately."

"How do you have time to be distracted? You spend day and night trying to figure out how to get your job back and put Mary Kennedy out of the business, and you're telling me that memories of Liza are distracting you?" Elizabeth pushed back her hair and took a sip of her coffee. "I don't get it, Peter. You've been stewing about a telephone call for two weeks?"

"And a letter."

"She sent you a letter? In the hospital?" Elizabeth furrowed her brow. "I didn't see anything come here."

"She sent it on CompuServe."

"And?"

"Randy's been tough on her and apparently hasn't had much time for their kids."

For the next five minutes, Peter fed a few morsels of general information that Elizabeth quickly chewed on before offering comment.

"So Liza sent you a letter on CompuServe. You wrote her back?"

"I did."

"And you said?"

Peter knew that it was less what he said than what he felt that he needed to be telling Elizabeth, but he couldn't bring himself to do it. The feelings that stirred within him were unlike any he had felt in many years. "I told her about our family, about being sorry I had missed her when she and her husband came to visit, about my career and about you."

"And what did you tell her about me?" asked Elizabeth. "That I'm exhausted from being a mother? That some gray is creeping into my hair? That I've added a few pounds here and there and that I'm not as beautiful as she is?"

"All of that and more," said Peter with a grin. "No, I told her that you're a good mother and wife and that I love you."

Kristin crawled up into her mother's lap. "Do you feel guilty about that?"

Peter nodded sheepishly. "I guess so."

"I bet with all her skills as a nurse, Liza would be great at changing your dressings," Elizabeth said, still joking. "Why don't you ask her to come up and stay with us as a live-in nurse for a while."

Peter continued the lighthearted conversation. "Let me call and ask her if she'd like to do that."

"I've got a better idea." Elizabeth's face lit up. "Since you're just taking up space around here, eating us out of house and home now that you spend half your day at the refrigerator, and," she raised her eyebrows, "since you don't have a job to go to, why don't you fly down to Mississippi and let her take care of you down there for a while, and you can take your computer and files and stacks of index cards with you!"

The two laughed in unison but for entirely different reasons. Elizabeth thought the notion preposterous. Peter knew the words were almost identical to those written by Liza in sincerity.

Elizabeth handed Kristin a corner of her toast as Jonathan opened the screen door and bounded to the table to take another bite of his cold eggs before racing back to the yard. When the phone rang inside, Peter was first to stand. "I'll get it."

"Thanks, I think I've answered it a thousand times this week."

*   *   *

Erecting a tall building on a barge at the entrance to Bayou Caddy did more than provide a lot of square footage for slot machines and gaming tables. It afforded an exceptional view of the fishing boats entering and leaving the narrow waterway. It also extended the horizon so that far more of the Gulf waters could be scanned for the boats used by law enforcement officials to interdict drug-smuggling vessels.

Kevin Daugherty was taking advantage of that grand view, noting in his mind the movement of the boats, most of them loaded with shrimp, others carrying oysters and a variety of fish. One Coast Guard cutter was less than a mile off shore traveling west to east. It had just passed through the wake of the *Miss St. Loo,* which was making its slow run to the bayou. Daugherty checked his watch.

*   *   *

"Who are you?" Peter interrupted, not able to identify the voice.

The man continued telling the story the way he wanted to tell it. "On Monday I saw Mary Kennedy."

Every nerve in Peter's body went to red alert.

"Yesterday I saw her again, with Patrick O'Hearn."

"Who's that?"

"They're after me, I know, and I have no place to turn."

While the man spoke, Boget leafed through the phone book to find the area-code map. From the display on his caller ID box, he could identify the area code, and the fact that the call was being made from a pay phone.

"Why are you calling me?"

"I don't know, but when you stopped to help me on the beltway, I knew you were a very special person and I'll never forget that. I've wanted to say I'm sorry, but didn't know how, and I was going to call Mike Downes, but I don't know if he's mixed up with Mary or not. But someone tried to kill me and only he knew where I was, so . . ."

Peter listened, but the story was too bizarre. The caller was telling him that two people who were supposed to be dead were in fact alive. He interrupted.

"If you are Barry Whitehead, which I don't believe you are, you would know that Mike Downes is not in league with Mary Kennedy or anyone like that. Secondly, if you are Barry Whitehead you'd be in Mexico, not in Louisiana."

"Who says I'm in Louisiana?" the man asked with a hint of panic in his voice.

"You're calling from a phone in the 504 area code, that much I know. Now whether in New Orleans, or Baton Rouge or somewhere in between, I can't tell, but I need more than what you've told me to believe you're Barry. Anybody reading the wire stories these past few weeks could probably fit together a story like the one you're telling me."

"Listen to me, I'm begging you." Desperation began to take over the man's speech. "You don't have to believe me, I'll understand, but I'm free and I don't ever want to go back to prison. I don't want anyone to ever find me again. But Mary has. She saw me when I was sitting in the office of Holland Engineering waiting to have a job interview, and now I know she's looking for me. I have no money, I have nothing. I'm staying in a shelter but I'm trying to get a job, and I could get out of here if I had some help. I'm asking—no, I'm begging you—help me get out of here and I'll be indebted to you for life."

Peter listened but found it difficult to believe what he was hearing. The singular bit of information that the man had offered that was not in the press was the name of Patrick O'Hearn. "Who's this O'Hearn character?"

"He's the one who made sure I got the goods to deliver, and he was the one I spoke with whenever I had a question. I think he's Mary's top man, because he was with her in Shoney's in Metairie yesterday morning."

"You saw them?"

"Eating breakfast. It's a long story, but I had to know if it was her I saw on Monday, so I finally got a chance to ask the man who followed her from Holland's office and—"

"Who's Holland?" Peter interrupted. "Where's Metairie?"

"Near the airport just outside New Orleans."

"Why are you telling me all this?"

"You don't believe me, do you?"

"I'm not sure."

"When you stopped you looked at me like you had seen a ghost, and we both laughed because we both thought we were looking at ourselves in the mirror and you asked me, 'Do you need some help?' I said, 'I've lost the key to my trunk' and you said, 'Let me get a flare first, then I'll call for a tow truck from my car.' "

Peter remembered the conversation and the man with whom he had it. Looking at Barry Whitehead *was* like looking in a mirror . . . perhaps not looking too closely and perhaps not looking at him when he walked, but their faces bore an uncanny resemblance. Even their hair was similar. Barry was not quite as tall and did not look like the athlete that Peter was, but if his only identification was the photo on his driver's license or Virginia Bell identification card, he'd have no trouble passing as Peter Boget.

"We heard you were killed in Mexico."

"Someone tried, but I was out of the car when the explosion bounced me across the road and into a ditch filled with water. I met a group of men from near Lafayette, Louisiana, who were helping to build a church in a village between Cancún and Mérida. They took pity on me and instead of turning me into the police, they patched me up and brought me back as far as New Orleans. They offered to take me to Lafayette, but years ago when I worked for Mary Kennedy, I frequently had contact with Holland Engineering and knew they were always looking for draftsmen, especially ones who could work CAD systems."

Peter wondered about the wisdom of going to work for a company that maintained ties with Kennedy.

"I'm not stupid," Barry replied. "I was going to talk with a draftsman who worked there, the man I used to talk to quite a lot, and see what else might be available in the area. I don't have a penny to my name and needed some work, quick. When I heard on the news that Mary was dead, I decided it was safe to apply for a job with Holland."

Boget was still skeptical. "And Kennedy just showed up the day after the crash?"

"Yes, but she didn't look the same. I think she was wearing a wig and she had changed her makeup and was wearing different clothes. But the way she looked at me, I knew it was her."

"And the other man—O'Hearn. Where'd you see him?"

"A man from Holland's office followed Kennedy after she left the office last Monday. I caught up with him on Wednesday. He wouldn't tell me anything, but I got a taxi and followed him to Shoney's where I saw Mary and O'Hearn."

"I thought you didn't have any money."

"I don't, but I did . . . a little . . . from the church people who brought me back here."

Elizabeth was surprised that Peter was still on the phone when she walked in and heard the tail end of the conversation.

"So why are you telling me all this?" Peter asked.

"As long as Mary Kennedy is alive, I'm a dead man." The brief self-assurance that Whitehead had displayed while talking about the job search melted into self-pity and another call for help. "I can't talk to the police or I'll end up in jail or be sent back to Mexico—and I can't go back there."

"So what do you want?" Peter said compassionately.

"I don't know. I thought you might have an idea. Mike said you were a man who was full of ideas. Money would help, I guess, but most of all I need someplace to hide. I'm afraid to go anywhere near Holland Engineering. With Kennedy and O'Hearn so close by, I know it will only be a matter of time . . ." His voice trailed off.

"Let me think about this and call you back. Where can I reach you?"

"I'll call you. When's a good time?"

"Two?"

"I think I'm an hour behind down here. I'll call you at one, my time."

"Fine."

Whitehead didn't speak for ten seconds. Then with a hesitancy in his voice he asked, "You won't tell anyone, will you?"

Peter agreed to maintaining confidence, at least for the time being, then hung up.

"Who was that?" Elizabeth asked. "You look like you've been talking to a ghost."

Peter excitedly relayed Whitehead's story. Before he was finished, Elizabeth interrupted: "So don't just stand there, call up Agent Giddings and tell him that Mary Kennedy is alive in New Orleans. They'll go and pick her up."

Peter looked long and hard across the kitchen table at his wife. "If I make that call, I'll be written off as a paranoid lunatic. Think about it. Even if I could tell them where I got the information—which I can't—I'd be the laughingstock of the law enforcement community. The last vestiges of credibility that I'm banking on to redeem me at the phone company would be shattered."

"No it wouldn't."

"You don't think there would be a few snickers if I called and said that a dead man just told me that a dead woman is alive?"

"I see," she said as the reality of her husband's words registered. "We'll just have to think of another way!"

* * *

One thousand miles away, Mary Kennedy, posing as Kathleen McKenna, visited the office of Jack Holland. The exchange of greetings was cordial but the conversation that followed was not.

"Why do you have a man following me around this city?" demanded Kennedy.

"I like to be careful. Your presence poses a risk to my operations," said Holland, hostility evident in his voice. "I always dealt with Miss Kennedy from afar and we both preferred it that way. I understand your interest in the upcoming delivery. It will be in Norfolk on Wednesday as scheduled."

"I can't take delivery in Norfolk, it's too dangerous. I want my merchandise today so I can get out of town as soon as possible," said Kennedy. "I have an associate who will assist me with transportation, relieving you of responsibility sooner than you expected and reducing your transportation costs."

"Sorry, I had a deal with Kennedy. Once the stuff gets to Norfolk, you can do with it whatever you want, but I don't know you, and I'm not changing the rules for you or anyone else." Holland stood up and walked away. Then he turned and looked at Kennedy sitting on the sofa. "Look, lady, you could be a cop, a fed, a con artist, a lot of things. If you didn't look so much like Mary, I'd have kicked you out of here by now. I don't know what your game is, but you'll never find me associated with any transactions that in any way might jeopardize my business, my company or my life. If you are who you say you are, you ought to head back to Virginia and be prepared to take delivery on Wednesday."

Kennedy glared at the man, "And if I'm not?" she asked indignantly. "Then what?"

"Then don't expect me to go along with any request you make."

"And if I drop by to verify that my shipment is on the way?"

Holland started to respond with a threat, but caught himself. "Be my guest, but I will take no responsibility."

                              *   *   *

Peter Boget's impulsive nature had him back at his computer while awaiting Whitehead's call. Peter logged onto CompuServe, just as he had several times a day since sending his letter to Liza on Monday. With all the disappointments he was facing, Liza's daily notes were becoming a welcomed escape from the realities of his postoperative world. He eagerly read her letter.

My Dear Peter,

Finally, a day off! Working the day shift has been exhausting—not getting in at 6:30 for the shift change, but getting up at 5:00, and slipping out of bed without waking Randy to read your words of encouragement and jot you a sentence or two. You have given me life where there was so little before. You have helped me see that I am somebody, after all. I've had to force myself to eat this week, because food is just not on my mind. When I work days, I miss all the kids' meals at home and I hate that, but I love not having a refrigerator full of leftovers to tempt me.

I begin nights on Sunday, so I thought about taking the kids shopping for some summer things tomorrow over in Gulfport and get myself a new outfit—something special, something I'd like you to see me in. But Eric wants to go fishing with some friends and Amy's doing a car wash with the youth group at church, so, if I can get away without Randy, I just might have a good day. I'm looking forward to it.

How I wish, though, that you could be with me. We could slip into a lot of little shops pretending we were husband and wife, cruising the mall, stopping for some lunch and then heading down to the beach for the afternoon to just sit and talk. On second thought, the mall would be out and so would the beach. Too public and too many chances we'd be seen, especially if Randy decides to come looking. He'd do that.

When I went back to school to get my RN, I'd be sitting in class down in New Orleans, and he'd walk in and sit down in the back row for half an hour and then leave, only to show up again in my rearview mirror all the way home. And I've walked out of a dressing room in a store in Biloxi and he was there standing with the children. He drove an hour to check up on me and dragged the kids around the mall for almost two hours looking for me. He told them it was to surprise me and take me for lunch, but he was just checking up on me. He was angry when we got home and he complained that I wasn't in the store that had the sale I said I was going for. Then he slapped me around.

I know I shouldn't be bothering you with all of this, but I just can't think about how much different life would have been with you. I know this is out of bounds, but I want so much to roll back the clock and start over. I want to go back to Mirror Lake and not let you go until you promise to come back for me. I want you, Peter, more than I've ever wanted anything in my life.

Peter's heart was racing when he finally finished Liza's letter. It was racing with anger, and it was racing with desire. His response was short.

Dear Liza,

You're right, you are out of bounds. But at this moment I'd like nothing better than to come and take you away from Randy, even though we both know that's impossible. Someday, somewhere I'd love to spend an hour or two with you and catch up on old times, but as I have written before, we can never be what you would like us to be. The Mary Kennedy story isn't over yet, and I have to make some important decisions today. Trying to explain this on this computer is too frustrating because my typing is so slow these days. I'm going to try to call between 1:00 and 2:00 your time and try to explain myself better. If it's a bad time, just say, "You've got the wrong number," and I'll understand.

17

Friday, April 27

A beautiful spring morning served as a great backdrop for Frank Mazzetti's short ride from Virginia Bell's downtown building to St. Mary's Hospital in the West End. He drove west on Grace for a dozen blocks, skirting the urban campus of Virginia Commonwealth University before turning left on Lombardy and right at the huge monument of General Stonewall Jackson astride his horse. At Libbie Avenue Mazzetti turned left and circled into the parking lot of the hospital.

Within minutes he was at the door of Earl Hendrick's room. He knocked gently and walked in. Emily Hendrick, who had been sitting beside her husband, stood and greeted him.

"Hello, Frank," she said. "I'm glad to see you again." The tone of her voice contradicted her words.

Mazzetti smiled, then asked the company president how he was doing since his transfer from the hospital in Kilmarnock.

"Much better, Frank, thank you," he responded cheerfully. "My head is back to normal, if there is a normal for a head like mine."

His wife chuckled.

"And the Chesapeake Bay has been pumped out of my stomach and lungs, and my heart is strong."

"He's coming home tomorrow," said Emily.

"That's good. I'm glad to hear you're doing so much better. You sure are a lucky man. The company—"

"It has nothing to do with luck," Hendrick interrupted. He reached for his wife's hand. "I have learned an important lesson from this. When a man faces loss as I faced when I saw my Emily bobbing in that water in the midst of the storm, and when a man faces death as I did struggling to hold on, he stops believing in luck. I knew that the God I had paid lip service to all these years was there in those waves and in those winds and in that rain. He gave Emily and me a second opportunity to discover what he really is. No, this is not about luck. But it is about a new lease on life—a new perspective, if you will."

Mazzetti wasn't interested in God or sermons on life, so he cordially side-stepped the issue. "I certainly understand where you're coming from, and I know the company will appreciate your new perspective when you return."

"I am afraid I am going to disappoint them. I spoke with Dan this morning," he said, referring to Mid-Atlantic Bell's chief executive officer, "and made some calls over to the office. The doctors are suggesting another week or two for recuperation, but Emily and I have decided on something more permanent—like seventy-something days of accumulated vacation. Then I am going to retire."

Mazzetti looked surprised. "You're not coming back?"

"With Mike and the others taking care of things, they will get along fine without me, and I—" he looked lovingly at his wife who was sitting on the end of his bed, "—that is, Emily and I are going to make sure we take advantage of our second chance and spend the rest of our lives doing the things we always talked about doing. And maybe we will add a few things to our schedule we never thought about doing . . . like helping others less fortunate than ourselves."

Mazzetti was elated with the news. "I've been thinking a lot about Peter Boget this past week. I know how much you and Mike respect the man, so I've talked with Dan and some of the others. I'm recommending that, instead of offering him a job in some remote community, we downgrade him and offer him a position in Washington."

"Funny you should mention Peter. I discussed his situation with Dan this morning, and he mentioned that possibility, but I reminded him that that would create quite a hardship for the family financially." The president, looking thinner but more robust than he had in weeks, scanned Mazzetti's face for a hint of emotion. He saw contrived compassion. Mazzetti was wearing an impeccably tailored black suit, a fitted white shirt monogrammed on the cuff and an almost iridescent maroon and gray silk tie that suggested a man who enjoyed the finer things in life and who had a pocketbook to afford them. But despite his dashing appearance and his pleasant, almost disarming personality, Mazzetti always seemed to be hiding another Frank Mazzetti. Hendrick believed that it was only the surface personality who was responding to his comment.

"It's such a shame," Mazzetti said, "to see a man with so much going for him throw it away so recklessly."

The president nodded gently and then looked up at the ceiling and over to his wife before resuming. "He seemed so content, though, when he and Elizabeth came by yesterday. I think he's planning on leaving and is already looking for employment elsewhere. He said he has some résumés circulating."

Mazzetti liked what he heard. With Boget out of the way, a major thorn would be removed from his side. With Downes tied up with his legal defense and with Hendrick gone, the path to the presidency was clear. But it was not just the top spot at Virginia Bell that Frank Mazzetti sought. His ambition was greater, his goal higher.

*   *   *

Elizabeth was sitting next to Peter when the phone rang.

"Mr. Boget," said the caller.

"Call me Peter."

"Okay, Peter, you haven't said anything to anyone, have you?"

"Only my wife."

"Look, I think there's a man following me," said Whitehead, "and I think he's going to try and kill me. I can't leave this shelter I'm in except at night, and they won't let me stay here another day unless I report my concerns to the police or go out to look for a job."

Peter listened as the man's voice became increasingly remorseful.

"I'm trapped. I can't call anyone because I don't know anyone to call. I could call my dad, but he'd have the FBI down here in an hour. And my exwife, if she believed me, would laugh and tell me I'm getting what I deserve. Mike Downes would turn me over to the police, and I'd be back in that hellhole in Mexico before sundown. I don't have anybody. Through all these years, I've never really had any friends, and I realize that the few people I know really don't know me. You helped me once, and I know I shouldn't ask to have you help me again, but I just don't know what to do. The people here have given me some clothes, and I've gotten some good food, but my life is about over, and I'm not ready to die." The quavering voice suggested that tears were running down Whitehead's face, or soon would be.

"Maybe I can help," said Peter, looking at his wife, who nodded her agreement. "We can send you some money, enough to get to Richmond. In the meantime we'll talk to people here in the church and see what can be done, and to the police, to see what would happen to you."

"Not the police! Remember, I was driving a car full of drugs. I don't want to end up in jail."

"Let me call the woman handling the Mary Kennedy case. I bet she'd be happy to provide you a new identity in exchange for helping them find her."

"You don't understand. I'm sorry I bothered you."

"Wait!"

"What?"

"Let me come and get you." When Peter spoke the words, Elizabeth pulled away from the phone and glared at him, shocked. She shook her head at what she perceived was another of her husband's ill-conceived ideas.

"Where are you?" Peter asked.

Overwhelmed with the offer of help, Whitehead let down his guard and named the homeless shelter in downtown New Orleans.

"Stay put. I'm coming to help you."

After Peter hung up the phone, Elizabeth looked at him long and hard. "You can't go anywhere," she said, "not in the shape you're in. And you certainly can't go to New Orleans, because we don't have the money. And even if we did, you don't want to get mixed up with Mary Kennedy and Barry Whitehead again. Peter, Whitehead left you to die on the beltway and Kennedy tried to kill you. The last place you should be is out in the open, where they could find you. Did it ever occur to you that maybe he's trying to coax you out of the house so someone can get us? Look, I know you want to get Mazzetti, and you think that getting Kennedy will help you pull that off. You also think that if you go see Whitehead you'll wrap this all up. But it doesn't work that way. They caught Randolph and had you traipse all the

way to Norfolk—and for what? Nothing!" She paused for a deep breath and
continued. "If God wants you to get your job back, he can do it without
sending you to New Orleans when you're still weak, when your dressings
still need to be changed every day, and when you're so preoccupied with
getting Frank or Mary or whoever you think you've got to get that you're
not thinking straight. This is for the police. This is what they do. Don't go
and do something we'll all end up regretting."

"Elizabeth, I've almost got this whole mess figured out. I'm going to make
Frank Mazzetti apologize publicly for what he did to you and what he's trying
to do to us. I'm going to see Mary Kennedy in jail. And, by God, I'm going
to find Patrick O'Hearn. And if he's the man who tried to take Jonathan,
and if he's the man who tried to kill me, I'm going to see him dead."

Elizabeth didn't like what she was hearing. She shook her head gently.
"No," she said quietly. "This is wrong."

"It's not wrong," he shot back. "The meek may inherit the earth, but
sometimes God calls us to take a stand against evil." Peter stood. "That's
all I want to do. I'm not buying a gun or anything like that, I just want to
see that justice is done, and right now I think we've got a chance to do that.
And what about Whitehead? The guy's desperate. You heard him. Maybe
we can help him."

"Don't fall for that victim stuff. Whitehead's in the drug business big time.
He tried to rape Debbie. This is not an upstanding citizen who just happens
to be down on his luck. We should be calling up the police and letting them
figure out what to do."

Peter, looking at the floor, slowly walked away. When he reached the
counter, he turned and leaned back and placed the heels of his hands on
it. He took a breath and, without looking his wife in the eye, he conceded,
"I'm sorry. I'm not thinking straight. Let's just drop the whole thing. Let me
call Barry," he said, stepping to the phone. "I'll tell him we're sorry, but he's
going to have to tough it out." Peter lifted the phone and started dialing
directory assistance for the 504 area code. "Then I'll call the FBI and tip
them off." He turned his attention to the phone. "Yes, ma'am, I'm calling
for the number for Good Samaritan House." He jotted down the number,
depressed the switch hook briefly, and then dialed a second time.

Elizabeth stepped up to him and took the phone from his hand. "Maybe
I'm wrong. We can't leave Barry hanging in the wind. If they kill him, at

least some of that blood will be on our hands. And if he disappears, Mike Downes might never get a fair hearing." She set the phone in its cradle. "If Mary Kennedy is down there and if Irish Eyes is with her, maybe, just maybe, we can stop them from killing someone else."

"And what do you propose?"

"I've got an idea."

*   *   *

"You're supposed to be a cop!" Patrick O'Hearn was shouting at Roland Hanks as they sat in a rented car in the parking lot of a strip shopping center north of downtown New Orleans. "You've had three days to find Whitehead, and you're telling me you can't locate him? We have work to do and we can't let anything or anyone get in our way. Do you understand?"

"I did find him," said an indignant Hanks. "But he keeps moving. He was at a homeless shelter last night but left for the day. That's the way those places work. I didn't know he was there until I checked this morning."

"You should have known! I saw him myself looking in the window at Shoney's a couple of days ago. Unfortunately, he disappeared before I could get out and find him. Somebody got to him in Mexico—if he ever was in Mexico—and sent him up here to work with Holland. I don't know what Whitehead or Holland are up to, but my guess is that they are trying to bypass us. The next shipment comes in tomorrow night. We're going to make sure we get what's coming to us, and we don't need Barry Whitehead screwing things up. Do you understand?" The final question wasn't so much a question as it was an admonition.

Hanks was boiling, and it wasn't because of the heat outside. He was sitting two feet away from the man who had shot him in the hospital in Baltimore, two feet away from the man whom he suspected killed two of his former coworkers. But instead of being able to take revenge, he was cowering. He was staring into the same killer's eyes that he saw as Patrick O'Hearn had backed down that hospital corridor with Jonathan Boget, and he was powerless to do anything but listen and obey. He had sold his soul to the devil, and the devil was demanding payment.

"Whatever it takes, make sure Whitehead cannot interfere with our work. And make sure he is not able to testify about his relationship or work for anyone."

"You want me to kill him?"

"I didn't say that. Now go." O'Hearn motioned to Hanks to get out of the car and waited until he returned to his own rental car and drove off.

Hanks headed back to the shelter that was a dozen blocks upriver from the convention center. O'Hearn followed for several blocks before swinging onto I-10 and heading back to the motel in Metairie.

*   *   *

Elizabeth Boget hung up the phone and scooped up Kristin, who was alternately standing and dropping to a sitting position on the kitchen floor. Each time the baby's diaper-padded rear hit the floor she laughed and cooed. In the adjoining room, where a warm breeze floated in through open windows, Jonathan sat on the floor applying crayon strokes to the line drawings of smiling, human-looking, embattled turtles of the teenage mutant variety. The coloring book that had been bought for Daniel three years earlier was nearly complete, with green dominating the pages and blue, red, yellow and orange showing up prominently on the waists and headbands of the fighting, pizza-eating amphibians.

Elizabeth climbed the stairs to the bedroom where Peter was sitting beside the phone. "Well, that *was* a good idea, Elizabeth," Peter said.

Elizabeth looked disappointed as she set her daughter on the floor and sat down on the edge of the bed. "If Josh can't do it, then we'll have to think of another idea. We can't ask Mike; he's already in over his head."

"And he's not allowed to travel . . ."

"If it was just for us, I'd say let's forget about it. But after all Mike's done for us, if we could somehow get Whitehead to speak to the prosecutor, we could probably get a huge burden off the man." Elizabeth walked to her dresser and pulled open the top center drawer. "When you were gone, I pulled out these two vouchers we have for a free round trip that you got when you and Daniel were bumped off that flight last summer. I thought we might need them to fly someone in to help out around here or to attend a funeral. Maybe now's the time to use one."

"One?"

"Me."

"Are you serious?"

"If he's not suspecting a woman, I should be able to get close to him before he takes off. And if he looks like you, I'm sure I'll be able to identify him. If someone is following him, they would never suspect me, would they? Nobody knows what I look like. But if you show up, and you look like him, they may . . . I don't even want to think of it."

"Your photo's been in the paper . . . and you've been on TV."

"But they certainly wouldn't be expecting anything!"

Peter looked thoughtfully at his wife. He admired her strength and courage. He admired her pretty face and the trim figure that belied the fact that she was the mother of five. He admired the way she loved him and supported him through all the trials they shared. But he seriously questioned her plan.

"A woman walking into who knows what . . . That's not reasonable. We're dealing with very dangerous people."

"I don't plan to come into contact with any dangerous people. I just want to get the information from Whitehead."

"You don't think he's dangerous? Less than thirty minutes ago you were telling me he was a criminal who couldn't be trusted."

"We're just getting a bit of information. We help him get out of wherever he is. Then we let the FBI take it from there."

"We should think this through."

"And pray about it. I know," Elizabeth added. "I have and I'm ready."

Despite the fact that almost everything within him was saying no, his tongue said, "Okay."

Elizabeth smiled, feeling suddenly empowered by her husband's support. For many years Elizabeth had to sublimate her feelings and desires to the rewarding but difficult, tiring and often thankless task of raising children. Now the thought of actually stepping into harm's way exhilarated her. "I'm going to call Debbie Steinbaugh and get her input on Barry."

"Before you do, I want you to know I'll be worried every moment you're gone. What if something happens?"

"Nothing's going to happen. And if it does," she said innocently, "I'm sure that Liza will come running up here to take my place."

"Speaking of Liza, maybe you can go to see her while you're in her neck of the woods," Peter said with mock seriousness.

"Let me call Debbie."

"I'll call Pat over at Travel Consultants," he said, "and see about booking a flight, a hotel and a car. And I'm going to order you a cellular phone so you can stay in touch."

*   *   *

One o'clock came and went. Liza waited, but Peter's call didn't come. A hundred reasons why he hadn't called raced through her mind. She reread his e-mail and her own. Yes, she had to agree, they were, or at least she was, way out of bounds, but the thought of letting go was something she refused to entertain. She decided to tackle the bathroom cleaning she hated to do . . . anything to get her hands working on something besides typing messages to Peter or playing love songs on the piano.

*   *   *

On the few occasions when she had traveled to see her family or to visit friends, Elizabeth had always had one or more of the children with her. Now she was going to board a plane by herself for the first time in sixteen years. The thought made her smile.

Her plan was simple. She was going to find Whitehead, have him show her where Mary Kennedy was, and then call the FBI. She would call her friends in Houston and ask them to take Whitehead for a few days until he could get settled. Then she'd put him on the bus for the six-hour trip.

She packed quickly even though she had three hours until her flight took off at 5:40. When the phone rang she picked it up and almost sang her hello.

The voice on the other end was pleasant, if reserved. "Elizabeth Boget?" the female caller asked tentatively.

"This is Elizabeth."

"Hi. This is Debbie Steinbaugh. I got a message that you called and had to speak to me right away. Is everything okay?"

"Yes, I just wanted to ask you about Barry Whitehead."

Debbie cringed at the sound of the name. "Barry Whitehead? Why?"

"Why?" Elizabeth paused. "That's a good question. First, I need you to promise that this conversation stays just between the two of us, at least for the next forty-eight hours."

Debbie liked the intrigue and agreed.

"I think Barry Whitehead is alive."

The gasp on the other end told Elizabeth she had Debbie's complete attention.

"He called this morning and is in . . . let's just say he's back in the States and he has some information that could lead the authorities to the people who put Peter in the hospital." Elizabeth stopped long enough for Debbie to absorb what she said. "I'm going to meet him tonight."

"Not alone."

"Yes, alone. Why?"

"You don't want to meet Barry Whitehead alone, assuming he's alive. But I don't understand. Mike said he was killed in Mexico."

"We don't know all the details yet. That's why I'm going."

"But you can't go near that man alone. I've seen him much too close. The very thought of him makes my skin crawl. He seemed nice, but he turned into a hideous monster in a heartbeat. I can't describe it, but one minute we were talking and the next he was trying to rape me. But he wasn't raping me, he seemed to be raping every woman who had entered his life. Hatred just poured out of his mouth and he started tearing off my clothes and it was terrible. I don't know what this is all about, but the last place any woman should be is near Barry Whitehead." She concluded her comment with a deep-throated growl that further expressed her utter disgust.

The two women talked for ten minutes. When she hung up the phone, Elizabeth Boget was subdued. She sat down in a soft chair near the window of her bedroom. She looked out at the verdant green front lawn and the three dogwoods, white with blossoms. Then she bowed her head in her hands and prayed silently. *Father, what am I doing? Guide me, please, and let me know you're out here. Show me what to do. Give me wisdom, Lord.* She wrestled with God for several minutes before getting up and walking downstairs and outside to where Peter was sitting in a lawn chair near the sandbox where Kristin was watching her younger brother play.

Elizabeth sat down on the corner seat of the sandbox. She wrapped her arms around her legs. Her long khaki skirt covered all but her casual cloth shoes. She looked up at her husband. "Peter, I can't go." She wiped her hand across her mouth and gently squeezed the soft skin above her upper lip, then she continued speaking. "I just talked with Debbie. I think she's right. A woman has no business being alone with Barry Whitehead."

"So you've come to your senses."

"Yes, I guess I have. I think . . . For sixteen years I've been working keeping this house together while you're out making sure the phone company looks good and taking care of half the people in the church. And when you're not doing that, I'm running the house while you run out to play tennis or basketball or coach soccer. And right now we've got bills to pay, and this big mortgage hanging over our head, and you may not have the income you once had, and none of this would be happening if it wasn't for some woman who doesn't care about life or the people she's destroying with her drugs. Not to mention Irish Eyes and Mazzetti . . . If we have an opportunity to get those jerks, I'm ready to do it, but I do have this family to care for. I've got enough sense to know that, while I'd be able to handle myself in New Orleans, and I could find Whitehead and probably do a better job than you or the police when it comes to getting him to cooperate, I value Debbie's judgment. I don't want to do something that might take me away from the kids or you."

Peter slid to the edge of the chair and listened intently.

"If you can, Peter, I want you to go," said Elizabeth. "Do this for our children, do it for Mike, do it for me. I truly believe this is a door that God is opening for us and I want us to step through it before it closes." She stopped and scooped up a handful of sand and let it slip through her hand onto the ground in front of her. "If you're able to fly, I say go for it. We'll never rest as long as there is any question in our mind." Elizabeth stood up and brushed the back of her skirt. Then she bent down and snatched Kristin from the sand. She began brushing sand from her daughter's feet and legs, looking down at Peter. "I'll help you get ready. We can change the reservations when we get to the airport."

"Two hours ago you didn't want me to go. What's changed?"

"I don't really know. I only know we've got to seize the moment. Talk to Whitehead tonight, and if this is all a hoax you can catch a flight back in the morning. That would cost us maybe a hundred at the most. We can squeeze that out. That's a small price to pay to put this behind us."

Peter stood up. "To put this behind us or to get revenge?"

Elizabeth looked coolly at her husband. "Maybe a little of both. Will you go?"

18

L iza Morgan grabbed her phone on the first ring. She tried not to
sound too excited when she said hello.

"What are you so happy about?" scowled her husband through the
phone line. "Look, I'm calling to tell you that I won't be home for
dinner. Derek just went home with a stomachache and I've got to finish
pulling these cables by myself. They're starting the sheetrock on Monday,
so I've got to get this done. When Eric gets home, send him up here to help.
I don't want to be here all night and all day tomorrow," he said. "Can you
drive him over when he gets home?"

Liza was irritated. How could the man live in this house and not know
that Eric was playing baseball every afternoon? She felt like giving Randy
a piece of her mind, but decided it was too valuable to share with him. Her
answer was pleasant and casual. "He won't be home until after practice. I'll
bring him up then."

"What's he doing tomorrow?"

"He's going out with some of his friends. I've heard him talking about
it all week. Isn't there anyone else you can call?"

"Well, what are *you* doing tomorrow?" Randy's question was more like a
demand.

Liza always got frustrated working with her husband. The few times she had done it, she could not please him. He ended up being verbally abusive, and she ended up in tears. "That depends," she responded carefully. "I was planning to do some summer shopping over in Gulfport."

"You're not going to Gulfport without me, understand? I'd like some help out here," he said with some hesitation in his voice. "But, no, you'd only screw things up. I'll talk to Eric tonight."

"Fine, but I do need some summer things and so do the kids. If you're going to be working, it just makes sense for me to get out, do the shopping, and get a change of scenery."

"You know I don't like you going over to Gulfport alone. It's dangerous for a woman to be out alone."

"I was thinking of taking Amy and Eric, but they're busy so I called Miriam Haskell."

"We'll talk about it later!" he growled.

"Randy," Liza said with her newly acquired assertiveness, "if you don't need me, I'm going shopping."

She hung up, leaving an enraged husband holding a dead phone.

After the conversation, Liza was feeling a rage of her own. She hated the way she had to conform to her husband's whims and demands, or his "preferences" as he would call them. Sometimes she wanted simply to take the children and leave. But she had always believed the marriage union was sacred and that she had a responsibility to submit to her husband's authority, even if that authority was abused.

Since Peter stepped back into her life, however, Liza had begun to see the world from another perspective. She began to question her belief system, particularly as it related to staying in a relationship in which she and her children were abused emotionally and physically. Now she felt empowered to reach out beyond the confines of a world largely defined by Randy. She didn't yet know where her steps would take her, and she expected repercussions no matter which way she turned, but she had passed the point of no return.

Moments after Liza hung up, the phone rang again. She feared it was Randy calling back to blow off steam. She didn't want to talk to him, but realized that if she didn't, he might be back in her face all too soon. Reluctantly, she lifted the phone to her ear. "Hello," she grumbled.

"Liza?"

She breathed a sigh of relief. "Peter, is everything all right? You didn't call."

"I think so. I'm at a pay phone at a convenience store and can only talk for a minute. I know this is bizarre and totally unexpected, but I'm flying to New Orleans this evening."

"What?" said a shocked Liza.

"I'll be very busy for a while . . . how long I don't know. Any chance I can meet you somewhere—just to see you for an hour or so? There's some things we've got to talk about."

Nothing had prepared Liza for this possibility. The idea brought a dozen conflicting thoughts and concerns to mind. It was risky. But this time she decided to let instinct, not rational thought, guide her speech. "I can meet you in New Orleans."

"I don't know the city very well," Peter said. "But I have to find a man at a mission down along the river. I don't know what's going to happen after that, but tonight I'm staying at the Rodeway Inn near the airport."

Liza was processing the information as fast as Peter supplied it. "On the east side of town there's the Plaza Shopping Center. It's at the Read Boulevard exit. There's a Days Inn right across the street. I can meet you in the parking lot at ten. If I can't get there, I'll call the motel and leave a message." She took a deep breath. "This is so exciting, I'm shaking. I can't believe I'm going to see you." The tempo of her voice speeded up. "Are we crazy? Can you imagine me telling Randy that I'm going to meet a man at a motel in New Orleans? He'd die. No, he'd kill me. I better not think about it. You know, we can leave my car at the mall and go down to the French Quarter. Oh, Peter, this is so romantic."

"Liza, slow down. Please don't make this out to be more than it is. I want to see you, but . . ." Listening to her voice on the phone electrified Peter, and concerned him at the same time. "Look, I have to go. If there is any problem on my end, I'll leave a message at the Days Inn. What are you driving?"

"A white Escort. A dirty, white—no, tomorrow it will be a clean, white Escort."

"Goodbye, Liza."

What am I doing? she thought to herself as she walked into the bathroom. She was trembling as she switched on the light and stared into the mirror

for a long time. Writing to a man was one thing. Seeing him face to face
was quite another. She placed her fingers on her face in half a dozen
places, pulling the crow's-feet away from her eyes, pulling the loose skin
back from her jaw. She pushed her hair up and pulled it down and then
pulled a comb through it. She wanted to do a lot to look just right for Peter,
but knew that anything she did beyond washing her hair and putting on
some lipstick would raise suspicions.

Randy never wanted Liza to dress nicely except when they were out
together. He preferred she stay as dowdy as an attractive woman can to
avoid inviting a pass from another man. But now she wanted to throw
caution to the wind and look stunning for Peter. She flipped through her
dresses hanging in the closet and finally settled on the floral print short-
sleeved dress that buttoned down the front from the neck to the hem. She
pulled it from the closet and held it in front of her as she looked at herself
in the mirror. She took in the whole Liza Morgan.

A broad smile allowed her lips to frame a set of teeth that looked like
they belonged in a toothpaste commercial. The upper front tooth had been
chipped and darker than the rest when Peter last saw her—a reminder of
a fall from a tree when she was a teenager. But now it was as pretty as all
the rest. The restoration was expensive, but, as Liza looked at the face in
the mirror, she knew it was worth it. She had taken her first paychecks after
going back to work and had the tooth fixed. Randy had threatened to knock
it out the day she came home from the dentist and flashed him her new
smile. But he decided that since the money was already spent he'd leave
her alone. And, from that day on, he demanded every paycheck before it
was cashed to make sure she wouldn't indulge in any more foolishness.

But Liza didn't want to think about Randy and she didn't want to see him,
at least not for a while. She walked to the kitchen, scribbled a note on the
white noteboard on the refrigerator, and scurried out the door.

*   *   *

From three until four, Peter and Elizabeth were busy. Not only did they
pack Peter's suitcase and change his bandages, they made more than half
a dozen calls. Peter lined up a job interview with a friend at the phone
company in Baton Rouge to provide a legitimate story for anyone who
might ask about his whereabouts. Elizabeth alerted a few friends that Peter

would be out of town for the weekend to ensure that she could get the kids to their soccer games on time.

Then the entire family piled into the station wagon for the forty-minute trip to the airport. The children viewed the trip as an outing, especially since Elizabeth promised to take them for pizza after they put their dad on the plane. Elizabeth saw the trip as a grim necessity. She was torn between worry for her husband's safety and a strong inner assurance that this final act was necessary to close the book on this difficult period of their lives. Peter didn't know how to feel. Nothing had prepared him for the mix of emotions he was experiencing. The chatter in the car helped to distract him from the real possibility that he might come face to face with someone who wanted him dead—and someone else who just wanted him.

"Hey, you guys," he said, glancing back to the children, "tomorrow, I'm going to call you after your games, and I'd like to hear that you all won."

"Don't worry, Dad," said Daniel. "This one's for you."

David added, "Reams will be a piece of cake!"

"Don't get too cocky," Peter advised.

"They always give you a good game," reminded Elizabeth.

David laughed. "If we don't win 3-0, I'll consider it a loss."

"When are we going to stop for pizza?" asked Jonathan, nestled in a car seat between his parents. "I'm hungry."

"First we have to take Dad to the airport," Elizabeth explained for the third time, as the station wagon circled downtown and headed north on Interstate 95. "Lauren?" she called to her daughter who was listening to music on her portable tape player. Raising her voice, she called again.

"What?"

"Would you pass the crackers? We have a hungry boy up here," Elizabeth said.

Without a word, the box of crackers arrived over Peter's left shoulder as Elizabeth exited onto I-64 east.

*   *   *

Just a half block from where U.S. 90 crosses St. Louis Bay, a delightful, well-stocked bookstore occupies one of several homes that have been converted to stores overlooking the main highway. Bookends introduces patrons to its fare on the enclosed porch where paperbacks and secondhand books line the bookshelves. Inside, each of the house's four rooms is filled with elegant slant-faced cases that a century earlier lined an apothecary shop in New Orleans's French Quarter. Now, however, the glass fronts are removed and the shelves are filled with books, featuring a selection as wide as might be found in a far bigger store. The house's kitchen doubles as the display room for cookbooks and a place for browsers to enjoy a cup of coffee. A small office is set up in an alcove off the kitchen.

On this Friday afternoon, when Liza Morgan walked through the door, the proprietor's cat was asleep atop a stack of invoices on the office's large wooden desk.

"Hi, Liza," said the owner, Sarah Digger. She was standing behind the counter near the front door waiting on Nancy Pleasant, another regular who lived a short walk away. "Don't you look like something's boiling up and ready to overflow," she said to Liza.

Nancy looked at Liza, with whom she had talked about dealing with difficult men, and agreed. "What's got into you? Did you finally divorce him?"

Liza continued to smile, unable to control the joy that spilled out across her face. "No," she said, "but I'm tempted."

The women laughed. Sarah finished recording Nancy's sale in her book of the few special customers to whom Sarah extended personal credit.

"Let's get a cup of coffee and talk about it," Nancy said.

"There's really nothing to talk about," Liza replied. "I've just come to browse."

Sarah leaned across the counter and lowered her usually loud voice. "You think you're going to come in here looking like you do and try to get out of here without telling us what's going on? Not on your life, sister! You usually look like Randy's just knocked you over the head with a salami or something; now you look like you've met Prince Charming. What gives?"

Liza glanced around the store.

"Don't worry, there's no one else here."

For two weeks, the emotions that had swept through her body and played havoc with her mind had been searching for release. She had good news—no, *great* news—but couldn't tell anyone. She felt like the elder who skipped church to play golf and hit his first-ever hole in one—and couldn't tell a soul. But she couldn't hold it in any longer.

"It's a long story," she whispered. "If Randy gets wind of this I'll end up at the bottom of the Gulf. But in a nutshell, here's what's going on . . ."

*   *   *

Peter Boget set his watch back one hour as the pilot announced the local time in New Orleans. The change of planes in Charlotte had gone smoothly and the flight to the home of Bourbon Street, Mardi Gras and jazz was uneventful and on time. Within thirty minutes, Peter had picked up his rented Bonneville and checked into the aging but well-kept motel across the street from the airport's entrance. There he dropped off his luggage before making the trip to the address Barry Whitehead had given him.

With map in hand and a good sense of where he was going, he picked up Interstate 10 and followed it into the city. After exiting he rounded the Superdome and headed south through the downtown area, reaching his destination ten minutes later. The neighborhood wasn't particularly attractive, and it was dark except for the white storefront in the middle of a block of closely spaced buildings. Above the front door, a large red and white cross hung from a pole protruding six feet from the building. The pole also supported two halogen lights that bathed the building in a blue-white glow. Written in white letters across the red horizontal arm were the words *Good Samaritan House.* Boget easily found a place to park half a block from the shelter's entrance.

He was surprised at the greeting he received when he stepped through the glass front door. The man at the painted steel desk looked up and pulled his head back as if startled. "Mr. Norton?" He studied Peter's face. "Are you all right?"

Surprised, Peter said, "I'm sorry, I'm not Mr. Norton. I'm Peter Boget, and I'm looking for a man who looks like me who is staying here."

The man behind the desk called for Father Jacobsen, a man whose ministry to the homeless of New Orleans spanned four decades. The gray-haired priest emerged from a small office behind the reception desk. He was dressed in a black short-sleeved shirt with white clerical collar and jeans that were a size too small for his portly body. He looked at Boget, then at the man who had been sitting at the desk, but who was now standing. "What do you need, Emile?"

Emile raised his hand in Boget's direction and said nothing. Peter took the cue and extended his hand and repeated his request. "I'm Peter Boget, and I'm looking for a man who looks like me. I believe he is staying here."

Jacobsen gave Peter a look not unlike the one given him by Emile. "You said Boget? But you look just like Mr. Norton. I can't believe it. Are you twins?"

"No. It's a long story. Mr. . . . uh, Norton . . . called me today and said he would be here. He said he has some very important information that could be of great value to a number of people, and I've just flown in from Virginia to hear it."

"He said you would be coming."

The priest beckoned Peter to follow him into his office and, lifting a stack of mail off a wooden chair, motioned for him to sit down. The office was cheerful, if cluttered. Articles about the shelter hung in picture frames amidst framed certificates of recognition from the city and several civic groups. A dozen or more wall hangings of various sizes, made from a variety of materials, also adorned the walls. They depicted the good Samaritan helping the man who, in Jesus' parable, was beaten and robbed along the road between Jerusalem and Jericho.

"Excuse me for looking at you like I did. Your appearance threw me. Mr. Norton said you would be coming, but, quite frankly, I wasn't expecting someone who looked that much like him, if you know what I mean." The priest's friendliness put Peter at ease. "Now, son, tell me about Mr. Norton and why you are looking for him."

"Is he here?"

"No, I'm afraid not."

"But he was here?"

"Yes, all week."

"And he's coming back tonight?"

"I don't know."

"What did he tell you about me?"

"Only that you were a friend."

"So where is he now?"

"For two days," said the priest, "a man has been inquiring about him—a private investigator from Maryland. He said Mr. Norton's name was really Barry Whitehead, and that he had stolen merchandise from his employer, and he was trying to track it down. And all day today he—"

"Did you get his name?"

"Hanks, somebody."

Boget didn't believe what he heard. "Did you say Hanks?"

"I think so."

Peter scratched his head. He was surprised that Hanks was actually here in New Orleans. "So what happened?"

"All day today, Mr. Hanks sat in a car, right across the street. When he came in here several hours ago, a couple of the men told me that Mr. Norton went out through our emergency exit. That's the last anyone has seen of him."

"Hanks is right; he is Barry Whitehead. The only question is why is Hanks looking for him."

"Do you have any idea?" asked the priest.

"Either the man wants the same information I am looking for or—and this is a distinct possibility—Hanks is working with someone who doesn't want anyone to find out what Whitehead knows."

"And what is it you want Mr. Whitehead for?"

Peter took a deep breath. "Mr. Whitehead is supposed to be dead, or at least that's the official word from Mexico where he was in jail for manslaughter. The people who thought they killed him are drug dealers. Those drug dealers mistook me for him and tried to kill me because they thought I stole some of their drugs. A friend of mine, Mike Downes, who was looking for me found Whitehead instead and took him to Mexico to confess to the manslaughter so that a friend of mine who was convicted of murdering her friend would be let out of prison. Now Mike Downes is being prosecuted by the government for helping Whitehead. If I can find Barry, there is a good chance the government will drop charges against Mike. But apparently Whitehead knows where the drug dealer is—somewhere here in New Orleans. That's why he called me. And if we can help get the dealer thrown in jail, Whitehead will probably get special treatment from the government."

Father Jacobsen looked up at Peter and laughed. "You lost me back in Mexico. And anyway, I don't want to know all the gruesome details." He looked somberly at Boget. "We don't ask the men here why they're here unless they volunteer the information or want our help. We try to give them dignity by accepting them as they are today and not requiring them to tell us about their pasts."

Boget looked at his watch. "It's almost ten," he said. "I'm going to hang around here for an hour or so, if you don't mind. Then I'm heading back to the Rodeway Inn. Here's a number where you can reach me." He pulled out a business card and wrote the motel's phone number on the back. He added another number beneath it. "Here's the number of the cellular phone in the car. Please call or have Whitehead call if he shows up." Peter pulled some money from his pocket and handed the priest a twenty dollar bill. "I'm a bit short of funds right now, but please take this as a small token of thanks for helping Barry this week."

Both men stood together. The priest extended his hand, then pulled it back as he realized that Peter would have a hard time shaking his bandaged hand. "I'll keep my eyes and ears open, and help you if I can."

"Thanks so much."

"By the way," Father Jacobsen said. "You're welcome to wait here in our lobby for Mr. Whitehead or go on back to the bunk room. I haven't been outside lately, but Hanks was gone the last time I checked." He walked to the door with Peter, stepped out onto the sidewalk and scanned the street. "I believe he's gone." Both men looked deathly pale in the glow of the halogen lamps.

"I'm going to sit in the car for a while and observe," Boget said, "if you don't mind."

"That's fine, son," said the priest. "Stop back in anytime up until 11:30. That's when we lock the doors."

"Thanks again," said Boget. Then, disappointed, he turned and walked to the car. From there he called Elizabeth.

When she answered the phone, Elizabeth was chipper. After only a few sentences, she was sharing her husband's disappointment. "So what are your plans now?"

"I'm going to sit here for an hour. If he doesn't show, I'm heading to the motel. I passed a Shoney's out by the airport; he said something about seeing Mary there before. I thought I'd swing by and see what I can see."

"Don't get yourself into any trouble," she cautioned.

"Have I ever gotten myself into trouble?" he responded with mock indignation.

Elizabeth laughed. "Are you asking about since we've been married or just the last twenty-four hours?"

"Would it make a difference?"

"No, it wouldn't. Call me in the morning."

"Don't know if I'll have time," said Peter lightly. "I'm thinking that if I don't find Barry and can't find Mary Kennedy, maybe I'll run over to Waveland and see if Liza wants to change my dressing."

"Do that and you *will* get in trouble!" Elizabeth said. "Leave the poor woman alone before she gets into hot water with her husband."

                              *   *   *

After six days on their boat, the crew of the *Miss St. Loo* was looking forward to unloading their shrimp and getting rid of the cocaine. But Holland's men weren't ready to take delivery for another twenty-four hours; so, with a good early-season catch already on board, the shrimp boat's crew finished its last steak and broke out the playing cards.

The boat's captain was the first to jump to the wheelhouse at the sound of another boat closing quickly. Jerry Plante knew that a boat speeding toward him in the dark could mean Coast Guard or the Drug Enforcement Administration. It was neither.

Within a minute, three men in army fatigues and brandishing automatic assault weapons had boarded the *Miss St. Loo*. A fourth individual remained at the wheel of the yacht. All wore black ski masks.

Using only their weapons to signal their intentions, the men made it clear that they wanted the fishermen out of their cabin and onto the deck.

"There must be some mistake," Plante protested as he stepped through the door, his hands raised only to his shoulders. "We're fishermen making our last run before heading in to unload. What do you want?"

As the other three fishermen filed out of the cabin, Patrick O'Hearn signaled them to lie face down on the steel deck.

"We're shrimp fishermen, that's all," one complained loudly before Liam O'Donnell pressed the muzzle of his gun into the nape of his neck. O'Hearn pulled one of the blankets from the cabin and draped it over the heads of the four fishermen.

While O'Donnell kept a gun trained on the fishermen, O'Hearn and Billy McMillan quickly searched the small vessel. Within five minutes O'Hearn found the device he was looking for behind a few canned goods in a small cabinet. He carried the transmitter to the yacht and carefully disassembled it to get what he needed. Then he reassembled it to gather the information. When he was finished, he returned the device to the exact location, he found it. Then he reached into the cabinet and dragged everything out, letting it all crash to the floor. For another three minutes, O'Hearn and McMillan, without saying a word, continued to turn the ship upside down while O'Donnell ran his gun barrel over the backs of the men lying on deck.

Then, as quickly as they arrived, the visitors jumped back onto their yacht. Before the four fishermen could scramble to their feet, the boat disappeared into the night with Adams at the helm.

"What was that all about?" one of the fishermen said as he scanned the ransacked boat.

"Gotta be pirates looking for drugs," Plante replied with a smile. "By now, they're probably wondering why they bothered to come aboard."

After a quick walk around the fishing boat, the men agreed that while the cabin's contents were scattered and overturned, nothing seemed to be missing. Plante had to dig through a stack of tin cans and broken dishware before he found pieces of the transmitter he had used to activate and deactivate the electromagnet holding the cocaine-filled canister to the underside of the boat. The circuit board was smashed, and wires dangled from the device. He didn't know what had been inside the transmitter, so he didn't notice that what was missing was the computer chip in which the digital activation code was stored.

"They didn't get what they came for," Plante told his crew, "but they sure don't want us to tell anyone they've been here. They've smashed our cellular phone and broken everything that even resembles a radio."

19

Warm moist air seemed to slow down the morning as Mary Kennedy made her way across New Orleans to the home of Jack Holland. Few cars and even fewer pedestrians were in evidence as she parked on tree-lined Carondelet and climbed the porch stairs.

Inside, Holland ignored the knock and ringing doorbell. But it was persistent, and finally the sleepy man walked downstairs. When he arrived at the door, he was wearing a paisley silk robe and a look of disdain.

"What do you want?" he shouted belligerently through the door.

"We've got to talk."

He shook his head. "Not now."

Kennedy considered how best to get inside the door before someone noticed her on the steps. She could demand he open the door but suspected that approach would meet with resistance. She could ask O'Hearn, who was sitting in a car on the next block, to come and open the man's door for her. Instead, she did something she found totally repugnant but effective. She began unbuttoning her blouse, slowly, seductively. By the time she reached the fourth button the door was open and she was inside.

"Are you going to finish, Miss McKenna?" Holland asked, surveying the woman.

Kennedy reached out and pressed her fingers against his chest. He backed up and rounded the corner to the living room. "Sit down," she said.

He liked sex, but was wary of women, especially this woman, on a delivery day. Still, he sat down on a newly upholstered antique sofa and watched her sit down across from him. She buttoned her blouse as he spoke.

"What do you want?" he asked.

"What do you think I want? I just heard that you exercised your option and took control of Kennedy and Associates."

"I thought you were only interested in Mary's other business," said Holland. "Anyway, we discovered that someone at Kennedy and Associates was transferring assets to a leasing company. If I waited until the end of next month, I might have discovered that not only would I not have payment for my goods, but I would have handed over twenty-five percent ownership in my company to someone I don't know—in exchange for a company that has no value. As it is, the goodwill value of Kennedy and Associates has dropped dramatically now that Mary is gone, and a cloud is hovering over her business."

"Not her business, Jack," said Kennedy, removing her wig. "Mine. We had a deal, and you crossed me."

Disbelief raced across his round face, but without hesitation he continued. "You have no intention of paying for the delivery, do you? You just want to get into my business, and you were going to do it by raiding your own company and giving me some worthless paper."

"It's not like that, I—"

"Well, I don't work like that. I said I'd deliver the merchandise, and I'm a man of my word. It'll be delivered on Tuesday just like we agreed."

"Not Tuesday—today!"

"I've got your company, and you have twenty-five percent of Holland Engineering. If you want to cancel the deal, you have thirty days to make payment and the deal is killed."

"I take delivery today—all thirty-two kilos."

"Are you listening to me?" asked Holland.

"And are you listening to me?" she shot back. "Delivery today."

Holland paused and studied the woman closely. "I can't believe you're sitting there," he said quietly. "You're dead. I saw it on the news."

"Listen, Jack, I am dead to anyone who asks. Do you understand? I don't have any safe way to take delivery in Norfolk; I want to make a pickup today.

You just tell me when and where."

Holland stood up and pulled his robe snug around his belly. Then he walked toward the front window. "You remember where we went to the casino two weeks ago?"

"Yes."

"Instead of turning into the parking lot, stay to the right and follow the road past Terry's Seafood and go up over the one-lane bridge that takes you to a parking area. Make a quick left over the bridge. We'll look for you." He paused. "Only one car. What are you driving?"

"They'll be driving a rental. A blue van."

Holland shook his head. "No vans."

"Okay, they'll be in the Buick Park Avenue I rented yesterday. It's dark green."

"Who's they?"

"My men. Three of them . . . and a woman," she said as she visualized how O'Hearn and the others would be making the pickup. "I won't be there. Remember, I don't exist."

Holland shook his head. "Mary, you're crazy."

"My name's Kathleen now." She extended her hand. "Kathleen McKenna. And I own twenty-five percent of your business. No tricks tonight, do you understand?"

Jack smiled broadly. "Speaking of tricks, now that we're partners, we ought to get to know each other better." He swept his hand in the direction of the archway to the hall. "You know the way to the bedroom."

Kennedy turned abruptly. "I also know the way to the door."

                              *   *   *

Elizabeth had to head out the door to take her children to a soccer game but didn't want to miss Peter's call. She dialed his motel and woke him up.

"Hello?" came the groggy voice over the line.

"Peter, good morning."

"Hi, Elizabeth. Is it morning already?"

"It's 8:15." Her voice was bright and cheerful.

"Not here it isn't," he said.

"I'm sorry. I just wanted to know that you are okay and find out if you located Barry."

"I struck out, but I'll be doing some checking today. I'm gonna go by the FBI office here and let 'em know what's going on. If nothing else, they can think I'm crazy, but if something happens to Whitehead, they'll know that I at least tipped them off. It must have been three o'clock this morning—I couldn't sleep—when the thought popped into my head that what if Whitehead ends up dead down here and somebody figures out I was in town and . . . well, you get the drift. I think the FBI should know what I've found out so far. That way they can at least verify that Barry was at the shelter."

"So you're going to the FBI this morning?"

"As soon as I wake up." Peter yawned. "Then maybe I'll do some sight-seeing and head back to the shelter tonight on the off-chance he gets back there."

"You won't have much fun sightseeing alone," Elizabeth said.

"Maybe you're right," he said teasingly. "I'll have to find a woman around here and let her escort me around the city."

"Just make sure she's old and married and sees your chest. That'll keep the two of you at a safe distance!"

"Are we talking 'old' like you?"

"At least as old as you. That way you can both save some money using senior citizen discount cards."

"You got it. I'll only talk to serious senior citizens. She'll be a lot older than me."

Both laughed.

"I'll call you the moment something turns up," Peter added. "In the meantime, you can always try to reach me on the mobile phone."

"At a dollar a minute? I don't think so."

"Fine. I'll call you at six your time."

Peter was in good spirits, but as he hung up the phone a heaviness fell on his heart. He had told his wife the truth, but he hadn't been truthful. And, as exhilarating as the thought of meeting Liza was, a quiet voice was whispering in his ear. It was a word of warning, a word of reason. "Don't play with fire," it was saying, "or you'll surely get burned."

Peter didn't want to hear that voice. He walked to the sink just outside the bathroom and switched on the fluorescent light above the mirror. He ran his fingers through his hair and slowly shook his head. At that moment, he realized that the reunion with Liza was going to have to be less than what he wanted.

He wished he had had a chance to talk all of this through with Elizabeth before he left. Excitement had clouded his judgment. And the distractions of Barry Whitehead, Mary Kennedy, Irish Eyes, Earl Hendrick, Mike Downes, the FBI—all had prevented him from taking the time he needed to sort out the situation in which he found himself.

He walked away from the mirror and took his Bible from his suitcase and flipped it open. He knew the verses he wanted to avoid—the ones that spoke about adultery, the ones that talked about love. He turned pages aimlessly, then stopped to read a verse that he had underlined years before. "Walk by the spirit, and you will not carry out the desire of the flesh."

He realized that since that awful incident in the hospital, he was preoccupied with controlling his life. He was trying to do it all in his own power— pursuing a relationship with Liza he knew would only end in heartache, going after Kennedy and Irish Eyes believing that their capture would erase the emotional scars in the minds of his family, and, more important in his mind, keeping Frank Mazzetti from taking away his job, and now taking an ill-advised trip twenty-two years backward in time.

Peter put down the Bible, bowed his head and prayed.

When he finished, he walked back to the mirror. The same man stared back at him. His desire to see Liza was just as strong, but he had a better perspective on what he was feeling. His desire to track down Whitehead and Kennedy was still strong, and he still wanted to personally see to it that Mazzetti went down in disgrace. His emotions were still overflowing, but, like a mighty river after a flood, they at least were back within the banks.

Had he any idea what the next twenty-four hours would bring, he would have driven across the street to the airport and caught the next flight to Richmond. But he didn't. And being a person who was always up for an adventure, Peter prepared for his ten o'clock rendezvous with Liza Morgan.

*   *   *

A woman answered the phone in a house overlooking the Severn River from a bluff two miles north of Annapolis, Maryland.

"I'm calling for Mike Downes, please."

"He's not here right now. He's down at the dock. May I give him a message when he gets back?"

"This is Debbie Steinbaugh."

"Oh, hi, Debbie, this is Jean Maxwell," said the woman, with a deep but warm and friendly voice. "Mike told us all about you last night."

"He did?"

"Oh, nothing to worry about. He spoke of you in the most glowing of terms. Sounds like I'll be needing a dress for the wedding."

Debbie was both embarrassed and flattered that Mike was speaking to his friends in those terms. But she hadn't gotten up at six on a Saturday morning to conduct a friendly chat with a woman she didn't know. "I need to speak to Mike right away. When will he be back?"

"Is something wrong?"

"Yes."

Jean waited for more, but when nothing came, she continued. "It's a two-minute walk down the hill to our dock. I could run and get him."

"Please, it's urgent," Debbie said. "Tell him Elizabeth Boget is with Barry Whitehead."

*   *   *

If Liza slept at all, it was only when she drifted off while imagining what a reunion with Peter would be like. She imagined stepping out of the car in the hotel parking lot and floating across the asphalt into his arms. She imagined the world around her disappearing, leaving the two of them alone in a virgin gulf-coast forest—alone to give and receive love, alone to enjoy all of God's creation, alone to share a lifetime of peace and happiness.

But the fantasy was short-lived as the icy fear of discovery awakened her to the reality of her world—a world in which she was a captive of her husband, her circumstances and her insecurities. She knew that even if she and Peter could do everything she dreamed of doing in the few short hours they would be together, and even if everything went without a hitch, tomorrow's pain would be nearly unbearable. To watch Peter leave her life a second time would be devastating. Still, she felt her life would be poorer if she didn't seize this opportunity to see him again.

She wished she had never said anything to her friends at the bookstore because she knew they would want a report, and she wasn't sure she wanted anyone to know of the actual meeting. To dream, to write, to fantasize was okay, she reasoned, but actually being with another man stirred a host of doubts. She tried to dismiss them as nothing more than the misplaced guilt associated with years of teaching that she should be submissive to her husband—even when she assumed that the physical and emotional abuse Randy had dished out to her and the children disqualified him from the role he demanded. Her heart was beating faster than normal, and she was aware of her quickened breathing. She wrapped her robe around her and headed for the kitchen.

*   *   *

"Debbie?"

"Mike! Good morning."

"It doesn't sound like a good morning," said Mike in his calm, reassuring voice. "What's this about Whitehead and Elizabeth? Have you had a bad dream?"

"I wish it were just a dream. I promised Elizabeth I wouldn't say anything, but I couldn't sleep all night and had to tell someone. Elizabeth called me yesterday and told me the most fantastic story, and then she said she was going somewhere to meet Barry Whitehead."

For the first time since leaving the Mexican prison with her, the thought crossed Mike's mind that this woman's brain was not wired right. Either that or she was still asleep. "Now let me get that straight," he said. "Elizabeth called you and said she was meeting Barry Whitehead?"

"I told her she shouldn't, but she said that he said he had seen Mary Kennedy."

"Debbie, are you awake? Barry's dead, and so is Mary. I'm sure no one is going anywhere."

"I know you may not believe me, but it's true."

She didn't sound like she was dreaming or that she was asleep. She was direct and forceful.

"Please," she went on, "at least call the Bogets and find out what's happening. She could end up like me with that man. She asked me not to say anything to anyone for forty-eight hours, but it's too crazy and I had to tell you. I don't know what to do, but maybe you do."

Minutes later, Mike dialed the Boget residence.

"Hello?" came Daniel's voice singing across the line.

Mike wasn't sure if he was talking to Daniel or Lauren, but took a chance on the former.

"Daniel?"

"Uh huh."

"This is Mike Downes. I was calling for your mother."

"Just a minute. I'll get her."

So Debbie had gotten the story wrong. Probably there wasn't any story at all—except the story behind what was going on in Debbie's mind. Then Elizabeth picked up the phone.

"Good morning, Mike," she said with little enthusiasm. "Debbie called, didn't she?"

"What's going on?"

"You'll never believe it," she began, "but Peter is in New Orleans right—"

"Where?" Downes was more than surprised. He was nearly speechless.

"He's looking for Barry Whitehead. He apparently wasn't killed in the explosion and got out of Mexico and has been at a homeless shelter in New Orleans for a few days. That's when he saw Mary Kennedy alive and called Peter for help because he said he doesn't know another soul in the world. In fact, he believes you might have been involved in setting him up, so he didn't want to call you. So Peter went down and found out that Hanks, the policeman from Maryland who was at the hospital with us, visited the shelter before he got there. Apparently, Whitehead saw him first and ran away."

Mike's head was spinning. Nothing she said made sense.

Elizabeth continued. "Debbie probably told you that I was originally planning to go down. But after talking with her, we decided that it wasn't smart for me to go."

"Why didn't you call me?"

"With all you've got going, Mike, we didn't want to say anything until we were sure. You have to admit, the story sounds rather bizarre."

Mike thought for a moment. "Is there a number where I can reach Peter?"

"That might be a good idea." She read off the hotel number and the number for the car phone.

"He's not planning on doing anything foolish, is he?"

Elizabeth laughed. She knew that her husband was often spontaneous, but he was not a wild risk taker. "I sure hope not."

"I'll give him a call."

"Thanks, Mike. Sorry you got mixed up in this."

"Are you kidding? If Barry is alive, that's the best news I've heard all week!"

The phone rang again as soon as Elizabeth had hung up. It was Barry Whitehead.

"Peter's in New Orleans looking for you," said Elizabeth, after a brief exchange of greetings.

"Where can I reach him?"

*   *   *

Peter was dressing when the phone rang.

"This is Barry Whitehead."

Boget had to shift his thinking 180 degrees. He had been absorbed with thoughts of Liza, not Barry. But this was what he came to New Orleans for. "Where are you?"

"Safe for now," Whitehead said with a distinct lack of conviction. "Can you meet me in Gretna?"

"Where's that?" Peter asked, opening his New Orleans map on the bed.

"If you take the ferry that crosses the river a few blocks from the Good Samaritan House, you'll be in Gretna. When you come over the levee, you'll be on a wide street. Pull over to the curb before Fourth Street. I'll be there."

"Looks like I can get there quicker on Route 90 from where I am."

"Take the ferry. I want to see you coming alone over the levee. There's a ferry every thirty minutes, and it only takes about ten minutes to cross. I'll look for you. What are you driving?"

Peter checked his watch and did some calculations. If all went well, he could still get to Read Boulevard by ten. "I can be there in an hour," he said. "I'll be in a blue Bonneville."

No sooner had he cradled the handset when the phone rang again. Peter thought it was Barry calling back. "What?" he said.

"Peter, is that you?" It was the familiar voice of Mike Downes. "*What* are you doing in New Orleans?" he asked.

"I'm going to catch a ferry."

Downes thought that was the most unusual response he had ever heard. "You what?"

"Barry Whitehead just called—if you got this number, you surely know by now he's alive. I'm meeting him in an hour and I have to take a ferry to get there. Then I've got an appointment at ten. Let me call you back from the car phone. This is going to be close."

"You don't need to," he said, sensing Peter's urgency. "I just wanted to know if you're all right."

"I feel great, just rushed. Give me a number and I'll call you back later and let you know what's going on."

He supplied the number and concluded, "Be careful, Peter. Don't do anything . . . ah . . . stupid."

"You mean like fly him to Mexico?"

*   *   *

For the crew of the *Miss St. Loo,* the unsettling night was over. They slowly knifed through the waters of the Gulf toward the entrance of Bayou Caddy. They didn't know who had boarded their boat in the night but suspected that whoever it had been was probably watching them. They also knew that Daugherty, their contact, had them in view from his vantage point atop the casino. They didn't know who he worked for and didn't care. Daugherty paid Plante, the boat's owner, ten thousand dollars in cash after each pickup. Plante in turn paid fifteen hundred dollars to each of the three who worked with him to assist in the pickup and to keep their mouths shut.

The fishermen spent their morning putting their clothes and personal things in order so that when they did reach land they could quickly unload the shrimp and head for their homes. None of them had the desire to hang around and find out when and how the torpedolike container attached to the boat's hull would be retrieved. They were paid simply to make a pickup and bring it to shore.

Once home, they would tie up their boat along a dock that ran parallel to the channel and just over a small bridge linking the docks, where the fishing boats unload their catches, and a parking lot. It was where Holland told Kennedy to pick up her merchandise.

It was also where Billy McMillan was, at that moment, staking out the rendezvous site.

*   *   *

While McMillan was busy at Bayou Caddy, eighty miles to the west, Peter Boget was driving toward the center of the city on Airline Boulevard, alternating his glance from the map in his lap to the street signs. He zigzagged over to Jackson and arrived at Tchoupitoulas Street, which ran along the levee. When he learned he had a twenty minute wait for the ferry, he pulled out of line and drove to the Good Samaritan House to view the facility by daylight. Then he returned to the ferry terminal and within five minutes was driving onto the partially enclosed, steel auto deck of the ferry. As soon as he stopped, he stepped out of his car and watched as half a dozen additional cars drove on and parked. Then he walked around to the steps that led to the enclosed passenger deck above.

With a deep-throated growl, the idling diesel engine sprang to life. The entire vessel shuddered as it pushed away from the dock to begin the ten-minute crossing of the swift river. Boget walked back and forth through the cabin area alternately looking back at the waterfront warehouses and forward to the low buildings on the Gretna side of the river that were growing in size as the ferry proceeded south. He wondered where Barry Whitehead was waiting. He wondered what was going through the man's mind, and what he would do with him once he met him. For Mike Downes's sake, Peter knew he would try to persuade Whitehead to turn himself in.

He checked his watch. His continued pacing was one way he could release some of the nervous tension that gripped him as his mind shuttled between Whitehead and Liza.

The river crossing did not last long enough to allow Peter to bring order to the confusion in his mind. Before he started his engine, Peter folded his arms and leaned forward on the steering wheel. He was tired and distracted.

A rapping sound jarred him to attention. The sound came from knuckles pounding on his window. The person standing beside the car was hard to see in the glare of the morning sun. Then the face registered, and the confusion in his mind turned to chaos. Nothing made sense, yet everything made sense. He began to fit the pieces together and the picture was becoming clear. But it was not the picture he expected to see. He rolled down the window, and both men asked the same question at the same time.

"What are you doing here?"

"Looking for the same person, I bet," Peter replied.

"I want to talk to you," the man said. "Pull over as soon as you can when we get off this boat."

"I'm meeting a friend at ten. Give me a phone number. I'll call you when I'm through."

Roland Hanks peered through the partially opened window just as he had looked into the driver's side windows of thousands of motorists during his years with the Maryland State Police. He could tell a lot about people just by looking at their faces, their hand movements, their breathing patterns. When he looked at Peter, he could tell that the man was telling the truth, but he could also tell that the man was very nervous. "Are you meeting Whitehead at ten?" he asked.

Peter knew that the only way to deflect the man's attention was to startle him with the truth. The ferry had already docked, and most of the motorists had started their engines. He only had thirty seconds. Only the truth would do. "I came to town because Whitehead called me. I went to the Good Samaritan House last night to meet him, but he was gone."

"I know."

"I thought I'd check again this morning before I head out to meet a friend I haven't seen in over twenty-two years. My wife thinks I have a meeting with the FBI this morning. I've got an hour and a half to kill so I decided to take a ferry ride." Boget started the engine in his car. "I've got a thing about ferries," he added with a shrug. "I like to ride them whenever I can."

"Pull over when we get off here." This time it was a command, not a request.

*   *   *

Everything worked out perfectly for Liza. Randy was in a good mood when he left at 8:30 with the boys. He didn't object to Liza's casual mention that Miriam wanted to go to New Orleans instead of Gulfport to shop. She was dressed and cleaning up the kitchen when her friend drove into the driveway. Liza walked outside. Her friend rolled down the window of her aging Toyota. "Are you ready, Liza?" she asked cheerfully.

"Just about. Would you like me to drive?"

The mere suggestion was enough for Miriam. She responded with a quick "Sure."

"I should have thought about this last night. You can leave your car here, or I can run by your place."

"You see me," she said after she stepped from the car. "I'm dressed for trying on clothes. The stores will be opening at ten." Her good humor was infectious. "Let's not keep them waiting."

Liza raced into the house, grabbed her purse from the kitchen table, and called to her daughter who was waiting for her ride to the car wash.

"Bye, Mom. Bring me lots of stuff!"

Liza was back out in less than thirty seconds. "Let's roll," she said.

*   *   *

In his rearview mirror Peter Boget watched Hanks climb into a car five vehicles behind him. He couldn't stop to see Barry with Hanks around, but if he abandoned Whitehead, all hope of finding Mary might be lost as well. Unless he could get Hanks to lead him to her. He looked quickly at his map and then scribbled directions on a piece of paper. The first cars were beginning to drive off the boat when he opened his door, ran back to Hanks's car and handed him the note.

"It's called Mel Ott Park. It's just past the elevated highway; that's what he told me. I'm supposed to pick him up at 9:30. But if I do that, I'll miss the most important meeting of my life. Here's my phone number in the car," he said as he wrote on the slip of paper. "Call me when you pick him up, and let me know where you're going." Peter tried to look more harried than he really was. He noted the model and license number of Hanks's car.

A member of the ferry's crew was yelling for Peter to get back to his car and get off the boat. He yelled back over the sound of beeping horns, "Just a minute," and raced back to his car. He had accomplished what he wanted. All the cars in front of him were well clear of the ferry. Boget jumped into his car and drove off the ferry much faster than the posted speed, bounced over the railroad tracks and sped to Fourth Street where he turned left just as Hanks, following slower cars, crested the levee. By the time Hanks reached Fourth and drove the one block to Lafayette, Peter was out of view.

Hanks turned right, heading south on Lafayette toward the park. Boget, who had made a left at Lafayette and pulled over to the curb in midblock, watched in his mirror as Hanks's car disappeared. Then Boget pulled out, drove to the end of the block, turned left, then left again on Huey Long Avenue. He slowed to a crawl searching for Whitehead. The man whom Peter had encountered over six weeks earlier on a cold night on the Capital Beltway in suburban Maryland dashed from out of nowhere toward the car. Peter stopped, unlocked the door, and Whitehead jumped in. He was pale, unshaven, and looked as if he hadn't slept in forty-eight hours—which he hadn't.

"Get down," Peter said, as he turned right onto Fourth and headed west. "I'm taking you to my motel. You can sleep for a while, and then we can decide what to do. I've got to meet a friend on the other side of town at ten."

Whitehead laid his weary head back on the headrest. "Thank you for coming, Mr. Boget. When you drove by the first time, I thought you had decided to abandon me. Then I saw the man who was at the shelter. I couldn't believe it."

"Where's Mary Kennedy?"

"She's registered under the name of Kathleen McKenna at the Shoney's Inn, next to the restaurant, in Metairie. At least, she was on Thursday."

"And you saw her?"

"Twice. It's her, believe me."

"I do," Boget said with conviction. "Hanks—he's a policeman from Maryland or was one before he got kicked off the force for trying to play hero at the hospital—is mixed up with Kennedy, I'm sure, or he wouldn't be down here looking for you."

"I know. I saw him with O'Hearn outside the shelter two nights ago."

Boget kept watching the mirror for signs of Hanks. "I was out at the Shoney's last night," he said. "I didn't see anyone who looked like Mary or anyone who looked suspicious."

"Well, Mary's changed her hair, " said Whitehead. "She's got a lot more of it now, and she's done something else to look different. I'm not sure what. But she's different."

Peter listened to Whitehead but couldn't concentrate on all he was saying. Too much was competing for his attention. He was hard pressed to imagine that he could make it to the Days Inn by ten, yet he didn't want to get caught speeding and be made even later. He knew he should call the FBI and let them know what was happening, but he wasn't sure he had enough of the story. He knew that for Mike's sake he had to get Whitehead to the police, but guessed that Whitehead wouldn't go.

As he drove, he began to shake inside. He continued checking the mirror for Hanks, but the man wasn't in sight as he began his assent of the Huey Long Bridge to cross the Mississippi.

He was happy for the distraction of the railroad train that had inched its way up the long approach to the trestle bridge and was now just a few feet away, crossing the bridge beside him. Watching the slow-moving train reminded him of the "Little Engine That Could" story and board game that was one of his children's favorites. The thought of his kids sitting around him playing that game brought a smile to his face. He wondered if David's early game had gone well and if the kids were back home for snacks before going back to the Coalfield Soccer Complex for the other games.

In all the thoughts of his family, it never occurred to him that Elizabeth's hectic but enjoyable morning might take a sudden turn for the worse.

* * *

"I'll get the phone," Lauren said as the Boget children all tried to push through the front door at the same time.

"No, I will," said Daniel, racing to the ringing phone. "I called it first."

The eight-year-old was quicker but his sister was stronger, and strength won out as Lauren wrenched the handset from Daniel. That caused him to howl in fake pain and plead for justice to his mother, who was entering the kitchen. "She knocked me down," he wailed. "You need to spank her."

Lauren interrupted and pointed the handset toward her mother. "It's for you."

Elizabeth walked to the phone and held her hand over the mouthpiece for a moment while she instructed the children to stop fighting.

"Is this Mrs. Peter Boget?"

"It is."

"Mrs. Boget, this is Detective Brown with the New Orleans police," the man on the other end said solemnly. "We think your husband may be in trouble. A man we were pursuing was picked up by someone driving the car your husband rented at the airport. Last night the man swore to the others at the homeless shelter where he was staying that he was about to take revenge on the man who had caused him to lose everything."

"Whitehead?"

"You know Barry Whitehead?"

"My husband was meeting him this morning." Panic was setting in.

"When he drove off the ferry, he eluded the policeman who was following him. Do you know where he might be going?"

Elizabeth tried to concentrate on the call, but her children continued their bickering. Lauren was slow leaving the kitchen and Daniel used the opportunity to run up, shove her against the wall, and race to his mother's side with an angry Lauren right behind. Elizabeth cupped the phone, glared at Lauren and Daniel and shouted, "Children!"

The shout subdued the two who were teasing each other, but caused a frightened Kristin to burst into tears. Elizabeth lost her train of thought and answered the caller reflexively. "He's staying at the Rodeway Inn near the airport. Do you need the number?"

"Please."

The moment Elizabeth hung up the phone the voice of the caller registered in her mind.

"Oh, dear God," she whispered. Then she dropped her head into her hands.

20

They were within a mile of the motel when the car phone sitting on the seat between Peter Boget and Barry Whitehead signaled that a call was coming in. The two men looked at each other, then down at the phone. Peter knew it couldn't be Hanks because he gave him a bogus number. With his bandaged right hand, he lifted the phone to his ear.

"Elizabeth?"

"I just got a call, and I think it was Hanks." Elizabeth's voice reflected her deep concern. "He said he was a New Orleans policeman, and before I realized who it was I gave him the name of your hotel. He said you were in trouble, and that he was going to help you."

"You sure it was Hanks?"

"What's going on, Peter?"

"When did he call?"

"Two minutes ago, no more," she said, then almost pleading for information she said, "What's going on down there?"

"Everything's going to be fine," he tried to assure her. "Barry's with me, and I'm going to run by the motel, pick up my stuff, and disappear. I ran into Hanks twenty minutes ago and gave him the slip, that's why he's probably calling. I'm at the motel right now. Let me run, and I'll call you back within the hour."

"Be careful, Peter . . . I love you."

He hung up the phone and spoke to Whitehead as he turned on his left blinker and crossed the road to the motel's parking lot. "We probably don't have but a minute, so as soon as we stop I want you to help grab everything in the room and throw it in the back seat. We can sort it out after we get out of here."

Boget was glad he had a first-floor room. He backed the car almost to the door, jumped out, opened the room, and, while Whitehead gathered up clothes, Peter opened both the door to the backseat and the trunk. The room was vacated in under a minute. Peter left the key on the table, closed the door and departed. Within five minutes he was at the auto rental counter in the Avis parking lot. "I need a new car, and I need it quick," he said.

The attendant looked quizzically at him. "Is there something wrong with the car?"

"No, it's fine. I think someone's following me and I want to change cars."

Without further questioning, the woman picked up several sets of keys on her counter. "I've got a white Caprice, a green Park Avenue, a red—"

"The Park Avenue will be fine."

The switch was made and Peter and Barry drove out of the parking lot. As they passed the Rodeway Inn, they saw what looked like the car Hanks had been driving and a man standing at the door of the room they had cleaned out fifteen minutes before. Peter anxiously turned onto the airport access road and headed for the interstate. The digital clock on the radio showed 9:53.

"Well, Liza," he thought to himself, "you are going to be in for a shock."

*   *   *

"Miriam," said Liza as she pulled the Escort to a stop outside Maison Blanche, "I'm not going shopping with you."

"You're not what?" said the woman who was already opening the door.

Liza took a set of keys from her purse and handed it to the surprised woman. "Here's some keys so you can put stuff in the car during the day. I'll park back here in this general area. But I'm not going."

Miriam pulled the door closed to keep the car cool under the hot sun.

Liza had not turned off the engine.

"All night and this morning I have been trying to think of a way to tell you this, but don't know how. I've got to meet someone in five minutes over at that Days Inn." She motioned toward the motel across Read Boulevard from where they were sitting.

Not much shocked Miriam. She spent too much time watching daytime television and reading the women's magazines she would pick up while standing in line at the grocery store. But when Liza, the woman she respected more than any other for her faithfulness despite her difficult marriage, said she was going to meet someone at a motel, Miriam was more than a little surprised. "Not you, Liza!"

Realizing that her words were communicating the wrong message, she quickly replied, "It's not what you think."

"Liza, what's got into you? No . . . don't tell me, I don't think I want to know."

"Miriam, an old friend of mine is in town on business. I haven't seen him in over twenty-two years—since before we were married. For anyone else in this world, seeing an old friend would be no big deal. But with Randy, I can hardly go shopping without him grilling me on everything I'm planning to do. If I told him I was planning to see a man, he'd chain me to the kitchen sink and lock the house."

Miriam's surprise turned to sympathy as she listened to her friend. "If it wasn't for you coming along, I couldn't even be here today. Please don't say anything. Peter, that's his name, is going to meet me in the motel parking lot, then we're going to bring my car back here and head down to the French Quarter and see a bit of New Orleans. I've got seven hours. Maybe less. Do you understand?" Liza's eyes sparkled with delight even as tears welled up in the corners. "I've never been unfaithful to Randy and I'm not going to be today. It's just that I have an opportunity to see a friend—and I just want to do it.

"He's probably already over there, waiting," Liza continued. Then she reached out and placed a hand on Miriam's arm. "I can't ask you to never breathe a word of this to anyone, even though that's what I'd like to do. It's not fair to ask someone to keep a secret after the fact, but you know that if Randy were to ever find out, there's no telling what might happen to me . . . or the kids."

Miriam smiled compassionately as she wrapped her hands around the car keys Liza handed her. The attached chain with the miniature baseball at the end dangled over her forefinger. "You better not keep him waiting," she said.

"I'll meet you at five in misses sportswear, okay?"

"And when you don't come home with anything, what will Randy think then?"

A grin crawled across Liza's face. "I already called and ordered a sundress, some shorts and a shirt. They're holding them for me. And they're supposed to be sending two things over from the juniors for Amy."

"You sly devil, you," said Miriam, opening the door. "Have fun and stay out of trouble."

As she stood up outside the car, Liza leaned over. "How much trouble do you think a girl can get into in seven hours with a guy who was near death just six weeks ago and is recovering from a bullet wound in his leg and a skin graft on his chest?"

Miriam was smiling when she leaned over and stuck her head back into the car. The additional information, bizarre as it was, tickled her and triggered a thought. "You probably can get into a lot of trouble, but I'd go for it! This sounds like a great Oprah story: 'Women who cheat on their healthy husbands with disabled men'!"

"That's not funny!"

"You ought to be hearing this from my side. It's a riot." Both women were laughing by the time Miriam said, "I'll see you at five," and withdrew from the car.

With a heart that was beating as erratically as her head was processing information, Liza drove out of the mall parking lot, crossed Read Boulevard and pulled into the lot at the Days Inn.

*   *   *

After calling and leaving a message for Liza at the hotel, Peter Boget pulled a piece of paper off the dashboard. He handed it to Whitehead as the two raced from west to east across I-10 through Metairie. "Here's the number where Mike Downes is staying. He might be there. Pick up the phone and call him, please."

Whitehead had placed his trust in Peter Boget and felt obligated to do as the man said, even though he was leery of making the call. He asked how to use the cellular phone and then dialed. Downes was near the phone when it was answered by his host. After he came on the line, Whitehead said, "Mike, this is Barry, Barry Whitehead. I'm with Peter Boget."

The two men talked for ten minutes about Mexico and Barry's miraculous escape. They also talked about Downes's need for Barry to testify on his behalf and perhaps spare him a conviction.

"Mike, this week has been a living hell for me. There's not much joy in being free if you have to look over your shoulder all the time. I don't want to go back to jail, certainly not to Mexico. But living like this with someone like Mary Kennedy on your back isn't living at all."

"Barry, call the FBI, or let Peter take you in. They've got ways to protect you and give you a new life."

"I know. Maybe now's the time. But first I've got to sleep." He handed the phone to Peter, who estimated they were five minutes from Read Boulevard.

"Hello, Mike?"

Downes spoke firmly. "I thought you weren't getting involved."

"I was surprised."

"So I heard. Barry said someone is after him . . . and now you, is that right?"

Peter didn't want to admit that he was doing several things that would classify as involvement. "Remember Roland Hanks?"

"Of course."

"That's who's after us," said Peter. "We had an encounter on a ferry boat this morning. I dodged him, but he called Elizabeth and got the name of my hotel."

"Are you serious? Where's Hanks now?"

"Probably running around the city looking for us. I'm sure he's on Mary's payroll. And if Barry's right, she's here or was here. Something big must be happening."

"If I were you," Mike cautioned, "I'd get on the horn to the FBI quick and let them know what's going on."

"I will, Mike, as soon as I get Barry tucked away."

"Where?"

"There's a motel at the next exit. I'm going to stop there and try to get a room."

"Good. Then you better lay low until you talk with the cops."

"I will," said Peter. Then he turned off the phone. It was 10:20. He was at the Read Boulevard exit and began to slow. He hoped Liza was still there.

*   *   *

The waiting was making Liza Morgan more nervous than she ever remembered being. What-ifs filled her mind, and sweat soaked her back as she waited in her hot Escort. She studied each car coming from the interstate and strained to see someone who looked like the man she had said goodbye to so many years before. The sun was reflecting off the windows of the cars she was watching, but still she was able to see the faces of the people behind the wheel.

As the minutes ticked by, she became increasingly anxious and thought about going to check for messages at the hotel desk but didn't want to miss seeing Peter driving down the boulevard. Then she saw him. He glanced twice in her direction as he maneuvered his green car into the turning lane. She knew he saw her because the moment he looked directly at her his marvelous smile lit up his face. That was a smile she had never forgotten.

Her heart leaped and the nervousness was intensified. The magical moment had arrived. What would she say first? What would he say? Would he touch her? Would she touch him? Should she touch him? She remembered the kisses they had enjoyed so long ago. Dare she let him kiss her again? Would he want to? Would he feel free to? She waved to him, and he waved back. She couldn't believe it was finally happening.

As her eyes followed his car, she saw a person in the passenger seat. In the initial glare she hadn't noticed the other occupant. At the sight of a second person, her elation was tempered. Perhaps her eyes were playing a trick on her. Maybe there wasn't really a second person, but she knew there was. In that moment she wondered if by some cruel twist of fate the person in the car was Elizabeth. She forced the thought out of her mind. Maybe it wasn't Peter she saw. No, that was him, it had to be. She would remember that face forever. But who was with him and why?

She turned on her engine and flipped the air conditioning on high, hoping to cool herself off a bit before she met Peter face to face. Her mind seemed to freeze time as it processed half a lifetime's worth of memories starting from the moment the two first met. When she returned to the present, she saw his car backing in beside her. When they were directly across from each other, he began to roll down his window and signaled her to do the same.

Faces that had been hidden from each other's view for so many years were gradually revealed as the glass curtains descended. They could have touched one another if they had extended their hands, but neither moved. With their eyes they traced every feature of the other, speaking to one another as clearly as if they were speaking with their lips.

Despite his utter weariness, Barry Whitehead looked past Peter Boget's shoulder into the face of Liza Morgan. There he observed something he had never seen in another woman. Had his mother even once shown him the kind of acceptance he saw on Liza's face, he knew his life would have been radically different. If his teachers or his girlfriends had exhibited such love, his view of women would be far healthier. If his wife had even once communicated such adoration, he knew that he would be with her today. He observed more communication in that silent exchange between Liza and Peter than he imagined was possible without the spoken word. He turned away to allow the two the privacy of the moment.

Finally, Peter inhaled deeply and spoke quietly. "Hello, Liza."

At the sound of his voice she wanted to jump into his arms. She wanted to turn off the ignition of her car, climb in beside him and drive off to the mountains of Colorado. She wanted to leave with Peter and never return to Waveland or to Randy or to her job or her home. She even forgot the fact that she had three children. Finally, she responded with a weak but melodic, "Hello, Peter."

"This is Barry Whitehead," Peter said as he leaned his head back so Liza could see the man seated next to him.

Unlike most people who were startled when they saw Whitehead and how much he looked like Peter, Liza barely noticed that the two shared so many physical features. When Liza looked at Barry, she saw a man very different from the one behind the wheel. Her greeting was a cordial "Hello."

"I need to go in and get a room for Barry and unload all of my stuff," Peter explained. "Then we can head out of here, okay?"

"Okay?" The word passed through her beautiful smile. "Anything you suggest is okay!"

"You want to wait here," he asked Liza, "or would you like to go in with me?"

She had six hours and thirty-five minutes to be with Peter, and didn't want to waste a single one, so she said she'd come along.

Peter got out of his car first, closed his door, and then opened hers. Whitehead opened his door but didn't get out. "I'd like to wait here, please. Can you give me the key so I can roll down the windows?"

Peter handed off the keys and walked beside Liza into the motel lobby. Their arms brushed as they walked through the door, fanning the flames they both were experiencing. The electricity that was coursing through the air was not lost on the woman handling the registration. When Peter asked for a room for two, the woman didn't look at all surprised. Nor did she make any comment when Peter asked if one was immediately available. But she did, unconsciously, raise her eyebrows when Peter asked for two double beds. She handed Peter a key, and he asked for a second. Liza said nothing.

"I hope you enjoy your stay," said the woman.

"I'm sure we will," Peter responded.

*   *   *

Whitehead was asleep when Peter and Liza returned to the parking lot. Peter awakened him as he drove around to the rear of the building, jumped out and, with Liza's help, began carrying clothes and luggage to the room. "This is a mess," said Liza as she scooped up some wrinkled shirts. "Looks like you cleared out in a huge hurry."

"I didn't want to keep you waiting," said Peter. The two arrived at the room, opened the door, and walked in. Peter set the suitcase on the floor and his computer on the bed. Liza dropped the clothes she was carrying onto the other bed as the motel-room door swung shut.

They were finally alone. They extended their hands and in the dim glow of the light sneaking around the opaque curtains on the window, slowly drew close to one another. The din of the air conditioner drowned out the pounding of their hearts.

*   *   *

"We're ready," said Patrick O'Hearn. He was talking to Mary Kennedy from a phone in the lobby of the Bayou Caddy Casino. "Looks to me like they're keeping two guards on the boat and one in the parking lot."

"Can you do it?"

"Just give me the word."

Kennedy had planned to steal fifty kilos of cocaine from Jack Holland and use the proceeds from their sale to pay off her indebtedness for the thirty-five she was buying. But once she learned that Holland had already exercised his option and seized her company, the stakes were raised dramatically. She was angry. "Get a hundred."

"I can't ma'am. I've only sixty pounds of sugar, and I don't want to be seen going back to any of the stores around here."

"Okay," she said with a hint of resignation, "get what you can."

*   *   *

"Oh, excuse me," said Barry Whitehead as he walked through the motel-room door that had not fully closed. He looked with embarrassment at the two who were just inches apart. "I wasn't thinking."

Peter took a step backward. "There's nothing to think," he said, trying to cover the awkwardness. "We're just straightening up so you can get a shower and get to bed. I've got some extra clothes; wear whatever you want." He picked up a pair of slacks and walked to the closet to hang them up. "I'll be back around five or five-thirty. Then we'll call the FBI. If you want to go sooner, go ahead and call them. If you're not here at five, I'll assume you've taken off, and I'll still call them. Do you understand?"

Whitehead was too tired to understand much of anything. "Yes, that's fine," he said, dropping onto one of the beds. "You'll probably have to wake me up when you get back."

Liza, who had said almost nothing up to that moment, could not resist answering the comment in a way that revealed her heart's desire. "We may never come back," she said. She wanted to take Peter's hand, but thought better of it. The two turned and walked out the door.

"Let's do New Orleans," Peter said as they walked to the car.

"Yes, let's," Liza replied.

*   *   *

After dropping their car in a hotel garage, Peter and Liza headed to Café DuMond, a famed coffee shop that seated several hundred people both inside and out. There they sat at a tiny table and savored the restaurant's *café au lait*. There they munched on the powdered-sugar-covered, deep-fried pastries called *beignets*. There they gazed at each other, oblivious to the waiters and waitresses who scurried through the tight seating taking and filling orders with amazing efficiency. They abandoned the notion of trying to carry on a conversation above the clamor of the crowd and the bold music of the nearby jazz band. They communicated with one another with their eyes.

From the café they walked a few steps to the levee, the earthen mound that stretched for miles along the river to protect the low-lying city from floods. In front of the French Quarter the levee is topped with a walkway, dubbed the "Moon Walk," on which a variety of musicians try to earn a living by performing and then passing a hat through the small clusters of people who gather to hear their music.

Peter dropped a dollar in the hat of one middle-aged saxophonist who accompanied a tape that played through his boom box. The song he was playing when Liza and Peter walked up was "Climb Every Mountain," and as the strains of the horn wafted through the sultry air, both Peter and Liza allowed their memories to drift back to the drive to the top of Pikes Peak while Liza sang that same song. Before the last note faded and the musician took a sweeping bow, the two were holding hands under the partial shade of a young oak tree. Without saying a word they strolled to the end of the Moon Walk and walked down the stair-stepped concrete wall to the water's edge. They were as alone as is possible in so public an area.

"I can't believe you're really here," Liza said, looking admiringly into Peter's face. "You'll never know how long I've dreamed of a moment like this, a moment alone with you." She shook her head from side to side allowing her black shoulder-length hair to lift ever so gently from the sides of her face and fall again on her fair skin. "I just can't believe it." Her voice was a whisper. "I just can't believe it."

Peter looked at the face that he had almost forgotten. His memories of her were what she said and how he felt when he was around her, not how she looked, and now he was more than surprised. She was beautiful. Not as attractive as Elizabeth, but beautiful in her own special way. As he studied her, he realized she wasn't the woman he had kissed while standing on a rock in the middle of that creek so long ago. She was so much more.

He couldn't put his thoughts into words. In fact he couldn't even organize his thinking. He only knew that the attraction he had to Liza was based on so much more than physical beauty or memories. He continued to study her and in that moment, he let down his guard. He allowed his heart to outrun his head. More than anything in the world, he wanted to envelop her and give to her all of who he was. He wanted to leave his world behind and walk into a new one populated by just the two of them.

Tears welled up in his eyes—tears of sadness that Peter Boget and Liza Bellamy had missed each other when that magical Colorado summer came to an end . . . tears of joy that they were reunited again . . . and more tears of sadness that, all too soon, they would have to part again and return to their separate worlds.

When Liza saw the tears, she saw a man who was radically different from any man she had ever known. The Peter she had always remembered was rugged and athletic, but she never thought of him as being strong the way her husband was strong. In the tears, she saw a strength that Randy never possessed—a strength of character, a self-assurance that allowed him to express his emotions through his tears as only a truly strong man can. If there was any doubts about her feelings toward Peter, they were washed away with the salty water welled up in his eyes.

She knew it was hopeless to fight against the feelings they were both experiencing. Her tears trickled across her cheeks. "Oh, Peter," she said almost worshipfully. She had to force the words out through the sobs. "So many times, I dreamed you'd come back for me. I'd sit on a rocker on our back porch . . . sometimes rocking a baby in my arms . . . sometimes just looking up at the moon . . . but always with tears in my eyes and a heaviness in my heart, and I'd call your name." Liza's voice broke completely as the painful memories flooded her mind. "Oh, Peter," Liza sobbed uncontrollably. "Peter, you've come back." She leaned forward while, gently and tenderly, Peter Boget wrapped his arms around Liza Bellamy Morgan and drew her to him.

Before she finished crying he pushed her away and sadly but firmly said, "Liza, we've got to stop. This is wrong."

She reached into her pocketbook, pulled out a tissue, and blotted her eyes, but as soon as she removed the tissue, the tears resumed. She could hardly speak but managed a sorrowful, "I know."

As Liza regained her composure she spoke again. "I know this is wrong, I have always known it was wrong, but . . . but I never wanted to give up the dream."

Peter's eyes were red and watery. "Liza, please forgive me," he said. "I never should have called you."

Through her sadness, a smile broke across her face. She lifted a finger to his lips. "There is nothing to forgive. No matter what the pain, to have experienced these two weeks and to know that you love me . . . well, you have made my life complete in so many ways."

He lifted his hand to her face and brushed away the streaks of moisture. "Maybe the best thing to do is to let it stop right here. I think I need to get some things straight with God and with Elizabeth."

"I know," she whispered. "And I think it's time for me to make some decisions about my life as well, decisions that won't—that can't—include you."

21

Miriam Haskell was eating a leisurely meal in the food court at the Plaza Shopping Center. She didn't mind shopping alone, but was disappointed about not having Liza around for lunch. She was munching on a salad while reading a new novel she had picked up at the mall bookstore earlier in the morning. So engrossed was she in her story that she didn't notice the man sliding into the chair across from her. When she looked up, she nearly gagged on a piece of raw broccoli.

"Where's Liza?" Randy Morgan asked in a not altogether friendly tone.

"Not here," said Miriam.

"I know that. Where did she go?"

Miriam always felt uncomfortable around Liza's husband, and sitting directly across from him gave her a bad case of the jitters. "I don't know, exactly," she said. "We're just doing our own thing today and meeting back here at five."

Randy could tell that Miriam was hiding something. He leaned over, pushed her book out of her hands and glared at her. He liked the frightened look on her face. It gave him a sense of power. "Who's she with?"

"I don't know," she said, wanting to run.

"You're lying. You're covering up something."

Miriam had heard stories about Randy Morgan, but a real-life encounter was worse than she had imagined. She couldn't believe that Liza had put up with this for over two decades. She decided to say nothing.

"It's this Peter guy, isn't it?"

Miriam quivered, but didn't answer.

"So she's with Peter. Now where are they?"

Miriam's hands were shaking. She tried to stand up, but Randy's glare seemed to generate a force that locked her to her chair.

"The motel across the street, isn't it?" he said, nodding his head and trying to get her to do so as well. "That's why she came here, because there's a motel across the street. That's where she went, isn't it?"

Miriam began to cry as several people in surrounding tables looked on. She didn't have to answer, but she felt compelled to tell it straight. "She's going to spend the afternoon in the French Quarter and meet me back here at five."

"You're lying. She went to that motel."

A plainclothes security agent for the mall walked to the table where Randy continued his inquisition. His arrival broke the spell that had held Miriam hostage. She jumped up and backed away from the table.

"Is this man bothering you, ma'am?"

"Yes."

Morgan interrupted. "I'm leaving. I've found out what I needed to know."

*   *   *

Jack Holland and Mary Kennedy were marking the occasion of their uneasy merger with a lunch in The Rib Room overlooking Royal Street in the heart of the French Quarter. Conversation was light as the two sipped "washbucket" martinis while awaiting their meals.

Holland gave not the slightest hint that he suspected Kennedy's people were involved with the overnight boarding of the *Miss St. Loo*. He also didn't mention that he had selected a pickup point that gave his people complete control over the transaction. The location for the exchange of cocaine was, for all intents and purposes, an island with the bayou's main waterway to the south, an inlet to the west, marsh to the north, and a small inlet to the east. A narrow, wooden, one-lane bridge with an arched roadway and wooden railings provided the only way a vehicle could get in and out of the parking lot. Holland was wary of Kennedy and was still trying to figure out how she had managed to stage her death.

"So are you going to stay here in New Orleans?" Holland asked.

"I don't know yet," Mary said thoughtfully. "I've thought about returning to Ireland and expect that's what I'll do eventually. It's a beautiful place. I just can't make the kind of money there that I can here."

"And now that you're wanted by the police . . ."

"I'm not wanted by anyone," she reminded him. "I'm dead, remember? And the only people that know I'm here are you and me and a couple of close associates who help me run my business and who make sure that people who try to interfere with that business are prevented from doing so—whether they are friends or business partners."

Holland grinned. "I'm guessing that's a threat, but I've always ignored threats—not that I've had many—because I run a clean operation."

"So I've seen," Kennedy said. "And your engineering work is excellent, too."

"We've got some real good people because we pay top dollar. I'd say our future looks pretty bright."

Mary dabbed her mouth with her cloth napkin and then casually asked, "If your business is going so well, why would you want to risk it all getting involved in—"

"I do it for the money and I do it for the fun. Mostly I do it because I like to gamble, and gambling takes money. I know because I owe a lot to a lot of people. Or did. I've gotten it down to a reasonable level . . ."

The leisurely pace of the meal gave the two plenty of time for discussion and for watching the tourists cruising Royal Street.

*   *   *

One thousand miles away Elizabeth was beside herself with anxiety. Peter had said he would call in an hour. Three had elapsed since then. He wasn't at the motel, and he wasn't answering his car phone. She tried to reach Mike Downes, but there was no answer at the number he had given her. Finally, she picked up the phone and called the FBI.

Both Giddings and his partner were off, but everyone in the Richmond office knew about the case. Ronnie Gearheart eventually took the call. He listened attentively to the unlikely tale and then offered some advice.

"I know you're very upset, but we have nothing here to go on. I'll pass this information to New Orleans. At least we'll try to locate your husband, but with so many visitors there, this will be a back-burner item. Look," he added, "if you don't hear from him by midafternoon, call back and I'll see what I can do to light a fire under this."

*   *   *

Liza and Peter were enjoying a beautiful day in one another's presence. From their vantage point along the Mississippi, they looked out across a body of water that seemed unchanged from one minute to the next, yet tens of millions of gallons of water were passing in front of them every minute. Like the river, so much about their lives had changed over the last twenty-two years, yet so much remained the same.

Peter knew he had already said too much, but his feelings were running ahead of his brain and once more he spoke the words that Liza so much wanted to hear. "I love you, Liza, nothing will ever change that."

"And I love you . . . "

He interrupted her. "I know, but I—we—must control the expression of that love." Peter struggled with the right words. "We can never be the lovers that we would have been had we taken a different road back then. We'll never be husband and wife. We've got to accept the fact that we live in separate worlds and we will forever have to keep them separate."

Liza didn't want to hear those words any more than Peter wanted to speak them, but she knew he was right. "Before we go, Peter, will you sing me the song, the one you said you wrote for me last week? Just once, just for us?"

"I shouldn't, Liza."

"Please . . . just once."

Peter's response was slow in coming. The emotional attachment to Liza was greater than he expected. What began as a pleasant diversion had become a consuming passion. He knew the song would only fan the flames of desire. He tried to say no, but Liza was persistent.

He slowly nodded. His voice, still weak from the effects of his injuries, was filled with emotion. As he began to sing, Liza remembered one more reason why she had fallen in love with Peter so many years before.

The melody was slow and thoughtful. Liza closed her eyes and allowed herself to be washed in memories. He sang of whispers in the wind. As she listened, she understood why he didn't want to sing it. She heard his pain in every line. His voice trembled as he began the last stanza. She reached out and took his hand in hers.

When he was finished, he stood up and wiped his eyes with his shirt sleeves. "I think we'd better go."

"I think you're right," said Liza as she pulled her last two tissues from her purse. She handed one to Peter and used the other for herself. "Will you let me show you the rest of the French Quarter?"

Peter looked at his watch. "I'm sure Barry's sound asleep and . . . oh, no." He put his hand to his forehead. "Elizabeth. I forgot to call Elizabeth. She's probably a wreck right now. I told her I'd call as soon as I met Whitehead, and . . . How did I forget?"

Guilt overtook Liza. She knew that she was the reason he forgot to make the call. "Let's find a phone," she said stoically.

*   *   *

Randy Morgan was ten miles away, standing at the front desk of the Days Inn waiting for the woman behind the counter to hang up the phone. When he decided she had spoken long enough, he reached across the counter and, to her great surprise, hung it up for her. He wasted no words. "What room is Peter Boget in?"

The woman had been trained to decline to give out that information, but the look on Morgan's face alarmed her. This man wasn't merely asking for information, he was demanding something that he was obviously going to get one way or another. She wished there was someone else around, but she and Morgan were alone. With trepidation she haltingly explained the motel's policy.

"I'm not asking you what room Peter Boget is in; I'm telling you to give me that information now. This is a matter of life and death."

The woman didn't have to look through the card file to get the room number of the only people who had checked in that morning, but she decided to get it anyway. It gave her trembling hands something to hold on to.

"They're in room 322." As soon as she said "they're" she wanted to retrieve the word. She remembered the couple who stood at the desk. She remembered the unusually early hour they checked in. And she remembered their peculiar request for two beds, as if the request would deflect suspicion from what she thought they were planning to do. It dawned on the clerk that she was probably looking into the face of the woman's husband. The jealousy, the rage—it was all there. She froze with the card in her hand.

Morgan leaned across the counter and snatched it from her. He read only as far as the number *2* above the word *guests*. Then he stuffed it into his back pocket. As soon as he was outside, the clerk picked up the phone, dialed an outside line, and punched 911.

Morgan was outside of room 322 in less than a minute. He was aware of the midday heat, but that alone did not explain why he was boiling. The *DO NOT DISTURB* sign hanging from the door handle only intensified his anger. He yanked it off and checked to see if the door was unlocked. It wasn't. So he knocked. But he got no response. He knocked again, straining to listen above the sound of the air conditioning for any sounds from inside. The third time he pounded on the door.

A drowsy man, wiping sleep from his eyes, cracked the door and peered out from the dark room. Without saying a word, Randy Morgan drove his shoulder into the door, knocking Whitehead to the carpet. Only the light from the opened door illuminated the room.

"Where is she?" Morgan demanded as he stood over the cowering Whitehead. He reached back and flipped a light switch near the door. A lamp came on and a quick glance revealed nothing. He walked toward the sink area and flipped on a light there. "Where is she?" he bellowed. He walked into the bathroom and pushed back the shower curtain. He stepped back into the main room and lifted up the bed skirts. By the time he was done, Whitehead, wearing only his underwear, was standing, a frightened look etched deeply into his face.

"Are you Peter Boget?" Morgan yelled into Whitehead's face as he pushed the man onto the bed.

"No, he's not here."

Despite the fact that Morgan had jarred him awake, Whitehead's brain was still in neutral. He didn't think about the ramifications of what he was about to say, only that he wanted the man who was bullying him to get out of the room and let him get back to sleep.

"He said he was going to the French Quarter with Liza."

At the sound of his wife's name Morgan lost what little control he had. For no logical reason he pulled back his hand and swung a fist at Whitehead's head. The seated man dropped backward onto the bed just as the blow brushed his forehead.

"That woman!" Morgan said.

Fearing a more disabling hit, Whitehead volunteered additional information that he hoped would cause Morgan to leave. "They won't be back until five."

Morgan turned to go, then looked back at the man sitting on the bed. "If you tell anyone I was here, I'll be back for you. Do you understand?"

Whitehead nodded, and Randy Morgan exited the room. He knew his wife and he knew the French Quarter. If she had her way, and she hadn't shacked up in some hotel room with Peter, she would be shopping on Royal Street.

*　　*　　*

From the levee, Peter and Liza walked back down to the French Market, found a phone, and called home. He dialed both lines, but all he got were busy signals. So he and Liza strolled through Jackson Square, the handsome garden park in the heart of the French Quarter. The once-dusty parade ground, where the city welcomed her heroes and held public meetings, was alive with visitors and musicians. Peter paused to admire the equestrian bronze of Andrew Jackson that stands in the middle of the park, serving as a silent reminder of the military leader who defeated the British in the Battle of New Orleans.

As they left the park, the couple stopped to look at some of the hundreds of paintings and photos that artists, eager for sales, hung from the iron fence that rings the park. Liza pointed out the red, three-story brick apartment houses adorned with ornate cast-iron balconies that flank the park and told Peter the story of Baroness de Pontalba who erected them in 1849. The two made a quick stop at St. Louis Cathedral and then walked narrow Toulouse Street two blocks to Royal. Peter made an additional attempt to call home at one of the hotels they passed but continued reaching the same busy signals. So they began to window shop.

That's what they were doing when Mary Kennedy glanced out the window of The Rib Room, where she was finishing her lunch with Jack Holland, and spotted them. From her table across the street, Mary noticed only Peter's face before he and Liza stopped and looked into a store window. To her eyes, it was the unmistakable face of Barry Whitehead. Holland followed her gaze.

"Who's that?" he asked.

"Don't you know? He was in your office when I visited you on Monday."

Holland waited for Peter and Liza to turn around. When they did, he said, "I don't remember seeing him. Maybe he was visiting one of the staff."

"Then you don't know who that is?" she demanded, her voice a near whisper.

"No, I don't. Who is he?"

"Trouble," she said, not convinced that Holland was telling the truth. She stood up. "Keep an eye on them. I'll be right back."

She quickly walked to the maitre d'. "I've got to use your phone," she said, picking it up. "It's an emergency."

She dialed a number that was written on a pad she pulled from her large pocketbook. It rang twice.

"Hanks here."

"Whitehead is in the French Quarter at Royal and St. Louis. He's with a woman, moving slowly from shop to shop. Where are you?"

The reception on Hanks's rented phone was scratchy, but he knew he was talking to someone from Ireland. He wouldn't have believed it was Kennedy even if she had said so.

"I'm over near the convention center," Hanks said. "Maybe five minutes away."

"Good, come get him."

*   *   *

Hanks was excited. He had just visited the Good Samaritan House to see what he could learn about Peter Boget's visit and was heading to another shelter when the call came from Kennedy. He raced north on Fulton, turned onto Canal, and then turned into the Vieux Carre on Chartres. He pulled into the first parking garage he saw, jumped out, and sprinted one block to Royal. When he reached the intersection of St. Louis, a middle-aged man with more stomach and less hair than he was born with intercepted him.

"Mr. Hanks?"

"Yes, who are you?"

"You don't need to know." He stopped, then pointed toward a store. "They're in there." Jack Holland said nothing more and then turned crisply back toward The Rib Room.

Hanks hated his role. He joined forces with Kennedy because he was intrigued with the idea that through the drug business he could earn five times what he was making as a cop and, in the process, he could expect some "action." He was being asked to do some dangerous and adventurous missions, but somehow what he was getting wasn't what he expected. He checked the hip bag he was wearing on his belt. His Sig Sauer 9mm semi-automatic pistol was there, along with an extra clip of ammunition.

From the window, Hanks saw the man that he had been told was White-head, but he knew that whoever had given him that information was wrong. He stepped away from the door and waited. Soon Peter and Liza emerged. They were laughing until Liza looked up. Never in her life had such a wave of fear washed through her body.

Sixty feet in front of her stood Randy Morgan. She didn't know why he was there or how he had found her, but for the first time since they were married she feared for her life. No one walking along Royal Street could miss the anger that caused his eyes to narrow and his jaw to tighten. He was holding something in his hand that seemed to be covered with a plastic bag. She feared it might be a gun, even though she was fairly certain he didn't own one. To be safe, she grabbed Peter and pushed him back into the store. Not understanding what was going on, Roland Hanks stepped in behind them.

"Randy's here," she breathlessly informed Peter. "I just saw him. We've got to get out of here."

Though he saw the fear in her face, Peter found the idea that Liza's husband was just outside the door a bit hard to believe. "Are you sure it's him?" he asked.

"Absolutely!" she said. "Let's see if there's a back way out."

As she said it, Peter felt a nudge in his back. He began turning when the voice said, "Mr. Boget, I'm going with you." Liza's heart stopped. She looked to see who knew Peter, but before she could speak, Hanks added, "Ask the clerk for a back door."

They emerged from the back of the store quickly. Peter had felt the gun in his back and decided to comply fully with Hanks's request. Liza was frantic but took her lead from Peter.

"My car is two blocks away. Follow me," Hanks said.

Five minutes later, Peter was driving Hanks's car out of the garage while Hanks, in the passenger seat, held a gun on him. Confused and frightened, Liza trembled as she lay on the back seat praying that her husband wouldn't see her while they picked their way through traffic. At Conti Street, Hanks ordered a right. At the next corner he ordered another. They would be out of the French Quarter in a few seconds. Peter hoped that also meant they would be out of danger, at least from Randy.

But before they reached Canal Street, the right rear window exploded, raining glass chunks on Liza. Peter stared in shock in the rearview mirror as a fist followed the glass. Before Hanks could turn around, Randy Morgan reached through the window and grabbed his wife's hair. "Get out of the car, Liza!"

Peter acted instinctively. He swerved the car to the left. Liza screamed as her head slammed into the door. Randy was pulled off his feet and dragged along the street while clutching his wife's hair. Liza's scream filled the car as it approached Canal. Peter blasted the horn to scatter the pedestrians.

Randy yelled threats as the car turned the corner, then he finally let go and dropped to the ground. Despite a bleeding arm and scraped knees that showed through torn jeans, Randy was shouting loudly as he sprang to his feet. "I'm going to kill you, Boget!"

Liza trembled as the car snaked through traffic. She knew that there would be a heavy price to pay when she got home . . . if she got home. She also knew that Peter's life was now in danger as well. She wept bitterly.

Peter drove three blocks north on Canal and then turned right and reentered the French Quarter.

"What are you doing?" demanded Hanks.

"The cops are going to be on my tail before I go another block. And now Randy knows what we're driving. My car is a couple of streets over."

Once they made the switch, Peter zigzagged through the city streets, heading north.

Once the atmosphere in the car relaxed, Hanks introduced himself. "My name's Hanks," he said.

"I know," said Peter. "You were with my wife in the corridor at the hospital. And you've threatened my family. And you tried to take out Barry Whitehead. Probably still are."

"No, I'm not."

"Really," said Peter sarcastically. "And you're holding a gun on me because you're glad to have me along as company? Look, I know you and you know me. If you're here to do something, go ahead and do it. But the woman in the back seat has nothing to do with this. Let me take care of her and then we can talk."

"You don't understand. I really want to help you, and—"

"Look, Hanks, I've figured you out already. You were working for Mary Kennedy when you came to the hospital on Palm Sunday. That's how Patrick O'Hearn knew your name when your badge was covered."

"That's not true."

"And she paid you to threaten my family not to testify against her or Mark Randolph. And she sent you to Mexico to kill Barry Whitehead." Peter continued to alternate left and right turns as he drove through the east end of New Orleans. "And she called you and told you she saw Whitehead here and wanted you to come and finish your job."

"You have a fertile imagination, Mr. Boget," said Hanks with a smile. "First of all, I guess you haven't heard that Mary Kennedy is dead."

"I did, but she isn't."

That comment took Hanks by surprise. "Oh, really?"

"Really. Why else would she have you down here? She saw Whitehead and she knows that Whitehead saw her. And she and O'Hearn are obviously too busy with something else to run around town looking for Barry, so they called you."

"A very good imagination," Hanks added.

"Look," Peter shot back, "this isn't about imagination. I think I got it all."

"So let's hear it."

"Mary wasn't on the plane to London because Barry Whitehead saw her here on Tuesday and again on Thursday."

Hanks just shook his head in disbelief. "She's alive?"

"What did you think?"

"I came down here for one reason," Hanks said emphatically. "To get the man who shot me. I don't know why he's here, and I never imagined that Mary might be here. But it was obvious to me that something was going down, and, if he was here, I'd find a way to get him. He's slippery . . . they both are, and I've been embarrassed more than once by them. When I heard Whitehead was alive, it was a relief. I could live with the other stuff, but not with killing someone. I tried to buy back the contract, but it was too late."

"If you're not playing with them, then why the gun on me?"

"Someone's watching me. Someone wants to make sure I do my job. That's why I had to make it look good."

"And the calls to my family?"

"I thought he worked for Kennedy," Hanks thought aloud, trying to fit the pieces together. "A guy named Mazzetti said he might—"

"Mazzetti!"

"He didn't tell me his name, but I had my friends trace his license plate."

"Mazzetti?"

"He said he'd be able to take care of an out-of-work policeman, and he gave me $5,000 to see to it that you kept your mouth shut."

Peter's mind was in high gear, reconstructing the puzzle in his mind. "The New Jersey connection," he said. "It all fits."

"What fits?" asked Liza, who was leaning over the front seat.

Peter didn't answer her. He looked at Hanks. "So what do you want with us?"

"Whitehead. I've got to find out what he's up to and get him out of New Orleans. I'm supposed to kill him, but I'm through with Kennedy's games. When I find him, I'm turning him in to the police and getting him into protective custody."

"And us?" asked Liza.

"That's up to you."

Peter glanced over his shoulder at Liza. "Do you know someone who will take you in till Randy calms down? Maybe someone at the church?"

Liza, who was still trembling intermittently, thought for a while. "Angie might. She's in the choir. Or Linda. She might be more understanding . . . and her children are all grown and gone."

"So where's Whitehead?" Hanks asked.

Peter had already placed Liza in danger; he wasn't sure if he should place Whitehead in that same path, but he didn't see a reasonable alternative.

"Where are we? Does anybody know?"

Liza checked the street signs. "We're near the fairgrounds, I think. If we keep going in this direction we should run into the interstate."

"We're in a motel east of town," Peter told Hanks.

Hanks glanced back over his shoulder and looked at Liza, who was brushing pieces of glass from her hair. "How'd your husband find you? You wearing some kind of an electronic collar?" he said with a laugh.

"I don't think so," she said evenly.

"Unless he was behind us and we didn't see him, how did he find us when we pulled out of the hotel garage?"

Liza thought about it. Since the incident in Biloxi when he spent several hours wandering through the mall looking for her, he never had any trouble locating her anywhere around town.

"May I check your purse?" Hanks asked.

"I guess so."

In twenty seconds Hanks completed his search. He held up her keys. They were on a ring connected to a small plastic baseball by a short length of braided wire. The baseball was emblazoned with the logo of LSU. It was identical to the one that Liza had given to Miriam. "Have you had this long?" he asked.

"A year, maybe. Randy gave each of the kids one and placed the extra set of car keys on another."

"I don't mean to spoil anything here, but I think this is a transmitter," he said, holding the baseball. He placed his finger on the braided wire. "And this is the antenna. Mind if I try to open it?"

Liza shook her head.

Hanks slid a knife edge between the two hemispheres of the ball and popped it open. When he looked at the electronics and the battery, he knew he was right. "Probably has a range of a quarter of a mile or so," he said as he removed the battery. "That relieves us of one problem. Now we've got to get Mr. Whitehead."

* * *

From the *Pollyanna,* a shrimp boat tied up along the dock at the southwest corner of the fisherman's parking lot in Bayou Caddy, Billy McMillan, wearing a black wet suit and using a snorkel and mask, slipped quietly into

262 □   VENGEANCE IS MINE

the cool, dark water. Liam O'Donnell and Eileen Adams, dressed in jeans and T-shirts, were washing out plastic ice chests on the deck of the boat. In the boat's cabin Patrick O'Hearn set up the equipment for the transfer.

The boat's owner was a quarter mile away at a slot machine seeking to double the three hundred dollars O'Hearn had given him to use his boat.

Moving quickly but carefully beneath the dock's pilings, McMillan reached the *Miss St. Loo* and, on his second dive, located the container filled with cocaine midway between the boat's keel and the water line. He unfastened the small radio transmitter encased in plastic that hung from his belt and removed a rubber wedge from beneath the only button that protruded through the case. When he pressed the button, the torpedo-shaped container dropped away from the boat. He grabbed it so it wouldn't strike the boat's hull and rouse the suspicions of the guards on the boat. After tying a line to it, he pulled it away from the boat and retraced his underwater route to the *Pollyanna*.

Five minutes later, after shrouding the container in fishing nets, O'Donnell, Adams and O'Hearn helped McMillan bring it on board the *Pollyanna*. Continually checking to see that no roving eyes were watching them, the four carried the torpedo into the cabin.

*   *   *

Although he had lost track of Liza's transmitter, Randy Morgan felt certain his wife would try to contact her friend Miriam and possibly make a run for the car at the mall. He didn't know who was with her, but he didn't like the idea that she was with not one but two men, one of whom looked young enough to be his son. He reached the Read Boulevard exit ahead of Boget, Hanks and his wife, but then had to decide whether to go first to the mall or the motel. He chose the mall.

He chose wrong. While he was disabling Liza's car, the other three breezed into the motel, grabbed Whitehead and headed to Waveland.

*   *   *

"The radio worked perfectly," McMillan said as O'Hearn studied the steel container to ensure he could put it back exactly as he found it.

"If Mary hadn't got the information she did, we'd be under that boat right now trying to pry it off," O'Hearn responded.

"There's still the matter of putting it back on. They may not have heard me taking it, but it'll be tough to reattach it without banging the hull."

O'Hearn smiled. "We'll make sure they don't hear it," he said as he removed the container's nose and pulled out the flat plastic packs of cocaine. Noting that each was numbered, he began to record the order in which they were removed. O'Donnell dumped the contents of each container into a zippered plastic bag and then placed the first bag into a second one and set it into one of two ice chests. Adams and McMillan carefully refilled the empty plastic containers with powdered sugar and set them aside to be reloaded into the steel tube.

* * *

Hanks took over the driving. After they crossed the Lake Ponchartrain causeway, they exited at Slidell for a restroom break and to take stock of their situation. While Liza called her friend Linda, Peter called his wife.

"Hello, Elizabeth. This is Peter." He spoke more loudly than was necessary, but he was trying to compensate for the road noise coming from just beyond the telephones.

"My gosh, Peter, where have you been? Is everything all right? Are you okay? And where *are* you? I've called the FBI, and even the local New Orleans police are looking for you. Are you in a hotel?"

"Elizabeth, I can't begin to tell you everything, but right now things are sort of under control. We're just on the run." Peter wasn't about to give her a rundown on the whole day.

"Who's 'we'?" Elizabeth asked suspiciously.

"You remember Hanks?"

"Yes."

"And Whitehead?"

"Of course."

Peter wasn't sure if he should add the third name. Without having time to explain, that information would only leave her confused and probably angry, so he said, "That's who I'm with."

She wanted to ask why, but could tell from the fact that he wasn't offering the information that he probably wouldn't give her a straight answer. Instead she asked, "Where are you?"

"Slidell."

"Where's that? You're not calling from the car phone, are you?"

"No."

She waited, but he didn't say anything else. Elizabeth was frustrated and worried. She was sorry she had ever suggested he go to New Orleans. "Come on, Peter, what are you doing and where are you going? Are you being held prisoner or something?"

"No, it's nothing like that. Let me call you from the car."

"No, Peter," she shouted into the phone. Her voice was breaking up as she fought back tears. "Don't hang up on me. Right now, I've got to know what's going on."

Minutes later, he concluded a rundown of the previous five hours. "I'm sorry for causing you hurt like this. I know this is awkward for all of us, but we'll get things settled soon. We're going to Waveland to find a place for Liza to stay, then we'll try to figure out what we need to do. Please don't say anything else to the police until I can sort things out with Hanks and Barry. Okay?"

Nothing was okay. Feelings of anger, disappointment, fear and jealousy crisscrossed Elizabeth's mind. The feelings were colored by the realization that she had practically ordered her husband into the line of fire—and now the Liza connection was beginning to sink in. She couldn't understand why her husband, the man she had loved for so many years, the man who had loved her for just as long, was now with another woman. It didn't make sense. In Peter's time of need she wished she could encourage him. She wished she could give him a poem or verse from the Bible to uplift him. She wished she could tell him she loved him. But the words would not come.

"Don't waste your sorrys on me," she finally said. "You better save them for Liza and her husband and her family."

Before Peter could respond, she hung up the phone and began to cry.

22

Saturday, April 28

Frank Mazzetti was sitting at Earl Hendrick's desk, checking and dou-
ble-checking his records on his laptop computer. He was comparing
them with those he took from Peter Boget's computer while Peter was
in the hospital. There was only one place the data on the two
sets of files intersected. Over and over again he asked himself how someone else might interpret that information. He picked up the phone and
dialed the Boget residence.

Just when Elizabeth thought that nothing else could go wrong, she had
to talk with Frank Mazzetti. She was angry with her husband and concerned
about his well-being. Now she was conversing with a man she loathed. She
wanted to spit into the phone, but instead she silently asked God for
strength, sucked in her breath, and with as much grace as she could muster
she said, "Good afternoon, Mr. Mazzetti. What a surprise to hear from you.
Why are you calling on a Saturday?"

"Well, I'm in town this weekend and was just wondering how your husband is doing," he lied.

"Great, really great." She lied too.

"I wondered if I could come by and see you folks this evening."

"Oh, I'm sorry, Peter is going to be tied up. Perhaps Monday or Tuesday
would be better."

"I'm sorry, too. Could I trouble you to ask him to come to the phone?" He was extremely pleasant, as he usually was, and smooth. "I owe you both an apology."

She was in a bad mood and a little sarcasm seemed in order. "Really, now? What are you trying to get from us?"

"Nothing, nothing at all. I just wanted to make you aware of some job possibilities that I have been researching for Peter. Is he available?"

"Not at the moment, actually. He's working with a needy person to try to locate some temporary housing. Is there something you can tell me?"

He hemmed and hawed, then said, "There's a new position that is being created in New Jersey to work on the new cable TV project. It's a downgrade, but Peter would be back at his current level within one year, and there is a financial differential to cover the higher cost of living."

"Does he have a chance for it?"

"I may be able to swing it," Mazzetti said, "if I could be assured that we all could put our differences behind us and that Peter would publicly apologize for, shall we say, inadvertently misusing company property."

"And I'm supposed to forget what you did to me, to us, in Peter's office?"

"That would be best for all of us, don't you think?"

Elizabeth was furious. The man had her right where he wanted her, and they both knew it. Peter's future at the phone company was bleak, and she hated the thought that she would ever have to be dependent upon Frank Mazzetti for a favor. But she thought about her children and the family's financial security. "I'll talk to him," she said. "Where in New Jersey?"

"Westfield. It's a beautiful community about twenty miles outside of Manhattan."

*   *   *

The closer they got to Waveland, the more nervous Liza got. She had called three friends, and none were at home. She directed Hanks to turn down Lakeshore Drive and follow the signs to the casino. Before he got there, she told him to pull off by a group of houses that backed up to what looked like a canal. Two shrimp boats and several pleasure boats were docked along the shore behind the few homes that lined the unpaved road. At Linda's house she ordered the car stopped. There was no car in front of the house and it looked vacant, but she checked nonetheless.

"She could be anywhere," Liza said when she returned to the car. "Maybe we can see if she's at work."

With Liza giving directions, they arrived at Beach Boulevard and turned toward the casino, where a nearly full parking lot suggested that business was going well.

"Just stay around here to the right," she said as they hit the gravel road beyond the casino parking lot. They bounced on the uneven roadway to the blue building on which was painted a large sign announcing Terry's Seafood.

"There's her car," Liza pointed out with relief.

When Hanks stopped the car, all four got out. They were feeling good about being so far from New Orleans. Liza quickly mounted the concrete stairs to the office door.

Before she reached the counter, Linda was on her feet. The pretty, middle-aged woman, dressed in jeans and an oversized blue T-shirt sporting the fishery's logo, walked toward her quickly. When the two met, Linda took Liza's arm and nudged her back toward the door. "I'll be right back," Linda told the woman behind the counter. Then she escorted Liza out the door and around to the outdoor work area where a group of men were removing sacs of roe from a catch of mullet.

Out of earshot of anyone else and hidden from the view of the parking lot, Linda said nervously, "Randy left five minutes ago. He said someone was after you and that if you showed up I should hold you and call for him."

"Someone's after me all right—him!"

"What's wrong?"

"I need a place to stay tonight."

"You're welcome at my house, but he'll probably be back." She narrowed her eyes and furrowed her brow. "Let me make some calls. In the meantime," she stopped. "How'd you get here?" she asked.

"Three guys brought me back from New Orleans. They're out front."

"I wouldn't stick around here. Go on over the bridge to the new parking lot. Give me a few minutes to make some calls. If you stay near this end of the lot, I can signal you when I've got some information, and you'll be able to spot Randy if he comes back."

"Thanks," said Liza as she reached out and hugged her friend. "I'll tell you all about it later."

*   *   *

Less than two hundred yards away, Patrick was completing his work. From where he stood beside a pickup truck he observed that the man who had been in the parking lot had switched places with one of the men on the boat, but all three continued to act as if they were mechanics working on the boat's engine and a winch used to raise and lower the fishing nets. O'Hearn nodded toward the *Pollyanna*. McMillan, Adams and O'Donnell carried the torpedo-shaped container from the boat's cabin to the end of the boat's work area and carefully lowered it to the water. McMillan, clad in a wet suit, slipped into the water alongside it. O'Hearn climbed into the cab of the pickup and cranked the engine. It groaned but it wouldn't start. He tried several times without success. He got out and raised the hood. After thirty seconds of fiddling, he walked around the truck and set out across the parking lot toward the *Miss St. Loo*. As he approached the man he believed to be the parking lot guard, he asked in a friendly voice, "Excuse me, do you think you could give me a hand? I can't get my truck to start."

"What's wrong?" said Todd Chamberlain.

"Don't know, thought you might be able to help. You're a mechanic, aren't you?"

"The boys on the boat are, but they just work on diesel engines."

"Oh, I see." As casually as he could, O'Hearn walked past Chamberlain and headed toward the *Miss St. Loo*. He continued to talk as he walked. "What are you working on?"

Nervously, Chamberlain, a big man with a ruddy complexion who weighed ninety pounds more than the wiry O'Hearn, tried to intercept the visitor, but O'Hearn walked quickly. The two men were side by side as they stepped onto the wooden dock. O'Hearn jumped down onto the deck of the boat. Chamberlain remained on the dock.

O'Hearn greeted Horace Bolton, the man who appeared to be oiling the winch, a task he had performed a dozen times since beginning his watch of the boat. "Afternoon, mates. Was wondering if you could give me a hand. My truck won't start."

Nick Duane emerged from the engine compartment. He was the only mechanic among the three, and knew that he needed to get O'Hearn off the *Miss St. Loo* immediately, because the stranger's presence had to be considered a threat to the integrity of the shipment. "Maybe I can help you. What's wrong?"

"I can't tell. It cranks, but won't start. I'm thinking it might be a fuel pump."

"Or a timing chain," said Duane as he wiped his greasy hands with a rag. "I'll take a look."

Out of view of O'Hearn, Chamberlain was shaking his head. He was in a high state of alert. He knew that if one of his men was diverted from his primary task of guarding the *Miss St. Loo,* the boat became more vulnerable.

O'Hearn glanced at his watch. "Oh, I didn't realize it was so late. Maybe I should just walk over to Terry's and call my wife and let her come get me. And get back over here with a mechanic tomorrow."

"Nonsense!" said Duane. "Let's have a look at it."

O'Hearn glanced down at his watch again and began counting the seconds in his mind.

Eight, seven, six, five . . .

He eyed the open steel toolbox on the ship's deck, just two feet away. He took a step backward so that, when he turned to leave the boat, the toolbox would be directly in his path.

Four, three, two . . .

"Thanks," he said to the mechanic as he turned quickly.

One . . .

O'Hearn caught the edge of the box with his toe, and just before Chamberlain could yell a warning, the tools were clattering and crashing across the deck.

Expressing humble apologies, O'Hearn scrambled to pick up the scattered tools. Duane and Bolton laughed and began helping him. But Chamberlain wasn't laughing. Something was wrong but he couldn't put his finger on it. He was afraid O'Hearn was up to something. He didn't know that O'Hearn's job was done—that while tools bounced along the deck of the *Miss St. Loo,* Billy McMillan had activated the electromagnets that secured the cocaine and sugar-filled container to the hull of the boat.

While the last of the tools were returned to the toolbox, Todd Chamberlain turned toward the sound of a car crossing the bridge to the parking lot. The moment he saw the dark green Buick Park Avenue, he believed that trouble was on its way. The car fit the description of the car that was to come later at night to make a pickup, and in it were three men and a woman, just as Kevin Daugherty, Holland's operations manager, had warned him. Without turning back to the boat he announced, "Company's coming."

O'Hearn stepped up from the deck of the boat to the dock. Nick Duane was by his side. Horace Bolton walked quickly to the boat's cabin and disappeared within. For the Irishman, the sight of what looked like Mary's rented automobile surprised him; the sight of Roland Hanks and Barry Whitehead in the front seat made him livid. He stepped off the dock and walked quickly back toward his rented truck.

"I'll be with you in a minute," Duane called after him.

Cautiously, Chamberlain walked to the car that stopped a few feet short of the dock. His hand was inside his shirt, wrapped around the handle of his semi-automatic. He approached the driver's door of the car. Hanks had already lowered the window. "Why are you here so early?" Chamberlain asked. "Get out of here and don't come back till ten."

Hanks was confused. *Who is this man? What's supposed to happen at ten? What's O'Hearn doing here?* Then it clicked. To Chamberlain he said, as casually as his racing heart would allow, "We're just checking the site. We'll be back later." Then he put the car in reverse and pulled away.

As he turned he looked into his rearview mirror and saw O'Hearn lower the hood on a pickup truck.

"We're in trouble," he said to no one in particular. "I think we've just stumbled onto something." Nodding his head back toward the parking lot, he said, "That's the man who's been giving me orders to get rid of Barry."

"That's Patrick O'Hearn," Whitehead added, looking over his shoulder through the back window. Then glancing at Peter Boget he added, "Your 'Irish Eyes.' "

As he turned the wheel and gunned the engine, Hanks handed the mobile phone to Whitehead. "Dial 911. Tell them there's been a shooting at Bayou Caddy."

"No one's shooting," Boget interjected.

"They will be before I'm done."

*   *   *

Randy Morgan walked through the screen door and into the kitchen. "Amy!"

She jumped from the couch where she slept while movie credits scrolled across the TV screen.

"Your mother's out with another man," he announced to the startled teenager. "She'll probably come by to pick up her things. Don't let her go without finding out where she's headed. She's going to have to answer for her actions to you and me and to the church and the courts. I'm heading out to look for her. If you hear from her, beep me."

*   *   *

Nick Duane approached the idling truck as Patrick O'Hearn quickly tied the plastic coolers under the tarp to ensure that they wouldn't slide around. "You got it started, I see," said Duane.

"Must have been some dirt in the fuel line."

"Whatcha got in those coolers?" Duane asked as he eyed Eileen Adams, who was standing near the passenger door of the truck. "Most people coming in have empty coolers, not full ones," he observed.

"Just some shrimp for home."

Billy McMillan chose the wrong moment to emerge from the water. He was spotted by Todd Chamberlain, who was walking up the dock toward the *Pollyanna.* Chamberlain leveled a gun at him.

A moment later, Duane flashed his pistol and ordered O'Hearn to open one of the containers.

"What's going on here?" demanded O'Hearn. "I'm just a fisherman."

"Like hell you are," he said, looking at O'Hearn's pale face.

Between the two of them, Chamberlain and Duane had enough firepower to send O'Hearn and his associates to their graves three times over, but they wanted to be sure before asking Daugherty for permission to take action. "Just open the cooler and let me have a look," Duane demanded.

Storm clouds were gathering quickly above them.

Liam O'Donnell maneuvered himself within five feet of Chamberlain while the man concentrated on McMillan, who was peeling off his wet suit. Suddenly O'Donnell sprang into action. More quickly than Chamberlain could react, the martial-arts expert was airborne and traveling vertically, his right foot poised to intersect with Chamberlain's wrist directly behind the gun. Before he knocked the firearm free, Eileen Adams reached for the gun in Duane's hand and yanked the man forward. Before he could react, she drove her foot into his right knee. With a swallowed scream, Duane dropped to the ground, releasing his pistol in the process. Adams followed with a devastating open-handed chop to the back of the man's neck. Taking out Chamberlain proved more difficult. Finally, after a series of exchanges, O'Donnell was able to land a foot to the man's jaw, taking him out of the fray.

Horace Bolton leaped from the deck of the *Miss St. Loo* armed with a "street sweeper," an automatic shotgun. He fired in the direction of O'Donnell, and some of the pellets caught the man in his midsection. Before Bolton's second shot exploded from the chamber, Patrick O'Hearn fired one rifle shot from behind his pickup truck. The bullet struck Bolton in his midsection and knocked him off his feet. Adams raced to her fiancé, who was doubled over but walking toward their car. McMillan raced to the truck and jumped in beside O'Hearn. Both the truck and car sprang to life and headed for the narrow bridge. Three fallen men writhed on the parking lot's hot asphalt.

The bridge was steep, and Patrick O'Hearn didn't see the stopped car blocking his exit out of Bayou Caddy until he reached the bridge's crest. He took the matter in stride until he saw that no one was in the green Park Avenue. He was outraged. "Get out and back that car out of there," he ordered McMillan. The strong redhead was out of the truck before O'Hearn finished speaking. What he saw discouraged him.

All four tires were flat and the keys were gone. He threw up his hands to signal to O'Hearn that it was hopeless. Patrick gunned the truck's engine and smashed into the car. It barely moved. In the packed dirt that covered the wooden bridge, the truck's tires spun uselessly. In less than a second O'Hearn made his decision. He signaled to the others and, with McMillan by his side, he ran toward Terry's Seafood. He targeted a Ford Taurus that was backing away from the building.

Beyond the Taurus, running as hard as they could manage, Peter, Barry and Liza reached the casino's parking lot when the first volley of gunfire rang out. All three stopped and turned. O'Hearn was dragging the driver of the Ford from behind the steering wheel. O'Hearn took his place as McMillan jumped in beside him. Hanks, who had hidden behind a parked car, stood and from twenty feet away pumped two bullets into O'Hearn before Adams, arriving last at the car, dropped him with a single shot from her Glock. McMillan yanked the slumped O'Hearn from behind the wheel. Adams jumped in and spun the car out of the parking area.

Mary Kennedy's most reliable employee had taken a bullet in his neck and another in his chest and was bleeding profusely. He couldn't speak but he signaled Adams to go fast. With Hanks out of the way, and the police not knowing that they were in the Ford, Adams knew that her chances of getting out of the immediate area were good. She headed to the paved road that swept to the left past the casino parking lot and then followed the beach through Waveland to Bay St. Louis. Three cars were in line to exit from the casino as the Ford reached the paved road.

Realizing that the car carrying O'Hearn was going to be able to drive right past the incoming police cars, Peter, who was approaching the exiting cars, pushed Liza back toward the casino. "Run!" he said. Then he yanked open the front door of a ten-year-old Chevy Caprice that was first in line to exit. The driver was a fiftyish woman who wasn't belted in. He pushed the startled woman across the seat. As her foot came off the brake, the car rolled into the path of the oncoming Ford. "Get out of here," he yelled as he reached in and threw the gearshift into park. The woman yanked opened the passenger door and jumped out.

The thunderstorm that had been gathering for nearly an hour splattered a few large drops on the ground before unleashing its fury in torrents.

With an oncoming police car filling the lane to her left, Adams cranked the Taurus's steering wheel hard to the right to avoid the Chevy. Her car hopped the curb but was going too fast to avoid hitting the Chevy's rear fender. In the driving rain, it careened into the parking lot and struck the second car in line.

Peter, who had been knocked to the ground when the Chevy was hit, scrambled to his feet and yanked open the car door as Adams and O'Donnell leaped from the Taurus, pistols in hand. In frustration as much as anger, Adams fired one shot at Peter as he ducked into the car.

From behind a parked car, Liza saw Peter lurch violently forward and drop from view. She cried out in horror, but her scream was drowned by the pounding of the rain on auto rooftops and the roadway. Then she saw eight county policeman, guns drawn, taking up positions in the road. With her hands raised to show she was unarmed, Liza raced to the Chevy and dived in.

Adams ran around the disabled Taurus toward the second car in line. O'Donnell had already reached the car that had been vacated earlier. He pulled open the back door so McMillan could throw in O'Hearn, but before he could slide behind the steering wheel, the police were shouting orders for them to drop their weapons. O'Donnell and Adams opened fire. The policemen returned it.

In the front seat of the Chevy, Liza pulled Peter's head onto her lap. She saw the blood oozing from his back. She was investigating the wound when he reached up and grabbed her head and pulled it toward him. "Lay down before you get killed."

"Are you okay?" she asked.

He looked into her face. It was closer than it had been at any time since they were together. So close that he had trouble focusing on her eyes. Rain beat on the windshield and poured onto Peter's back through the shattered left window. Peter spoke loudly above the din of the storm. "I promised Elizabeth I wouldn't do anything stupid." He couldn't prevent tears of pain from commingling with the water that dripped from his hair. The bullet seared his shoulder and spread a burning sensation throughout his body. Liza put her arm around him and held him close.

A shotgun blast shattered the car's windshield, raining glass and water over Peter and Liza as they huddled together. Adams, though hit in the abdomen, had managed to take up a position behind the Chevy and used her marksmanship to disable three officers, but the shotgun blast took her out of the firefight. O'Donnell was already down. With four bullets sucking life from his body, only McMillan's enormous strength allowed him to continue firing from behind the car door.

"I hurt, Liza," Peter said as explosions filled the air. "I really hurt."

The deafening sound of gunfire filled the air for nearly thirty seconds. Then, despite the rain, an uneasy calm fell upon the street and parking lot. Adams, O'Donnell and McMillan were dead. Boget, Hanks, the driver of the Taurus, four policemen and O'Hearn were among the wounded.

*   *   *

Jack Holland listened as Kevin Daugherty relayed the grim news. "How could something like that happen?" Holland demanded.

"I don't know."

"I pay you to know!"

"All of our men are alive; I evacuated them by boat. Looks like we have a broken knee, a broken arm, a smashed face and a bullet in the abdomen. We're not sure if any of the merchandise is missing."

"It better not be missing. How could they have gotten it? Were you watching it?"

"Of course we were watching it. I'm not sure what happened, but some people are dead. I don't know who they are. The four who were supposed to come here tonight showed up and some others were there as well. I don't know yet who's who."

After he hung up the phone, Holland dialed Kennedy's hotel room.

"Hello," she answered pleasantly. She was expecting a call from O'Hearn.

"Mary, this is Jack."

Kennedy didn't like his tone. It was surly but controlled.

"What do you think you're doing?" he asked.

"What do you mean?"

"Let's get right to the point. You tried to screw me. When I say a ten o'clock delivery, I mean a ten o'clock delivery, not four in the afternoon. Do you understand?"

"I don't know what you're talking about," she said with quiet innocence.

"They carted your people out of Bayou Caddy in ambulances and hearses," he told her. "What the hell's going on down there?"

"I don't know what you're—"

"Shut up and listen! We figured out your scheme. You were going to take over my business from your 'orphanage' in Ireland. You cooked the books so I'd end up on the short end of your power grab. But what'd you expect to gain from coming early for your merchandise?"

"Look, Jack, this is business, strictly business. I do what I have to do."

"And I do what I have to do."

*   *   *

Liza Morgan sat in the ambulance with Peter Boget as it sped toward Hancock Medical Center. She was trained in emergency medicine, so she was sent alone with Peter while the medic who would ordinarily be in the ambulance remained at the scene to attend to the injured who didn't need hospitalization.

Liza couldn't hold back the tears. For years she had seen people in her emergency room who were injured far more seriously than Peter, but the emotional attachment made the injury seem so much worse. She wasn't thinking about her husband or what awaited her at home. She only knew that a day that had started out so bright and with so much promise had turned bleaker than she ever could have imagined.

The rain beat on the roof of the ambulance and thunder crashed nearby, rattling her bones. To her it seemed like the voice of God, who was trying to get her attention. She waited for a message, but all that came was a song. She reached out and took Peter's hand in hers. In her mind she could hear the orchestra playing *Finlandia*. She waited until the music got soft near the end of the piece. Then she began singing, "Be still my soul: the Lord is on thy side . . ."

Peter squeezed her hand as she sang. After she finished, he said, "I've always had trouble being still, Liza . . . in my body . . . in my mind . . ." He remained quiet while he formulated his next sentence. "I'm here because I refused to be still. Some people would've thought I learned my lesson up on the beltway in Washington, but, you know, that all happened to someone else. But not this time. I wanted to take charge." He coughed as he spoke and blood drooled from his mouth. She tried to quiet him, but Peter continued. "I wanted it all . . . to help my friend Mike . . . to catch Irish Eyes . . . to see Mary Kennedy go to jail, and . . ." He struggled with the words. "I wanted to see you, even though I don't belong here." He drew a deep breath and winced as the bullet wound sent sharp pain racing across his back. "I'm sorry, Liza. I'm so very sorry."

The ambulance turned into the driveway at the hospital and stopped in front of the double glass doors that led to the emergency room. Two policemen helped Liza and the driver pull Boget out of the ambulance and roll him into the hospital. Liza's presence surprised no one.

"Glad you're here, Liza, we need all the hands we can get."

"How many?" asked Liza.

"He's the third."

"Two are on their way to Memorial."

The conversation turned to the matter at hand. Peter's vitals were good. Those of the man in station two were not, so that's where the most attention was focused.

Liza glanced over and immediately recognized the man whose neck was a bloody pulp. She wanted to tell her coworkers to save their time and effort and let the man go, to come and work on a real man, one whose family is dependent on him, one who's making a difference in the world. One . . . one whom she loved. She wanted to say that the world didn't need Patrick O'Hearn, but a quiet voice within her reminded her of the line in the song she had sung in the ambulance: "Leave to thy God to order and provide."

She whispered a prayer and began prepping Peter for surgery.

*   *   *

It was five after nine Virginia time when the call Elizabeth didn't want finally arrived. David answered it and announced that a Liza Morgan was on the line.

At once Elizabeth was angry and jealous. She had been worried all evening and fought back the insidious thought that Peter and Liza were doing more than just finding her a place to stay. She expected Peter to at least have the courtesy to place the call himself. As she walked to the phone her anger toward Peter turned to loathing of Liza, who, she was convinced, had lured her husband into some kind of tryst. She half expected Liza to announce that she and Peter had decided to head to who-knows-where to save her from her husband, and that Peter was too tired to call and that she had changed the dressing on his chest, and he was fine and they were in a motel but that he was asleep and that nothing funny was going to happen. Elizabeth's imagination was running wild when she took the phone from her son. Her greeting was not friendly.

"Elizabeth, I don't know how to say this."

"Just say it."

"Peter's just come out of the operating room."

That was the other thing Elizabeth imagined she might hear from Liza— that Peter had been shot by her husband.

"He's going to be okay," Liza went on. "He had a bullet removed from his shoulder." Liza's businesslike demeanor melted and she started to cry. "I'm sorry, Elizabeth, for all the pain and hurt I've caused you and Peter and your family. I never expected this. I never wanted this."

Elizabeth's anger was lowered a notch, but she still didn't know what happened and was feeling a knot tighten in her stomach at the realization that Peter was in a hospital bed a thousand miles away. The fact that Liza was tending him was less of a concern than was Peter's well-being.

"What happened?" Elizabeth asked. "Was it your husband?"

"Oh, no. Nothing like that. It was a woman with Patrick O'Hearn. Peter drove a car in front of them, blocking their escape from the fishery over by the casino . . ."

Elizabeth rolled her eyes and tried to imagine a fishery and a casino and drug dealers, and Peter ramming a car, and a woman shooting him. It had to be real, she thought, nobody could make up a story like that.

Liza continued. "After Hanks shot O'Hearn, they were trying to escape when the police arrived. That's when Peter did his thing and the driver of the car that wrecked jumped out and, while Peter was at the door, she shot him in the back. She shot the man named Hanks too, after he shot Patrick O'Hearn, but he went to another hospital so I don't know what his status is. Peter told me to tell you that O'Hearn is Irish Eyes. He's here and he's not doing well at all."

With no visual clues to orient her, Elizabeth was only hearing words, not seeing the picture Liza was trying to paint. All she could firmly see in her mind was her husband in a hospital bed. She had a hundred things to ask, but couldn't think of any of them. She did get a phone number and the name of the hospital before she hung up the phone.

When she did, she noticed the six eyes of her oldest three looking at her intently. "Your father's in a hospital. He's been shot." The six eyes got bigger. "So has Irish Eyes." That revelation brought a collective smile to the children, but Elizabeth cautioned them not to rejoice over O'Hearn's situation. Then she added, "I was wrong. His life and death is not our responsibility; it's God's. I think we better pray for him and Mr. Hanks and your father."

*   *   *

On the third floor of the federal courthouse in New Orleans, in the office of the U.S. marshals, an exhausted Barry Whitehead awaited word from the prosecutor in Norfolk. From the time that Elizabeth Boget had notified the

FBI about her husband's mission, prosecutor Heather Priddy was brought on board and the FBI office in New Orleans was asked to locate Mary Kennedy. Whitehead's call from the casino following the shootings gave them a place to start the search.

The ten o'clock news was starting when the call arrived. Whitehead qualified for witness protection services, but no one was going to do anything until after they watched the televised news coverage of the Bayou Caddy firefight and drug bust.

*   *   *

Sitting in a chair next to a sleeping Peter, Liza watched the same coverage. In the dark room, only the light from the TV screen offered flickering illumination. The words and the images told a very different story from the one she had witnessed, but she didn't know why. No mention was made of Hanks, Peter, Whitehead or herself. Even the woman whose car blocked the path of Adams, O'Hearn and the others didn't recall being pushed from her car. The rain had washed away the blood and the tire tracks, and had driven most of the witnesses indoors, leaving the reporters with little to show except the back seat and trunk of the car that O'Donnell and Adams had been driving onto the bridge when the incident started—and the back of O'Hearn's pickup truck. The former contained enough weapons and bomb-making materials to supply a small army; the latter, enough cocaine to destroy the lives of thousands.

Before the weatherman began his report, fear had once again overtaken Liza. So much had happened since she had returned to Mississippi in the middle of the afternoon. Thoughts of Randy's wrath had been pushed aside in her frantic effort to save lives. Now as the reality of what she yet had to face began to sink in, the anxiety began to tie her in knots. She turned off the TV, plunging the room into darkness. In that darkness she called out to God to bring her comfort. She knew that her husband was looking for her, and she knew her children would be concerned. But she took solace in believing that Amy was out of the house for the evening.

Randy's actions earlier in the day finally convinced her that she could never return. But where to go? And how? It was all too much to think about at the end of so exhausting a day. She closed her eyes and soon her fears gave way to sleep.

*   *   *

Randy Morgan wasn't sleeping. He was walking into the emergency room at Hancock Medical Center. A frustrating afternoon and evening of searching had yielded nothing. Then on the news he had heard about the action in Bayou Caddy. He knew that Liza's commitment to duty would send her to her job.

A calm had returned to the emergency room. The night staff, wearing their teal uniforms with floral print jackets, were taking inventory of the stock so they could replace some of the critical supplies that had been used in record number earlier in the evening. Randy didn't wait for someone to acknowledge his presence. "Where's Liza?" he bellowed.

Cindy Woodson was closest to him and quickly responded. "She doesn't come in until tomorrow night."

"Was she here earlier?"

"Yes, but she's gone."

Morgan was still steaming. "Where'd she go? Was anyone with her?"

"Mr. Morgan, I'm sorry," Cindy said quietly. "There have been a lot of people in and out of here tonight, and one man is still in the operating room. I'm sorry I don't know any more than that."

"If Liza comes in, tell her to call home, will you, please?" Randy's "please" was little more than window dressing on an order that was strident and filled with vituperation. He headed to the door that exited into the main part of the hospital, but a security guard, walking through the door, blocked his path.

"May I help you?"

"I'm looking for my wife!"

"I'm afraid visiting hours are over," the officer responded.

"She's a nurse!"

The policeman looked in the direction of Nurse Woodson. "Have you tried to call her?" he asked.

She responded, "He's looking for Liza Morgan. She's off today."

The policeman peered into Morgan's face. He saw the anger but didn't know what it represented. He did know that an incident of domestic violence would serve no one any good. "I don't know what's wrong," he said, "but you don't look too good. Why don't you just go home and sleep on it."

Morgan thought better of confronting the officer, turned and walked toward the double glass doors. He walked past the postcard-sized wall switch that opened the doors and almost drove his hand through the glass when the doors failed to yield to his push. Without turning back to face the three people who were watching his every movement, Morgan stepped to the switch and with the side of his fist, slammed it against the wall. When the doors swung open, he walked out of the hospital.

23
___

Jack Holland had been in bed less than an hour and had just drifted off to sleep when the knock came at the front door. He looked at the digital clock next to his bed: 3:07 a.m.

He waited for his personal guard to answer the knock. Then he pressed the button on his bedside intercom to hear the conversation.

"Yes?" he heard Larry Crozet say from inside the door.

"FBI. We'd like to talk with Jack Holland."

"Can't it wait till morning?"

"No."

Crozet allowed the men to enter. "Just a minute. I'll wake him."

"No need for that," said Holland, wrapping a bathrobe around himself as he walked down the stairs to the central hallway. "I'm awake."

When he reached the bottom of the stairs, special agent Gene Longue told him, "Mr. Holland, we're sorry to bother you again, but you said you've not seen Mary Kennedy in weeks."

"That's right. Maybe a week before she died."

"Now, is it possible," asked Longue, "that she might have visited you last week, after she was supposedly killed?"

"What do you mean 'supposedly'?"

"We have reason to believe that she may not actually be dead. An eyewitness says he saw her leaving your office on Monday."

Now fully awake, Holland did some fast thinking. The only people he remembered who could have seen him with Mary were his secretary and the receptionist. "Whoever said she saw her must have been mistaken. A relative of Miss Kennedy, a Miss McKenna, did stop by to follow up on some business. She bears some resemblance to Miss Kennedy, but I haven't seen Mary Kennedy since she visited two weeks ago."

"And that was when you finalized your corporate merger?"

"Yes."

"Do you know where we can find this Miss McKenna?" the agent asked.

Holland weighed the risks of exposing Mary and having her end up on a witness stand or allowing her to go on her way and, possibly, come back for him later. "I think she said she was staying out by the airport."

"Was she with anyone?"

"What do you mean?"

Agent Longue held up a photo of Patrick O'Hearn. "Have you seen this man?"

"No, I don't think so. Why?"

"He's one of her employees and, I guess, now he's one of your employees. He was with that group of people shot in Bayou Caddy earlier this evening."

"Really?"

"Really. You'd better be careful," said Longue. "When you got Kennedy and Associates, you may have gotten more than you bargained for."

*   *   *

Before Jack Holland had returned to his bed, Elizabeth Boget's best friend, Joyce McGuire, pulled into the driveway of the Boget residence. Several lights already were on in the house, and the front door opened before she knocked.

Mike Downes was standing in the hallway.

"Is she ready?" Joyce asked.

"I think so," said Downes, looking fresh despite the early hour. "We've got over an hour until the flight, so we're in good shape." The two walked into the kitchen, where a half-filled glass coffeepot was beckoning. "Would you like a cup?" Mike said, playing the role of the host.

"Would I ever," she said, wiping the night from her eyes. "I don't usually get up quite this early."

"I didn't."

She looked at him quizzically.

"I drove down from Annapolis after I got the call from Elizabeth. I stopped at home to freshen up and got here about five minutes ago."

Joyce looked over the handsome vice president. Elizabeth had kept her apprised of the trials of this man who had done so much to bring Peter home. Yet, as she allowed her eyes to search his face, she didn't detect any of the strain that she expected to see on a man who was in such a difficult position. "You're looking good for a man who's been up all night."

He sipped some of his coffee, then confessed, "Actually, I got about six hours' sleep yesterday afternoon."

"I'm sorry you had to come so far to help Elizabeth."

"I'm not just helping Elizabeth. From the sound of things, I may be getting the help I need to get the feds off my back."

Joyce hadn't heard that part of the story, and she listened intently to Downes's explanation.

"I take it as a good sign that my prosecutor granted me permission to make the trip." He drank some more coffee and switched subjects. "I think it's wonderful that Elizabeth has a friend like you who is willing to drop everything and come to look after her family like this."

"No big deal," she said. "A lot of people in the church would have done this if they had only been asked. She just called me first."

Elizabeth walked down the stairs and into the kitchen. Joyce could not remember seeing her friend look so stunning. Given the circumstances surrounding the trip and the early hour, she expected Elizabeth to look dour, thrown together. Instead she was resplendent in a red suit and ivory-colored silk blouse. Her thick brown hair looked as if it had just been coifed at the beauty parlor.

"Wow, Elizabeth, don't you look great."

"Thanks. This is Peter's favorite outfit. I thought he might like to see me in it."

Joyce issued a knowing nod. The two women had had a long conversation eight hours earlier, during which Elizabeth confided to her that Peter had been to see another woman. For Elizabeth, this trip was as much to ensure Peter's commitment to her as it was to bring him home. "Any man would like to see you in that."

Elizabeth reviewed a list of things she thought Joyce should know and gave her a second one that she had made up for another friend who would be taking Joyce's place after the morning church service. "We better get on our way," Mike interrupted. "We've both got to get tickets and I'll have to park my car."

Joyce reached out to her friend and embraced her. "Don't worry about anything here. Everything will be fine."

*   *   *

Sunday had always been Liza Morgan's favorite day, but this one was different. For the first time in many years she didn't want to face the morning light. Her two weeks of ecstasy had ended. Even with the man she loved lying just inches away from where she sat, the inexorable pain of loss was setting in.

Whispers, she remembered. *He sang about whispers in the wind.* But today there would be no whispers . . . only the mournful cry of a wounded heart.

She felt safe in the darkened room, but knew that she would soon have to come into the light. She feared the exposure. She feared the inevitable confrontation with Randy. But most of all she feared the future. To be forty-two and alone in the world was a prospect she didn't want to face. To be forty-two and married to Randy Morgan seemed worse.

She walked to the bathroom, turned on the light and looked in the mirror. Her hair hung in strings. Her makeup had been washed away. Her once-beautiful dress was torn and spotted with blood. As she pulled the door shut, she heard Peter's voice.

"Liza? Is that you?"

She opened the door, allowing a shaft of light to stretch across the room and faintly illuminate his face. All he could see was the silhouette of her frame against the light. "Yes, Peter, it's me."

"Why are the lights off?" he said, trying to prop himself up with his one good arm. He groaned as pain shot across his back.

"It's the middle of the night."

"Would you turn them on?"

She did and returned to the side of the bed.

"I didn't expect to see you here."

"Why not?"

"I don't know," he said quietly, trying to maneuver into a comfortable position. "After last night . . ." He stopped, groaned again and dropped onto the pillow, wincing during the long silence that followed.

"I called your wife last night," Liza told him.

He closed his eyes. He didn't want to have to face his wife or his five children or his friends.

"She's going to try to get down here today."

"Elizabeth? Here?" He wasn't surprised, just fearful of the encounter. "I'm sorry, Liza."

"I know," she said softly. "You've told me that quite a few times."

"I'm sorry," he said again.

She laughed, then sat down on the bed near his knees so he could see her without straining. "I'm the one who should be sorry," she said. "I allowed myself to believe that you were my knight in shining armor who would ride in here on a white horse and carry me away . . . and I did everything within my power to make that happen." She turned aside and looked wistfully at the blank wall. "Now I've got to face the music. I'm going to have to go home, if only to get some clothes. Once morning gets here I'll call one of my friends and see if I can get an escort. I'm afraid of what Randy is thinking right now."

"Me too," said Peter, smiling weakly. "Maybe it's time we did something we used to do in Colorado; maybe it's past time."

"I don't think so. It's never too late to pray."

*   *   *

Sunday, April 29

After four hours of sleep, Randy Morgan was back in Diamondhead checking the work his assistant and his son had done the day before. He walked from room to room checking each of the cable runs against the blueprints. Satisfied that everything was in order for the insulation crew, he headed out. His watch showed 11:10 a.m.

Liza hadn't come home by the time he left at eight. He didn't care. He had a good idea where she was, and he had stayed up half the night thinking through how he was going to deal with her. By the time his plan was worked out in his mind it was nearly midnight. It took him another three hours to secure what he needed to make the plan work. He made visits to six drinking establishments before he found what he was looking for. In a bar featuring country music, beautiful girls and wicked drinks, he found someone willing to sell him a gun. It wasn't fancy and it wasn't powerful, but the .22 caliber target pistol was more than adequate.

*   *   *

After the short connecting flight from Richmond to Baltimore, the USAir flight from Baltimore to New Orleans was smooth and quick. It landed a few minutes early. Elizabeth and Mike walked the long corridor through the baggage claim area past the rental car counters and out to the waiting courtesy bus that took them to the Avis rental car lot. Within minutes they were driving onto Airline Boulevard.

"That must be where he stayed on Friday night," Elizabeth said, pointing out the Rodeway Inn. "I can't believe so much happened since I talked with him there less than twenty-four hours ago."

"I'm sure there's lots to this story we haven't heard," said Mike.

"And some I don't want to hear."

"I understand," he replied compassionately.

Mike and Elizabeth continued the conversation they began on the plane from Baltimore. She avoided discussing Peter's relationship with Liza; instead, they talked about Frank Mazzetti's peculiar offer of a job in New Jersey, the good news that Barry Whitehead was alive, and the fact that they were a major step closer to putting a whole range of problems behind them.

Even as they talked, Elizabeth frequently caught herself not really listening. The hurt and betrayal she was feeling were eating away at her insides. She didn't know the whole story, but what she did know made her unhappy and angry. She was angry with Peter, with Liza, and with herself. As they drove the last few miles through Waveland, anger was displaced by trepidation. Her memories of the near-disastrous reunion in Maryland still were fresh in her mind.

Downes drove into the parking lot of the low building accented with four blue pyramids, the two larger of which formed canopies at the building's entrances. Although the structure seemed pleasant, Elizabeth's greatest desire was to grab her husband and leave as quickly as she could. She didn't want to encounter Liza, but at the same time hoped that she'd get to see her again so she could understand what attracted Peter. She also wanted to see Patrick O'Hearn, but knew that seeing him would do her no good.

They stepped from the cool car onto the hot pavement. The moist air clung to their skin, reminding both of them of Richmond in July.

Once inside, they were briefed by a doctor before they entered Peter's room: "He's in good shape, especially considering what he's been through. The bullet struck his shoulder blade, was deflected down into his chest cavity and grazed his lung before lodging against a rib. He's still coughing up a little blood, and both the shoulder blade and the rib are fractured. The skin graft on his chest is partially abraded, but it's not too bad. He should be ready to travel by the end of the week, I would imagine."

"A week?" Elizabeth was surprised and disappointed. All the way down she had imagined that she and Mike would stay overnight and take Peter home in the morning. She didn't want to be away from her children more than two days. She filed that problem in her mind and proceeded into Peter's room.

He was awake, and he was alone. He greeted his wife and Mike with a strained version of his patented smile. Elizabeth walked to his bedside and gave him a tentative kiss. Neither the excitement nor the joy of discovery that had been so much a part of their reunion four weeks earlier was present in the bright room. He looked up at his wife and over to his friend. His smile disappeared. In its place was a look that reflected his penitent heart. "Please forgive me," he said as tears welled up inside his eyes. "I'm sorry, I'm so, so sorry."

Elizabeth took his hand. "I know you are. That's why I've come."

The room remained quiet for a long time.

Finally, Elizabeth spoke again. "Do you want to tell us what happened?"

The sedative was taking hold so Peter found it difficult to focus. "We got Irish Eyes. And I found Barry. And Hanks . . . now, he's an enigma."

"Was," Downes said quietly. "He died this morning."

"Oh, no." He closed his eyes as if by doing so he could resuscitate Hanks. "We needed him."

Elizabeth and Mike looked quizzically at each other, then at Peter.

"He had the answers."

"What answers?" Mike asked.

"I thought I had everything figured out, but now I know less than I did before." He paused. "Is Hanks really dead?" Then he started to tremble as he realized the impact he had had on the lives and deaths of people during the previous twenty-four hours. "He can't be dead," Peter cried aloud. "I was just with him. He's a hero. He helped us out when we saw Randy, and he came up with the idea of blocking O'Hearn so we could take him out. He can't be dead."

Elizabeth didn't care about Hanks. She wanted to know what was going on with the other woman in her husband's life. "When did you meet up with Liza?" she asked. She wasn't sure she wanted an answer, particularly if the meeting took place on Friday evening and he was going to say that they had spent the night together. She pulled away from the bed and waited.

Mike was growing increasingly uncomfortable. "Would you excuse me?" he said. "I'd like to talk with some of the police officers here in town and contact Barry." He disappeared out the door.

Elizabeth sat down on the edge of the bed. Peter looked like he was falling asleep but he shook his eyes open and began retelling what happened after he had spoken to Elizabeth early on Saturday morning.

*   *   *

After driving by her home in the back seat of a friend's car, Liza Morgan made a quick stop to grab as many clothes as possible, including her uniforms for work. She wasn't surprised that Randy wasn't there, but she was worried that she didn't know where he was. She hoped the absence of her children meant that they had gotten a ride to Sunday school. She scribbled notes to each of them and slipped them under their pillows. She thought about going by the church to check on them, but she was in no shape to meet anyone, and she worried that Randy might be lurking about. She dropped her clothes off at another friend's house and then, dressed in her uniform, returned to the hospital. She was in the emergency room when a message was passed to her that Peter Boget would like to see her.

She had heard through the hospital's efficient grapevine that Elizabeth Boget and a male friend had arrived around noon. She wondered if they had left already. A call to the nurse's station serving Peter's room delivered the news: Peter's guests were still in the room. With more than a little trepidation and a healthy dose of embarrassment she headed down the hall. She paused briefly outside Peter's door, grateful that she had had the opportunity to shower and change into her uniform. She looked rather official, and that made her feel a little better about the situation. She knocked, then entered.

Mike, who had returned, and Elizabeth didn't especially notice the nurse who stepped gingerly into the room. But when Peter saw Liza his mouth fell open. *Not now,* he thought to himself. *Come back later.*

But Liza was in and looking at Peter. She asked, "Did you call for me?"

"No, there must be some mistake," he said nervously.

But it was too late for Liza to leave. Elizabeth recognized the face; the nametag confirmed it. She stepped forward. She tried to suppress her anger and let compassion come to the fore. She knew from Peter's story that the past twenty-four hours had been rough on Liza as well. Elizabeth extended her hand. "Hello, Liza."

Mike Downes felt the electricity in the air as the two women shook hands. He was surprised that Liza would walk in on the group the way she did. Intruding like this seemed inconsistent with the woman Peter had described. Peter, too, thought it was strange. Liza was above pulling a stunt like that, he thought. He enjoyed seeing her, but the timing was all wrong.

Elizabeth sized up the woman. She was prettier than she remembered— or maybe hoped—and she looked very professional in her uniform. Elizabeth was glad she had gone to the trouble to look her best, because the competition was strong—and she could not overcome the feeling that this woman *was* competition.

In the awkwardness of the moment, Liza lowered her gaze to avoid eye contact with Peter's wife. "I'm sorry you've come under these circumstances."

"I'm sorry too."

"I was in the ER when I got a message that . . ." She didn't want to say it, but she already had come this far. Turning to Peter she said, ". . . that you called."

Elizabeth looked at her husband. So did Downes. Both awaited his response.

"I didn't call for you, Liza," said Peter.

"No, I did!" bellowed the man walking through the door. The shout startled the four already in the room. "So here's the little . . ." Randy Morgan groped for a word, and finding none finished the sentence, "who's cheating on me."

His revelation answered the questions running through the minds of Elizabeth and Mike, who were standing by the bed, to Peter's right.

"Where have you been all night, woman?" he demanded of Liza, who was near the foot of the bed. His voice was sharp, abrasive. He stepped around Liza and walked to the head of the bed across from Mike and Elizabeth.

"You must be 'darling Peter.' You're the one who's come a thousand miles to take my wife to a motel. And don't tell me you didn't." He pulled a card from his pocket and turned toward Liza. "Your friend Miriam told me you were meeting at the Days Inn," he sneered. "And the motel clerk told me you were both at her counter when she rented a room for two. See here?" He waved the registration card from the motel. "I've got it in black and white." He motioned in the direction of Elizabeth but continued talking to Peter. "Is that your wife?"

Peter nodded.

"Mrs. Boget," Morgan said, "why do you keep a bum like this around?"

Elizabeth didn't have a ready answer.

"And who are you?" he asked of Downes.

"Mike Downes. A friend of the family."

"Well," said Morgan, "I'd like you to leave. This is strictly a family matter."

Downes didn't move. "I'm sorry. I don't understand," he said.

"Well, maybe you'll understand this." Morgan unzipped the leather Bible case he was carrying and yanked out his newly acquired pistol. A collective gasp hushed the room as he pointed the gun first at Mike and then waved it toward the two women. He took a step closer to Boget's bed and placed the cold steel muzzle on Peter's left temple. A wicked smirk took possession of Morgan's face.

For Peter, Elizabeth, Mike and Liza, time stopped. It stopped long enough for Peter to feel greater fear than he had ever experienced in his life . . . and greater sadness than he had ever known. He wasn't ready to die. He had too much life to live and too much love to give: to his wife, his children, his friends, even the strangers in need who so often crossed his path. The issue of life after death and whether he was going to heaven or hell had long since been settled, but this was not the way he wanted to begin his journey.

His body reacted to the threat by pumping adrenaline into his system, heightening his senses, shutting down unneeded activities, and preparing every extremity for flight or the fight. But Peter was incapable of either.

Elizabeth trembled with horror. She couldn't believe that once again she was watching as someone she loved was a nervous twitch of a finger away from eternity. She wanted to cry out for mercy, but words choked in her throat. She wanted to leap across the bed and knock the gun from Morgan's hand or at the very least have him turn it on her instead. In that instant, her anger toward Peter, the hurt, the disappointment and the embarrassment faded. All she could see was the man she loved. The wonderful father to her children, the good friend to so many, the, until now, faithful husband. She didn't want him to die.

Mike turned on the pragmatic portion of his brain as he processed the scene. Where the others saw the impossibility of the situation, he calculated the probabilities. Physical assault would not be possible, but appeals to the gunman's heart and mind might work. Unfortunately, he knew very little about Randy Morgan. Mike did know that far fewer people were dependent on himself than were dependent on Peter Boget. The thought crossed his mind of offering himself in Peter's place. Now he had to figure out how to make that offer palatable to Randy Morgan.

Liza was beyond the point of feeling. Her worst nightmare was playing out before her and there wasn't anyone to waken her from it. She knew Randy, and meting out punishment for grievances—real or imagined—was a common pattern. She saw the fear in Peter's face. She felt Elizabeth's pain and desperation. But she was the one Randy really was after. She had to convince him of that. As tears blurred her vision, she began to speak.

"Don't do it, Randy," she said quietly but forcefully.

The man cackled with hate. "You're going to watch the destruction of someone you love, just as I have watched the self-destruction of the woman I love. You destroyed yourself by failing to be the kind of wife God called you to be . . . you never submitted to my authority . . . you abandoned your children and our home to become a wage earner, and for what? To indulge yourself in fancy clothes and expensive teeth. And then you condemned yourself to eternal damnation for leaving the marriage bed for this man." He pushed the muzzle into Peter's flesh, forcing his head to one side.

"You're wrong, Randy. It's not like that at all. We never did anything, I swear, we never even kissed."

"That's too bad," he said, enjoying the anguish he heard in his wife's voice, "because you'll never have the chance again."

"Put down the gun, Randy, I'll do anything you want me to," she pleaded.

Morgan laughed, but there was no humor in it. "That's right, Liza, you will do anything I want, because we're leaving here today, and you're never coming back—to see Peter, or to work, or anything else. You're coming home with me and you're going to do what you said you were going to do on our wedding day, aren't you?"

She nodded her head sheepishly as tears dripped to the floor. She didn't dare wipe her eyes for fear that any movement might give him a reason to pull the trigger.

"You're going to love me and cherish me and listen to what I tell you to do and stay home and care for our children!"

Liza was trembling. She brought her hands up in a praying position. Her voice quavered. "I'll do anything, anything you want me to do, but please don't shoot anybody. Please, Randy, please put away the gun. I'll go with you right now."

"No, you won't," he smiled. "You can't do everything I want, because I want you to stop loving Peter Boget. And you can't do that, can you?" Before Liza could answer, his voice dropped to a vile whisper. "The only way I can stop you from loving this man is to kill you or kill him, and I'm not going to give you the easy way out. I want you to watch as I pull the trigger and splatter his brains all over this bed. I want you to go through life remembering that you killed Peter Boget. You killed him because you abandoned me."

"If you pull that trigger," Mike interrupted, "it will be you they send to the electric chair, not your wife."

"Shut up."

"Let me tell you something about love."

"I said shut up!"

"My wife died two years ago," Downes continued. "I grieved terribly, and I certainly didn't stop loving her just because she was dead. But recently I met another woman and have fallen in love again, and all the pain of my wife's death is fading into obscurity." He was casting in the wind, but Downes felt he had to do something to distract Morgan. "Maybe you and Liza can fall in love again, but shooting Peter will make it impossible."

Liza stood motionless, unable to control her sobs. Elizabeth was paralyzed with confusion and fear.

Ignoring Mike's comments, Morgan looked at his wife and shook his head. "Don't cry for Peter. He's not worthy of your tears. He came down here to commit adultery. He should be taken outside of town and stoned. And you should be too. But this is much more satisfying."

With a leer worthy of the devil himself, Randy Morgan pulled the trigger.

"Bang!" Randy yelled as the hammer slammed against the empty chamber. Peter remained still as if in shock. But Morgan broke into uproarious laughter, tossed the gun onto the bed beside Peter's legs and grabbed Liza by her arm. His plan had worked flawlessly; he had accomplished exactly what he wanted. "No bullets!" he said, continuing to laugh, and headed for the door.

Elizabeth could not move. Peter had yet to register what was going on. But Mike Downes wasn't about to let Randy leave with Liza. He sprung so quickly that, even though Morgan was slightly taller and thirty pounds heavier, he could not prevent the takedown. But before Downes could control the man, Morgan rolled over and swung his left fist into Downes's skull just behind his ear. The two men rolled into the bedside tray, sending a vase full of flowers shattering to the floor.

Liza stepped toward the door, but Randy grabbed her ankle with one hand and pulled her to the ground.

Elizabeth let out a powerful scream for help and pushed Peter's bed to the wall to move it away from the two men fighting on the floor. Liza scrambled to her feet and reached the door just as a nurse pushed it open. A security guard followed. Moments later two policemen raced into the room and broke up the fight.

Sore and bleeding from his nose, Mike slumped into a chair. Randy continued to flail at the arresting officers as they dragged him from the room.

As if some dam burst within her, Liza sat down on the end of Peter's bed and wept uncontrollably. Years of pain and sorrow rode that river of tears. So, too, did years of abuse and neglect. The cleansing process that had begun when Peter reentered her life was nearing completion. She called out to God to bring order to the chaos of her life.

Elizabeth stepped to Liza's side and placed her arm on the woman's shoulder.

*   *   *

American Airlines flight 100 to London's Heathrow Airport sat at the gate in Atlanta. Mary Kennedy knew that the doors would be closing at any moment, and she would be on her way. She had wanted to check on Patrick O'Hearn, but thought better of it. She also figured that the possibility existed that Holland might tip the police to her whereabouts, but didn't encounter any resistance leaving the Crescent City.

She began to relax when she noticed the nicely dressed man who was standing in the aisle near her seat. Then she noticed the gun inside his jacket. He was beckoning to her. But he didn't call her by the name listed on her ticket. Instead he said quietly, "Miss Kennedy, please come with me."

*   *   *

Eventually, Liza lifted her head and wiped away her tears. "Thank you, Elizabeth."

The two women stood up. The gulf that had separated them had closed dramatically in their shared fear of what would happen to Peter.

"I think it's time for me to go," said Liza.

Peter wasn't ready to release her. Despite the pain that he felt when he moved, he propped himself on his good arm and looked down the bed. "Where will you go? What will you do?"

Elizabeth wasn't happy that Peter was extending the farewell, but she said nothing.

"Do?" Liza responded almost wistfully. "I don't know what I'll do. But I'll never go back. I guess we'll have to wait and see." She inhaled deeply and exhaled slowly. "I'm a survivor. God has carried me and my children all these years. I'll just have to trust him a little more now." She walked to Peter's side, leaned over and kissed his cheek as tears trickled from his eyes. Then she turned and gave Elizabeth a gentle hug that wasn't returned.

Trying to keep her trembling lip from opening up with the sobs that were rising within her, she said a hurried "Goodbye" and walked out of Peter's room and his life. But she didn't leave empty handed. She walked away with two weeks of glorious, if bittersweet memories and a portion of a man's heart that she would cherish forever.

Elizabeth turned to her husband. She wanted to thrash him—she wanted him to explain what was going on in his head. At the same time she wanted to crawl into the bed beside him—to comfort him and to take comfort in his arms. She could not remember ever feeling so confused.

He reached out to take her hand.

"Elizabeth, if there were two of me this wouldn't be so difficult." He tried to construct the next sentence in his mind before he spoke it. "You surely know that I love you. You've always said that love isn't words, it's actions, and in thousands of ways for twenty years I've tried to show you just how much I love you. I've made mistakes—some really big ones—but I've never made the mistake of not loving you. I didn't come here for Liza. I came for Barry Whitehead. In the process we got Patrick O'Hearn—that's what we wanted, isn't it? And maybe, because of what I've done here, someday someone will get Mary Kennedy. And I came to try to help Mike, and I think I've done that too." He stopped and the two remained in silence for a long time. "But I guess what I want to say is I've never stopped loving you, I just got distracted. I'm sorry, Elizabeth. Can you ever forgive me?"

Elizabeth had spent half a lifetime helping others: caring for children, kissing away hurts, setting aside some of her own desires to serve those around her. Now it was she who needed comfort, and in her husband's words she found some of the comfort she was looking for. But the hurt ran deep and even in her confusion she knew that the trust that had been an integral part of their relationship was seriously damaged. "I do forgive you, Peter. But . . ."

"I know," he said, answering for her. "It'll never be the same."

24

Friday, May 4

Since she arrived home Monday afternoon, Elizabeth Boget was preparing her children for their father's return and was trying to get her heart and head ready for the next phase of her life with Peter. She was glad she decided not to stay on in Mississippi. She needed some distance to rethink her marriage, and her children were having problems dealing with another round of newspaper articles and classmates inquiring about their father.

What Elizabeth was also preparing her children for was the possibility that the family would have to move to take another job with the phone company, or to get into a house that had lower interest payments. At the breakfast table with David and Lauren she reminded them that their father would be arriving at two. "I'd like to come by and pick you up at one, David, and then we'll stop at Swift Creek for you," she said to Lauren, "and then we can pick up Daniel and head for the airport."

"Why can't we just stay home?" Lauren asked. "It'll be too embarrassing to have you come and pick me up to go to the airport just to meet my father."

"Don't tell anyone," David said. "They'll never know."

"They know everything. I can see it now, an article comes out in the paper about how Dad got shot stopping a major drug deal and he'll say something like, 'The best part was seeing the shining faces of my children at the airport when I arrived home,' or some gush like that. You don't understand. I'm always being embarrassed by the things you and Dad do."

"Okay, Lauren, I won't come for you. I'll ask Mrs. Rogness if you can go to her house after school until we get back, all right?"

She thought for a moment. She really did want to go to the airport. "I'll go with you, if you promise not to tell anyone."

Elizabeth smiled. "Cross my heart."

*   *   *

This was coming-home day for Earl Hendrick as well. He was dressed and sitting in a chair in his room while flowers and cards were being loaded on a cart by a hospital volunteer. His wife, Emily, beaming with delight, was gathering up his personal belongings. She opened his attaché and pulled out the vial of tiny fragments of skin in the dark solution. "It's really too bad that you never got to take this to Washington," she said. "You would've really caused quite a stir."

"We will never know. I am afraid it would be a little outdated right about now. It certainly has lost its shock value."

She agreed, and returned it to the attaché case. "Well, anyway, it was nice of those Worthingtons to come here to the hospital and return your case. I think I paid a hundred fifty for it."

"I remember."

The phone rang, and after answering it, Emily handed it to her husband. It was Mid-Atlantic Bell's CEO.

"Earl, Dan Hart here. I want you to know that all of us here in Washington are cheering for you as you get out of the hospital today. I'm real glad you pulled through so well. You know, you gave us a real scare," said the fast-talking executive.

"I think I scared everyone, including myself."

After exchanging a few minutes of pleasantries, Hart changed the subject. "There's something else I have to talk to you about that can't wait until you get back."

"I'm not coming back, you know that."

"That's what I need to talk to you about. We had an emergency meeting of the executive committee last night via conference call, and I'm sorry I didn't think to include you. But I think you'll want to go on record on this one."

"Oh?"

Hart slowed his speech to something approaching normal. "The committee unanimously voted to call for Frank's resignation."

Hendrick was dumbfounded. "Mazzetti?"

"I know that you and Mike Downes had expressed some concerns about his dealings with Peter Boget. And sooner or later we would have gotten around to investigating the allegations, but on Wednesday one of Frank's employees brought some very damaging information to my attention."

"What kind of information?"

"It goes back a few years, but it involves a letter that Frank found when he worked in New Jersey and used it to, shall we say, advance his career. Well, one of the people he was blackmailing decided to stop playing ball and so Frank began altering e-mail messages to make it appear that the man was involved in wrongdoing. Yesterday, we found hundreds of altered messages involving lots of people. We confronted him with the evidence yesterday afternoon and gave him an hour to clean out his desk."

Hendrick was beaming. "Put me down for a yes vote, and let me call Mike. He will certainly be surprised . . ."

"He was. I reached him at his hotel in New Orleans."

"And Peter, what about Peter?"

"I think that man needs a leash," said the CEO. "We do have a real problem that he went into another employee's electronic mail, and some of the other stuff that Frank brought up looks bad. But I'm not ready to pass judgment. We'll look at his case after he gets back, and we can talk with him about the specifics."

"I understand . . . but Mazzetti, that is unbelievable!"

*　　*　　*

To be so close to Peter yet to be so far gnawed at Liza Morgan for the entire week. Her four-night tour of duty at the hospital had come to an end, but she didn't want it to. Even though she stayed away from his room, she was thrilled to be in the same building with him. And she received regular reports on his progress from other nurses. Now she was torn between what was right and what she wanted. She looked at her watch. Mike Downes would be arriving from New Orleans in an hour to take Peter home. She couldn't let him go without saying goodbye.

She was still in uniform when she walked into his room. He looked as good as he did when she first saw him six days earlier. He smiled broadly when she entered. "I thought you forgot me," he said.

"You know I can never forget you, I just thought it would be best to stay away while I put my head back in gear." She stood at the end of the bed, wanting to get closer, but knowing that she shouldn't.

"They sent Randy to the state mental hospital for evaluation, and the district attorney says when he comes out he'll face some firearms and assault charges. So I'm back home now and I probably won't have to worry about him for a while. My kids are okay, I think, and I earn enough here at the hospital to keep up the house, so that's good." She gripped the end of the bed and gently rocked back and forth, thinking about her next words. "It's just I wish you weren't heading home today and that somehow you could come and be part of my life. I know you can't, but if circumstances ever change, I want you to know that you're welcome at my place anytime."

"I know." Peter nodded slowly. "I'd like to stay and yet I really want to go home. I've done a lot of thinking this week. I don't understand what this episode was all about. Hanks is dead and O'Hearn is alive. Does that make sense?" He answered his question with a shake of his head. "I've lost the trust of my wife and gained a friendship that I can never enjoy. Does that make sense?"

He shook his head again. "And there's one man, Frank Mazzetti . . . I've spent hours and hours and hours trying to find a chink in his armor, and now that I've found it, Hanks isn't around to tell what he knows. Without him, nobody will believe me.

"But that's not what you came in here for, is it? You didn't come to hear me complain. I'm sorry. I just don't want to face up to the feelings that are swirling within me."

Liza moved to the chair near the bed and sat down. Neither spoke for several minutes. Then Liza stood up and took Peter's hand in hers. She was losing the battle with her emotions and felt the flood rise within her. "I better go," she whispered.

He nodded a goodbye. She released his hand and walked out of his life for the last time.

*   *   *

No sooner had Liza departed when Mike Downes arrived with a triple helping of good news. "Good morning, Peter, are you ready to go?"

The usually ebullient Peter was strangely somber. Propped against his pillow, the man of many words had none for his friend. Slowly, almost reluctantly, he nodded his assent.

Downes waited until Peter eased himself out of bed before speaking in a voice much less sunny than was his greeting. "Barry's in protective custody, and last night they arrested Jack Holland, who I hear ran the operation in Bayou Caddy, and, get this, Mary Kennedy had sold him her company in exchange for stock in his." Peter acknowledged the comment with a grunt. "But the best news is the U.S. Attorney in Norfolk, last night, dropped the charges against me."

"You must be feeling pretty good right about now."

"In more ways than you know."

"Debbie?"

"Yes, her too," he said almost sheepishly. "With the charges lifted I hope I can give her more of my time. We've got some planning to do," he said with a twinkle in his eye. "How about you?" Mike asked.

Peter carefully walked across the room to the closet. His left shoulder was bandaged into place to restrict movement. "It's tough to leave Liza, but she'll survive." He reached for his slacks. Mike helped him get the rest of the clothes from the closet. "It's taken all week, but I think I've finally got Mazzetti."

Downes waited for more as a faint grin spread across his face.

"This is it in a nutshell," said Peter, eager to get his mind off Liza. "Somebody, maybe Mark Randolph, was selling cocaine to a manager in the New Jersey company who in turn was selling it to some employees. Mazzetti was a director there and saw the opportunity to cash in on what he knew. He threatened to take the story public unless he was rewarded with a promotion. Too many had too much to lose, so they opted for the cover-up." Peter's countenance lifted as he presented his thesis. "I think they didn't want the cocaine story to become front page news right in the middle of a rate case, so Mazzetti used a blackmail scheme to his advantage even after a few of the key players got eased off the payroll. That's how he got to his present position. That's what I found out on the computer bulletin boards and had it confirmed when I picked up things in his e-mail."

Downes looked mildly amused. "You figured all that out on your computer?"

"And the phone. I told you I was going to nail him, and if it wasn't for Hanks's death I could."

"What's Hanks got to do with it?"

"The way I got it figured, Dan Hart has Mazzetti's number and is forcing him to prove his worth on his own. That's what the security roundups are all about. They make Frank look good. But when he discovered I was on to him, he had to take me out. As long as I was discredited within the company nothing I said would amount to a hill of beans. It wasn't until he thought I might be testifying in court in the Randolph case that he panicked. He knew that under oath, I would have implicated him, and that would destroy him."

"And Hanks, what about Hanks?"

"He said Mazzetti hired him to call us and threaten our family to keep me from testifying."

That revelation caught Downes off guard.

Peter continued. "But if Hanks is dead, it comes back to my word against Mazzetti's, and I know what that means. So I thought a lot about what I'm going to do. When I get back to Richmond, I'm going to walk up to Mazzetti and confront him with what I know. Even if no one believes me, I want him to know that I know, and then I'm going to tell him 'I quit' and that I'm going to write a book about this whole mess and name names."

Mike's smile broadened. "You're serious, aren't you?"

"You're darn straight I am. This week I've written the first chapter."

"I thought we talked about this revenge stuff. Didn't you say it wasn't your responsibility?"

Mike helped Peter slip on his shirt while Peter continued. "The way I figured it, if no one else was going to get the job done, I had better take care of things on my own . . . for my family . . . for the company . . . and for me."

With a shake of his head Mike signaled that Peter's thinking was wrong, as were some of his actions. Then, quite matter-of-factly he dropped the bombshell. "Mazzetti's gone."

"What?" Disbelief widened Peter's eyes.

"I was going to save this for our trip to the airport, but Mazzetti was fired last night."

"You're kidding!"

Downes shook his head.

The incredulity on Peter's face was transformed into a curious expression of anger and resignation. He knew that he had almost nothing to do with stopping O'Hearn or apprehending Mary Kennedy or busting up a drug operation. But he was convinced that in exchange for all the pain and suffering of the previous two months, he would still have the satisfaction of nailing Frank Mazzetti.

"He can't be fired," Peter implored. "I haven't shared the rest of my findings with anyone."

"They must not have needed them."

"But don't you see, Mike, I've done all this work. I'm the one who figured it all out."

Downes stepped away from Peter. He walked to the window and opened the blinds. Then he turned around and folded his arms across his chest. "Maybe you should've been resting and getting your strength back, 'cause it looks like someone else was getting the job done for you."

Peter slumped into the chair by the bed. He stared blankly at the wall and slowly bobbed his head as he processed Mike's statement and correlated it with his values system and the accumulated wisdom of four decades. He turned toward his friend, who was silhouetted against the bright window. "Isn't it strange how easily we can allow ourselves to believe that we are in control of the world?"